The Ocean under

the Moon

By Tony Stubits

The Ocean under the Moon

No man is an island, entire of itself; every
man is a piece of the continent, a part of the
main; if a clod be washed way by the sea,
Europe is the less, as well if a promontory
were, as well as if a manor of thy friend's or
thine own were; any man's death diminishes
me, because I am involved in mankind, and
therefore never send to know for whom the
bell tolls; it tolls for thee.

John Donne, 1624. Devotions upon
Emergent Occasions, XVII.

The Ocean under the Moon

ACKNOWLEDGEMENTS

The famous passage on the preceding page denotes that all mankind is connected and no man stands alone. This is particularly true when one writes a book. Although writing a novel is essentially a solo experience, it is also an accumulation of small experiences and contributions that come together like mortaring bricks together to make a building. I would like to acknowledge some of the people who helped me build this book into its final form.

First and foremost, I need to thank my wife, Donna, for her support in this endeavor and for transcribing my long-hand scribble into the computer for editing. I also need to thank my children, Tracey and Troy, for the time they allowed me away from their affections. Next, I would like to thank Charles Tomlinson, M.D., my childhood friend and golfing rival, for reviewing the medical aspects of this book. Hopefully, the proceeds of this book will allow me more time to work on my game, in order that I may beat you at golf again one day.

Sincere gratitude must go to Barry Woods, my former classmate and real-life captain of the *Island Girl* for educating me on the everyday working life of the modern-day shrimpers and allowing me to go on his boat so I could write about the shrimper's way of life realistically. Janie Thomas, executive director of the Florida East Coast Shrimp Producers Association, deserves my thanks for delineating the economic problems facing the domestic shrimpers these days. Nobody works harder to promote Florida wild-caught shrimp and to improve the lot of shrimpers in Florida.

I would like to thank all of the local people and friends who allowed me to use their names as minor characters in the book. The plot is entirely fiction, but some of the names are real, as my nod to them for their friendship.

I would like to thank Frank Green's writing group for showing me how high the bar needed to be set. I would be remiss if I didn't thank Linda McClane, my partner's wife and freelance writer, for her input and initial editing. Much gratitude goes to my office staff for functioning as a focus group and for their encouragement, comments, and proof-reading. I would particularly like to thank Karen Bell for her IT assistance and word processing skills. Last, but not least, in the editing department, I owe major thanks to Emily Carmain, of Noteworthy Editing Services, for helping with the structure of the novel and for making the final product as professional as possible. Also, my sincere gratitude goes to Heuland Simpson of Go PC, Inc. for tech assistance on the interior of the book layout and the book cover.

Finally, I would like to thank my parents, Jackie and Joe, for having the good sense to move to Amelia Island in the 1950's, so that I could be born and raised in such a beautiful environment and also for making me into the man I am today.

The Ocean under the Moon

Author's Note

Although my central character, Nick Stamos, is a creation of my imagination and his story is a work of fiction, the place where I have set this story is a very real one.

Like Nick, I grew up in the idyllic setting of Fernandina Beach, a beautiful small town located on Amelia Island in the far northeast corner of Florida. This fourteen-mile-long island is surrounded by serene marshes, rivers, and the Atlantic Ocean. Known as the "Isle of Eight Flags," it has a long and colorful history — as the only territory in the United States that has been under eight flags or jurisdictions.

The history is unique, but a bit convoluted. Therefore, in order to not bog down my story, my editor suggested I remove some of the history from the body of the novel and place it in this section. For you history buffs and readers who want to get a better understanding of the setting, please read this brief synopsis of the history of Amelia Island. Those of you who fell asleep in history class in high school can skip forward to the prologue.

The first Europeans to discover the island were French explorers in 1562. They named it "*Isle de Mai*" in honor of its month of discovery. They encountered the tall, statuesque Timucuan Indians, who were adorned with tattoos covering most of their bodies. The original inhabitants of the island had thrived in the area for centuries due to its abundance of game, fish, shellfish, and

The Ocean under the Moon

fertile soil.

Next to arrive were the Spanish. Their soldiers marched up through the swamps from St. Augustine and defeated the French at Fort Caroline, on the nearby St. John's River, driving the French from the area. The Spanish renamed the island "*Santa Maria*," and then developed a mission here. They ruled uninterrupted for the next two hundred years. Sadly, it was during this time the Timucuan people disappeared as a race due to the diseases the Europeans brought with them.

In 1763, all of Spanish Florida was traded to England for Cuba, and the British flag flew over Amelia Island for the next twenty years. James Oglethorpe, Governor of Georgia, had earlier named the island Amelia, after Princess Amelia, daughter of King George II, when the island was still under Spanish control. The Earl of Egmont ran a large indigo plantation here during the British rule, and English colonists populated the town of Fernandina. Then, at the end of the American Revolutionary War, Britain returned Florida to Spain. However, the name Amelia stuck, even after the British left.

The next century brought more changes. Thanks to the Embargo Act of 1807, restricting trade between the United States and the United Kingdom, and the abolishment of the American slave trade, Amelia Island became a hot spot. As the northernmost port of Spanish Florida, it became the center for smuggling goods and slaves into Georgia, which was right across Cumberland Sound. During this period, as many as three hundred square-rigged sailing vessels would be in the harbor.

It was also during this time of prosperity that the town of

The Ocean under the Moon

Fernandina was platted — in what later would later be known as "Old Town" — and named in honor of King Ferdinand VII of Spain.

The next group to take over this prized spot would be the "Patriots of Amelia Island." Annoyed by the continuing smuggling and prosperity of their neighbor to the south, on March 17, 1812, an independent group of American citizens, secretly backed by the United States government, seized control of the island and raised the "Patriots of Amelia Island" flag. Spain strongly protested this action, and since the United States wanted to maintain civil relations with Spain because of the looming War of 1812 with Britain, the United States relinquished the island back to Spain.

After the War of 1812 ended, the Americans were again free to covet Amelia Island. A Scottish military adventurer named Sir Gregor MacGregor, with funding from the Americans, overtook the island in 1817 and raised his "Green Cross of Florida" flag. Soon, however, due to lack of funds and reinforcements, MacGregor left the island for the Bahamas, leaving his lieutenants in charge. The lieutenants soon lost control of their men due to desertion, drinking, brothels, and the lack of funds to pay the soldiers.

Luis Aury, a Frenchman and known pirate, sailed in to rule the island next. Aury had been the leader of a pirate gang on Galveston Island, Texas, flying the Mexican Rebel flag, when he heard MacGregor had captured Amelia Island from the Spanish. Ever aware of an opportunity, Aury sailed his warships around Florida to Fernandina.

With the island in disarray, Aury soon seized control, declaring himself military and civilian commander. The next day,

The Ocean under the Moon

he raised the Mexican Rebel flag and annexed Amelia Island to
Mexico. His reign didn't last long, for in December of 1817, U.S.
forces invaded the island, running Aury off, and held Amelia
Island in trust for Spain, until all of Florida was ceded to the United
States in 1821, and the American flag went up.

Florida became a state in 1845 and the Army started
building Fort Clinch two years later. After the outbreak of the
American Civil War, Confederate forces took control of the fort and
port and used the latter for blockade running. The National Flag of
the Confederacy only flew for about a year, and then the Union
sent a large flotilla of gun ships to take the island. General Robert E.
Lee had already given orders for the Rebel troops to leave, so by
the time the ships arrived the fort was empty.

After the war, Reconstruction was followed by the boom
of tourism during Amelia's Golden Age — the 1880s and 1890s.
Steamers and trains from up North brought crowds of well-dressed
tourists to enjoy the elegant Victorian hotels and the balmy
weather.

But by the end of the century, the casino and hotel at the
beach had been destroyed by a hurricane, and the railroad had
been extended, first to St. Augustine, then to Palm Beach, making
those towns the new desired locations.

Fernandina, as a tourist destination, would be mostly
forgotten for the next several decades. After the turn of the century,
it was shrimping that spurred the local economy, and the island
became known as the "birthplace of the modern shrimping
industry."

After a severe downturn during the Great Depression, the

The Ocean under the Moon

island's economy was stabilized by the construction of two paper mills. More recently, the latter part of the 20th century harbored in the second era of tourism and development with the establishment of a major resort, the Amelia Island Plantation, on the south end of the island, and the addition of the Ritz-Carlton Hotel, in the middle of the island. Now, in the present century, the Great Recession once again has slowed the island's economy.

Therefore, like a beautiful, but unattainable woman, Amelia Island has attracted many men to try their luck — to see if they could succeed where the Timucuans, French, Spanish, British, American patriots, pirates, and Confederate soldiers have failed to succeed. I hope you enjoy this modern-day tale of Nick's trials and tribulations.

The Ocean under the Moon

Prologue

July 13, 2008

3:16 p.m.

Nick had consumed a six-pack of beer and was feeling just right. The alcohol coursed through his arteries and made its way to his brain and he felt strangely relaxed, considering what he was about to do. He'd put the nets back out and the boat was on autopilot, doing a slow drag to the south. Since there wasn't anything to do now but enjoy the scenery, he opened a fresh beer and went up to the bow of the shrimp boat.

The sea breeze kicked in about thirty minutes ago, and he sat down on the storage box in front of the pilothouse to enjoy the breeze and the apparent wind created by the forward movement of the boat.

The *Resurrection* motored about three and a half miles off the shoreline of Amelia Island, working its way south, parallel to the beach, toward Big Talbot Island. The boat droned forward on this familiar route, like an old plow horse that knew its way. He could easily see the tall skyline of Amelia Island Plantation and its rows of high-rise condominiums. He could even make out the small, ant-like movements of people on the beach enjoying their summer vacations.

The Ocean under the Moon

The island wasn't the same anymore, he lamented, as he eyed all of the high-rise condos on the south end. When he was growing up on the island, if he and his family went out at night to a restaurant, they would know about ninety percent of the people in the restaurant. Nowadays, when he and Monica went out to eat, they were lucky if they saw anybody they knew.

Between all of the tourists on vacation and wealthy retirees moving down from up North, the previous inhabitants of the island, like the shrimpers, crabbers, mill-workers, and the Afro-Americans at American Beach, were getting squeezed off the island by the constantly rising property taxes. Maybe it was best that he would leave this place; there wasn't room on the island for his type anymore.

He laid his head back against the pilothouse and closed his eyes. He felt the warm sunshine on his face, the cool breeze across his skin, and smelled the fresh salt air. He'd miss these kinds of moments. As bad as his life and financial situation had become, he still loved his job. If he could make any profit out of what he was doing, he would be willing to work his way out of debt. But since the profit had gone out of shrimping, it was like treading water; a lot of effort expended without getting anywhere.

He'd left Gator's old boom box blaring out old-time rock songs on the classic rock station, from its post just behind the pilothouse. He was just about to fall asleep for a little catnap when he heard the opening keyboard notes of "Free Bird" come over the radio. He listened to the languid beginning of the song and instantly thought of his friend. He had sworn to never listen to the song again, but this time, he did not get up and switch it off. He'd

11

hear the song one last time.

"Well, if it worked for Gator, maybe it'll work for me," he muttered to himself, and stood up from his resting place. He was a little woozy from all the beer and it took him a few seconds to get his sea legs, once he stood up. Then he made his way around the side of the pilothouse and stepped inside to grab the broom. When he came out, he moved to the stern of the boat. He jumped up on the transom of the boat, clutched the wooden end of the broom in his left hand and waited for the fast part of the song to begin.

Just before the beginning guitar licks for the up-tempo part of the song, he swiveled the broom into position so his left hand could work the imaginary frets on the broom handle and his right hand could strum the imaginary strings on the straw end. When the fast part of the song kicked in, he jumped off the transom onto the afterdeck and started working his imaginary guitar.

His goal was to play the most frantic air guitar solo ever, and, if he was lucky, he would keel over. The beer gave him a bravado he did not normally possess and he played his fake guitar like a man possessed.

He crouched down low, then reeled way back. He ran from one side of the boat to the other, all the time playing his fake guitar. He jumped on the icebox for a few licks on the guitar, and then jumped off. He played behind his back, between his legs, and with his teeth, *a la* Jimi Hendrix; then he duck-walked across the afterdeck like Chuck Berry. The song got faster and he ran to the bow of the boat then stopped to do some more gyrations, as if playing to a different section of an audience. Then he ran back to icebox and stepped up on it and then onto the roof of the crew's quarters.

From the perch on the roof, he discovered why Gator had loved his ritual so much. On top of the crew's quarters, twenty-something feet above the sea and looking down on everything for miles in every direction, he felt omnipotent, like the king of the ocean. He could imagine how rock stars felt, on a raised stage, looking down on a sea of admirers.

He flopped down and started doing the "Gator," the infamous dance that his friend used to do when he was drunk. He was on his belly, moving his arms up and down like an alligator trying to run on ice. He rolled onto his back and gyrated his arms and legs up and down like a dying cockroach.

The song reached its crescendo so he jumped back up to his feet, grabbed the broom, and pretended to belt out the last few guitar licks and danced in a circle, hopping on one leg.

When the song finished, he held up the broom in mock triumph, to imagined thunderous applause. Then he dropped the broom and collapsed on his back on top of the crew's quarters. He waited for a heart attack, but none came. Just heavy, laborious panting, as he was out of breath.

Damn, dying was not going to be easy.

He laid his head back against the roof of the crew's quarters and tried to make his mind go blank—to blot out all the memories, the pain, the struggles—even the good times and the people he loved. But it didn't work. Forgetting was impossible. It is said that right before a person dies, their whole life flashes before one's eyes. Nick hoped he was going to die tonight, so he closed his eyes, thought about his life, and what had transpired to bring him

The Ocean under the Moon

to this point of desperation.

The Ocean under the Moon

Chapter 1

July 31, 1960

The earliest memory that Nick could recall from his mind was a day when he was about four years old. He was standing next to the oyster pit his father built in the back yard. The pit was a circular brick structure, about three feet high and four feet in diameter, but was open at the top except for the grate that the oysters were placed on to roast. His father, Abe, had just taken a batch of steamed oysters into the house, leaving him alone by the fire when he had seen his opportunity.

Earlier in the day, he'd discovered a box of .22-caliber bullets in his father's nightstand. His young mind had been fascinated with fireworks, since the Fourth of July just a few weeks earlier, and having seen his father load bullets into the pistol and shoot at cans in the back yard, he'd grabbed a small handful and stuck them into his pocket.

When his father took the oysters inside the house, young Nick saw his opportunity and threw the bullets into the fire. At first, nothing happened, then there was a loud explosion and a bullet ricocheted off the brick structure sending shrapnel past his head. Only then did his young mind realize the potential danger involved.

His father came running out of the house, almost

knocking the door off its hinges.

"Nick get down!" His father yelled at him to take cover, but it was unnecessary as Nick had already started for the corner of the house, sprinting for the safety of the front yard.

He would never see his father as mad as he was that night. Red-faced, his father screamed at him that he could have killed himself. However, due to good fortune, and the circular brick wall sending the bullets off in fortuitous angles, nobody had been hit. He was sent to his room for what seemed like a week, and it was then that young Nick realized there were consequences for your actions in life.

* * *

Nickolas Markos Stamos had been born on May 19, 1956, at Humphrey's Memorial Hospital in Fernandina Beach, Florida. The town was located on Amelia Island, a fourteen-mile-long barrier island in the very northeast corner of Florida, next to Georgia. As related to Nick later, his birth had been difficult, being his mother's, Isabelle's, first child. Labor lasted over fourteen hours and for a while there was concern for both the mother and child because of the position of the fetus and the lack of progress, but the baby finally turned and presented itself to the world.

The long delivery had been a blessing in a way because it allowed Nick's father, Abeiron, or Abe as everyone called him, to make it back from sea just in time for the delivery. Not that he saw the birth, as in those times the father was confined to the waiting area. But he was there for the delivery of the news and to pass out cigars. He was excited about the birth of his child and for it to be a boy, was almost too good to be true.

The Ocean under the Moon

His father had a reason to be excited beyond the usual primal need for a man to have a son. Abe was a second-generation shrimper, a man who made his living from the sea. Thirty years old at the time of Nick's birth, Abe was of Greek heritage. At the time, he possessed dark, jet-black hair highlighted by his brilliant green eyes. His Mediterranean skin was tanned from years at sea, but he was young enough that his face was empty of the permanent lines and flaws that all fishermen develop over time.

That day, however, the corners of his eyes were wrinkled somewhat because his smile was so large. He now had a son, who held the promise to fill many needs for him. For now there was someone to teach the ways of the sea and to use as a deckhand, first mate, and eventual successor when he got too old to go to sea.

* * *

Nick would learn later, all of his father's hopes and dreams were centered on his son following in his legacy. His difficult birth rendered his mother unable to have any more children. This would place the continuation of the Stamos shrimping dynasty squarely upon his young shoulders.

The Ocean under the Moon

Chapter 2

June 23, 1967

"Hurry up, Bobby. Time's a' wasting," Nick yelled to his friend
who was struggling to ride his bicycle up the short, but steep,
Fourteenth Street Bridge while holding on to his sandboard. Now
eleven years old, Nick had grown into the confident leader of his
small band of friends. He and his friends, Chuck Tomlinson and
David Crumpler, were sitting on their bikes at the top of the bridge
waiting for Bobby Peters to catch up to them.

The bridge spanned Egan's Creek, whose freshwater
beginnings started in the center of the island and ran north, in a
curve like a paring knife, getting saltier, and lined by marshes on
each side, until it passed under the bridge they were sitting on and
emptied into the Amelia River at the northwestern end of the
island. The creek, at the boys' location, separated Old Town, a
small community of shrimpers and crabbers living on the bluff of
land on the south bank of the creek, from the north bank.

Old Town was where Nick lived. Even at his young age,
Nick knew he lived on the wrong side of the railroad tracks. From
his schoolwork and his grandfather's stories, Nick knew that, even
though all the important history of the island, up to the middle of
the last century, had happened on the bluff of land where he lived

18

now, with the coming of the railroad all that changed. When the Spanish owned the island, the main mode of transportation was by ship. Therefore, they'd platted the original town of Fernandina on the large bluff overlooking the deep harbor in the Amelia River.

Later, after the Americans took over the island, the town was moved south, on the other side of a marshy area just south of Old Town. This was due to the construction of a railroad line onto the island; they didn't want to build a bridge over the marshland. The new, larger town was platted and also called Fernandina. The new Fernandina would boom in the late 1800s due to an influx of tourists coming by train or steamship from the North to enjoy the mild climate. The old Fernandina would be forgotten and left to the fishermen and crabbers.

Nick, however, liked living in Old Town. For a young boy growing up, the area possessed a lot of opportunity for adventure. Today, he and his friends were about to embark on a new one. From his perch on his bike looking north in the direction they were headed, Nick knew there were only two directions to go.

One road turned to the left and followed the north bank of the creek to the pogy plant. The pogy plant was a dilapidated fish processing facility that sent boats out into the ocean to catch pogy fish, or menhaden, as Nick had learned they were more properly called. Nick didn't care for the pungent odor the plant produced when it ground up the oily fish up to be used in oils, fertilizer, animal feed and even perfumes. He hated when the wind came out of the wrong direction and the smell wafted over his house on the bank across from the plant.

The other road at the bottom of the bridge going north

was the back way into Fort Clinch State Park. The huge park, over a thousand acres, wrapped around this end of the island from its campground on the northwest corner of the island, to the Civil War era fort located on the northern tip overlooking the entrance to Cumberland Sound, to the fishing pier beside the southernmost jetty that demarcates the entrance to the sound. The park extended southward, with a winding road through the maritime forest, to its main vehicular entrance on Atlantic Avenue.

Since the main entrance was about a three-mile bike ride from Old Town, the boys never used the real entrance. Even if the boys had the fifty-cent entrance fee to spare—which they never did—it was much more fun and adventurous to sneak in the back way. The only problem was, if the park rangers caught you in there without a sticker on your bike proving admission to the park, they would escort you out. This cat-and-mouse game with the rangers just heightened the adventure for Nick and his friends.

Once inside the park, the boys had all kinds of options. They could go to the campground area on the edge of the Amelia River, which offered great climbing trees and tall, wooded sand dunes to run up and down. Or they could go to Willow Pond, a swampy area with several algae-covered ponds, complete with alligators and the occasional otter.

Sometimes the boys caught fiddler crabs along the shore of Egan's Creek, put them in a bucket, then grabbed their cane poles and bikes and rode into the park to go fishing at the jetties. The jetties were large boulders or jettison that'd been brought in to line the north and south sides of the entrance to Cumberland Sound—the waterway separating Amelia Island from Cumberland

The Ocean under the Moon

Island in Georgia. On this side, the big rocks started at the beach just east of Fort Clinch and extended in a line eastward into the Atlantic Ocean for about a quarter of a mile, to keep shifting sand out of the channel.

Nick and his friends would climb out onto the barnacle-encrusted rocks with a cane pole in hand and, using the fiddler crabs for bait, try to catch sheepshead that hung around the huge boulders. They had to pay attention to the tides, however, fishing around the low tides when the rocks were best exposed.

Due to the seven-foot variance between low tide and high tide, if the boys didn't head back to shore soon enough to beat the incoming tide, they would find themselves stranded on the high rocks with the lower spots submerged, cutting them off from shore. Swimming back to shore was out of the question, due to the treacherous currents and waves pounding the rocks, so if you got stranded you had a long wait until the tide went out again. They also wore tennis shoes to protect their feet from the barnacles and oyster shells, because even if the tide didn't catch them, one slip on the algae-covered rocks could lead to a painful gash from the sharp crustaceans and a long, painful bike ride home.

Nick's favorite option, however, was to ride to the five-sided brick fort overlooking the sound. The fort came complete with a moat, a drawbridge, rifle ports, cannons, and a two-story bastion on the end of each of its five points. The boys would divide up into two teams and play a form of hide-and-seek with each team trying to capture the other.

If you were tagged by the seeking team, then you had to go and sit in the old jail, which had four cells complete with bars on the doors and windows. A player could be released from jail by a tag of one of his teammates, if that player could get in and out of the jail without being tagged himself.

There were hundreds of hiding places in the fort and the game would sometimes last hours. There were long chases along the top of the brick walls, up and down stairs, and through the numerous hallways and tunnels. The boys would be almost too exhausted at the end of the day to ride their bikes home.

"Hey, guys. Wait up," Bobby said. He dismounted his bike to push it up the bridge, since he was struggling to hold onto the handlebars, carry his sandboard, and pedal the bike up the steep incline.

Today, the boys were going to do something different. Just a week ago, Nick and his friends had seen the surfing movie, "Endless Summer." The documentary about two surfers on a worldwide quest to find the perfect wave motivated the boys to try their own surfing safari. Since none of the boys possessed the money for a real surfboard, David came up with the idea of making a sandboard and looking for the perfect dune instead of the perfect wave.

For the last week, the boys had been busy working on their sandboards. They each took a one-inch-thick, six-inch-wide board and cut it about five feet long. Next they used a file and curved up the front edge of the board. Then they'd nailed a one-inch by one-inch strip of wood about five inches long to the board, slightly more forward than halfway on the board. After some paint and decals, their sandboards had been complete.

Now the trick was to find a dune with just the right

steepness of grade. Sand has a lot more friction than water, so a dune needed to be found with a grade steep enough to overcome that friction, but not so steep the boys would tumble over the front of their boards.

"Where do you think we should go?" Chuck asked, while they were waiting for Bobby to reach the top of the bridge.

"The area just east of the fort, toward the Jetty Lodge, has the best dunes," Nick said.

While he, Chuck, and David waited at the top of the bridge for Bobby to catch up to them, Nick took in the view of his surroundings. To the southwest, he could see the white cottage that he lived in with his parents, Abe and Isabelle, and grandparents, Eber and Catherine. The two-story, wooden house stood on the high bluff overlooking where Egan's Creek flows into the Amelia River. Nick knew his grandfather acquired the land at a tax auction back in the 1930s, during the depth of the Great Depression. This was now the base of the family shrimping business.

He noticed the docks were empty, as the three shrimp boats that were berthed there were all out to sea. This meant that his grandfather, father, and the other boat that the family leased out to another shrimper, were all out trying to catch shrimp.

The bluff of land that his family lived on owned quite a long history. A few months ago, his parents had taken him to a play performed in the courtyard of Fort Clinch, called "The Eight Flags of Amelia," reenacting scenes from the past of the island.

The first Europeans to land here brought the flag of France. The French encountered the Timucuan Indians, a native tribe that was located here for centuries. They'd apparently loved

The Ocean under the Moon

shellfish—something Nick could relate to, as he and his family did also—and he even knew that the mounds that he and his friends played on near his house were the covered-up remains of piles of oyster shells that the Timucuans had thrown into enormous heaps, called middens.

The Spanish drove the French from the area and developed a mission, named Santa Maria, on the bluff where Nick now lived with his family. The streets in Old Town still maintained their Spanish names, and the site where the fort used to be located was now a grassy field by the river—a great space for Nick and his friends to play.

England held the island for awhile in the 1700s, and it was the British name that had stuck—after Princess Amelia. But Nick's favorite part of the play was about the three groups of adventurers who each seized control briefly, raising their flags—the "Patriots of Amelia," Sir Gregor MacGregor's "Green Cross of Florida," and the pirate Luis Aury with his "Mexican Rebel" flag.

The local story was that the pirate Aury left in such a hurry, he buried some of his treasure somewhere on the island. Other pirates possessed their own legends that were also part of Fernandina's rich lore, and Nick and his friends spent a lot of their time searching for buried treasure. But after weeks of digging holes around Old Town, all the boys found for their hard work was a collection of old bottles and arrowheads.

Eventually, Florida of course became part of the United States. At the start of the Civil War, the Confederate flag flew over Fernandina for about a year. But when the U.S. gunboats showed up, the Rebels retreated without firing a shot. From then on, "Old

The Ocean under the Moon

Glory" reigned supreme.

Nick knew from his grandfather's stories that Fernandina had been a booming tourist destination during the Reconstruction a hundred years before, but then the tourists went farther south and the town became a quiet little village, undisturbed by the passing of time. After the turn of the century, it was fishing and shrimping that brought prosperity — until the Great Depression hit. After the depression, it was the construction of two paper mills that drove the island's economy.

Nick looked south, past his house, and he could see the larger of the two paper mills, on the island. Container Corporation was located on a marshy area of land near Old Town. It was a sprawling, mechanical behemoth running day and night, spewing noise and smoke. On hot, summer nights when his mother opened all the windows in the house to get a breeze, Nick had trouble sleeping from all the noise coming from the gigantic mill.

Trains and trucks constantly brought pine logs there, and they were chipped, mashed and cooked into pulp, which eventually made its way into brown paper for paper bags and cardboard boxes. Since the end of the1930s, when the two mills had been built, reviving the economy, most Fernandina residents worked either at one of the two mills or in a business that supported the mills, or that served the workers. All of Nick's friends' fathers worked at one of the mills — only the fishermen, crabbers and shrimpers, like his family, were independent of the mills.

Rayonier, the smaller of the two mills, was located south of the city docks downtown, out of Nick's sight and mind. That mill turned the southern pine trees into cellulose fibers that were used in all kinds of products, like toothpaste and film. Besides the greater distance from his house, Nick had another reason to like Rayonier better than Container. Rayonier maintained a pipeline that ran from the mill across the island to discharge straight into the Atlantic Ocean, and the mill's liquid by-products contained a large amount of ammonia.

Whenever the ocean got rough during storms, like in a common "nor'easter," the ammonia caused massive banks of foam to build up along the shoreline. The crashing of the waves would build up banks of foam up to five feet high. When Nick was younger, he and his friends played hide-and-seek by disappearing into the walls of foam. It was hard to breathe inside the foam banks, due to the strong, acidic smell, so the boys would run into the banks of foam, holding their breath as long as they could, then dash back out to daylight and clean air, when they ran out of breath. They also used the foam to create fake beards and moustaches on their faces.

"Hurry up, Bobby," Nick implored. "The sand dunes took over a hundred years to get as big as they are, but they may be gone by the time you make it to the top of this bridge."

"I'm coming," Bobby responded, as he dropped his sandboard for about the tenth time.

While he waited for Bobby, Nick looked over the side of the bridge at the creek below. Nick wondered if there were any trout lying in wait in the trout hole today. He knew that it wasn't the best time of the year to catch trout because it was too hot, but if there were any, they would be hanging out in the cooler water,

The Ocean under the Moon

deep in the trout hole just east of the bridge.

Whenever he was not in school, and Eber was not out
shrimping, his grandfather would take him fishing. Some of his
fondest memories were of himself, as a small boy, scurrying about
the shoreline trying to catch fiddler crabs before they could
disappear into their little holes. His grandfather had shown him
how to catch the small crabs to use as bait. Then, using the fiddler
crabs or live shrimp they caught with a cast net, they would fish for
red drum, spotted sea trout, or flounder.

If the tide was coming in, they would float up Egan's
Creek, casting along the shoreline. They would always stop at the
trout hole, just on the other side of the bridge, to see if the trout
were biting at that time and tide.

Nick couldn't wait until his grandfather retired from
shrimping. Then he and Grandpa could go fishing all the time. His
grandfather had told him that this coming fall's shrimp run was
going to be his last and that next year they would have plenty of
time to go fishing together.

Bobby finally made it to the top of the bridge and shook
Nick free from his random thoughts.

"Are you guys ready to go on a surfin' safari and find the
perfect dune?" Nick asked.

"Ye-ah!" the others yelled.

"Then let's go!" Nick exclaimed as he pushed his bike
forward and started coasting down the steep incline of the bridge
followed closely by his friends.

The Ocean under the Moon

Chapter 3

August 8, 1968

"Grandpa, why don't you trade in this old wooden rowboat and get an aluminum Jon boat with a motor?" the boy asked, as his grandfather rowed them toward their favorite fishing spot on this hot August morning.

Nick was twelve years old now, old enough to question his grandfather's old-fashioned ways. He knew that his grandfather, Eber, came from the old country, having emigrated to the United States in 1913, from the Greek island of Ikaria. Grandpa came from a long line of fishermen from the island town of Agios Kirikos.

His grandfather was still spry for his age, the boy thought as he looked with admiration at the stubborn old man. He was a short, wiry man, his face weathered from years at sea and reflecting his Mediterranean heritage.

"Rowing gets my blood going, and keeps me young," Grandpa responded. "Besides, all those years of trying to keep those old diesel engines running on my shrimp boats has left me with a bad taste in my mouth for anything mechanical."

His grandfather quit shrimping eight months ago. At seventy-four years old, he no longer felt like getting up early and spending several days at sea. He relinquished that hard life to Abe, his son and Nick's father, who was supporting the family now by shrimping full-time on one of Eber's boats. The other two boats that he owned, he leased out to other shrimpers for extra income.

If the weather was good and the shrimp were running, Grandpa would still go out on occasion with Abe or one of the other crews as an extra hand. Otherwise, the seasoned old shrimper would hang out with the other old shrimpers at Joe Tringali's dock or David Cook's dock downtown and swap sea stories about the good old days. If he wasn't at the docks telling tales or at the Marina Restaurant eating lunch, he was out fishing in his little boat, either with Nick, or by himself, or with one of his old shrimping buddies.

Nick inherently loved fishing. It was a gene that was passed from Eber to Abe and then to him. He loved everything about fishing, from catching the bait, to baiting the hook, to understanding the currents and tides, to casting in the proper spot, to setting the hook, then battling the fish to the boat, and seeing what came out of the water. Every day of fishing was like Christmas Day, and Nick couldn't wait to see what presents the waterways held.

They would usually head up the creek to try and catch red drum or spotted sea trout. If the fish weren't biting up the creek, they could try catching sheepshead around the rocks next to the old pogy plant. Their plan on this day, however, was to row out the river toward Fort Clinch and fish for flounder.

"Whew!" Nick said, as his grandfather rowed them past the plant that morning. "The pogy plant is really stinking it up today."

He and Grandpa could put up with the foul odor that the plant produced, because the rocks that were placed where Egan's Creek met the Amelia River, to control erosion around the plant, made for great structure for sheepshead to hide in. Nick liked fishing for sheepshead, because they were both easy and hard to catch. Easy, in that the equipment and bait needed were simple. All that was necessary was a cane pole, fishing line, lightweight sinker, and a small hook.

Also, since sheepshead like to hang around rocks and pilings, they eat oysters, clams, barnacles, and fiddler crabs — all readily available to Nick and his friends by catching fiddler crabs in the marshes, scraping barnacles off the rocks and pilings, and raiding the oyster beds.

The challenge to catching sheepshead was that with their small, hard mouths and several rows of stubby teeth — resembling a sheep, thus the name — they like to crush their prey and eat slowly. So, unlike most other fish that tend to gulp their prey, resulting in a hard tug on the fishing line signaling a bite, sheepshead tend to grind their food. Nick knew the trick was to feel the gentle pull of the sheepshead as it started to nibble on the bait and allow it enough time to get the food well into its mouth, but not waiting too long as to let it steal the bait off the hook.

Today, though, they were not out for sheepshead. To take advantage of a west wind and an outgoing tide, they had left at eight-thirty that morning. This time of year, they knew that the wind would be nonexistent, or a light, west wind in the morning; then, as the land heated up, a cooler, stronger sea breeze would blow in from the east, off the ocean.

They planned to go north, past the pogy plant and around the northern end of the island into Cumberland Sound to the rocks around Fort Clinch. The currents were significant there, running in and out of the sound to and from the ocean, so they would have to hug the shoreline and pay close attention to the tides. Rowing easily with the current since the tide just started going out, they passed the pogy plant and then the small campground on the northwest end of the island.

"Not many people in the campground today," Nick commented.

"Well, it is the hottest time of the year. The heat has probably scared everybody away," Grandpa said, as he wiped his brow with the sleeve of his shirt.

On this morning, with the wind at their backs, they headed toward one of their favorite fishing spots just west of the fort. A series of small jetties had been placed there to help slow the erosion of sand in front of the fort. The still, shallow water between the small jetties was perfect for catching flounder, which Nick knew to be an ugly, but great-tasting fish. He also knew that flounder are flat-fish, or side-swimmers—both eyes on the same side of the fish. Ambush predators, they lie flat on one side, half-burying themselves in the soft mud or sand, waiting for their unsuspecting prey to swim over them. Their top half, where the eyes are located, is a spotted light brown to match the muddy bottom. Their underside is a soft white color. Their meat is a delicate, white texture and wonderful to eat fried, broiled, or baked.

The Ocean under the Moon

Another reason Grandpa and Nick liked taking flounder home was that they are easy to eat. Since flounder don't have scales, there's no need for the time-consuming, labor-intensive task of removing the scales—just cut off the head, scrape out the guts, dip each side in uncooked egg, then flour and fry it till done. The fish also has only one set of bones radiating down the middle of the fish. The meat can be scooped off one side of the fish and eaten, then the fish can be flipped over to eat the other side, leaving just the skeleton in the middle.

It was with these thoughts of the delicious flounder that he and his grandfather set out that morning. After reaching their fishing spot between the two small jetties, just west of the fort, Nick stood up and threw out the anchor. Using some live finger mullet they'd caught earlier in Egan's Creek with the cast net, they cast towards the small jetties and then slowly retrieved their lines across the smooth bottom.

It was a glorious morning; the wind was light, the water calm. They'd been sitting in the shadow of the fort, but as the sun crept up over the walls, it illuminated the area in the golden morning light. Nick looked around and thought how beautiful everything was. The sun coming up over the fort, the white beaches glistening in the early morning sun, to the windswept sand dunes, followed by the wind-carved oak trees... the surroundings seemed surreal. He also noticed after several days of calm weather how clean the water had become. He loved these days fishing with his grandfather and glanced over at the old man, who looked energized and happy.

"Have I ever told you how I came to this island?"

The Ocean under the Moon

Grandpa asked as he reeled his line in slowly.

"Well," Nick said, "I know you came from Greece, a long time ago."

Grandpa grinned at him and continued reeling. "I guess you're old enough for the full story now," he said. "You might even remember it, when I'm dead and gone."

"You are too mean and tough to die, Grandpa," Nick said with a smile.

"Nevertheless, it's good to have history pass from one generation to the other," the old man said.

Nick knew his grandfather loved to tell stories but they were mostly about shrimping, the storms he survived, and the places he'd gone to in search of shrimp. He'd never talked to Nick in detail about his early life.

"What was it like when you were my age?" he asked.

"Well, when I was growing up on the island of Ikaria, we owned a two-room cottage by the sea, but we didn't have much money. Everything we earned, and ate, came from the sea." The hook on his fishing line came over the side of the boat devoid of a fish, but his bait was still intact so he cast it back out toward the rocks.

"Ikaria got its name from an old Greek myth, you know," he said. "It was named after Icarus, who was the son of Daedulus, the architect hired by King Minos to build the labyrinth on Crete to hold the Minotaur—"

Nick cut off his grandfather. "Yes, Dad has told me that story many times when I get too full of myself, to take me down a notch. He's always telling me not to fly too close to the sun, lest I

33

fall into the sea."

"Well, my departure from Ikaria was not as dramatic as Icarus' departure from Crete," Grandpa began. "We'd been ruled by the Turks for several centuries, until Ikaria was liberated by the Greek army in 1912. We had high hopes being back under Greek rule, our rightful heritage, but the Greek government ignored our island and did not invest in helping our economy. We were all still very poor and that made us mad. Several men left, to seek their futures elsewhere, and some ended up in the United States. Soon, stories of the riches in America, and money, began to make it back to those of us left in Ikaria."

"Hang on, Grandpa. I think I got one," Nick said, as he set the hook in a flounder's mouth by standing up and jerking the tip of the rod back behind him. He started reeling in the line and felt the fish on the other end fighting to get away.

Soon, he maneuvered the fish by the side of the boat and his grandfather got up from where he was sitting, grabbed the net and slipped it under the struggling fish. Grandpa scooped the catch out of the water, grabbed his pliers, removed the hook, and let the fish splash into a five-gallon bucket filled with seawater in the back of the boat.

"Now, where was I?" he started again. "Oh, yes, now I remember. Being nineteen years old at the time, I saw no future on the island for myself, so I hired on as a seaman on a small freighter that serviced the island once a month. The freighter took me to the Greek port of Athens where I caught a larger freighter that took me to New York."

"But weren't you lonely, being all by yourself in another

country?" Nick asked.

"No, I lived with my cousin Ianos, who worked as a
fishmonger at the Fulton Fish Market—and that was a big
operation, let me tell you. It was where fishing boats from all over
the East Coast, but especially from New England, brought their
catch. We unloaded the boats in the middle of the night, then
transported the fish by wagons and carts down the pier and across
the cobblestone streets to the fish market. There, fifty to sixty
vendors, including the one we worked for, would sell their fish to
the buyers from New York's hotels, restaurants, and retail markets,
early in the morning of each business day."

Grandpa reeled his line over the side of the boat and
noticed that his bait was gone. He frowned at his lack of attention
and put a fresh live mullet on the hook and cast it back toward the
small jetty, then resumed his story.

"I worked there about six months before I realized that I
would rather be out catching fish, instead of slinging fish from cart
to cart to get them ready for sale. Fortunately, about that time, I met
Salvatore Versaggi, who was from Sicily but now was living in
Fernandina. Versaggi had come to New York to try and make
contacts at the fish market to distribute shrimp, he and his brother-
in-law, Mike Salvador, caught off the shores of Amelia Island."

"I know some kids named Salvador," Nick put in, and his
grandfather told him the Salvador family had been part of the
community since the century before.

He explained how shrimp used to be caught long ago
around Amelia Island using cast nets and rowboats in the inland
waters. Then around 1902, Mike Salvador started using a power-

driven boat pulling a haul seine net out in the ocean in pursuit of larger numbers of shrimp. Mike was successful and the shrimp were plentiful, so he then convinced Versaggi, and his other brother-in-law, Antonio Poli, to move to Fernandina from Sicily to join him in the shrimping business.

"After awhile," Grandpa said, "they were catching so many shrimp they were having trouble selling all of it before it spoiled. With shrimp selling for only a nickel a pound in the poor local economy, Mike sent Versaggi to New York to find contacts where they could distribute their shrimp."

Nick noticed Grandpa kept glancing to the west, where a significant thunderstorm was building in the summer heat. On Amelia Island, most of the time the summer mornings would start out clear, with very few clouds in the sky. But as the heat and humidity built up during the morning, the hot air over the land would rise, taking moisture with it and causing cumulonimbus clouds to build up over the land. The rising of the hot air would suck in cooler air from off the ocean at the surface level, causing the sea breeze, usually much anticipated, to kick in around one or two o'clock every afternoon. Often the heat and moisture would build up in the clouds until it reached a breaking point and all that energy would be released in severe and sometimes violent thunderstorms.

Grandpa dismissed the storm as too far away to concern them, and watched his fishing line. "Anyway," he went on, "Salvatore Versaggi told me of the money to be made catching shrimp around Amelia Island. During the spring and fall, he said the shrimp were so plentiful they practically jumped into the boat.

The Ocean under the Moon

He and Mike had just figured out how to pack the shrimp in iceboxes on rail cars, with a repacking in North Carolina, to get the shrimp to New York without spoiling. The Fernandina shrimp were catching on as an exotic delicacy in the restaurants of New York," he said.

"Salvatore also told me how beautiful the island was. Compared to cold and hectic New York City, with its dingy apartments and overcrowded streets, his stories made the island sound like a paradise. In fact, the fishing village of Fernandina sounded a lot like my home village of Agios Kirikos. So it was no wonder that when Salvatore returned to Fernandina, I went with him with just the promise for me to be able to work as a deckhand on one of the shrimp boats."

Nick smiled as he watched his grandfather's face. He couldn't imagine Grandpa ever being anywhere but here.

"I never regretted deciding to leave New York," Grandpa said with a grin. "I was a hard worker, and I exhibited the seamanship Mike wanted, so soon I was captain of one of his boats. After about five years, I'd saved enough money to have the Tiliakos brothers build me a boat of my own."

"And you ended up with three boats," Nick said.

"Yes, and along the way I married a local girl, Catherine Oxford, your grandmother. That was in 1925, and the next year we had a son, your father. So, Amelia Island attracted another man to try his luck, to see if I could succeed—following in the footsteps of the Timucuans, French, Spanish, British, pirates, soldiers and adventurers."

He laughed as he ended with his dramatic flourish. "Well,

that's my story. What do you think?"

"I think—I got another fish," Nick said, as he set the hook and proceeded to reel in another nice flounder.

For the next couple of hours they concentrated on their fishing. It was a perfect morning, and even the fish were cooperating. By eleven o'clock, they'd landed seven flounder of various sizes—more than enough for dinner that night. They kept on fishing however, waiting for the tide to change and the sea breeze to begin so their row back home would be easier.

At around eleven-thirty, it was still very hot and humid, as the sea breeze had not begun nor the tide changed yet. Dead low tide was not slated for another hour and the tide was still flowing out to sea past the fort.

The wary old fisherman kept glancing to the west, noting the progression of the dark, angry clouds that were building up over the eight miles of marshes that separate Fernandina from the little town of St. Marys, Georgia. The squall line had almost reached Tiger Island, a small spoil island just to the west of the Intracoastal Waterway. If the storm moved any farther east, it would soon cut off their escape route back to Egan's Creek.

"I don't know if we are going to be able to wait until the tide changes before we head back. That storm is coming faster than I would like," Grandpa said.

"But the fishing is so good. Can't we stay just a little longer? The sea breeze will keep it back."

"That's what I'm afraid of, son. The sea breeze hasn't kicked in yet."

Nick looked around and saw his grandfather was right.

The Ocean under the Moon

The water around them was dead calm, without the hint of a chop, and the air was hot and still, without a breath of the cooling breeze.

Just then, a bolt of lightning made up their minds for them. It seemed to come out of the sky directly toward Tiger Island. The flash of light was followed by a loud slap of thunder less than a second later.

"Let's go," Grandpa said. Nick did not argue.

With the thunder rumbling increasingly louder and the sun disappearing behind the clouds that were making a slow march to the east, Grandpa started the hard row against the current toward the northwest end of the island. Nick offered to row, but his grandfather refused him, since he was still bigger than his grandson and felt responsible for getting them home safely.

The stubborn old fisherman had been rowing hard for about twenty minutes, making painfully slow progress against the swift, outgoing tide. Nick glanced to his right and noted they were just even with the campground area.

He had moved to the bow of the boat to get out of his grandfather's way and also to start cleaning the fish, because the storm would not probably give them time to do that when they got back to their dock. He was just about finished, dropping the heads and guts over the side of the boat, when he heard a thud and felt the boat slipping sideways in the current.

He'd been facing forward concentrating on his task and he whirled around to see his grandfather slumped over on the floor planks of the boat.

"Grandpa!" he yelled.

There was no response. He scrambled to the back of the

boat and shook his grandfather, who lay still and silent.

Nick glanced around, noting that the boat was rapidly drifting with the current back to the fort. He did not see any boats nearby, so he knew he needed to row toward the campground and get to shore as quickly as possible to find help.

After rowing for what seemed like an eternity, he finally made it to shore, just east of the campground. He dragged the boat onto the beach as far as he could and then sprinted toward the campground.

"Help! Somebody help!" he yelled.

The first person he came to was a doctor vacationing with his young family by camping out at Fort Clinch. The doctor, an earnest-looking man about forty years old and wearing black horn-rimmed glass, yelled at his wife to watch their two young children and ran with Nick back to the rowboat.

The man scrambled into the boat, rolled the old man over and felt for a pulse. After finding none, he then checked both pupils, which were fixed and dilated. Nevertheless, the doctor dragged him out of the boat and laid him flat on the beach. He started doing cardiopulmonary resuscitation, which had only gained acceptance in the last several years.

The doctor worked on his grandfather for about twenty minutes, while Nick looked on helplessly. Nearing exhaustion, he looked up at Nick with sad eyes and shook his head from side to side.

"I'm afraid he is gone, son."

Nick, who stood just outside the boat, screamed, "Do something!"

The Ocean under the Moon

The doctor stood up, knowing there was nothing else that could be done, and tried to console the shaking boy.

"Now, now, son," he said.

Nick pushed the doctor away and started to sob. He'd never encountered death before and for it to be his beloved grandfather, who was here one minute and gone the next, was too much to bear. He sat down on the beach, as the first raindrops from the thunderstorm started pelting the ground.

He thought about the tough old seaman, who'd regaled him with stories of all the storms and sometimes hurricanes he'd ridden out. Now he'd been killed by a routine summer thunderstorm, trying to guide his grandson to safety.

Nick drew his knees to his chest and looked up to the black sky. With tears streaming down his face, he screamed his frustration at the cruelties of life. He was answered by a flash of lightning, followed by a cracking boom of thunder that was so close, the doctor had to drag him to safety.

Since there were no phones at the campground, the doctor left his wife to comfort the boy, while he drove off to find a park ranger. But Nick could not be consoled. At first, he sat under a tarp, bundled in a blanket that the woman had given him. He was sobbing and staring at his grandfather's body being pelted by the rain on the beach.

Finally, he couldn't take it any more and ran back out in the rain carrying the blanket. He reached where his grandpa lay and propped him up and sat down behind him, wrapping his arms around him and draping the blanket over the both of them.

Nick and his grandfather's body remained there under the

41

blanket, until the doctor and a couple of park rangers returned, followed closely by an ambulance.

* * *

Grandpa Eber was buried at Bosque Bello Cemetery three days later. The service at St. Peter's Episcopal Church had been overflowing. In his fifty-plus years on Amelia, he'd accumulated a lot of friends. There were shrimpers, crabbers, net makers, boat builders, store owners, bankers, teachers, and coaches.

When Eber was not out shrimping, due to inclement weather, or because it was the off-season for shrimp, he'd done a lot of volunteer work. Always one to promote the shrimping industry, he was instrumental in starting the annual Isle of Eight Flags Shrimp Festival. He'd also been one of the charter members of the Fernandina Beach Chamber of Commerce. He loved baseball and for many years he helped sponsor and coach Little League teams.

Bosque Bello, meaning "Beautiful Woods," had been established by the Spanish around 1798 and was located just south of the entrance to Old Town. Fitting its name well, the cemetery possessed abundant old oak and cedar trees, combined with subtle swales of well-kept grass, creating a serene atmosphere.

Earlier, Eber bought a large plot, large enough for eight family members. It was here, on a side of a small hill, underneath a decades-old cedar tree, that he was laid to rest. The old shrimper was the first Stamos laid to rest in the plot. He would not be the last.

The Ocean under the Moon

Chapter 4

July 31, 1973

Nick was seventeen years old when he first met Monica Johnson. He'd grown into a tall young man, six-foot-one, weighing one hundred eighty pounds and inherited his father's dark, curly hair, green eyes, and strong Greek features.

That summer, he worked as a lifeguard for the City of Fernandina Beach at Main Beach, the popular area at the end of Atlantic Avenue. He'd grown muscular lifting weights all spring, getting ready for his senior football season in the coming fall. This was his second summer as a lifeguard, and although the pay wasn't great, the fringe benefits were rewarding.

First of all, he got to hang out with his friends at the beach all day long, working on his tan, and getting paid for it. Secondly, he was getting in shape for the upcoming football season, because, as part of their training, the lifeguards ran five miles on the beach one day. The next day, they would lift weights for an hour at the recreation center a couple of blocks away.

But the most important fringe benefit, for a seventeen-year-old boy, was meeting girls. Tanned and muscular, wearing a red bathing suit with the word LIFEGUARD stitched in white down the side, sitting in a position of authority high in his lifeguard chair looking through mirrored sunglasses, Nick was a magnet for girls.

Like a minor rock star, he'd obtained his share of groupies, particularly the young ones. They'd come to the beach early in the day, setting up their beach towels near his stand. Then, the girls made up excuses to try to talk to him, asking dumb questions, and sometimes even faking jellyfish stings to try to get some attention from him.

He either answered their questions curtly, maintaining his focus on the swimmers in the ocean, or, if it was towards the end of the day and he was bored, he flirted with them a bit, raising their hopes, and sending them back giggling triumphantly to their girlfriends, who waited on their beach towels.

But he didn't have much interest in the local girls, most of whom he'd known since grade school and who were more like sisters to him. No, his interest was in the new, exotic south Georgia girls, who were vacationing with their parents in the wooden cottages that were rented out by the week during the summer months.

The Georgia girls held several advantages over the local ones in his eyes. They were strangers and therefore interesting — he didn't remember them as seven-year-olds, as he did the local girls. Their syrupy Southern drawl and general naiveté made them irresistible. Besides that, they were usually just staying at the beach for a week, before they went back to their mundane lives on their farms or in the little towns of southeast Georgia.

This last factor was important in his eyes, since it compressed the relationship into only a short time. The normal cycle of dating, complete with the societal and peer-group pressure, including corresponding judgment, did not exist at the beach. Free from worry about what their classmates and friends would think about them, the fresh young girls from small towns like Nahunta, Hoboken, Waycross, Blackshear, Pearson, Douglas, and Alma would come to the beach looking for a little summer romance and they knew they had to hurry.

Nick, with his dark hair, sea-green eyes and flashing white smile, was like a beacon in his lifeguard chair, attracting girls— much like the Egan's Creek lighthouse, a quarter of a mile away from his chair, beckoned boats back to the port. From his vantage point high in his chair, Nick surveyed the scene below him, as though he were a lion on a hill in Africa surveying a large herd of wildebeest on the savannah below him, looking for the easiest, most attractive prey.

It was the end of July. So far, it had been a successful summer for him. He was now tan and fit and saved almost all the money he had made from working as a lifeguard that summer. All the weightlifting and running had made him stronger and faster for the two-a-day football practices he would start in a couple of weeks. The romance department was also successful, evidenced by the letters he received from love-struck girls from all over south Georgia.

On this sweltering morning, Nick who was wearing nothing but his bathing suit, mirrored sunglasses, and a little zinc oxide on his sunburned bottom lip, was broiling in the sun radiating off the surface of the ocean. The ocean was calm, without waves, as there wasn't a breath of wind, and it would be several hours until the sea breeze would give its cooling relief. He leaned back in his unpainted, tall wooden chair and closed his eyes behind his sunglasses, since he had been out late the night before. It was so hot he could feel beads of sweat run down his chest, across his stomach, and pool into his belly button.

He almost drifted off to sleep, but a seagull's cry from directly overhead brought him back to reality. When he opened his eyes, he thought he was seeing a mirage. Right in front of him, silhouetted against the brilliant light of the mid-morning sun reflecting off the ocean, was a perfect figure in a white bikini.

He blinked twice to make sure he wasn't dreaming, then the girl moved to his left, out of the direct reflection, and he knew she was real. Long blond hair, slender waist, with just enough curves to show this was a girl turning into a woman, without being overly voluptuous—a vision of loveliness.

The girl walked toward his lifeguard chair, the sunlight reflecting off the ocean behind her like an angelic halo. He squinted into the sun, trying to make out her features. When she reached the front of his lifeguard chair, he could look down at a steep enough angle that the sun was not blinding him.

Sun-bleached hair, cerulean eyes, and perfect white teeth formed in a mischievous smile. He was overwhelmed.

"You know, I've been looking for shark's teeth on the beach for two days and I haven't found one yet. What's the secret?" she said in her soft, Southern drawl.

Nick, despite his considerable experience talking to girls on the beach, was momentarily speechless.

"Cat got your tongue, or are you just the strong, silent

46

type?" she said.

He broke out of his stupor and leapt out of the chair to land on the beach beside her.

"Hi, I'm Nick." He was trying to act confident, without letting her know how intimidated he was by her beauty.

"I'm Monica. Monica Johnson from Hazlehurst, Georgia."

"Hazlehurst," he said, with mild surprise. "We don't get many girls from Hazlehurst."

"Oh, I bet you 'get' girls from all over," she said.

Nick realized his words had come out wrong and decided to change the subject.

"The secret to finding shark's teeth is the color and shape," he said. "First of all, you look along the edge of the water where the ocean leaves the broken shells. It's best to look at low tide, where the pockets of shells are scattered along the beach. Then you look for something black and triangular."

"They're black?" she asked, raising her eyebrows.

"Most people think shark's teeth are white." He grinned at her. "But that's only true if you pluck them from a shark that's just been caught. The ones that wash up on the beach have been in the sand under the ocean for awhile and are fossilized, so they're dark like coal."

He was an expert at finding shark's teeth. When things got boring and he got tired of sitting, he would take a stroll around his lifeguard stand. With one eye on the bathers out in the ocean, he would cast a practiced eye on the beach around his stand and would usually spot a tooth or two. He kept a small collection to amaze the tourists who would approach him asking if he had seen any sharks in the water that day.

He would always respond that he hadn't seen any sharks, so far, but he reminded them that there were some out there and he would show them the teeth he had found, as proof that somewhere out there in the ocean, there were sharks swimming around. This was sufficient to keep most tourists out of the water that day, which made his job easier.

He felt a little guilty about that, and he was sure that the Chamber of Commerce wouldn't approve, but the truth was, there were plenty of sharks out there under the surface. He knew this to be true because whenever he went out to help his father shrimping, they would always catch some sharks in the nets as by-product. Black-tip sharks, spinner sharks, sandbar sharks, nurse sharks, hammerhead and bonnet-head sharks would all be routinely found in the nets. Also, after they'd hauled in the nets and separated the shrimp from the by-catch — like crabs, pogy fish, jacks, etc. — they would dump the by-catch off the back of the boat and a feeding frenzy of darting fins of all sizes would take place behind the boat.

In addition, he once caught a ride up in the pogy-spotting plane that located the schools of fish for the pogy plant. Nick's friend Billy was the son of the pilot for Nassau Fertilizer Company, which ran the pogy plant. Billy's father's job was to fly a single-engine Cessna airplane up and down off the coast of Amelia Island and its surrounding waters and find the pods or concentrations of the fish. He would then guide, by radio, the pogy boats to the area to haul in the pogy fish in the long, purse seine nets.

That day had been his first time up in a plane of any sort and the perspective from the air was a revelation. The green marshes with all their creeks and tributaries were spectacular and better visualized from above. And, as they'd flown along the beach, they could see dark silhouettes of sharks swimming just offshore— and sometimes quite near clueless bathers. This proved to him that there were more sharks swimming around in the murky water of northeast Florida than most people would like to admit. But due to the abundance of other prey, and also probably to a dislike of the taste of human flesh, shark attacks in northeast Florida were rare and likely accidental.

But there was nothing accidental about his finding some shark's teeth near his stand that day. While he talked to Monica, he pointed to an area of crushed seashells and periwinkles near the edge of the water that should be prime shark's teeth hunting ground.

When she turned her attention to the spot he was pointing at, Nick reached into the storage cubby below the seat of his lifeguard stand and retrieved a few pointed teeth from his small collection. These were not his best shark's teeth; he stored those in a glass jar he kept at home.

He clutched three of the teeth in the palm of his right hand and walked over to where she was stooped over, staring at the ground. The tide had receded, leaving shards of shells lying in thick collections. With her unpracticed eyes, Monica stared at the thousands of broken shells of all shapes, sizes and colors, looking for something black and triangular.

"Oh, here's one!" she said.

She placed the shell in Nick's outstretched left hand. He took one glance at it and shook his head and let the shell fragment fall back into the mass of shells on the ground.

"Not even close," he chided, with a smile.

"Drat." She took a few more steps.

"Oh, oh!" She giggled and bent over to scoop up another object.

He examined the object carefully. "It's the right shape and color," he said. "But it's just a smoothed piece of seashell."

She furrowed her brow and went back to her task with a determined concentration. After a few unproductive minutes, he spoke up.

"Here, let me find one for you."

"It's impossible."

"No, it's not," he countered. "You just have to have a trained eye."

She continued to stare into the mass of shells. He stood beside her to her right and a little behind her. He dropped one of the shark's teeth he was clutching in his hand onto the beach beside his right foot.

"There's one!" he said. She turned in his direction as he bent over and picked up the tooth to then show it to her.

She stared at the smooth and shiny shark's tooth in his outstretched hand.

"Oooh, it's beautiful," she purred in her soft drawl. He allowed her to pluck the tooth from his hand and she examined it.

"You can keep it if you like," he said.

"Oh, I couldn't."

"I have plenty at home. Go ahead and keep it."

"Okay. Thank you," she said. "But I'm going to keep

looking until I find one of my own." She returned her focus to the jangled mass of shells on the beach.

He let her search awhile, amused by the look of concentration upon her face. He watched her scurry about, and laughed every time she screamed with excitement whenever she spotted a piece of shell that looked anything like a shark's tooth, only to let her shoulders sag as close inspection revealed the object to be a false alarm.

After a few minutes, he let another shark tooth fall from the grasp of his right hand.

"Here's another one," he said. He scooped it up with his left hand and presented it to Monica, who stared at it in disbelief.

"How do you do that?"

"I'm just good."

"Oh, I bet you say that to all the girls."

"I have my talents."

"I bet you do."

They stared at each other for a moment, and then she turned back toward the beach.

"I'm not leaving this beach until I find one of my own," she proclaimed.

He had saved the largest of the shark's teeth that he grabbed earlier. He sauntered over to a flat area of hard-packed sand that was almost devoid of shells. He dropped the last tooth onto the barren patch of beach when her back was turned to him. He wandered back over to her and made a suggestion.

"Why don't you try an area of the beach where the shells aren't packed so close together? Sometimes they are easier to see that way." He gestured in the general direction of where he'd dropped the tooth.

Monica looked frustrated, but after a moment of hesitation, headed that way.

He walked back to his stand and leaned against it, facing the ocean, to give the appearance at least that he was working and watching the bathers in the water.

But his gaze kept returning to the barefoot girl in the white bikini. He couldn't imagine a more gorgeous creature. Long, pale blond hair, about halfway down her back. Smooth, flawless skin tanned to a golden brown by hours spent at her backyard pool. Tall, about five-foot-nine, but not too tall, with long slender legs. She looked like the perfect beach-bunny, surfer girl, even though she was from south Georgia and only spent one or two weeks a year at the beach.

He could see the lone shark's tooth lying in the barren area of sand even from where he was standing. He watched her flutter about looking everywhere, but where he wanted her to look. Finally, just when he was about to divert her attention to the area where the tooth lay, she zigzagged her way close to the spot.

He thought she was going to bypass the tooth, but she turned and scooped it up. After a quick inspection, followed by an excited squeal, she came running over to him, waving her hand while holding the tooth up in the air.

"I found one! Please tell me I found one," she implored, holding the tooth in her outstretched palm.

"Ooooh, that's a nice one."

"I found one! I finally found one!" she shouted. She

skipped around in a circle doing a little jig, and then she came over and gave him a hug.

"Thank you for showing me how to find shark's teeth."

Nick, taken aback by her effusiveness and public show of affection, remembered he was on duty and stepped back to try to maintain some semblance of professionalism.

"You're quite welcome." He turned his gaze back to the water away from her amazing eyes.

"You can repay me by agreeing to go out with me tonight," he said.

She paused and looked thoughtful. He guessed that she was wondering what her parents would allow.

"I'll meet you at the skating rink at eight o'clock," she said at last.

"See you then," he said, grinning.

She gave him a smile. Then she turned and walked away, back toward the beach cottage where her family was staying, the shark's teeth in hand. Every so often, she bent down to pick up something from the sand to examine it more closely, then look back at him and shake her head and throw the object back down.

He watched her until she was almost out of sight. He glanced at his watch, noting it wasn't even noon yet. He sauntered back to his stand, climbed up in the tall chair, and settled in to a long afternoon, preceding what he hoped would be a special evening.

The Ocean under the Moon

Chapter 5

July 31, 1973
7:30 p.m.

When Monica met Nick that day at the beach, she was only sixteen. She came from a close-knit family. She knew her mother would never approve of her going out with a boy whose parents she didn't know, in a town she was unfamiliar with, unescorted. So, she devised a plan.

Her little brother, Bud, was eleven years old, and usually, she had little use for her younger brother, who loved to try and annoy her, but tonight he would be her ticket out of the little wood-frame cottage where they were staying. She knew that after three days here, with Bud's constant questions and need for attention, her parents were in need of a break. After dinner that evening, she made her move.

"Hey, Bud, do you want to go to the skating rink with me?"

He eyed his sister warily, not sure if he wanted to go or not.

"They have an arcade next to the skating rink," she added.

That did it for him, because he loved games of all kinds, but particularly pinball machines.

The Ocean under the Moon

"I'll go," he said.

She turned her attention to her parents, who were clearing the dishes from the table.

"Mom, can Bud and I go to the skating rink tonight? I'll drive him there, and we promise to be home by eleven." She had recently acquired her permanent driver's license.

Caroline, who was eager to have a quiet evening in the cottage alone with Buck, acquiesced somewhat.

"You and Bud can go to the skating rink, but first you must wash the dishes. Then I will take you and pick you up at ten-thirty."

Monica knew better than to argue, or she wouldn't be able to go at all, so she agreed to the compromise. She just hoped Nick wouldn't be waiting outside the skating rink when she pulled up with her mom and little brother. That would embarrass her to no end.

She washed the dishes, taking care not to get the front of her sundress wet. Then she rounded up her brother, and they piled into the car for the short ride to Main Beach. When they pulled up in front of the skating rink, there were several kids lurking around the entrance, but Nick was not among them.

Main Beach was the term the locals used for the area where Atlantic Avenue intersected with South Fletcher Avenue. There was a U-shaped parking lot at the foot of Atlantic Avenue with a ramp at the end to drive down onto the beach. Driving on the beach wasn't allowed to the north, because this was the area patrolled by the city lifeguards for sunbathers only, but you could drive south on the beach all the way to the south end of the island.

The Ocean under the Moon

On the north side of the parking lot was the skating rink, a white block building about fifty feet wide by one hundred twenty-five feet long. To the left, and wrapping around behind the skating rink, was the Putt-Putt Golf Course. Illuminated by a series of bright lights, the tightly compressed, thirty-six-hole miniature golf course with its green artificial turf and orange wood side boards stood out sharply in the twilight.

To the right of the skating rink stood a smaller, nondescript block building with a large sign on the front that said simply "Arcade."

Next to the arcade, closest to the beach, was the Blue Seas Restaurant. It was a greasy dive, but the locals claimed it had the best cheeseburgers on the island. Across from it, on the south side of the parking lot, was a low, cement building called the Golden Sands. Despite its prime location, just south of the ramp down to the beach, this bar/restaurant was always changing owners and styles to not much success. A popular spot just west of the Golden Sands was the Aloha—a package store/lounge where the locals went to drink away their loneliness and boredom.

Moore's grocery store stood beside the Aloha. Once the site of a large dancing hall covering the entire southeast corner of this intersection in the 1940s and 1950s, it had been downsized to a neighborhood grocery store.

Monica and Bud jumped out of the car, said goodbye to their mother, and watched her drive away. Monica pulled out a bag of coins that she had been hiding in her purse and held them up to Bud.

"Have fun, little guy," she said.

The Ocean under the Moon

"Oh, I will." He snatched the coins from his sister and made a bee-line to the arcade.

Monica walked into the skating rink full of anticipation. She'd visited the rink often on previous trips to Fernandina when she was younger. It was old, but it had a certain character. Since the building was not air-conditioned, it was steaming hot during the day, but at night with the windows propped open, allowing the cool sea breeze to blow through from one side to the other, it could be quite pleasant.

She entered the building and heard "Hang on Sloopy," by the McCoys, coming from the loudspeakers. She looked around for Nick while her eyes adjusted to the light. Thirty or forty kids were skating counter-clockwise around the wooden floor. She spotted Nick leaning up against the wall, talking to two girls who were sitting up on the open windows, cooling off in the breeze.

Miffed, she went over to the counter, rented skates and sat down on the wooden benches to put them on. An expert skater, she was soon up to speed, flying around the wooden floor. Nick, who was still leaning with his hand on the wall talking to the girls in the window, had his back to the flow of skaters and hadn't spotted her yet.

She zipped by him, missing him by just a few inches, hoping to gain his attention. Her fly-by worked, for he stopped in the middle of a sentence and his eyes followed her down the rink. At the first curve she looked back at him and gave a coy smile, her long hair flying in the wind.

He left his spot beside the girls, without an explanation, and set off in pursuit of her. Dodging her way past the slower skaters, Monica maintained her lead over him. Realizing that he would never catch her this way, he took a shortcut across the rink to intersect her.

"Hey, slow down," he yelled to her over the music.

"Aren't you in a hurry to get back to your harem?" she said.

"Oh, they're just classmates," he said. "I was beginning to think you weren't coming. I waited outside for you for while, but I finally decided to come on inside."

"I had to wait until we finished dinner." Monica saw the sheepish look on his face and she softened.

"You're a really good skater," he said. He struggled to maintain his balance, even as she had slowed down somewhat.

"Well, there's not much to do in Hazlehurst."

They spent the next hour gliding around to the music. Even though it was the early 1970s, the rink played mostly nostalgic beach music like "Under the Boardwalk" by the Drifters, "Sittin' on the Dock of the Bay," by Otis Redding, or the tunes of the Beach Boys and Jan and Dean. If the older woman who ran the place went outside for a cigarette break, one of the younger workers might slip on something more radical like "Crossroads" by Eric Clapton and the Cream or even "In-A-Godda-Da-Vida," by Iron Butterfly. After skating to the slow, couples-only song, "Crimson and Clover," by Tommy James and the Shandells, Nick and Monica decided to go outside for awhile.

They sat outside on the trunk of a parked car, cooling off in the sweet ocean breeze. After a few minutes, she decided she better go check on her brother. She didn't want Bud to see her with

Nick, because he would surely inform their parents, so she told Nick to wait for her and she would be right back.

When she walked through the door of the arcade, she spotted Bud playing one of the pinball machines with zeal. Just as she'd suspected, he had blown through the bag of coins she had given him and there were only a couple of nickels left on the top of the glass of the pinball machine.

She pulled a second, reserve bag of coins out of her purse and placed it beside the two remaining coins on top of the pinball machine.

"Here you go, twerp," she said. "This is all I got, so try not to go through these as fast."

"Thanks, Sis."

He was busy trying to maintain that fine balance between nudging the machine firm enough to direct the ball where he wanted it to go and not tilting the machine.

"I feel a winning streak coming on. I think I've got this machine figured out."

Just then a distinctive pop was heard, indicating he had just won a free game and he gave Monica a triumphant smile. She turned and went back out to join Nick, knowing Bud would be occupied for quite some time.

"What do you want to do now?" he asked as she approached. He noticed the beautiful three-quarter moon that had risen above the ocean as night had fallen and hoped she would say that she wanted to go for a stroll on the beach.

Monica, however, walked up to him where he still sat on the trunk of the car, grabbed his knees and said, "Let's go play putt-putt."

It was not quite the answer he wanted to hear, but her touch on his knees and her imploring smile made him jump up.

"Okay, but I warn you, I'm a better putter than I am a skater."

"I would hope so."

"All right, you asked for it."

He grabbed her hand and pulled her toward the small building in the center of the putt-putt course. The side of the building facing the road was a concession stand serving cotton candy, snow cones, ice cream cones, and hot dogs.

They walked around to the counter at the other side, and signed up for eighteen holes. They selected their putters and colored golf balls. There were four colored light bulbs hanging from the corner of the building and for about five minutes at a time, one of the bulbs would light up. If you made a hole in one with a ball the same color as the lighted bulb, you won a free round of eighteen holes.

He'd spent many afternoons at this little course as a kid, and he was quite familiar with all of its secrets and quirks. He knew what to do and what not to do and all the angles. He won the first few holes and after building a commanding lead, sufficiently putting her in her place after her previous remark, he started coaching her and telling her how to play the course.

After letting her win a couple of holes, he noticed the light bulb on the building had switched to red, matching the color of her ball.

"Your light is on."

The Ocean under the Moon

"Ooooh, I need to make a hole in one."

"Well, this is a good one to do it on."

They'd reached the twelfth hole, one of the easiest on the course.

"Just follow my directions and you'll make one."

"Easier said than done."

"This hole is not as hard as it looks," he said. "Look, I'll show you."

He placed his ball on the small, green mat that had three indentions on it to hold the ball in place like a tee—one indention on the left side, one in the middle, and one on the right. From experience, he chose the one farthest to the right. The hole was a ninety-degree dogleg to the right with a board angled in the corner that would send the ball ricocheting toward the hole.

"Now, the secret is, you have to hit the ball against the angled piece of wood in the corner in just the right spot, where the ball will bank off of the back wall, then ricochet off the wall behind the hole, back into the hole."

"Sounds easy," she said.

"It is… watch the master."

He hit the ball about where he wanted to, the ball ricocheted off the board, banked off the long board along the far side, went past the hole on the left side, rebounded off the back board behind the hole, then headed to the hole and just lipped out.

"Arrggh," he groaned.

"Close, but no cigar. Now watch the real master," she said.

He gave way and she stepped up to place her ball.

The Ocean under the Moon

He walked down beside the hole while she got ready to putt the ball. He placed his putter on top of the board that was slanted across the right angle.

"Hit it right here," he said, indicating the spot with his putter head. "Hit it hard, too."

She did as she was told and the ball ricocheted off the wood, just where he had indicated. The ball grazed off the long board at the end of the hole, then banked hard off the board behind the hole and then went right into the hole.

"Hole in one!"

"You did it!" he said.

She ran toward him and jumped on him, clasping her legs around his waist. He caught her and supported her weight by hugging her as tight as he could.

She gave him a little kiss on the cheek and raised her arms in triumph.

"I'm the putt-putt queen!"

"That you are."

"We make a good team," she said, as she looked into his eyes.

"Yes, we do."

They looked at each other for a second or two, full of youthful hope and anticipation.

"You'd better go claim your free round, before they change the light," he said, lowering her to the ground.

She skipped over to the counter, received her prize and came back waving it triumphantly.

They played the last few holes, with Nick making a couple

of holes in one down the backstretch, but his light wasn't on so he didn't win anything.

"Want an ice cream?" he asked as they placed their putters back on the rack.

"Sure."

They walked around to the other side of the building to the concession stand and Nick bought two vanilla ice cream cones.

"Let's go down to the rocks and eat our ice cream looking at the ocean," he suggested.

"Okay," she said.

They headed toward the rocks about fifty yards away. Large boulders had been placed at the foot of the small sand dunes to keep the sand from eroding at extreme high tides. They found a flat, smooth boulder and sat down on it to gaze out over the sea and finish their vanilla cones.

The moon up over the water, illuminating the surface, and a brisk, southeast sea breeze had kicked up the ocean with two to three feet seas. They listened in silence for a minute to the ocean's roar, as the waves broke on the beach, while they tried to eat their ice cream before it melted, as it spilled over and ran down the sides of their cones.

"This is beautiful," Monica said softly, as she gazed out at the moonlit waves.

"The ocean is beautiful at night. I've spent a lot of nights shrimping with my father on his boat," he said.

"So your family is in the shrimping business?"

"Yes, my grandfather came here from Greece about sixty years ago and helped start the local shrimp industry. My father followed my grandfather into the shrimping business and when I graduate, I'm going to work a few years helping my father, save up some money, buy my own boat, and be the third generation to make a living from shrimping."

"Sounds exciting. What's it like out there?"

"Well, most of the time it's pretty boring. You drag the nets behind the boat, going slow, and in a straight line. Then when we dump the nets on the deck of the boat, we have to work fast to separate the shrimp from the by-catch. But there's always something to see. Porpoises, sea turtles, sharks—even sometimes a whale. I've seen it all. Plus, the surface is always changing. Some days it's calm, some days it's rough, but every day is a little different," he said.

"There are whales around here?" she asked, in astonishment.

"Well, not this time of year," he admitted. "But during the winter the Northern right whales come down from the Northern Atlantic to the coastal waters, from south Georgia to central Florida, to give birth to their calves."

"White whales?" Monica's face looked puzzled.

"No, silly. Not white whales … right whales. They're called that because it was the 'right' whale to hunt in the last century, because they were slow, swam close to shore, and—this was good for the harpooners—the whale floated after being harpooned. Now, they're an endangered species—seems there are only a few hundred of them left."

She stared eagerly out at the ocean, as if she was going to spot a gigantic whale any moment.

The Ocean under the Moon

"Oh, that's terrible. But it must be exciting when you see one."

"I was only about twelve when I saw one for the first time," he said. "I was out helping my dad on the boat one day. I didn't know there were whales here either. When the whale came to the surface, at first I thought it was a submarine, then I saw it blow air and water from its blow hole and I knew what it was. By the time I yelled at my dad to look, it went under the surface. My dad kidded me for the rest of the day about seeing 'sea monsters,' but he'd seen the whales sometimes himself, so he knew what I had seen."

She glanced at her watch, noting in the moonlight that it was five minutes after ten and her mother would be there soon to pick up her and Bud.

He noticed her uneasiness. "Do you have to go now?"

"Not yet, but my ride will be here any minute."

Nick, not wanting this romantic, moonlit evening to pass without at least stealing a kiss, moved closer to her.

"You know," he started, "of all the amazing creatures I have seen around the ocean, the one I saw for the first time on the beach today is the most beautiful one I have ever seen."

She turned to face him and, realizing that he was talking about her, she blushed.

Then she smiled. "I bet you say that to all the girls."

"Only the special ones." He leaned forward and kissed her.

A hormonal release of sensations cascaded through him, and she felt warm and yielding in his arms. After a long, passionate kiss, she opened her eyes and pulled back.

"I really must be going. My mother will be here soon to pick up my brother and me," she said, sounding a little breathless.

He did not want this moment to end and hesitated for a minute, not wanting to release her.

"Can I see you again?"

"Are you working tomorrow?"

"Yes."

"Then I'll come see you at your lifeguard stand tomorrow," she said.

He released his grasp and watched as she scrambled back over the rocks toward the arcade.

He turned around and gazed back out onto the moonlit sea, his body still tingling from the kiss and her touch. He realized it was love at first sight for his two main loves, the sea, and now this beautiful creature he'd just kissed.

The Ocean under the Moon

Chapter 6

August 1, 1973

He did see her the next day, but only to learn that she and her family were leaving that afternoon to go back to Hazlehurst. She and her family were supposed to stay three more days, through the weekend, but some of her father's cows were ill and he needed to get back to talk to the vet.

She apologized to him about their departure from the island. He was disappointed, but realized it was out of their control. She produced a notepad and pen that she'd tucked down the small of her back into the back of her bathing suit. She took down his address and phone number from him and promised she would write him. Then she tore off another page out of the notebook that had her address and phone number on it and gave it to him, as he sat in the lifeguard stand.

"You will write me, if I write you?" she asked.

Not given over to sentimentality, and having never written a letter to anyone, other than thank-you notes to relatives for presents, he gazed down at her imploring eyes, and knew he would comply.

"Positively," he said.

With a smile and a wave, she turned and walked away

down the beach. He followed her with his eyes as long as he could, thinking about what it would have been like if they had a few more days together.

The Ocean under the Moon

Chapter 7

August 8, 1973

Nick thought he would get over this girl in a hurry — after all, there were a couple of weeks of summer left before football practice started and there would be more vacationing girls to meet. But it turned out not to be so easy for him.

Every song over the radio that he kept on his lifeguard stand reminded him of her. Every gentle wind off the ocean reminded him of the kiss on the rocks that night. As it turned out, this would be one girl he would never forget.

The following week, Nick arrived home from a day at work on the beach. He wore just his bathing suit and a white t-shirt with "Lifeguard" printed across the back. He was tired, hot, and just wanted to take a shower to wash off the sand and suntan oil.

His father was out shrimping and his mother was still at work at the telephone company, but his grandmother, Catherine, was home as always, sitting in the living room watching TV. She was seventy-five years old now, but still maintained all of her faculties.

"There was a letter in the mail for you today," she said.

"A letter for me?" he said, his apprehension rising.

"Yes, a letter from a girl," she responded. "Who's

The Ocean under the Moon

Monica?"

"Just a girl I met at the beach."

"Then you won't mind if I open it," she said, picking up the letter from the coffee table in front of her.

"No, you don't." He rushed over to her.

"You won't let Grandma have a little fun?" She pretended to start opening the letter.

"Give it to me, Grandma."

"Oh, all right," she said. "You know, your grandfather used to write me the most romantic letters when we were courting."

He grabbed the letter and made a quick retreat to his room. He was dying to know what was in the letter, but he decided to get cleaned up first. He hid the letter under his pillow and then took a quick shower. He threw on a pair of shorts and a t-shirt and retrieved the letter from under the pillow.

Sitting on the edge of the bed, he held the letter in his hand, examining it. No wonder Grandma knew it was from a girl. It was in a pink envelope with a return address of Monica Johnson, 1601 Country Lane, Hazlehurst, Georgia. And the letter was scented. He held the sheet of paper under his nose, smelling the sweet perfume, and it reminded him of her and the night that they had kissed. He had barely noticed her perfume that night, but the second whiff from the letter had his senses salivating like Pavlov's dogs.

He opened the letter and read:

Dear Nick,

The Ocean under the Moon

You have probably forgotten me by now with all the girls you meet. Just to remind you, I was the one from Hazlehurst, Georgia, in the white bikini. Seriously, though, I hope you haven't forgotten me, because I sure remember you. I enjoyed our night at the beach, the skating rink, playing Putt-Putt and especially, our kiss on the rocks.

I'm sorry we had to leave so suddenly, but my daddy was worried the sickness that a couple of cows had would spread to the rest of the herd and wipe out the herd. Anyway, it turned out to be a false alarm and my mom was none too happy about cutting our vacation short.

It didn't make me happy either, because it interrupted our time to get to know each other. You seem like a great guy! The only problem is that you are in that lovely beach town and I am stuck in this boring, small town in Georgia. The only thing to do here is to cruise up and down Main Street, then hang out at the Dairy Queen. Please don't forget me and write to me!

Je t'aime,

Monica

He didn't know what the closing term meant, but he was thrilled with the tone of what the letter said. He had clearly made a positive impression on the girl from Hazlehurst. It was also clear, from the letter, that she yearned for more than Hazlehurst could provide, and it sounded like she didn't have a steady boyfriend there. This was all good news to him, so he grabbed a pencil and a piece of paper and wrote a reply.

Monica,

I've met so many girls this summer in white bikinis, remind me,

71

The Ocean under the Moon

which one were you? Just kidding! I have not forgotten you. The picture of you in your bathing suit remains imprinted on my mind. This past week, sitting on my lifeguard stand, gazing out at the ocean, every song I heard about lost love on the radio reminded me of you. Every beautiful scene, like the seabirds skimming over the ocean's surface, or the porpoises surfacing for air, reminds me of your beauty.

I wish you could have stayed longer. The kiss was wonderful! Is your family planning to come back to Fernandina anytime soon? It's kind of boring in Fernandina once summer time is over, also. Football practice starts after next week and that will keep me busy during the fall.

Please keep in touch,

Je t'aime,

Nick

He didn't have a clue about "*je t'aime*" — but by the way it looked, it must be French, he surmised. He didn't want to look unsophisticated, so he used it as his closing also. It was only after he had sealed the letter in an envelope and addressed it, that he walked into the living room to ask his grandmother a question.

"Grandma, your parents came from France, didn't they?"

"*Oui*," she said with a smile.

"Do you know what *je t'aime* means?"

She chuckled and raised her eyebrows at him. "It means I love you."

He was both pleased and horrified with her translation, but he decided not to reopen the letter and change his closing.

72

The Ocean under the Moon

Chapter 8

October 15, 1973

That letter became the first of many between Nick and Monica over the last few months. The summer had come to an end and he became busy playing football for the Fernandina Beach Pirates. He was the quarterback and also played safety. He was a pretty good running quarterback, but as a passer, his arm strength was suspect at best. Fernandina didn't pass much anyhow, since it ran the veer triple action offense that was popular at the time.

Nick also spent time working on his father's shrimp boats, and it took effort to balance it all. He'd learned how to get along without a lot of sleep. On the weekends, he would stay up late with his friends, then his father would wake him up, early, to go shrimping with him, as an extra deckhand, or when his regular deckhand was unavailable due to illness — or due to being thrown in jail for being drunk and fighting.

After they cleared the channel and made it out to their shrimping grounds, they would put out the nets. Then Nick could go below for a quick nap while the shrimp boat trawled back and forth. The rocking of the boat and the drone of the diesel engine struggling to pull the large nets through the water would put him almost instantly asleep.

The Ocean under the Moon

Every so often his father would pull in the small trail net to see if there were any shrimp in it. If sufficient shrimp were found in the trail net, then he would wake Nick up and they'd begin the lengthy process of pulling in the large nets.

Once the large nets were reeled in, the catch was dumped into the back deck of the shrimp boat for the arduous and sometimes dangerous process of sorting the catch. Along with the shrimp there was always a by-catch of fish, crabs, jellyfish, sting rays, sea turtles and small sharks.

With an excited flock of seagulls gathered over the back of the shrimp boat waiting for some easy prey, the deckhands sorted through the by-catch, returning all but the shrimp and the edible fish back to the sea. The good fish, they either kept themselves to take home for dinner, or gave to friends, or sold to the fish market, if it was a particularly valued species.

The "trash" fish, as they called the pogies and other smaller species that were not edible to men, were pushed out the scuppers to be devoured by the sharks and tarpons in the water that trailed behind the shrimp boats, and the seagulls that dived down to scoop all dead fish floating on the surface.

This procedure was repeated several times a day, and even into the night, if they were catching a lot of shrimp. In between, Nick would go below and catch some sleep when he could, so he had learned to fall asleep fast and wake up refreshed after just a short nap. He'd also learned very early that shrimping is an arduous job, for boat owners as well as deckhands.

* * *

That fall, Monica was a cheerleader for her home town

74

team, the Jeff Davis High School Yellow Jackets. They were having a successful year, so far, going five wins and two losses, which was better than usual and this kept everyone's spirits high.

Her mother, Caroline, had noticed the letters coming in the mail and asked her daughter what was going on. Monica told her about Nick and even showed her some of the letters. Caroline thought the letters were sweet, but she had higher ambitions for her daughter than to get involved with a shrimper from Fernandina.

Monica's father, Buck, was from a long line of farmers that had settled around the Hazlehurst area several generations ago. Over the decades, the Johnson family had made their living logging, collecting turpentine, growing tobacco, and raising pigs and cattle, always in connection with the land. Over the years, they had accumulated several thousand acres outside of Hazlehurst. Buck, himself, owned several tracts totaling about five hundred acres.

The family's main source of income these days was from raising chickens for both their meat and their eggs. About two miles from their house, on a ten-acre tract, ten large, white chicken houses each contained thousands of chickens. The rest of Buck's land was divided in several large tracts farther away from town that he leased to farmers and hunters, or grew pine trees to sell to the paper mills.

Caroline Johnson was a Southern belle, originally from Macon, Georgia. Her father owned a couple of car dealerships there and she grew up in a privileged, sheltered, and traditional environment, involving cotillion and debutante balls.

The Ocean under the Moon

After attending the all-girls Wesleyan College for two years, she had convinced her parents to allow her to go to Athens to the University of Georgia. It was there that she met and fell in love with Buck, who was on the "five-year program" at UGA. Buck, who had been idly making his way through his classes, doing just well enough to stay in school, fell hard for the beautiful, cultured girl from Macon.

Up until that point, Buck, who knew he would be returning to the small town of Hazlehurst to rejoin the family enterprises, was enjoying the college trifecta of fraternity parties, sorority girls, and football games. Meeting Caroline was good for him. The serious and elegant debutante motivated him to clean up his act to impress her family. Her family was not too happy that she was dating a small-town "hayseed," despite the fact that his family was fairly well off, by Hazlehurst's standards.

Despite her family's misgivings, they were married the year they graduated, and her family gave them a huge country-club wedding reception attended by five hundred guests. Then it was off to a quiet, comfortable existence in Hazlehurst, highlighted by attending all of the University of Georgia's home football games by custom motor coach in the fall.

* * *

Caroline allowed Monica to receive the letters, thinking it was just a passing crush and either the boy, or her daughter, would soon lose interest and the letters would cease. But the letters continued, one or two a week, all the way through October. As November approached, Monica started thinking about Homecoming.

The Ocean under the Moon

In Hazlehurst, Homecoming was a very big event, starting with a pep rally Thursday night, followed by a parade down Main Street Friday afternoon. The main event was the game, of course, on Friday night, with the presentation of the Homecoming Queen and her princesses at halftime. The homecoming dance, at the school, followed immediately after the game. And the evening ended with cruising up and down Main Street and a late night snack at the Dairy Queen, which stayed open late for this event.

Monica, who had been chosen as one of the princesses on the homecoming court, needed an escort. She wanted to ask Nick to come up for the weekend, to be her escort, and stay with her and her parents. She knew she would be the envy of all her friends, with the handsome, dark-haired young man from Fernandina. She just didn't know if her parents would allow it, and if he would come.

Finally, about two weeks before homecoming, she got up the courage to ask her parents. Caroline didn't like the idea, at all, at first. But teenagers have a way of pressuring their parents, and most parents want their children to be happy, so Monica's parents eventually relented.

Since Nick's football team had started its season earlier than Hazlehurst's team and his team had a bye week, before getting ready for the playoffs the following week, he was able to attend her homecoming.

The Ocean under the Moon

Chapter 9

November 8, 1973

He made the trip that weekend in his slightly used 1972 Pontiac
Firebird, his pride and joy. He bought the car at the end of the
summer with money he'd been saving for years, earned by
shrimping on the weekends and working as a lifeguard in the
summer. He hadn't intended to buy such a nice car, because it used
up his entire savings. But when he read the ad in the paper and
then saw the car, he had to have it. The owner, who had bought the
Firebird new, off the showroom floor, was a car enthusiast and had
taken excellent care of the sleek, bronze-colored sports car.

With a front bumper and grille molded out of Endura
rubber and a 350-cubic-inch V-8 engine rated at 255 bhp, the car
both looked and ran fast. Unfortunately for the man who owned it,
his wife gave birth to their second child, and the sports car, with its
small back seat, had to go. He sold the car to Nick for twenty-five
hundred dollars, and Nick had never seen anybody look as forlorn
as that man in his rear-view mirror when he drove away that day.

Now, he was enjoying the two-and-a-half-hour drive up to
Hazlehurst that fall day. Other than a couple of short trips into
Jacksonville, he hadn't really driven his car off the island. Today,
the open road beckoned him. He was familiar with the first half of

the trip, because his maternal grandparents had lived near Waycross, Georgia, which was on the way, about an hour and half into the trip. He had fond memories of going to their farm, near the small town of Manor, with all the farm animals, the tractor, the tobacco barn, the garden, and the pecan orchard. As a kid, he loved to go up there and shoot his B-B gun, and, as he got older, to go hunting with his shotgun. But Grandpa died about three years ago and Grandma sold the farm and moved into Waycross, where she died about a year later.

From his family trips up there, he knew there was a long, straight stretch of road between Folkston and Waycross that would be perfect to open up his new car. On this desolate stretch of road, lined by thousands of pine trees planted by the paper mills, he would see how fast the car would go. The speedometer on the car went up to one hundred sixty miles per hour and he wanted to see how close he could come to that mark.

He waited until there were no cars ahead of him or behind him, in either direction as far as he could see, then he pressed the gas pedal down. At eighty-five miles an hour, the overdrive kicked in and the car accelerated even faster. At one hundred twenty miles an hour, he noticed there was still space between the pedal and the floor. He pressed the pedal all the way to the floor. When the car reached one hundred forty miles an hour, he noticed how fast the ground was flying by and the car started to feel a little loose, so he eased up on the pedal.

He had no doubt the car would have reached the one hundred sixty mark, but suddenly he thought about what would happen if he had a flat tire or something mechanical broke at that speed. The wreck would be horrendous and he never would get to see Monica. So for the rest of trip, he was content going just a little over the speed limit.

After an uneventful drive the rest of the way through the pine forests and small towns, he arrived in Hazlehurst. He turned right on Uvalda Highway and, a couple of miles out of town, he spotted the long, white, three-board fence along the highway, which Monica had described to him. The large, brick ranch-style house sat on five acres of well-kept lawn, surrounded by forty acres of fenced pastureland where cattle grazed in scattered groups.

He pulled into the long, winding driveway, feeling nervous about seeing Monica again. Normally he wouldn't put out this much effort for a girl, but he felt she was special. Still, he had only gotten to know her those couple of days last summer and only really knew her through her letters. Now he'd driven over a hundred miles to see her and meet her parents.

He parked in the circular drive at the front of the house and looked into the rear-view mirror to check his appearance. His mind was racing as he asked himself, "What was I thinking when I decided to do this?"

His doubts were soon dispelled as Monica, wearing her cheerleader uniform, burst through the front door and bounded toward him. He got out in a rush and shut the door. She ran around the front of his car and met him in an embrace.

"I'm so glad you came. We are going to have the best time!"

He stepped back from the hug and looked into her exuberant face.

The Ocean under the Moon

"I'm glad I came, too," he said. "You look great in your uniform."

"Oh, I just came from school, where we had a pep rally. They let us out early on Homecoming day."

"Well, you look terrific and it's so good to see you again."

She glanced over at the front door, where her mother was waiting patiently.

"Let's go meet my parents," she said, taking his hand and leading him toward the door. "We'll get your luggage later."

He held her hand for reassurance as they walked toward the doorway. He saw a slender woman with perfect coiffed, shoulder-length blond hair. She wore a blue cocktail dress, with a pearl necklace and matching pearl earrings.

"It's so nice to meet you, Nick. Monica has told me so much about you," Caroline said in a refined Southern accent. She extended her hand as he climbed up the couple of steps to the doorway.

He clasped her hand with both of his and said, "The pleasure is mine, Mrs. Johnson."

"Come in and meet Mr. Johnson."

She took him by the hand and he allowed himself to be guided into the house.

The house, while very unassuming on the outside, was quite elegant inside. The large foyer gave way to a formal dining room on the left side and a living room on the right, with heart-of-pine floors, an Oriental rug in each room, and dark, antique furniture.

The far end of the foyer led down into a carpeted, sunken

81

family room that was less formal than the front of the house. A large, L-shaped couch sat in front of a stone fireplace. Over the fireplace was a family portrait of the Johnsons from a few years ago. He noticed Monica looked about twelve at the time and was wearing braces.

She saw him glancing at the picture and declared, "Nick, don't look at that hideous picture. See, Mom, I told you we need to do a new one."

"I like that one just fine. It reminds me of when y'all were young," Caroline said, as she continued to lead Nick through the house.

He looked out the large French doors, past the screened-in back porch, to the pool in the back yard.

"Y'all have quite a spread here, Mrs. Johnson."

"Thank you," she said, as she guided Nick into the spacious country-style kitchen.

"Would you like some sweet tea?" she asked.

"Yes, ma'am. That would be great."

She took a pitcher out of the refrigerator and poured a glass for him. "How was your trip up here?"

"Quite pleasant, actually." The image of him, going one hundred and forty miles an hour in his car, popped back into mind.

"Yes, it's not a bad drive. We've made it many times going to the beach. We're quite fond of your little town."

"Well, I'm the third generation of our family to live there, so we really like it too."

"So, Monica tells me your family is in the shrimping business." She smiled at him with grace. "Is there any money in it?"

The Ocean under the Moon

"Mom!" Monica frowned at her mother.

"It's fine," Nick said to Monica.

"I'm sure it's a lot like farming or ranching around here," he said. "There are good days and bad days, good years and bad years, depending on weather conditions, market prices, overhead, and demand. My grandfather came over from Greece right before World War I, when the shrimping industry was starting to boom, and got in on the ground floor, so to speak. He had the foresight to buy some land at the mouth of Egan's Creek, so we don't have to pay for dockage, like most other guys.

"The other good thing," he said, "is my father now runs two shrimp boats that are paid for already, so we don't have boat payments. Our only costs are boat insurance, diesel fuel, and ice. Even the deckhands work for a percentage of the catch, so if the catch is bad the labor costs don't eat you up. So my dad does pretty well, I guess."

"And do you plan to join in the family business when you graduate?" Caroline asked, although Monica had already told her of his plans.

"Yes, ma'am, I'm going to work on one of my dad's boats for a year or two and hopefully save up enough money to buy my own boat."

"You're not interested in going to college?"

"Well, I might take some business classes at Florida Community College of Jacksonville, but I don't really need a college education to do what I want to do." He gave her a big smile.

"But college is more than just a formal education, it is also a social education," she said.

The Ocean under the Moon

"Quit grilling him, Mom," Monica said.

"I'm not grilling him, I'm just trying to get to know him," she said, sweetly.

"Where's Dad?"

"Last time I saw him he was cleaning his shotgun in the den."

Nick didn't like the sound of that, but Monica grabbed his hand and led him down a hallway. They passed what looked like a guest bedroom on the left.

"That's where you'll be sleeping tonight," Monica said.

On the right side of the hallway, he saw a game room with a pool table, a ping-pong table and a lot of University of Georgia paraphernalia. The room was about thirty-five feet long and looked out over the porch and pool.

They came to another room on the left, and she knocked on the door, which was ajar.

"Daddy?" she inquired.

"Come on in, pumpkin."

She led Nick into the room.

Her father was sitting on a green leather couch, his shotgun disassembled on the coffee table in front of him. There was an open gun safe in the corner that contained several shotguns and rifles. On the wall behind the couch was the mounted head of a large buck, and on the wall opposite the couch, a boar's head. Over the large walnut desk at the end of the room was a mounted bobcat. The last remaining wall, next to the doorway, displayed a large mounted bass.

Buck Johnson wore blue jeans, a tan corduroy shirt, and a

John Deere cap. When he stood up to shake Nick's hand, Nick noticed how big a man he was. Six-foot-two, two hundred and fifty pounds, broad shouldered, but with a slight paunch, he extended his large, calloused, farmer's hand.

"So this is the young man you've been telling us about," he said. He looked Nick over, shaking his hand with a firm grip.

"Yes, he's nice and I like him. So don't go scaring him away," she said.

"I wouldn't dream of doing that," he said, with a gleam in his eye.

"Daddy, I mean it."

"Nick, are you going hunting with us in the morning?" Buck asked.

Startled by the sudden question, Nick didn't know what to say and hesitated.

"I'm taking Bud, Monica's brother, to the hunting camp in the morning," Buck went on. "We're trying to get him his first buck. He shot a doe last year, but now he's got his sights on getting a buck. You're welcome to come along. I've got plenty of guns, and you don't even need a hunting license because it's a private hunting camp and I know the game warden. Have you been hunting before?"

"I have a twenty-two and use it to shoot squirrels down by the cemetery in Fernandina. But I've never been deer hunting."

Buck looked at Monica, who was watching Nick anxiously. Nick glanced at her and then said, "Sure, I'll go."

"Well, it's settled then. I'll wake you up at five o'clock. We have to get out there before the deer start moving at dawn."

The Ocean under the Moon

Nick winced at the thought of getting up so early, after what he expected would be a fairly late night. He looked at Monica, who shrugged her shoulders.

Buck, for his part, was beaming. Nick figured he had planned the early hunting trip to make sure Nick and Monica ended their date early. Plus, he guessed her dad wanted a chance to get a measure of him—to see if Nick was worthy of dating his daughter.

They left her father to finish cleaning his guns.

Monica had informed Nick they would be riding in the back of a convertible for the parade as part of the homecoming court. After changing clothes, they headed downtown.

He soon found out, the homecoming parade in Hazlehurst was a big deal. It seemed the entire population of the town and the surrounding farms turned out to line the streets. The marching band led the way, with the student band leader, blowing his whistle, followed by the majorettes, in their sequined outfits, twirling and tossing their batons high into the air.

Following the band were floats from the different class years and clubs, all of them proclaiming how the Yellow Jackets were going to beat their opponent that night. Then came the homecoming court, in convertibles loaned for the parade by prominent citizens or car dealerships. Monica and Nick rode on the back of a brand-new, 1973 Mustang convertible.

Monica, looking very regal in her blue dress and long white gloves, waved politely to the crowd. She was also bathing in the adulation, knowing her friends and all of the old ladies in town would be wondering who that handsome young man sitting next to her was.

Behind the convertibles were two flat-bed trucks carrying the football players, dressed in their uniforms, minus their shoulder pads and helmets. The mayor of Hazlehurst followed in a convertible, waving and wearing his best political smile. Signaling the end of the parade marched a drum corps consisting of five members of the band with snare drums.

After the parade, they went back to the Johnsons' house, where Nick enjoyed one of the most delicious steak dinners he had ever tasted. Buck explained, while he was grilling the steaks out back by the pool, how they'd butchered one of the cows just for him. Nick had to admit it was one of the best cuts of meat he'd ever put in his mouth, although he felt a little awkward about eating it while looking out in the pasture at the cow's relatives.

After dinner, Monica changed back into her cheerleading outfit, and came out of her bedroom carrying a formal gown and a pair of shoes to change into for the halftime festivities. Nick put on the suit he had brought, and they all piled into Caroline's white Cadillac sedan with Buck behind the wheel.

He could see the stadium about a mile before they got there, it was so lit up by the bright lights. When they arrived, he noticed it was a typical high school stadium with large, concrete bleachers on the home side and a much smaller set of wooden bleachers on the visiting side.

Monica joined her cheerleading teammates, and Nick followed her parents up to the reserved section where all the movers and shakers of town sat to watch the game. It took about ten minutes for them to get to their seats, because all along the way her parents kept stopping and shaking hands, acknowledging people, and introducing him.

He put on his best demeanor and tried to act excited about meeting these people. After what seemed like an eternity, they reached their seats, about three-quarters of the way up, right on the fifty-yard line. He could tell by their location and by their welcome in the stands that the Johnsons were important members of the local society.

Soon after the game commenced, it became apparent that the home team had chosen their homecoming opponent well, as the Yellow Jackets soon jumped out to a fourteen-point lead.

Just before half-time, Caroline and Nick made their way down to the bottom of the bleachers. As time wound down in the final minute of the first half, Monica came around and met them, and she and her mother hurried off to the ladies' restroom for Monica to change out of her uniform. He waited at the edge of the bleachers, and when they emerged, Monica was looking gorgeous with a bouffant hairstyle and dressed in her blue gown, but walking with difficulty in her high heels on the uneven surface.

"Wow, you look amazing," he said. He extended his elbow out in a chivalrous manner as she approached.

Monica wobbled forward and put one arm through his, clutching the top of his shoulder with the other hand to steady herself.

"Yeah, we'll see how good I look, when I fall flat on my face," she said.

"That's what I'm here for, just hold on to me."

He was amused by this beautiful tomboy, who looked the

part of an elegant young woman, but who was clearly not comfortable in heels on the soft ground.

Caroline made them pose for a picture before she returned to the stands for the halftime ceremony. They made their way in front of the stands to a couple of folding chairs reserved for them as part of the homecoming court. The high school principal made a short speech, then he started calling out the names of the girls on the homecoming court.

"Most of these girls are seniors," Monica said. "I'm one of only two juniors who made the court."

He nodded and grinned at her.

Soon the loudspeaker announced Monica's name and Nick's name as her escort. They walked out onto the field to their appointed spot and waited as the rest of the court was announced. After all of the others, the homecoming queen was announced.

A mousy-looking brunette and her escort walked out onto the field.

"You look much better than she does," he whispered to her." Who does she know?"

She elbowed him in the side. "She's a senior, her daddy runs the bank, and she is very popular."

After the half-time ceremonies, Monica changed back into her cheerleader uniform and returned to the sidelines, while Nick went back to the stands.

The home team's dominance continued, and the final score ended up being forty-two to seven. The end of the game couldn't have come soon enough for Nick, for while he enjoyed playing football, watching two teams he didn't care about, while making small talk with Monica's parents, was not his idea of a good time. Besides, he was aching to be alone with her. It had been several months since their kiss on the beach in Fernandina, and he was ready to pick up where he had left off.

At last, the gun sounded, the game was over, and the celebration spilled out onto the field. He and Monica's parents came down out of the stands, found Monica among the throng, and congratulated her with hugs.

Back at the house, Monica and Nick changed into more casual clothes and then left in Nick's Firebird to go to the homecoming dance in the high school's gymnasium. Even though the outside temperature had become quite brisk, it was hot inside the gym from all the body heat. They walked in as a cover band was playing "China Grove," by the Doobie Brothers. The gym had been decorated extensively in crepe paper of the school's colors, hanging from the ceiling.

Since Monica had taken a while to get ready, the dance was in full swing by the time they arrived. She hustled him over to a table where her friends were located and introduced him to all of them. It was hard to hear over the blaring music and he caught only about half of the names.

Soon, she grabbed his hand and dragged him out on the dance floor, among the crowd in front of the stage. He was a reluctant dancer. He didn't really like to dance; therefore he didn't practice enough to be very good. Besides, in Fernandina, for a teenager, the only real chances to dance were the big events like homecoming and the prom.

She, on the other hand, was a natural dancer. She moved

about the dance floor effortlessly, like a butterfly with ballet training, inventing graceful moves as she went. He was captivated by her sensual movements and found himself mimicking her steps, and soon they were dancing in sync. The music was loud and rhythmic as each song gave way to another, each one more exuberant than the previous one.

After about forty-five minutes, the band finally took a break. The dancers retreated to their table for a much needed drink of punch. Now that the band had quit playing, he could hear the conversation.

It was obvious that the three girls at the table were Monica's close friends and their dates were from around here. He could tell that these were "good old" country girls and boys, ready to have a good time at one of the biggest events of the year.

After about fifteen minutes of small talk, the band cranked back up and Monica dragged him back out onto the floor. Before he realized it, it was twelve-thirty in the morning. Since she had a strict one o'clock curfew for that night, she pulled him out into the parking lot to cool off in the brisk, night air and to have some time alone.

They walked hand in hand over to his car, and sat down on the hood of the Firebird. They had both worked up a sweat from all the dancing and the cold air felt good on their steaming bodies.

"That was quite a dance," he said, taking her hand.

"Yes, there's not much to do around here. So when something fun comes along, we like to take advantage of it."

"The band was awesome," he said

"They were great, weren't they? I heard the band was

91

brought down from Macon and that they were going to get a record contract from Capricorn records, the record company that handles the Allman Brothers Band."

"I believe it."

"It was great of you to come all the way up here for this." She put her arm over his shoulder and leaned in to give him a kiss on the cheek.

"Well, I'm having a great time and, so far, I'm very glad I came," he said.   She snuggled closer, and he noticed she was shivering. The night air had cooled down their sweat-drenched clothes.

"You're shaking. Here, let me give you my coat."

He stood up and faced her, then reached out and draped his coat over her shoulders. She looked at him and his hands moved from the coat to stroke her hair out of her face, then he leaned in to kiss her, cupping the back of her head with his hands.

She responded to his kiss, sliding down the front of the car so she was straddling him. They spent the next ten minutes making out passionately, their hormones racing like runaway locomotives. The band was still playing inside, with the music coming to a crescendo, as this was the encore number signifying the end of the dance.

Just as Nick and Monica were about to reach a crescendo of their own, she gently pushed him away and reminded him that they had to be home by one and that he had to get up at five o'clock, which was only about four hours away.

The last thing he wanted to do was get up at five o'clock in the morning to try and shoot some stupid deer. His prey was right in front of him and he was ready to pounce. But reality set in quickly, as he realized he had to go hunting to impress her father, for hunting was a measure of a man in these parts. He did not want to overstep his bounds with her, either.

Just then, the music stopped and people started spilling out of the gymnasium, into the parking lot. He gathered himself, and with a sigh, gave her one last kiss on the cheek.

"To be continued," he said, staring into her eyes.

"Definitely."

The Ocean under the Moon

Chapter 10

November 9, 1973

Buck woke him up right at five o'clock. Nick was dreaming about Monica, and her father had to shake him awake several times, before he came to his senses. Buck tossed some camouflage hunting gear on the bed and told him to be in the kitchen in five minutes.

He turned the lamp on beside the bed and sat up and shook the cobwebs from his head. He looked over at the clothes on the bed. For a moment, he entertained the thought of lying back down, pulling the covers over his head, and going back to sleep. However, he knew he couldn't disappoint her father like that.

He donned the green thermal socks and slipped his legs into a large pair of camouflage overalls. He put on a long-sleeved shirt and a camouflage sweatshirt, and pulled the straps of the overalls over the sweatshirt. He slipped his feet into an old pair of hunting boots that were one size too big, and laced them secure. Then he put on a wool cap, grabbed the heavy hunting jacket off the bed and headed for the kitchen.

Buck and Bud were waiting for him, already dressed out in their hunting gear. Caroline had cooked sausage and biscuits the night before, and Bud handed him a warm sausage biscuit and a hot coffee in a Styrofoam cup.

The Ocean under the Moon

"Here, take these," he said, and he and Buck, with their heavy jackets already on, started for the door.

Nick put down the biscuit and coffee on the counter, for a little while, so he could put on his jacket, then followed them out the front door. Buck's hunting truck was idling out in front of the house to heat up the cab, since it was only twenty-eight degrees outside. The old Chevy was a faded red, with big tires and a few dents, and looked like a survivor of many hunting seasons.

The three of them piled into the front seat with Buck driving, Nick sitting by the passenger window, and Bud in the middle. They rode for several miles, trying to eat their biscuits and drink their coffee without spilling it in the cramped, front seat. He was just about done with his biscuit and was halfway down on his coffee, when Buck turned off the paved road onto a dirt road. The ride really got rough then, the suspension on the old truck feeling every pothole and rut and vibrating on the washboard sections. He gulped down the last of his coffee, to keep from spilling it all over the place.

After about a mile and a half, they turned down a narrow lane going even deeper into the woods. It was still pitch black and the truck's headlights only illuminated a small area right in front of them. Soon they pulled into a clearing and the headlights centered on a hunting lodge about thirty by twenty feet. Five men stood outside, warming themselves around a fire burning in a fifty-gallon steel drum cut in half.

Buck pulled up beside the other trucks and they climbed out. The men around the fire were laughing and carrying on in loud voices. They waved a greeting, as Buck and Bud approached, with Nick trailing behind.

"Hey, Buck. You missed quite a poker game at the lodge last night," a big, burly man with a dark beard said.

"Well, I'm sorry I didn't get a chance to take all of your money, boys. But I have my son with me, and Monica's boyfriend, and I didn't think they would want to spend the night here," Buck said. "Y'all remember Bud, and this here is Monica's boyfriend, Nick, from Fernandina."

Greetings, nods, and handshakes were given all the way around.

"Did y'all save us a good spot, so I can show these boys how to kill a deer?" he asked.

"Six and seven, just as you requested," answered the burly man.

Buck wheeled toward the lodge, motioning Bud and Nick to follow. They climbed up the three wooden steps and entered the lodge. The inside was one large room with wooden floors and wood-paneled walls. All along two walls were bunk beds, enough to sleep fourteen people. In the center of the room stood a big round table with cards still lying on top. There was a kitchen of sorts, along one wall, and a guy stood at the stove, frying some bacon. Beside the front door, to the right, was a blackboard with the day's assignments on it written in chalk.

It showed that they had indeed been assigned stands number six and seven. The stands were assigned on a rotating basis and Buck had called in a favor and done some trading to ensure they had the best stands for that day. Now, having confirmed their locations with his own eyes, he hustled Nick and Bud back out to the truck. He wanted to be sure to get to their spots and settled in their stands, before the sun came up. The other hunters were also piling into their trucks.

They crammed back into the front cab and soon were bouncing down a one-lane trail through the woods. They came to a small clearing and Buck pulled off of the trail and parked.

As they climbed out, he shined his flashlight into the bed of the truck and retrieved three guns, still in their soft gun cases. He unzipped one of the cases and pulled out a twelve-gauge shotgun and handed it to Bud, reminding him to keep the barrel pointed up and not at anybody. Then he unzipped the second case and pulled out a .270-caliber rifle, with a scope on it, and handed it to Nick.

Nick felt somewhat familiar with the gun, because the day before, after the parade, Buck had showed him how to use the rifle. Monica's father had a little shooting range set up in his back yard behind the pool, with a wooden stand for resting the gun upon to steady the shot. About eighty yards away was a silhouette of a fake deer on a piece of plywood with a mound of dirt behind it to catch the bullets. An orange target on the fake deer, about the size of a small dinner plate, indicated the kill zone on the deer.

Buck explained that the traditional kill zone was the best bet for a new hunter like Nick. Viewed broadside, the zone he demonstrated was roughly centered on the rear edge of the shoulder. If you hit the lungs, he explained, the deer would run away and then die. If you hit the heart, the deer wouldn't be able to go far at all. If you hit the shoulder bones, breaking them, the deer would fall on the spot, immobilized. He added that the traditional kill zone gave the most margin of error, although a more experienced hunter might aim for the neck in order to preserve the edible meat from damage.

After showing him where the safety was on the gun and how to load a bullet into the chamber, he had demonstrated how to use the scope and had squeezed off a round, striking the center of the orange target. Then it had been Nick's turn.

After his first couple of shots had missed high and to the right, Buck explained to him that he was pulling the trigger, instead of squeezing it. After a little more practice, he was able to hit the target with regularity and Buck was satisfied. There was nothing more wasteful to the members of the hunting club than to mis-hit a deer and have it run off to die without being able to find the dying animal.

Now, Nick held his gun with these thoughts on his mind as Buck reached to retrieve his own gun, his reliable 30-06. Then the three of them headed off into the woods. After a short walk of about one hundred and fifty yards they came to the first tree stand. This was his stand, Buck told him, and Bud would be with Buck in another stand, about fifty yards away, that faced in the opposite direction. He said that they would be hunting until about eleven o'clock and Nick should remain in his stand until they came to get him.

Buck reminded him not to shoot anything unless Nick clearly identified it as a deer through his scope. The experienced hunter warned him this type of hunting was long hours of doing nothing, combined with a few seconds of exhilaration, when a target presented itself. He told Nick not to be over-anxious and shoot the wrong thing, or move too fast and scare the deer off. He also warned him against shooting any does or taking any bucks unless they had four points to their antlers or more.

Nick nodded his understanding and checked to make sure his gun was on safety as he moved toward the tree stand. Buck kept his flashlight focused on the tree, as Nick climbed up the ladder-like steps nailed to the trunk. About ten feet off the ground, he crawled through the bottom of the stand and into the sitting area. The wooden stand was supported by two trees and was about four feet long and three feet wide. It was enclosed, up to about four feet high, with a rail to rest the gun upon when shooting. The stand was open, for about two feet above the rail, to allow for visibility, and above was a flat roof supported by two-by-fours to keep the rain off the hunters. There was a single wooden chair inside for him to sit on.

Once inside, he waved to Buck to assure him he was settled in all right. Then he watched the light fade away as the others moved toward their stand. After his eyes adjusted to dark, he noticed that dawn was coming; there was a faint glow to the east.

It was just getting light enough to make things out when he saw what looked like a large housecat coming down the trail beneath him. He had seen a bobcat once before at Fort Clinch, and as the creature came closer, he realized that it was indeed a bobcat, with its brown coat and black spots and its black-tipped, stubby tail. The bobcat didn't seem to realize Nick was there as it walked down the trail underneath the stand.

He swiveled his head as the cat passed beneath him, his

finger moving the safety off on his gun. He didn't think a bobcat would attack a human, but he had never been this close to a wild animal that could inflict damage if it wanted to, so he wasn't taking any chances. But the bobcat passed below the stand and meandered out of sight down the trail.

He settled in for what could be a long morning. He was suffering from lack of sleep and his mind felt a little foggy. He scooted his chair forward near the front on the stand and rested his rifle against the rail. He raised the gun and peered through the scope at the food plot in front of him, about sixty yards away. The stand certainly gave him a good, clear shot, if a deer came out to the food plot, and he felt confident he could make the shot, if one presented itself.

He sat there, listening to every bird chirp and squirrel bark in the quiet of the early morning. There was something primal about hunting. In the quietness of the woods, with the sun coming up, he felt the same connection with nature that he got when he was out on the ocean shrimping. Somewhere within him were centuries of training to hunt, buried deep in his DNA. He noticed his senses were heightened, as he noted every sound and movement around him.

He stayed in this attentive position for about an hour and a half, but nothing happened. He remembered what Buck had said about hunting being hours of boredom interspersed with a few seconds of exhilaration. He lowered his rifle, putting the butt of the gun on the floor and leaning the barrel against the front of the tree stand. He leaned forward, putting his head against the rail, and closed his eyes. It was warming up a little bit with the rising of the sun, but his toes were still numb from the cold.

He started daydreaming about Monica, who was the reason he was doing all this, and he realized how tired he was feeling. He was not sure how long he had been sleeping when he heard a sound of something large moving through the woods. The noise startled him awake and he tried to clear his senses and get his bearings.

Yes, there was something big coming through the woods. Maybe it was a big buck, or maybe a hog or even a bear. Buck had said there were both of them in these woods and it was all right to shoot if one presented.

He raised his rifle and peered through the scope. He could hear whatever it was coming toward the clearing, and the tops of the underbrush and fronds of the palmettos were waving back and forth as the animal approached.

It must be a huge buck. He readied his finger on the trigger as he looked through the scope trying to spot the antlers. He prepared himself to shoot, waiting for the animal to clear the thick underbrush and step into the clearing around the food plot.

After what seemed like an eternity, the creature began to step out into the open. The first thing he noticed was that it was black. Maybe it was a bear, he thought. Then he lowered his gun and looked around his scope, not believing what he had seen.

"It's a damn horse!"

A huge black horse had stepped out into the clearing, followed by a white dog. Maybe he was still dreaming and seeing an apparition. Maybe someone was playing a practical joke on him. He looked around.

The Ocean under the Moon

The horse lowered its head and started to eat grass from the clearing around the food plot. Thank goodness he hadn't pulled the trigger. That would have been very embarrassing, and hard to explain to Buck and his hunting buddies. He could imagine the jokes that would be made at his expense, if he'd shot a horse.

Now, there was a different problem, because the horse was in his line of fire and would scare away any game from his food plot. So he yelled out and kicked his feet against the floor of the tree stand to make noise. The dog looked up at the tree stand, startled by the noise, and ran off into the woods, soon followed by the horse. Now, he went back to his vigil, still shaking his head in amazement.

Buck, who'd heard the shouting, came over from the other tree stand to see what the commotion was about. Nick explained what he'd seen, hoping Buck would not think he was crazy. Buck laughed when he heard his story and assured him he wasn't going crazy. In fact, Buck told Nick that spotting the dog and horse on their hunting land was happening too frequently and was becoming a problem. A previous visit to the farmer, who owned the land next to their hunting tract, had ascertained that the dog was lifting the latch on the gate to the horse's pen and letting the horse out, so they could go exploring together.

The hunters had warned the farmer that if he didn't prevent the horse from getting loose and coming on their property, they were going to shoot it and mount its head with some antlers on it, on the hunting lodge wall. The farmer assured them it wouldn't happen again, but the dog and horse found a way to escape again today. Buck gave orders for Nick to shoot the horse, if it showed up again, and went back to his tree stand.

Nick went back to scanning the woods for signs of life and another hour and a half went by slowly. He hadn't heard many gunshots that morning, just a couple off in the far distance; he assumed most of the hunters were having the same luck as he was having. At about ten-thirty, just about when he had given up on the morning's hunt, a couple of does silently stepped out into the clearing. Heads up, and on alert, the does surveyed their surroundings. He sat motionless, watching the deer, his heart rate accelerating. His gun was leaning up against the front of the tree stand, but he didn't dare move while the does were looking around. One of them seemed to be staring right at him, as if she was daring him to move.

For a long time, he sat perfectly still. After awhile, the doe that had been staring toward him lowered its head and started feeding on the tender, young grass shoots that had been planted around the food plot. He slowly reached for his rifle and eased it up into position. He wasn't planning on shooting the doe, as Buck had warned him not to. But he'd also explained earlier, on their drive to the hunting camp, that a buck will sometimes use the doe to reconnoiter an area before the buck will show itself.

Nick had been wondering all morning how he would react if it came down to shooting a deer. On the one hand, he felt bad about taking an animal's life, especially when he did not need it for food or survival. On the other hand, he was competitive and wanted to show Buck what he was made of. As the morning had progressed, the hunting gene and boredom kicked in and now he was ready to shoot almost anything, even the horse if it came back.

The Ocean under the Moon

While he was studying the does through the scope, he noticed some movement behind and to the right of them. There at the edge of the clearing, he zeroed in on the head of a magnificent buck. He counted eight points on the antlers, making it qualified to shoot by Buck's standards.

He waited for the buck to step all the way out into the clearing, so he would have a clear shot. Half of him wanted the buck to turn and run, so he wouldn't have to kill it, and the other half of him was praying that it would step out, so he could drop it.

After surveying the scene for several long seconds, and sniffing the wind, the majestic buck stepped into the clearing and paused.

The sharp crack of his rifle pierced the mid-morning quiet. Birds took off on wing, the does ran away, and the big buck dropped to the ground in a heap.

Nick scrambled out of the stand, down the steps nailed to the tree, his rifle on a strap over his right shoulder. He ran toward the deer, removing the rifle from his shoulder and leveling it toward the deer, in case he had to deliver a *coup de grace*.

The buck lay motionless and he stooped over it. The large, pitiful eyes seemed to stare back at him as if to ask why he had done it.

He stood over the deer, partly full of regret and partly elated at his conquest. Soon, Buck and Bud arrived, attracted by the shot. Buck slapped him on the back. "Nice shot, well done, Nick."

Bud walked around the deer, admiring it, prodding it with the end of his gun. It was almost eleven by then, and the time, along with the fact that the shot would have scared off any other deer in the area, signified the end of the morning's hunt.

Nick and Bud started dragging the deer toward the truck and Buck went to bring the truck as far as he could towards them. Then, the three of them, after a lot of exertion, got the dead deer into the back of the truck.

When they reached the hunting camp, most of the other trucks were back, but the area where they butchered the deer was empty. That meant Nick's deer was the only one killed by the group, so far that morning.

Buck lay on the horn to signal the arrival of a successful kill. The other hunters poured out of the lodge, as he pulled up to the front. Soon, Nick was shaking the hands and having his back slapped by all the men, as they gathered around the truck admiring his trophy.

A couple of the members hauled the deer over to the cleaning area, hung it on a large hook and started butchering the deer. Nick didn't want to watch this process, so he hung back, sitting on the tailgate of Buck's truck, repeating the story of his morning hunt to a few of the club members.

Soon, one of the men butchering the deer returned, holding something behind his back. Nick was too engrossed in his conversation to notice the man's approach.

"Grab him, boys," the man said to the other hunters.

The two closest to him grabbed him by his upper arms. The burly hunter, who had been cleaning the deer, appeared right in front of him wearing a mischievous smile and holding a bowl of the deer's blood in front of him.

"It's a ritual in our club that whoever shoots a buck for the first time needs to be bloodied," explained the hunter through his dark beard. "That is, the victorious hunter must wear the blood of the deer who gave up his life for the hunter, so their souls will bond together and from this day forward will always be a part of you. It also signifies that you are not a hunting virgin any more." He gave what Nick thought was a maniacal smile.

Without further explanation, the two men holding Nick stood him up and removed his jacket so it wouldn't get ruined. The other hunter dipped his large, stubby fingers into the bowl and started smearing the blood all over Nick's face. The blood was still warm and he felt a slight revulsion, but continued to smile and act good-natured, as all the gathered hunters guffawed while the ritual continued.

Buck and Bud, seemed to enjoy themselves at his expense. Bud joined in to help smear some of the blood on him, jawing as though he was Nick's baby brother. Buck stood back, beaming like a proud father enjoying this ritual.

After they were done, Nick looked like a tourist with severe sunburn, red all over. They went inside the lodge so he could warm up, since he couldn't put his coat back on until after the blood had dried. He wanted to wash the blood off, but Buck and Bud would have none of it, because they wanted to parade him at home for Monica and Caroline to see.

The trio headed back to the Johnson home with a cooler full of venison and with the deer's antlers tied to the front of the truck. Nick's emotions were a combination of pride and feeling foolish. He was proud that he had killed his first deer, which was a rite of passage for the boys in this part of the country. He was the only one out of the entire hunting club who shot a deer that day and he was coming home with antlers and venison meat as his trophies. He hoped that, in some way, his successful hunt would prove to Buck and Monica that he would be a good provider for her and worthy of possibly marrying her at some point.

He was also feeling a little self-conscious. Unkempt hair, unshaven, and with dried blood caked all over his face and hands—he knew he was quite a sight. As Buck turned into the long driveway leading up to the house, he started blowing the horn.

When they came to a stop, Monica and Caroline appeared at the top of the steps, wearing amused smiles. Nick exited the truck with his blood-soaked face, and Monica realized what had happened and came bouncing down the steps.

She jumped on him, giving him a big hug. He forgot for a few seconds about his appearance and his probable unsavory smell and held her tight in a triumphant embrace, swinging around in a slow circle.

"You got one!"

"I sure did," Nick said, all remorse for having taken the deer's life now gone.

"You should have seen the shot, girls. Right through the heart, just like an old pro," Buck said.

"Did you bring back some meat?" Caroline asked.

"Got a cooler full," Buck responded.

"Good, we'll have venison steaks tonight, then."

The Ocean under the Moon

Chapter 11

In the guest bedroom, Nick shaved, then took a long, hot shower, scrubbing hard to get the blood off of his face and hands. Once he dried himself off, he put on some shorts, and lay down on the bed.

After a fifteen-minute catnap, he woke up, dressed and found Monica waiting for him in the living room, watching television with Bud.

Monica yelled to her mother that she and Nick were going for a drive, and Caroline came to the doorway of the kitchen to remind her to be back by five to help prepare for dinner.

They jumped into Nick's car and took off to explore the area. After driving around awhile, they ended up at the Dairy Queen on the outskirts of town. This was the local teen hangout spot, but since it was the middle of the afternoon, she did not spot any of her friends. They decided to have a large banana split anyway, and sat on the hood of his car to share the treat.

Since there wasn't anything going on in town, Monica suggested they go back to her house so she could give him a tour around their farm before it got dark. She directed him to park near the barn around the back of the house, and she went over to the barn and opened the large doors on the front. She went inside and soon re-emerged driving a large, green John Deere tractor.

He'd never ridden a tractor before, but climbed up on it

when she stopped and motioned to him. She stood up, to let him sit down in the low seat on the tractor, and then she sat in his lap, so she could drive. Soon they were bouncing around the fields, Monica driving, sitting in his lap, giggling. She showed him the hog pens, the peanut fields, the pecan orchard, the cow pastures, and the corn field. At the back of the property, near a pond, was an old tobacco barn.

"See that old barn over there? That's where they used to hang the tobacco to dry before taking it to auction back in the days when tobacco was the money crop in this area. Nowadays, hardly anybody grows tobacco any more because you can't make any money on it—there's too much cheap, imported tobacco driving the price down."

She stopped the tractor in front of the barn and they jumped off. She grabbed his hand and led him inside the barn. The old, dilapidated wooden structure had a dirt floor and a strong musty odor. She showed him the drying racks suspended from the ceiling.

He was gazing up at the drying hooks, still holding her hand, when she spun around in front of him and looked up into his eyes.

"I like you, Nick Stamos," she said, her azure eyes staring up at him.

"I like you, too, Monica Johnson," he responded, with mock formality.

He pulled her close to him, pressing her body against his, and their lips met in a passionate kiss. He felt an explosion of synapses and feelings in his brain and body. They kissed with the eagerness and optimism that only teenagers can generate.

Just when it seemed things were getting out of control, she stepped back from him and said she should get back to the house to help her mom with dinner and turned towards the barn's door. He gathered himself and followed her out of the barn.

Back at the house, he joined Buck, who was grilling marinated venison steaks. After awhile, dinner was ready. Caroline had prepared a Thanksgiving-like feast, served in the formal dining room. Besides the venison steaks, she'd prepared a ham, mashed potatoes, baked beans, green beans, squash, dressing, rolls, pecan pie and a pound cake. They sat down at the large table and Buck said the blessing, then Bud led the assault on the food spread around the table. The conversation flowed and Nick realized that even though he'd only known her family for a little over a day, he already felt at home with them. Monica kept giving him little, encouraging smiles all throughout dinner, as if she was proud of him.

After two helpings of everything, at Caroline's insistence, he thanked her for the feast. Caroline and Monica started clearing the table, while Buck, Nick, and Bud relocated to the soft couches in the living room to watch a football game.

About forty-five minutes later, Monica emerged from the kitchen and announced that she and Nick were going to drive into town. Her father glanced over to the kitchen doorway where Caroline was standing and she gave him a little nod.

"All right, but be home before midnight," he said.

"I will, Daddy," she said, bending over to give her father a peck on the cheek.

The Ocean under the Moon

Nick jumped up from the couch, excused himself, and followed her to the front door.

"Good night, y'all," she called to her family as she reached the door.

"Be careful, sweetie," Caroline said.

"Behave yourselves," Buck ordered.

"We will," she said.

They bounded down the front steps, hand in hand, and jumped into the Firebird.

Monica had told him there wasn't much to do in town but cruise up and down Main Street, so they made a couple of laps up and down the main drag in his car. Every now and then, she would recognize someone's car coming from the other direction and she would reach across him and mash the horn, waving to the other car excitedly, and the person in the other car would respond, in kind.

After awhile, she spotted some cars belonging to her friends that were parked in the Dairy Queen parking lot. She told him to pull in beside them. The teenagers looked impressed with Nick's car and excited to see Monica emerge from the vehicle, and welcomed them into their crowd hanging out, mostly sitting on their cars. He had met most of them at the dance, but she reintroduced him around to refresh his memory of the names.

They hung out there joking, laughing, and having a good time, until at eleven o'clock, the Dairy Queen turned off its lights, signaling that it was closing—time for everyone to leave. One of Monica's friends suggested they continue the party at Old Man Miller's barn, an abandoned barn that they sometimes used for impromptu late-night parties. Most of the kids agreed.

The Ocean under the Moon

To Nick's surprise, Monica demurred, saying they needed to be home soon. Despite protestations and pleas from her friends to continue the party with them, they left the dark parking lot and headed back down Uvalda Highway.

When they came to the driveway of her house, she told him to keep driving straight, as she wanted to show him something. He asked her where they were going, but all she would say was, "You'll see."

A few miles farther, she told him to slow down and then motioned him to turn off the main highway onto a dirt road. The dirt road meandered for a few hundred yards with him picking his way around the potholes and washboard ripples, due to the low ground clearance of his car.

After a very uncomfortable ride, with his sports car's stiff suspension shuddering over every bump and bounce in the weathered dirt road, they finally reached their destination. The pine trees and cypress trees gave way to a clearing that revealed a small parking area, then a white sand beach, followed by a wide, dark river with a brilliant full moon over it, making the surface sparkle like diamonds.

"It's beautiful," he said, in awe.

"It's the Altamaha River," she said. "The Oconee and Ocmulgee rivers come together just a mile or two upstream from here to form the Altamaha—it empties into the Atlantic Ocean at the Altamaha Sound near Brunswick, about one hundred and forty miles downstream."

"Is the moonlight deceiving me or is that a white sand beach in the middle of south Georgia?" he asked.

The Ocean under the Moon

She laughed. "Yep. The water is full of clay sediment coming down rivers from the north Georgia hills, and that makes the water look reddish-brown. But at certain bends and banks along the river the clay settles, and the sand gets deposited, like here—and it turns into a long, white sandbar."

"Let's go check it out," he said.

He turned off the ignition, put the car in park, and raced out onto the white sandbar on the bank of the river, with her just behind him. He stopped in the middle of the sandbar, twirling around to take in his surroundings.

On this cool, November night there was not a cloud in the sky. The full moon was as bright and large as he had ever seen, and he had seen plenty helping his father shrimp into the late evening. The hundreds of stars that filled the sky seemed even brighter in the absence of any manmade illumination for miles around, except for the occasional pair of headlights of a car passing over the bridge on Uvalda Highway, around the bend, several hundred yards away. Looking up and down the river in either direction, there was no sign of man's influence, just tree-lined banks and an occasional pale sandbar glistening in the moonlight.

Nick grinned at Monica and reached for her hand. "Is this where you take all your boyfriends?"

"Just the special ones," she responded, with a sly grim.

"Are you saying I'm special?"

"You could be."

He put his arms around her, his lips finding hers in a long kiss, pushing their limits. They stood embraced like lovers at the end of a play, with the sandbar as their stage, the moon as their spotlight, and with disinterested raccoons, opossums, and an occasional alligator as their audience.

Soon, the kiss had them both feeling weak in the knees and they paused to catch their breath.

"Damn, I wish I had a blanket in the car," he lamented.

She was glad they had not thought to bring a blanket, because if they had, she was not sure she could control herself. She sensed they were approaching a corner with too much speed and decided to tap the brakes.

"Let's just sit down here on the sand and talk."

They plopped down side by side, their knees drawn up to their chests. Both were shaking a little bit, either from the excitement of their embrace, or from the cool night air. He took off one sleeve of his jacket, pulled her close to him and draped half of the coat over her.

"I hate the fact that you live so far away from me and that after tomorrow, I won't see you, until who knows when," she said.

"I don't like it either."

"How do I know you don't have a girlfriend back in Fernandina or if you are going to meet some new girl at the beach?"

He laughed. "First of all, I don't have a girlfriend in Fernandina and secondly, nobody goes to the beach now — it's too cold until about April. Besides, you are my girlfriend now."

She turned to him, and he grasped her hand and slipped a ring onto one of her fingers.

"With this ring, I do solemnly swear to date the bearer of this ring, exclusively, and to look at no other girls that shall cross

114

my path," he said.

She looked down at her hand and even in the moonlight could see that it was his class ring. He had received it just two weeks earlier and it was his prized possession.

"Oh, Nick," she said.

Her eyes grew wide and serious. She gently pushed him back, so he was lying on the sand, and she threw one leg over him, so she could straddle him. She sat on top of him, her pelvic area resting on top of his, and gazed down at him, staring into his eyes. He looked up at her face, silhouetted by the full moon and adorned with scattered stars behind her head.

She leaned forward and starting kissing him, slow at first, then picking up steam. Soon she started rocking back and forth while kissing him. After a while, even though they still had all of their clothes on, he thought he was going to explode. This time it was he who applied the brakes.

He rolled her off of him and lay on top of her, while they caught their breath. He gazed down into her eyes, which were filled with desire and confusion, as she tried to compose her breathing.

"*Je t'aime*," he said softly, as he caressed her cheek with the back of his fingers.

"*Je t'aime*," she whispered, still almost breathless.

They sat up, side by side again, facing the river, and he draped his coat over their shoulders again. The reflection of the moon on the calm surface of the river seemed to create a ray of light shining right at them. They held each other in a firm embrace, knowing that he would have to leave in the morning, and they wanted this moment to last forever.

In a few minutes, Nick reached a hand up to touch her lips.

"I, Nick Stamos, promise that as long as you wear my ring, I will always be faithful to you," he said.

"And I, Monica Johnson, promise that I will wear your ring forever and, therefore, I will forever be faithful to you." She kissed his fingers with a loving smile.

"Now, since it's five minutes to midnight, I better get you home on time so your father won't shoot me and we end up with the shortest romantic relationship, since Romeo and Juliet," he said.

"Are you kidding? After your performance this morning, do you think he would shoot the great deer slayer? You are like his new favorite son, now."

"Just the same, I think he likes his guns and hunting a little too much. I wouldn't want to risk making him mad and having my head end up on his trophy wall."

"You don't think I'm worth the risk?" she asked.

She brushed the sand from her bottom with both hands while she wiggled her hips back and forth.

He sat there watching her and remembering the feel of her body against his a few minutes ago, when she was on top of him, and realized if there was a woman he would give up his life for, she would be the one.

"I do think you're probably worth the risk. But I'm going to have to get to know you a little better before I make that decision," he said.

"Well, I look forward to getting to know you better then,

The Ocean under the Moon

Nick Stamos," she said, with fake formality. She grasped his hand, swinging it back and forth as they left the sandbar and headed back to the car.

The Ocean under the Moon

Chapter 12

August 23, 1975
1:10 p.m.

Nick woke up with a start at the sound of his father's voice piercing the air over the drone of the diesel engine.

"Pull in the trail net," Abe demanded, from the doorway of the pilot house facing toward the back of the boat.

Nick was sitting on the ice cooler, leaning his back against the rear wall of pilot house, facing the stern of the boat. As usual, whenever there was a lull between putting out the nets and winching them in, he took the opportunity for a quick nap. Now his father's demanding voice had jolted him awake.

He rose from his resting space, walked over to the trail net winch and started cranking. He couldn't wait until he had a boat of his own. It had been over a year since he graduated from high school and started shrimping with his father, full time. Like any son, working with his father, he both appreciated the knowledge that was being passed to him and resented the constant directions being given to him. He felt like he'd learned all he could learn from his father and was anxious to get a boat of his own, be his own captain, and master of his fate.

The only problem was, his father was already running two

boats. The *Amelia Queen* was the flagship of the fleet, a large, wooden boat, eighty feet long, handed down to Abe from his father. It'd been in the family for thirty years and was his pride and joy. About three years before, he'd repowered the boat with an eight-hundred-fifty-horsepower Caterpillar diesel engine, and won the last three shrimp boat races at the annual shrimp festival. The three trophies were placed with pride on the mantel in his house.

Abe also owned another boat, a more modern sixty-five-foot fiberglass boat that he had acquired when another shrimper got into financial trouble. He'd bought the boat cheap from the other shrimper before the bank could repossess it. He promoted Billy Sutton, who'd been his first mate for ten years, to captain of that boat and named it *Island Girl*.

Billy was thirty-five years old and had been shrimping since he was seventeen. He was hard-working and dependable and Abe trusted him to run his boat for him. Billy hired Marty Jones, a weathered, forty-year-old local shrimper to be his first mate and the two of them ran the boat for Abe. They didn't receive a salary from him, but worked off a percentage of the catch. After the boat's expenses were deducted, the profits from the catch were divided fifty percent for Billy, twenty-five percent for Marty, and twenty-five percent to Abe. He wasn't getting rich off of his arrangement, but Abe was paying the expenses of the boat, providing income for Billy to support his wife and two kids, and getting a little extra income for himself, without having to do the work.

The third boat that Grandpa Eber operated had gotten too old to be dependable. Abe then sold it to a young shrimper out of Mayport, who was able to get a few more years out of the boat

119

before it sank one day at its dock.

His father could have bumped Billy off of the *Island Girl* and let Nick be the captain, but he'd let Nick know he wasn't going to do that. Abe told Nick that Billy was like an older son to him, and he was the godfather of Billy's children, so he felt responsible for him and his family. No, Nick would have to wait his turn and save up enough money for a down payment on his own boat, Abe had said.

Nick was still living at home, rent-free, and had no expenses, since his car was paid off. In a little over a year, he'd managed to save about five thousand dollars on the small deckhand salary that his father was paying him.

At this rate, it would take him several years to save up enough money to buy a decent boat, because even though he would have the down payment, no bank would lend him the rest of the money based on his income, unless Abe co-signed for him. Abe made it clear to Nick that he did not want the responsibility of a third boat in the uncertain climate of the shrimping industry, and that he didn't feel Nick was ready yet.

Nick, being headstrong and in love, wanted to establish himself so he could prove he was worthy to Monica and her family, and he was in a hurry to do so. Therefore, Nick and Abe were at odds with each other. Nick and Marty had even switched boats at times, with Nick working as a deckhand for Billy, for things to cool off between him and his father.

Meanwhile, Nick was still seeing Monica on an occasional basis, and had kept in touch by letters and phone. She'd come down for his senior prom the month before he graduated. It was the first time his friends and family had met her, and they were all impressed by her looks and Southern charm.

Before the dance, Nick took Monica to the Le Chateau Restaurant down in Atlantic Beach, the northernmost section of Jacksonville Beach. It was a scenic forty-five-minute drive from the south end of Amelia Island on Highway A1A, crossing the undeveloped Big Talbot and Little Talbot islands. On Fort George Island, they took the ferry boat across the St. John's River to Mayport, a sleepy, little fishing village, and drove another ten miles down A1A to reach the French restaurant. They dined at a small table for two, overlooking the ocean. It'd been daylight on their drive down to the restaurant, but by the end of their meal, night had fallen and they were able to see the moon creep over the horizon.

Afterward they drove back to the dance, which was at the Atlantic Avenue Recreation Center. The Rec Center, as it was known, was a large, brick structure with an Olympic-size swimming pool in the center, a large auditorium to the right of the pool, and meeting rooms to the left. The auditorium was the site of all the major high school dances.

The band was good that night, and they'd stayed until the band quit playing at twelve-thirty in the morning. The next day, he took her to Fort Clinch for a picnic and, on Sunday, they'd spent all day at the beach until Monica had to leave for home.

In July, she came down with her family for their annual summer vacation. He had to work most days on the shrimp boat, but he made sure to spend his nights with her. Using some of the money saved up from shrimping, he'd bought an old, four-wheel-drive Ford Bronco. He'd removed the top to make it a convertible and was using it as a beach cruiser.

It was still legal to drive on the beach in Nassau County at the time. The wide beach and hard-packed white sand made driving easy, below the high-water line. Like the more famous Daytona Beach to the south, Fernandina Beach was a great place to throw all your gear in your car or truck and drive down one of the ramps onto the beach, find a secluded area to dump your stuff out on the sand, and enjoy a relaxing day in the sun.

Beach driving was allowed on the southern ten miles of beach from the Main Beach ramp all the way to the ramp on the very south tip of the island. There were beach access ramps at Main Beach, Sadler Road, Peter's Point, American Beach, and on the south end of the island at A1A, right by the bridge.

Back in the 1960s, people were even allowed to drive in the sand dunes, but in the late 1960s, the Jacksonville Dune Buggy Club discovered Amelia Island and soon every dune on the island had tire tracks going over it. Every virgin dune became a challenge to the dune buggy enthusiasts and, like Mount Everest, each one had to be conquered.

The problem was, the thirty-foot or higher sand dunes, which had taken centuries to build up, could be destroyed in an afternoon of merrymaking followed by a few days of strong, northeast winds. The dune buggy tires would tear up the sea oats and other vegetation that held the fragile sand dunes in place. Without the protecting vegetation, any strong nor'easter or even a stiff sea breeze could flatten the sand dune in days. Therefore, by the 1970s, there was a five-hundred-dollar fine for riding in the

The Ocean under the Moon

sand dunes, although Nick and his friends were not above an occasional late night foray in their four-wheel-drive trucks.

That summer, while Monica was in town with her parents, he would pick her up in his Bronco and they would go to Main Beach, to skate or play putt-putt. Then, they would cruise around town for awhile. But they would always end their night by driving down on the beach and parking the Bronco. There, gazing out over the ocean, they would make out and talk about their future.

Nick wanted to be with Monica all of the time. He couldn't stand only seeing her every now and then. If he had his way, they would get married as soon as she finished high school, but she'd made it clear that her mother would never allow her to marry until after she graduated from college. So he'd kept his desires to himself, which wasn't easy with her lithe body beside him and a romantic moon out over the silvery waves.

"Are you going to crank that winch or just fondle it?" his father yelled from the side of the pilot house, looking back at him. "And you want a boat of your own?" he added, shaking his head in dismay.

Feeling sheepish that he'd been daydreaming about Monica instead of concentrating on his job, he started cranking with a vengeance. He chastised himself for his lack of concentration, as his father glared at him. He knew that this would just add to his father's argument that he was not ready for his own boat.

He had no way of knowing, however, that before the next day arrived, unforeseen circumstances would lead to him

The Ocean under the Moon

beginning the first steps toward realizing his dream.

The Ocean under the Moon

Chapter 13

August 24, 1975
12:54 a.m.

Late that night, Nick was hanging out in the parking lot at Main Beach with his friends, leaning against their vehicles, drinking beer, and solving the world's problems. These were good times for him and his friends, most of whom were recent high school graduates and making good money, either working at one of the two paper mills or shrimping.

They had the good fortune of coming of age at just the right time. In 1973, when Nick was just a junior in high school, the Vietnam draft lottery was abolished. This meant that they did not have the specter of receiving a low lottery pick and being drafted and sent to Vietnam when they turned eighteen, like so many of their older friends and brothers had.

Their second advantage was that the year before they turned eighteen, the state of Florida lowered the legal drinking age from twenty-one to eighteen. The state would later raise the limit back up to twenty-one, realizing its mistake, but for Nick and his friends, it was perfect timing.

Since there wasn't a law against public drinking, just public intoxication, they could hang out in the parking lot without the cops hassling them, as long as they didn't get too rowdy. In fact, Nick knew most of the cops on a first-name basis. When making their evening rounds in their patrol cars, the younger officers would stop and chat for twenty or thirty minutes at a time. Since there wasn't much crime in Fernandina, the cops were just killing time.

Most of his friends still lived at home with their parents, and the main thing they had to spend their money on was their trucks. The evolutionary path for most males in Fernandina at the time was to finish high school, then have your father get you a job at the paper mill where he worked. Next, you would buy a truck and carouse for a few years. Then, find a willing girl, marry her, buy a small house, and start the slow, mundane crawl up the paper mill ladder, until retirement thirty years later.

Nick's friends were enjoying the first, and most fun, phase of their life-cycle. Most evenings, they parked their Jeeps and big, four-wheel-drive trucks side by side in the northern part of the Main Beach parking lot, away from the tourists and putt-putt area. Then, they'd lower their tailgates and "hang out" —joking and kidding each other, waving at any pretty girls who drove by, and not doing anything special.

He would bring his Bronco, and not his Firebird, on those evenings. He'd just added large tires to the Bronco, for easier beach driving, and painted it a midnight blue to cover up the rusty spots and to prevent further oxidation, which was inevitable from driving on the sand. He'd also added a citizen-band radio under the dash, with a large antenna rising up from the back bumper.

It was nearing one o'clock in the morning, and Nick was

getting ready to leave his friends and head home, when a city police car pulled into the parking lot. The patrolman rolled his passenger window down to talk to them. He could see that it was Ben Johnson, one of the younger members of the force who often stopped to chat with them.

"You boys need to stay off the beach tonight," Ben said. He knew the teenagers liked to take a cruise down the beach before heading home.

"We're getting ready to lock down the accesses up and down the beach. A shrimp boat, loaded with pot, hit the jetties and then beached itself to keep from sinking. On the way in, they ditched most of their cargo, which is coming to shore all over the place on the north end of the island, next to the jetties."

"No kidding, man!" one of the kids said. "Wow!" The boys jumped down off the tailgates and most of them crowded around the patrol car to listen.

Ben grimaced at them and shook his head. "One of the park rangers, living at the Jetty Lodge, saw the boat come ashore and alerted us. We've called the Nassau County deputies and the state patrol to help us patrol the beach. If we catch you down at the beach, we are going to assume you're trying to pick up some pot and we are going to arrest you.

"In fact, the state patrol is going to be setting up some roadblocks along North and South Fletcher, only allowing residents to enter these roads," the officer said. "Since y'all have been drinking you might want to head for home now, before they set up the roadblocks."

Nick realized an opportunity, more with the boat than

with the pot. "Hey, Ben, what's with the condition of the shrimp boat?"

"Well, I haven't seen it, but they tell me it's pretty much intact, sitting on the beach with a pretty big hole on one side of the bow."

"Is it wood or fiberglass?"

"I don't know," he said, exasperated. "I'd like to sit here and talk about all things nautical, but I've got a job to do and you guys need to get on home." He rolled his window up, then sped off.

The boys hung around awhile, discussing several grandiose schemes about how maybe they could drive to the end of North Fletcher, then sneak into the state park by foot, and find a deserted area of the beach that wasn't being patrolled. Then, with luck, find a bale of marijuana and drag it back to their trucks, all without detection.

They weren't interested in the pot to smoke it; their idea would be to sell it and make enough money for a new truck—or, as in Nick's case, a slightly used shrimp boat.

After about ten to fifteen minutes of fake bravado and wild declarations, cooler heads prevailed and all of them headed for home, knowing that to be caught would be too embarrassing for themselves, and their parents.

But all the way home, Nick was thinking about the shrimp boat stranded on the beach. If the boat had not been damaged too bad by its collision with the jetties, and if it didn't get broken up by the waves pounding on it while it sat on the shoreline, then maybe it would be salvageable.

The Ocean under the Moon

He tried hard to think about the tide, his brain addled by the beer. Earlier that evening, he'd driven down on the beach, around seven o'clock, to see if anybody was setting up to fish for sharks that night from the beach. The movie *Jaws* was released that summer and shark fishing had become all the rage.

The procedure for shark fishing was to drive down on the beach, dump out a cooler full of beer and a couple of lawn chairs, then half-bury a three-inch-diameter PVC pipe in the sand, so it was sticking up vertically. The butt of a large Penn reel with eighty-pound test line was inserted in the PVC pipe, which served as a rod holder. Two or three pogies, acquired from the pogy plant, or Spanish mackerel caught earlier surf fishing, would be skewered onto the large hook.

Then, one unlucky fisherman would have to take the bait out into the ocean. This was accomplished by paddling out the bait, three or four hundred yards into the ocean, using a surfboard, dropping the bait, and paddling back into the shore. This was the part of shark fishing that Nick didn't like. He had the misfortune of paddling the bait out on two different occasions, earlier that summer.

Both times, he'd been terrified. Paddling out into the ocean, right before dark, legs dangling off the back of the small surfboard, the line tied to the buttonhole of his bathing suit so he could use both arms to paddle, the bait dangling down into the water a foot or two below his surfboard. This made him feel too much like bait. He imagined a shark hurtling up from the ocean depths, attracted by his paddling, biting into one of his legs, or worse, swallowing the bait on the hook, hooking itself, and pulling

The Ocean under the Moon

Nick down into the ocean depths, before he could untie himself from the line.

When the second time of taking the bait out didn't get any easier, he had made up his mind to leave that job to other people. However, he still liked to stop by to see if they were catching anything. Tonight, there hadn't been anybody down on the beach fishing.

He'd noticed from his foray down on the beach earlier that night, that around seven o'clock, that it had been low tide. That meant high tide would be about six hours later — right about now, in fact. That would explain why the boat had hit the jetties. With the full moon only a day or two away, the tide would be higher than normal. He knew from experience how treacherous finding the channel could be, having come in through the channel many nights returning from evening shrimping trips with his father.

If one approached from the south, the farthest third of the jetties that extend out into the ocean would be just submerged under the water at high tide. There was a buoy with a light on it that marked the eastern end of the jetties, farthermost out into the ocean, and you were supposed to go to the right of it when approaching from south. Another lighted buoy was about two hundred yards back toward shore, intended to further delineate where the jetties were. Some boaters, at night or in bad weather, would mistake the gap between the two lighted buoys as the entrance to the channel.

He could remember at least five boats that had made that error in his short lifetime. Most of the boats had sunk right after hitting the rocks, their crews having to be rescued by the Coast

Guard. He was surprised that the captain of the shrimp boat tonight was able to beach the boat before it sank. Maybe it wasn't running very fast when it hit the rocks, because they were searching for the entrance to the channel, so the damage was not as severe, he surmised.

He wasn't surprised, however, that the boat hit the rocks, particularly if the crew had been smoking some of their cargo. He looked up at the sky and noticed even though it was almost a full moon, the moon was obscured by a thick layer of clouds, making it a very dark night. Even he and his father, with all of their experience, sometimes had trouble negotiating the entrance to the channel, in times of poor visibility, like fog, or in a heavy thunderstorm. They had to make sure they didn't mistake the more western lighted buoy for the more eastern buoy that marked the actual end of the jetties.

When his father approached from the south of the jetties, he'd always told Nick, that if he was unsure of his position, to turn east and go out farther in the ocean and then turn and approach the channel from the proper angle, to better line up the markers that were farther back inside the channel.

He wondered about the condition of the boat and the overall situation. If the boat made it all the way to the beach, then the hole in its hull must not be too bad. If they beached it just after midnight, then after tonight's one o'clock high tide, the water would recede, leaving the boat high and dry on the beach, but out of harm's way as far as the waves pounding away on the boat, doing further damage.

He knew that for the next several days, the weather

131

report called for calm wind and seas. His father was angry that the weather was going to be perfect, but they wouldn't be able to go shrimping. Two days ago, they had been out shrimping all day and doing quite well, until the end of the day, when their net got hung up on some underwater obstruction that tore their main net to shreds.

Yesterday, his father had taken the net to Burbank's Net Makers, behind Standard Marine Supply, to see if they could repair it. The Stamos family had been doing business with these firms for many decades. Standard Marine, originally called Standard Hardware and Grocery Company, dated back to 1900 when the Hardee brothers, Ira, John, and Noble, opened it and sold food, supplies, nets, and engine parts to the shrimpers and other boaters along the city docks.

Burbank's was located right behind Standard Marine, in a large metal building where the family had been making shrimp and fish trawl nets by hand since 1915. Billy Burbank Sr. started the company when he couldn't find nets to his liking for his own boats so he began making them himself. The Burbanks made the nets and Standard Marine marketed them in other shrimping areas from Louisiana and Texas to Key West, the Caribbean and South America.

Nick's father knew Billy Jr. well since they were about the same age and grew up together. They'd been in the same grade and played on the high school baseball team together. Nick had gone to school in the same grade as David Burbank, with Billy III and Tommy being older than him and Johnny being a year younger.

Despite the closeness between the two families and Billy

The Ocean under the Moon

Jr.'s promise that he would start on their net as soon as possible, postponing other nets in progress, Billy Jr. had informed Abe that it was going to be two or three working days, until they could mend the damage.

This was frustrating to Abe, being land-bound during a week of good weather when the shrimp were running. However, it would not be a complete waste, as Billy and Marty would, with any luck, have some good days on the *Island Girl*.

Nick knew his father would be up at the crack of dawn, even though they weren't going to be able to go shrimping in the morning. He always got up early, even on his days off; it was just his way.

Nick went to bed as soon as he arrived home. His plan was to get up early and talk his father into going out to the jetties and seeing if they could attain the salvage rights to the boat, if it was worth saving. Abe was good friends with both Earl Baxter, the city police chief, and Herb McKendree, the Nassau County sheriff. Nick didn't know which one would have jurisdiction over the boat—or maybe the state would, since the boat came aground on the state park shoreline.

He felt confident that if they could get down there early enough, Abe could talk either one of them into letting Abe and Nick have the salvage rights. He knew it was a long shot, but he didn't know if he could stand working for his father for another two or three years, until he could save enough money for a boat of his own. He and his father were both headstrong and they were butting heads every day, while out on his father's boat.

Maybe this would be a way to speed up the process of his

133

becoming a captain. He went to sleep with images of himself behind the wheel of his very own shrimp boat.

The Ocean under the Moon

Chapter 14

August 24, 1975
6:00 a.m.

Nick woke up with a start to the loud sound of his alarm clock ringing. He reached over and shut it off. The clock said six, which was what he had set it for. Even though he had only had five hours of sleep, he jumped out of bed and got dressed.

He knew that his father would have already gotten up at five-thirty in the morning and would be sitting at the kitchen table having toast and coffee. Nick walked down the hall to the kitchen.

"Morning, Dad."

"What are you doing up so early on your day off?" Abe said.

"Funny you should ask."

He summoned his courage to tell his father about the boat and ask him for his assistance.

"Last night a very weird thing happened."

Abe looked up from his paper, a look of concern crossing his face, and Nick knew he was wondering if his son had wrecked one of his vehicles or gotten into trouble with the law.

"No, it doesn't have anything to do with me," he said. "What I'm trying to tell you is that last night a shrimp boat loaded with pot hit the south jetty and then managed to beach itself near the jetty lodge inside Fort Clinch State Park."

"What's this have to do with us? You didn't try to pick up any of the pot, did you?"

"No, Dad. I'm not interested in the pot. I'm interested in the boat."

"The boat is probably a piece of crap, or broken up by now." He returned his gaze to the newspaper.

"The boat can't be in too bad of shape, if it made it all the way to shore. It must be over a quarter of a mile from the end of the south jetty to the beach. I doubt it has broken up, because I was down on the beach earlier last night checking out the shark fishermen, and the waves were less than a foot high. You know it's supposed to be calm for the next couple of days.

"Besides it went aground at high tide, so it's probably sitting high and dry on the beach by now. I was hoping, since you know Sheriff McKendree and Chief Baxter so well, that we could go down there and see if we could get the salvage rights, if the boat is worth anything."

"You're not ready for your own boat," his father said.

He knew his father liked having him work on his boat. Abe had not spent as much of his time with him as his father would have liked to when he was growing up. His father missed many baseball games and other activities, chasing shrimp up and down the coast. If the shrimping was good, his father couldn't abandon what he was doing and head back to port just for a baseball game, when the family's income was at stake. Having his son work with him was Abe's way of "having his cake and eating it too." He got to provide for his family and spend time with his son.

Besides that, Nick provided him with a stable deckhand. Some of the helpers preceding him were less than dependable. One problem with shrimping is that it could be "feast or famine." In good times a deckhand could make fifteen hundred to two thousand dollars a week as his cut of the catch. Other times they might go two or three weeks without any catch at all because of bad weather or lack of shrimp. Either scenario, if one was prone to drink alcohol, was not a good one.

Some of the deckhands, after a week at sea and having received their money from a lucrative catch, would march straight down to the Palace Saloon, where they would drink late into the night, waving their money around and buying everybody drinks. Even if the good shrimp run continued, his father sometimes had trouble getting deckhands to go back out with him, since they were hung-over and unmotivated from being flush with cash.

On the other hand, if the boat had been having a stretch of bad luck, where they weren't catching anything, some of the deckhands would lose interest and fake illnesses or come up with other excuses, so they could stay home and drink. Either way, a good dependable deckhand was a valuable asset in the shrimping industry.

"But you've already taught me all you know," Nick said.

"You've only been shrimping with me, full time, for a little over a year."

"Yeah, but I've been going out with you part-time, since I was ten."

"Well, I worked on the same boat with Grandpa Eber for

137

eight years, before I got my own boat," his father said.

He had heard this argument before, so he was ready with his response.

"And for how many of those years you worked with Grandpa, did you wish you had your own boat?"

Abe thought about it for a minute, as if he was wavering, then responded. "You are not ready. We haven't really even been in any really bad storms yet, just summer squalls and such."

"Well, that's because you run for port every time the weather starts to get bad," he said, with an edge in his voice.

"That's because your mother would kill me, if I let anything happen to you. Me, she doesn't worry about—you, on the other hand, that's a different story. If your mother worries now, how much do you think she is going to worry if you have your own boat?"

He wasn't going to win this argument, so Nick decided to take another tack.

"Well, if we could get the boat cheap enough, wouldn't it make business sense to have a spare boat, for when the *Amelia Queen* or the *Island Girl* is out of commission? Just like having to have the *Amelia Queen's* net worked on now, you wouldn't lose shrimping time, like we're doing this weekend. Then, later on, when you feel that I'm ready, maybe I could start using the boat full time."

His father rubbed his chin and looked at his son. Aha, Nick thought—he's beginning to realize this idea does make a little bit of business sense. If they could get the boat cheap enough, without the need for a mortgage, and since they owned their own dock, the carrying costs for a third boat would be minimal. Between the *Amelia Queen* and the *Island Girl*, they did lose several weeks of shrimping time due to engine problems, net issues, and other equipment failures.

"All right, we'll go look at the boat," he said, giving in. "But we're only going to fool with it if the boat's in pretty good shape, and if we can get it for a song."

Nick was glad his father turned back to read the paper, so he couldn't see how broadly his son was smiling.

The Ocean under the Moon

Chapter 15

An hour later, they pulled up to the park ranger shack guarding the entrance to Fort Clinch State Park, which closed at sunset, and then reopened at seven in the morning.

When they pulled up, Abe and Nick saw the metal gate still in place across the road, blocking the entrance to the park. A park ranger appeared at the doorway of the guard shack and walked up to the car.

"The park's closed today, until at least noon," the ranger began. "You'll need to turn around and you can check back with us then."

"Yes, we know about the marijuana and the boat marooned on the beach. I was hoping to talk to Chief Baxter about salvage rights to the boat," Abe said.

"Well, my orders from the state police are not to let anyone into the park. But the city police are guarding the beach access. You may want to check with them to see if they will grant you access, by way of the beach."

"Thank you," Abe said, then swiveled his head so he could back up his vehicle and turn around.

Two blocks away, he drove up the little rise marking the entrance to the original parking lot at Main Beach, then down to the southeast corner, where the ramp began, next to the Golden Sands

The Ocean under the Moon

Restaurant. When they came over the rise, they could see two city police cars parked beside the ramp and a wooden barricade placed across the entrance. Abe parked his International Scout Harvester next to one of the police cars.

Abe loved his 1964 International Scout Harvester 80. The body of the vehicle was red with a white top. It possessed a fold-down front windshield, vacuum windshield wipers at the top of the windshield, sliding side rear windows, and an IH logo on the center of the grille. Its distinctive colors made him very recognizable, as he drove about town. Created to compete with Jeeps, the only other recreational off-road vehicle at the time, the Scout was an early incarnation of the sports utility vehicles that would become so popular later.

Back when Nick was young and the Scout was new, Abe often took his son riding in the sand dunes. Each time, he left the Scout in two-wheel drive while he and Nick raced off to see how far they could go until they got stuck in the sand. Then, Abe got out and turned the locks on each front wheel, engaging the four-wheel drive. Back in the vehicle, with the stick shift in four-wheel-drive low, the Scout could pull itself out of almost any predicament. That was back when almost all the dunes were virgin, before the dune riding ban, when you could ride anywhere, including inside the State Park, near the Jetty Lodge, where the tallest dunes were located.

They got out of the Scout and walked toward the two city police officers guarding the beach access ramp.

"Hey, Bobby. Hey, Joe. How you boys doing this morning?" Abe said to the officers who were leaning against the hood of one of the police cars.

Bobby Smith and Joe Stevens were in their late twenties and he knew them from Stamos Shrimping's sponsorship of a softball team that most of the younger members of the police force played on. Abe used to play a lot of softball himself, up until his early forties, when a knee injury from sliding into second base ended his softball career. He still liked to sponsor a team every year, which just meant buying the uniforms and hats, and he got to print Stamos Shrimping on the back for advertising, making it tax-deductible. He also liked to go hang out at the ball park, grab a hot dog, and catch up on the latest news from around town.

"Mr. Stamos, you're out early this morning," Bobby said.

"Well, son, I'm always up this early. Just usually, I'm out shrimping. But my net is all tore up, so I had to find something else to do," he said. "Is Chief Baxter out at the accident site?"

"Accident site? You mean where the shrimp boat and the pot washed up?" Joe said.

Bobby elbowed him in the ribs.

"Yeah, that's what I'm talking about," Abe said.

"I guess the whole town's probably heard about it by now," Bobby said.

"Well, I only know about it because one of your officers was kind enough to warn my son, Nick, here and some of his buddies, to stay off the beach late last night."

This news seemed to perk Bobby up a little bit. "Well, what can we do for you?" he asked.

"We're interested in the salvage rights for the shrimp boat, if it's worth saving. I was wondering if you would get on your radio and call Chief Baxter to see if he is interested in us moving it off the beach, after he gets done with it."

Bobby stared at him for several seconds, deciding whether he should bother Chief Baxter with this request. But since Mr. Stamos had always been generous, sponsoring the softball team, donating to the Fraternal Order of the Police, and knew the chief quite well, Bobby decided he would comply.

He got into one of the police cars and they could see him talking on the radio. After a brief conversation, he hung up the radio mouthpiece and stepped out of the car.

"The chief says you can come on out to the site," he said. "Just drive down the beach as far as you can to the north, until you get to the police barricade, and then you will have to go from there on foot."

"Thank you, Bobby. Good to see you, Joe."

Abe and Nick headed for the Scout. Nick was all smiles, as Bobby moved the ramp barricade out of the way.

"What are you smiling about?" Abe asked, as he turned the Scout north and drove up the beach.

"My plan is coming together."

"Your plan?" he snapped. "I haven't seen you do anything yet. I'm the one that got us past those two officers. If I hadn't sponsored the softball team for the last eight years, we wouldn't have gotten this far."

They remained silent for awhile while they drove toward the north end of the island.

"When we get to the police barricade, I want you to stay in the Scout while I go talk to Chief Baxter. I don't want the state

police or any of the other policemen out there mistaking you for
some pothead trying to pick up some free pot and arresting you,"
he said.

"But I want to see the boat!"

"You can see the boat from inside the Scout. I don't want
you leaving this vehicle. I will talk to Chief Baxter, and I will
inspect the boat, to decide if it's going to be worth our efforts. Do I
make myself clear?"

"Yes, Dad," he said, knowing that to protest would be
counterproductive.

They pulled up to the police barricades that stretched
from the dunes down to the waterline. Nick watched helplessly as
Abe exited the vehicle and walked up to the state policeman
guarding the barricades. He saw the patrol officer wave Abe inside
the barricade, Chief Baxter having obviously informed him of their
impending arrival.

Nick took this as a good omen and strained to see the
shrimp boat, which was two or three hundred yards further up the
beach. From what he could see, the boat looked intact, but he could
only see its deck, because when the water receded, leaving the
vessel high and dry on the beach, the boat had listed severely
toward his direction.

He would have to wait until Abe came back to find out if
the boat was salvageable. He changed his gaze to the large state
patrolman with a buzz cut, staring at him. He removed his cap and
shook out his long, curly hair, watching for the policeman's
reaction, and then reclined his seat, to try to take a nap while he
waited.

The Ocean under the Moon

Abe trudged up the beach, toward the stranded boat. He noticed the tide was dead low now. Nick was right, the water was calm, which wasn't unusual for that time of year, except when the sea breeze kicked in or an early-season hurricane was passing offshore, kicking up the swells.

He spotted Chief Baxter, along with a group of ten to fifteen other officers, all scurrying around the boat. Baxter was a heavy-set man in his mid-fifties. A jovial man, who had worked his way up from patrolman to become chief of police in Fernandina, Chief Baxter was from Ohio. He'd fought with the Marines to take Iwo Jima in World War II, then sought refuge in this small town to get away from big city stress and crime.

Baxter waved him over, as Abe approached. The chief left the men he was talking to and started walking toward him, to intercept him before he got too close to the boat.

"Hey, Abe," he said. The two men shook hands.

"I'm glad you radioed. I was just talking to Captain McElroy of the state patrol and we were wondering how we were going to get this boat off the beach after our investigation is done, when Bobby called," he said. "Bobby said you might have some interest in helping, in that regard."

"Well, I don't know if I'm interested yet. What kind of shape is it in?"

"There's a pretty good-sized hole in the hull on the starboard side, but other than that, it seems to be in pretty good shape. They must've had a pretty good bilge pump and raced the boat straight to the beach before the engine flooded out. They didn't even have time to throw all of the cargo overboard. Most of the pot was still in the boat."

"What about the owners?"

"One of the counselors at the halfway house at Jetty Lodge saw the boat come to shore and alerted the park rangers who called us. Luckily, all of the juvenile delinquents that are staying at the halfway house were asleep at that time. The last thing we needed was those kids breaking out and getting their hands on that marijuana. We'd still be pulling them out of the sand dunes.

"Well, anyway, two of the rangers that live at the lodge were able to apprehend the men on the boat, before they could get off the beach. The captain was a down-in-his-luck shrimper from Texas. His two deckhands were Panamanians, who don't speak English. The boat is registered in Panama to what I'm sure is a fictitious corporation."

"What's to become of the boat?"

"Well, after the state police get through taking pictures, fingerprints, and unloading all the pot, we'll want to get the boat off the beach, as early as possible, so it doesn't get broken up by the waves. We don't want leaking fuel and debris floating down the beach. My crews have been out all night and morning, just picking up the pot off the beach that those men threw overboard last night."

"How soon will the state police be done with the job?"

"Captain McElroy said they should be done by noon," the chief responded.

"High tide is supposed to be around one-thirty this afternoon. If I could patch the boat up well enough to float, I might could bring my other two boats around and drag it off the beach and refloat it at high tide. The tide should be a little higher this afternoon than last night, since the moon is getting fuller. But what's in it for me, if I do this?"

"I'll give you a letter granting you pure salvage rights. If you successfully salvage the boat, you'll need to take your claim to the federal court in Jacksonville, which will award salvage based upon merit of the service and the value of the salvage property. We'll have to impound the boat until after the trials for the captain and crew, since we'll need the boat as evidence. Then after the trials, if the present owners try to re-claim the boat, which I doubt they will since the boat is registered under a foreign entity and they will not want to incriminate themselves in the smuggling scheme, the owners would have to pay you twenty-five percent of the surveyed value of the boat," Baxter said.

"If the present owners don't try to claim the boat, we'll have to put it up for auction. Anybody that wins the bid on the boat will have to pay you twenty-five percent of the auction price to receive the boat. You can also bid on the boat yourself, which will give you a twenty-five percent advantage over all the other bidders, since you won't have to pay yourself for the salvage rights."

This sounded pretty good to Abe. Even if they didn't end up with the ownership of the boat, if the boat sold for forty thousand dollars at auction, twenty-five percent of that amount would be ten thousand. That would be a pretty good day's work, if they could get the boat off the beach, without damaging it or his other two boats. Nick had been smart to come to him with this idea.

"Well, let me take a look at her and I'll let you know if I

can get her off the beach."

Chief Baxter nodded in acknowledgement, relieved that somebody he knew and trusted might be willing to tackle the job. The sooner he could get this boat off the beach and the state police out of here, the sooner he could get back to his office and take a well-deserved nap. He'd been up since one o'clock in the morning, when one of his deputies had called him about the situation, and he had come down to the site to take control of the scene.

Abe walked over to the large, white shrimp boat lying on its side like a beached whale. He estimated the boat to be about sixty-five feet long. He noticed that the long metal booms, which were used to pull the nets when lowered in the horizontal position, were locked in the upright position, out of harm's way, and were straight and not bent. The raised pilot house, about fifteen feet long, seemed to be unharmed and all the windows were intact. He didn't see any nets hanging from the booms, but this didn't surprise him as they'd had no intent of shrimping, their cargo being of a different sort.

Satisfied with the way the topside looked, he walked around to the other side, so he could inspect the damage to the underside of the boat. As he walked behind the stern of the boat, he saw its name painted across the stern.

"Albatross" was painted in big letters, with "Panama" below it in smaller letters, indicating its home berth. How appropriate, he thought, thinking of the famous poem, "The Rime of the Mariner," by Samuel Taylor Coleridge.

He knew from reading books about the sea, that albatrosses are among the largest of flying birds and have wide range in the Southern Ocean and northern Pacific. In older times, the mariners considered spotting albatrosses in the open ocean to be a sign of good luck, and killing one of them was considered to bring on bad luck. In the poem, a mariner kills an albatross, then the boat becomes becalmed, and the other sailors make the mariner wear the dead albatross around his neck; thus the metaphor of "an albatross around his neck" for someone who has a burden or obstacle to overcome.

The captain and his crew didn't kill this "Albatross," but they severely wounded it. Now the albatross they'd wear around their necks would be in the form of lengthy prison sentences.

He looked down to check out the propeller. This was one of the areas of the boat he was most concerned about. To his relief, he saw that the propeller was recessed into a well, built into the stern of the boat, with a metal skid plate to protect the propeller in case of grounding. The weight of the boat was resting on its keel, and the metal skid plate and propeller were not bent or damaged.

He walked along the underbelly, until he reached the high, upswept bow on the starboard side. Here was the part of the boat that struck the rocks. It appeared the boat did not strike the jetty head on but struck at an angle, cracking some of the planks of wood just aft of the bow. Abe took a closer look at the damage.

The boat appeared to be constructed from thick mahogany planks. This made sense since the boat was from Central America, and Honduras mahogany was one of the best boat building materials there was for wooden boats. That's probably what saved the boat from sinking, he thought, since even though there was about a three-foot crack diagonally encompassing several planks, the wood had not given away altogether, slowing the influx of water long enough for the boat to reach the beach.

He circled around the bow and saw Chief Baxter standing next to the port side of the boat talking to some state patrol guys. He walked up to the group of men as they finished their conversation.

"Abe, I want you to meet Captain Ed McElroy of the state patrol and his lieutenant, Pat Eason," Chief Baxter said. Abe shook hands with each patrolman.

"What do you think?" Baxter said, nodding at the beached boat.

"It doesn't look that bad, so far," he said. "I think I can patch the crack in the hull with a couple of sheets of marine grade plywood and some epoxy, which should be good enough to get her around to the other side of the island to dry-dock her, until real repairs can be made. But I need to look inside to see how much water is there and what kind of shape the engine is in."

"Well, we're through taking all of the cargo out of the hold. We've still got to take some more pictures. But you're welcome to go on down and check it out—just don't touch or move anything," Captain McElroy commanded.

"I won't."

He stepped on the portside gunwale, which was only about three feet above the beach since the boat keeled over at about a forty-degree angle, and walked along the slanted top sides toward the pilot house. Although he had promised he wouldn't touch anything, it was impossible to walk along the slanted deck without touching or grabbing something to maintain his balance.

He just hoped he wasn't tainting some evidence or implicating himself by doing so, but he continued on.

Inside the pilot house, he noticed charts spread out on the bridge in disarray, but everything else seemed normal. There was a large, wooden wheel for steering the boat in the center of the bridge. A VHF radio was attached to the bridge to the left of the wheel. He saw a large compass, which he noticed was still working, straight in front of the wheel.

He stuck his head out of the door to the pilot house and yelled to the chief.

"Hey, Chief. If you will, go around to the stern of the boat and when I turn the wheel, tell me if the rudder moves in both directions."

"Okay, give me a few seconds to get back there."

Abe waited a few seconds, then turned the wheel hard in each direction. He'd noticed when he was examining the propeller earlier, that the metal skid plate also protected the rudder from damage and he felt confident it would still work, but he wanted to confirm that. Towing a rudderless boat, or one with a fixed rudder at an odd angle, was not an easy thing to do.

After yanking the wheel back and forth in both directions and not feeling any severe drag in either direction, he looked back out the door of the pilot house to see Chief Baxter behind the stern, giving the thumbs-up sign.

Now, Abe walked to the back of the pilot house to where a companionway led down into the hull. He climbed down the ladder two-thirds of the way but stopped short of going all the way due to the two or three feet of water in the bottom of the hull.

The Ocean under the Moon

From his vantage point, he could see all the way to the bow, where light from outside was coming in through the crack in the hull. Looking back toward the stern, in the dim light he could make out the engine compartment, which was on a raised platform about two feet tall with a short wooden wall around the engine to protect it from flooding. This configuration also enabled the boat to make it to shore without the engine drowning out.

He couldn't make out much detail in the dim light, so he tugged on the string that dangled from a light fixture that contained a single naked bulb. To his surprise, the light bulb lit up when he pulled the string, indicating the batteries were still functioning.

"Damn," he muttered to himself, when the light came on, because now he could see that the boat had a gas engine, instead of diesel. He preferred diesel engines in his boats. There were three good reasons.

First of all was longevity. Diesel engines can run for thousands of hours before requiring major maintenance, which is why most commercial vessels and trucks that run for long hours at a time use them.

Secondly, at the time, diesel fuel cost less than gas. He had noticed yesterday at the city fuel docks that the price of gas was up to fifty-three cents a gallon.

Thirdly, and most important, Abe knew diesel is safer than gas. Diesel oil vapors are not explosive like gas vapors. In the hull of a boat, gas vapors can build up in the bottom of the boat around the engine, and then when the engine is ignited there's a sudden chance of explosion. This is a rare occurrence, but when it

The Ocean under the Moon

does happen, it is spectacular.

He'd seen it happen once before. He had taken his boat to Key West for a couple of months, because the shrimp had been scarce in the waters around Fernandina and there'd been reports of the shrimp running good around the Keys. He was on his boat, in its berth, near the end of Duval Street, getting it ready for another couple of days and nights of shrimping in the waters toward the Dry Tortugas. All of the sudden, the stern of a shrimp boat, a couple of berths away, exploded in a ball of fire, sending debris a hundred yards out into the water.

He'd run along the dock to offer his assistance. When he got there, he saw that the entire back end of the boat had been blown off and the stern end of the boat was sinking. Fortunately, the captain had been in the pilot house and was unharmed.

Abe helped both shrimpers off the sinking boat and onto the dock. As the boat sank, the water extinguished the residual fire remaining after the explosion. The captain of the boat told him what had happened. Hung over from a night on Duval Street, the captain hadn't remembered to use the blower before turning on the engine, the second time that morning. The exhaust blower should be engaged for five or ten minutes before trying to turn the engine over, to suck out the gas and exhaust fumes that can accumulate in the bilge of an enclosed vessel, to prevent such explosions from happening. Most owners of gas engine boats, as a habit and precaution, always use the blower to vent the fumes before turning on the ignition. The blower is run by battery power and the switch to engage the blower is usually right next to the ignition.

On this day, the captain had remembered to use the

153

blower the first time he had cranked the boat that morning, but after they had idled the engine for about twenty minutes, while they were preparing the rest of the boat for the day's job ahead, the mate remembered that he had left something in the car. The captain had turned off the engine to save gas, while the mate left to retrieve his lunch. After the mate returned, brown bag in hand, the captain, in a hurry now to get on with his day of shrimping and his brain foggy from his hangover, turned the ignition, without first using the blower, causing the explosion.

Abe returned his mind to surveying the rest of the interior of the beached boat. It looked like the owners had removed the normal crew quarters that are in most shrimp boats and replaced them with just a couple of bunk beds built along the wall, in order to be able to get more bales of pot in the boat.

He then looked back toward the stern of the boat and noticed a rather large bilge pump sticking up out of the water beside the engine compartment. The smugglers had installed a large capacity bilge pump to better protect their cargo, since they knew the boat would be heavy laden.

He went back up the companionway back to the bridge to locate the switch for the bilge. The bilge pump was normally wired straight to the batteries, so it would keep functioning, even if the engine was not. He located the switch and flipped it and heard a sucking noise coming from down below. He walked out of the pilot house and looked over the side toward the back of the boat and saw water spewing out of the bilge exit hole in the side of the boat towards the stern. He hurried back to flip the switch off, not wanting to pump the water out of the bilge until he got the go-ahead from Captain McElroy.

He exited out of the other side of the pilot house on the port side and jumped the short distance down to the beach. Chief Baxter and Captain McElroy were milling around outside the boat talking to some of their underlings. When they saw him jump down off the boat, both cut short the conversations and approached him.

"Well, what do you think?" Chief Baxter asked.

"I think it's doable," he said. "The hole in the hull, I think I can patch, at least enough to get it around to a boat yard, where they can fix it the right way. The bilge pump appears to be in working order. So I can get the excess water that's in the hull now out, and pump out any water that leaks in, while we tow the boat around to the leeward side of this island."

"Good," said Captain McElroy. "We should be done with our part of the investigation in an hour or two. I'd like to get this boat off the beach at the next high tide. The park superintendent is anxious to open the park to visitors and I don't want any gas spills. We need to get it off the beach while the weather's good.

"Out of curiosity, how do you plan to get the boat off the beach?" McElroy asked.

"We've got about five hours until the next high tide, which is at one-thirty this afternoon. First, I'll patch the hole in the hull with plywood and epoxy. Once the tide comes in enough, I'll bring my two shrimp boats around and tie two lines to the bow of the boat. Using the large winches we have in our boats to winch in the nets filled with catch, we can drag it through the surf into deeper water."

The Ocean under the Moon

"Sounds like a good plan," Baxter said.

"Where do you want us to tow the boat?" Abe asked.

"Tow it to Deonas' place. The city has a contract with them to store confiscated vessels," the chief said. He was referring to the long-time family-run boat yard off of Clinch Drive.

"Will do," he said. "I'll be back in about an hour with the wood. Make sure your deputies know to let me back down on the beach."

"I'll radio them now."

Abe turned and started the long trek back to the Scout, where Nick was waiting. The Scout lacked air-conditioning, and the early- morning sun had cleared the horizon like a rising ball of fire. That, combined with the lack of wind, was going to make it a beautiful day, albeit a hot and muggy one.

When he opened the door and plopped down in the driver's seat, Nick woke up with an eager look of anticipation.

"Well?"

"It's a piece of crap," Abe said. He watched Nick's face turn into a dejected frown.

"But it might be our piece of crap," he added with a wink. Nick's frown turned into a big smile, as they drove off down the beach.

The Ocean under the Moon

Chapter 16

June 6, 1976

Ten months later, Nick and Abe were standing at the bottom of the front steps of the Nassau County Courthouse, just four blocks from the waterfront docks. The old brick structure, dating back to 1891, with its tall white clock tower was where the county auctioned off tax lien certificates every year on properties when the owner had not paid the taxes.

Five years ago, Abe had been on these very steps to bid on a tax certificate for the vacant lot just to the south of the Stamos home. He'd wanted to acquire the property so Nick could build a house on it, when his son got old enough to settle down and have a wife and kids, so they would be right next door and Abe could see his grandkids every day.

Abe won the tax certificate auction for the property at that time, and two years later when the owner failed to pay the tax debt, he bought the property at auction for twenty-two thousand dollars, including all of the back taxes, interest, and fees that were owed.

On this day, they were back at the steps of the courthouse for a different kind of auction. This was to liquidate confiscated vehicles, boats, and equipment by both the city and county law enforcement agencies. There really wasn't much crime in Nassau

157

The Ocean under the Moon

County and the public notice advertising the auction had listed only three vehicles to be auctioned and one boat, the *Albatross*.

Besides Abe and Nick, only a handful of potential bidders had gathered at the foot of the courthouse steps in anticipation of the auction. Nick was nervous, however, and could already feel the sweat running down his back, even though it was only ten o'clock on this June morning.

Nick had been waiting impatiently these last ten months, waiting for the trials of the captain and crew of the *Albatross* to conclude, and to see if the foreign owners of the boat tried to claim the boat. Finally, a month ago, the captain of the boat, the shrimper from Texas, was given fifteen years in prison as his sentence and the two crewmen got ten years apiece. No claim was made for ownership of the boat.

* * *

He thought back to that day, ten months ago, when they had pulled the *Albatross* off the beach. They'd patched the crack in the hull by nailing marine-grade plywood to it, bending the plywood to conform to the slight curve of the hull. They sealed the bond of the plywood to the hull of the boat and the nail holes with epoxy. While the epoxy was drying, the seawater was pumped from the bilge out onto the beach, using the boat's bilge pump and a manual pump they had brought from home.

Then he and his father had gone home to wait for the epoxy to dry and the tide to come in. Abe used the *Amelia Queen's* radio to call Billy on the *Island Girl*. Billy said they were about ten miles south of the jetty and hadn't been catching much shrimp so far that morning. After Abe explained the situation, Billy had

158

promised he would meet them around one o'clock at the south jetty. Abe and Nick finished their lunch and then took the *Amelia Queen* out the inlet.

They'd rendezvoused with the *Island Girl*, just outside the breakers. Abe informed Billy of the plan over the radio.

Before Nick had left his house, he'd grabbed his long surfboard from off the porch. He owned two surfboards, his long board, which was eight feet five inches long, and his short board, just a little over six feet long. The longer board had more buoyancy and was for surfing when the waves were small, and the shorter one was for carving up the big waves and was much more maneuverable.

That afternoon, Nick used the surfboard to paddle in to shore carrying a rope from each shrimp boat and attaching the ropes to the *Albatross*. The other end of each rope was attached to the cable on the winch that the shrimpers normally used to pull the nets.

As the tide had come in, Abe and Billy tried to winch the boat off the beach into deep water. The first couple of tries, the boat didn't budge. The strain on the lines was so great that Abe was afraid the winches would be yanked off their mounts.

As the tide came in further, however, the stern of the *Albatross* started to float and pivoted so that the angle was better to pull the boat out to deep water. The third attempt was successful and the *Albatross* came free with a great sucking sound.

Nick climbed aboard the boat and stored his surfboard on the deck. His job was to steer the *Albatross*, as it was being towed by the other boats. With two boats towing it from slightly different angle, the *Albatross* tracked in a straight line and very little steering was necessary. So, after they rounded the jetty and were coming into the channel, he closed his eyes for a moment and imagined himself coming back from sea, in his very own boat, and his large cargo freezers full of succulent shrimp.

* * *

Now, he stood beside his father on the sidewalk in front of the courthouse, shifting his weight from one foot to the other, waiting for the auctioneer to start the auction. He had managed to save almost ten thousand dollars, since he'd been working full time with his father.

He was worried, however, that the money he'd accumulated was not going to be enough to purchase the boat at auction. Through their own experience, plus talking to Jimmy Deonas at Deonas Boat Yard, and research through trade publications, they had determined that the boat, if it was in good working order, would be worth between thirty and forty thousand dollars. They knew, however, that there were several issues that would lower the value of the boat in the eyes of any potential bidder.

First of all, the hull damage would have to be fixed. Most of the planks of wood near the starboard bow would have to be replaced. If replaced with mahogany wood to match the rest of the boat, this would be expensive, since mahogany was an exotic wood for this area.

Besides that, the fact that the boat had a gas engine would deter some bidders. Most shrimpers looked at gas engines with disdain and preferred diesel engines. There was also the question of whether the engine worked at all. In order to prevent corrosion from possible saltwater intrusion when the boat almost sank, the workers at Deonas Boat Yard had drained the fluids out of the engine, so no one knew if the engine really worked. To re-power the boat with a diesel engine or even a new gas engine would be an expensive undertaking.

And, since his father had been awarded by the federal court in Jacksonville a twenty-five-percent salvage rights award, anyone else who made the winning bid would have to pay him twenty-five percent of the total price to pay off the lien he had placed on the boat.

A rotund man in a cheap brown suit approached the top of the steps. In a loud, distinct voice he introduced himself as Dick Stevens of Stevens Auctions. He explained that each bidder should already have received a bidding number from the clerk and to raise the number high in the air when intending to bid. He mentioned that a ten percent buyer's premium would be added to every successful bid, to serve as payment for the auctioneer's services. Any successful bidder was required to pay a twenty percent deposit of the winning bid, plus the buyer's premium, at the conclusion of the auction, and would then have five working days to pay the balance, or it would forfeit to the next highest bidder. The three autos would be auctioned first, with the boat going up for auction last.

The auctioneer launched into the first sale in a strong, staccato voice. Nick paced around like a nervous cat, watching to see who was bidding on the cars, figuring at least those buyers weren't here for the boat. He was pleased that there were only seven potential bidders and most of them seemed to be interested in the cars. By the time the cars were sold, all of the people with numbers, except for one, had made at least one bid on one of the vehicles.

The lone man who had not yet raised his bid number looked to Nick like he was a shrimper. The man, about forty years old, wore a faded t-shirt, blue jeans, and a worn red and black Georgia Bulldog hat. He had a full, dark beard and squinty eyes, combined with the crow's feet that all fishermen accumulated after years on the water.

"Now, we'll move on to the shrimp boat," the fat auctioneer said, sweating heavily and wiping his brow as he rattled off the attributes of the boat, as if it was the "Queen of the Seas."

"Now, who will start off the bidding at ten thousand dollars? Ten, ten, ten, ten thousand dollars," he said, in his rapid-fire delivery.

Nick's heart sank. Ten thousand was the maximum amount he could spend, nine thousand really, when you included the ten percent buyer's premium. He fell silent and grabbed his father's arm. His father had warned him to be patient and not to get carried away in the process.

Abe held the bidding number and stared at the auctioneer, who was watching all the bidders' faces. The winning bidders of the cars had already faded away, going over to the clerk's table to settle their finances. Their departure left only him and his father, the guy in the Georgia Bulldog hat, and one guy in his twenties who bid on each of the cars, but always lost out to a higher bidder.

His father gave Nick a stern look, indicating for him to be

patient. Nick glanced over to the guy in the Bulldog hat, who was watching the auctioneer with a stone face.

The auctioneer, seeing his effort to start the bidding off at the higher plateau wasn't working—and probably ready to get out of the stifling heat and into some air-conditioning—took a different tack.

"Do I hear five thousand dollars? Five, five, five, five thousand dollars?" he implored.

Nick nudged his father, who shook his head indicating not yet. The guy in the Georgia hat raised his number.

"Five thousand dollars!" the auctioneer said, glad to get the bidding started. "Do I hear six thousand dollars? Do I hear six, six, six thousand dollars?"

He glanced at his father who stood still, not moving a muscle.

"Five thousand five hundred dollars!" the auctioneer said, lowering the amount to generate interest. "Do I hear five, five, five, five thousand and five hundred?"

The auctioneer repeated the offer and Abe still stood motionless with Nick glaring at him.

"Come on, folks." the auctioneer said. "This boat's worth four or five times this amount. It's a boat you can make money when using it. Most boats are holes in the water you pour money into, as they say. This boat you can actually pull money out of the water, in the form of shrimp. So let's get the bidding going on this boat."

Again the auctioneer started with the five-thousand-five-hundred figure and again Abe held firm by not bidding. The auctioneer was sweating profusely by now, the damp stains seeping through the brown suit.

The auctioneer shook his head in resignation and started the final countdown. "Five thousand dollars going once, five thousand dollars going twice ..." He raised his gavel.

Nick was about to walk away, in disgust and disbelief, when his father raised his bid number.

"Five thousand five hundred," Abe said. The Georgia man's wide smile turned to a frown.

"Six thousand dollars," the Georgia man said, not waiting for the auctioneer to raise the bid.

"Six thousand dollars," the auctioneer repeated. "Do I hear six thousand five hundred?"

Abe raised his hand. "Six thousand five hundred," he confirmed.

Nick raised his eyebrows at his father's sudden change in tactics, but as his father told him later, his goal was to let the man think he had almost acquired the boat at a reduced cost, because of lack of interest. Then, after the man's disappointment at not getting a rock-bottom price, he wanted to show the man, that whatever he was going to bid, he was going to up the bid, so it was fruitless to continue to bid.

The bid kept going back and forth by five-hundred-dollar increments until it reached nine thousand dollars. This amount represented the maximum that Nick could afford and still pay the buyer's premium without borrowing money from his father. They had discussed beforehand the maximum they would spend. Nick was prepared to spend up to his ten thousand dollars. Abe, for his part, had said he would loan him up to five thousand dollars more, if need be, and that he could pay him back over time, from the profits he would make from working his own boat.

They looked at each other and his father raised the bid to nine thousand five hundred.

"Nine thousand five hundred dollars. Do I hear ten thousand? Ten, ten, ten, ten thousand dollars," the auctioneer said. The auctioneer repeated the number again, pointing at the man in the Georgia hat.

"Nine thousand five hundred going once. Nine thousand five hundred dollars going twice," the auctioneer declared.

Nick and Abe stared at the other bidder, watching intensely, expecting the man to continue the bidding. Instead, the man threw his bid number down, indicating he was through, and turned his back and walked away.

"Sold!" the auctioneer exclaimed. "To these two gentlemen over here."

Nick and his father hugged each other.

"Well, for better or worse, she's all yours," Abe said.

"I couldn't have done it without you, Dad. Thank you for helping me with my dream."

"Just remember that the first four hundred and fifty dollars you make goes to me, to pay me back, since we went over your budget."

"No problem, Dad. But it's going to be awhile before I can get the boat back in shape to go shrimping."

"Well, I'm not looking forward to finding a new deckhand, so I'm glad we'll be working together on my boat for a little while longer," his father said, as they started up the courthouse steps to finish the purchase. "By the way, what do you plan on calling her, anyway?"

"Well, I think since we rescued her from the dead, I'll name her the *Resurrection*."

The Ocean under the Moon

Chapter 17

December 23, 1976

Nick had spent the rest of the year getting the boat ready to go to sea. It'd taken all of his money to buy the boat, so he continued to work for his father to earn extra money to repair the boat.

The mahogany planks to repair the hull, with wood of the same kind, were both expensive and hard to get. Since the wood was a special order, he first had to save up the money for a fifty-percent deposit. Then it took almost eight weeks more for the wood to come in, which was just as well since it would take about the same amount of time for him to earn the money to pay the balance. After the hull was fixed and paid for, he had the engine overhauled to make sure it was functioning properly.

All of the work was being done at the Deonas Boatyard. Greek immigrants had been heavily involved in building shrimp boats on Amelia Island since 1912, when Michael Tiliakos arrived in Fernandina Beach from his native Greece. Mike Tiliakos came to the United States, planning to go to Tarpon Springs, on Florida's west coast, where there was a large community of Greek sponge divers. But he fell in love with a woman on Amelia Island and never left, establishing a boatyard at the foot of Beech Street, where it meets the docks. Later, his sons, John and Nick, joined him in the

167

business. When Dimitrios "Jimmy" Deonas, an experienced boat maker from the "old country," married into the family, he and the Tiliakos brothers ran the boatyard for several years until Deonas branched off on his own, first at site on the north end of Front street, then later at a site off Clinch Drive. So Nick knew the *Resurrection* was in good hands.

Nick and his father had been busy shrimping on the *Amelia Queen* all through the summer and fall. He'd resigned himself to the fact that the *Resurrection* would not be ready until the spring anyway. The fall season for white shrimp was almost over. January and February were not good shrimping months, because the weather was bad and the shrimp had all headed south for warmer water. Most shrimpers used those two months to work on their boats and nets. Nick still needed to have nets made for his boat and had just put a deposit down with the Burbanks, so they would get started on the nets he wanted.

He'd seen Monica only a couple of times since the summer ended. They, of course, saw each other every day or night, during the Johnson family's annual summer pilgrimage to Fernandina Beach. He had to work some during her vacation, but his father did make sure the *Amelia Queen* stayed close to port, with no overnight trips, while the Johnsons were in town. Buck and Bud even went out shrimping with them one day, while Caroline and Monica went shopping. Buck was impressed with the hard work necessary to operate the boat and nets and the similarity to what he did on his farm. Instead of tractors, the shrimpers used boats, and instead of harvesting combines, they used nets.

Bud, on the other hand, was amazed by the open sea and

the variety and exotic nature of the creatures in the by-catch. He loved playing with the crabs, stingrays, and jellyfish that were plopped down out of the net onto the afterdeck. The shrimp had to be sorted from the by-catch before pushing all of the unwanted sea creatures through the scupper holes, so they could return to the sea.

Buck and Bud had gone home that night, weary from a full day of rocking back and forth on a boat in the open ocean, a little sunburned, but with a cooler full of shrimp, and some fish out of the by-catch to show for their productive day. Abe and Buck had gotten on well that day, both hard-working men, who made their living off of the natural world with calluses on their hands.

* * *

After Monica went off to the University of Georgia for her freshman year, Nick only saw her once that fall. She'd been busy getting acclimated to college life and pledging a sorority, while he was working hard, shrimping with his father and fixing up his boat.

He did manage to get up to Athens for the Georgia football team's homecoming game against Vanderbilt. She invited him to be her date for the big weekend—a pep rally on Friday night, the game on Saturday afternoon, and a dance at the sorority house that night.

He'd enjoyed himself immensely in the college party town, but he couldn't help but feel a little out of place and worried whether she would stick with him since she was surrounded by so much other opportunity. He wondered if their two worlds were so far apart now, that she would spin off to another world, like electrons going from one atom to the next.

The Ocean under the Moon

The fall had gone by fast and, now, two days before Christmas, he was sitting in the Palace Saloon, at a small table by himself, thinking about Monica. He was also thinking that he needed to start looking for a deckhand for when the *Resurrection* was ready. Tomorrow was Christmas Eve and he and his father had shut down their shrimping early, so they could buy presents. The weather was supposed to be bad anyway over the weekend, so they'd decided to take off a couple of days before Christmas, along with Christmas Day and the day after.

He was looking forward to a few days off. Since the white shrimp started showing up in early October, he and father had gone out every day the weather permitted. Now he sat in the smoky bar, waiting for his friend Jason Strickland to join him on this Friday night. Jason was one of his best friends from high school. They used to do a lot together, but since Jason followed his father into working shift work in the paper mill, and Nick was out to sea shrimping for days on end sometimes, it was harder for them to hang out together.

Since the mill shut down every year for a week around Christmas to do maintenance, Jason was enjoying a few days off. They'd decided to meet at the Palace to catch up on things.

Nick always liked spending an evening in this historic bar, in a brick building that had been a landmark since 1903 on the corner of Second Street and Centre Street. The Palace, Florida's oldest continually operated saloon, had been intended to be a cut above the other twenty-two saloons that were open during Fernandina's golden years of tourism around the turn of the century.

The Ocean under the Moon

In Nick's opinion, the Palace remained a great place for drinking. After entering through the wooden swinging doors, the ambiance was of a New York tavern, crossed with an Old West saloon, with a pinch of Florida thrown in. Behind the bar was a custom-made English oak bar-fixture complete with two topless mermaids.

The walls of the bar were wainscoted with Italian marble and the upper walls between the windows were painted with a series of four murals, scenes from Charles Dickens novels. The old tile floor, which was perfect for dancing, coupled with the low-hung antique ceiling fans and red velvet curtains, gave the Palace an aura of timelessness that made every night seem like a recurring dream from the past.

A large figure plopped down in the chair opposite him, at the small two-person wooden table that was set up against the wall. He looked across the table, expecting to see his buddy Jason, but was surprised to be staring at the ruggedly handsome face of Travis "Gator" McDougal, smiling back at him like a Cheshire cat.

"Hey, Nick, how are you doing?" he said cheerfully, as if they were long-lost friends.

"Fine, Gator," he said, surprised that McDougal even knew his name.

The guy was famous about town for being the finest football player Fernandina Beach High School had ever produced. With a body strengthened by years of surfing as well as football, he looked like a Polynesian warrior, except that he sported a long, blond ponytail. A six-foot-three, two-hundred-thirty-pound middle linebacker, he'd been recruited by all of the colleges, but decided to stay close to home and play for the University of Florida Gators.

He'd acquired his nickname "Gator" even before he went down to Gainesville to play for Florida. One day, when he was a junior in high school, he and a couple of his buddies from the football team were walking home from practice when they spotted a seven-foot alligator sunning itself on the bank of Egan's Creek, where it passed under Atlantic Avenue. One of the boys bet him a hundred dollars that he wouldn't jump down and wrestle the alligator into submission.

Without hesitation Gator jumped onto the back of the unsuspecting alligator, flipped it over onto its back and rubbed its belly, until the alligator was in a semi-catatonic state. Covered in mud, but with a big grin, he released the stunned gator and collected on his bet. Ever since then, everyone had called him Gator.

Nick did not know him that well, since he was two years ahead of Nick in school. They did play on the same football team for one year, but Gator was a star and Nick rarely got on the field, since he was so young.

He'd followed Gator's career down in Gainesville, as did everyone in Fernandina. He knew that the strong, fast linebacker played in several games as a freshman, in an era when most freshmen were red-shirted. He'd been a regular starter as a sophomore and played well, but in the first game of his junior year, he tore all of the ligaments in his right knee. At the time, this kind of knee injury took one and a half to two years to fully recover, if at all.

A borderline student to begin with, and without football

to motivate him, he stopped going to classes and concentrated on sorority girls and drinking beer. After the fall semester, he was kicked out of school for poor grades and not going to class; his coaches were glad to reclaim his scholarship, to give to another recruit the next fall.

Nick knew Gator returned last winter to Fernandina, where the former football star continued to chase girls, drink beer, and get into fights. He'd heard Gator was given a cushy job at the paper mill, based on the goodwill he had earned playing for the Fernandina Beach Pirates football team, only to lose the job six months later for not showing up to work.

Gator tried to work for a couple of Nick's father's friends, as a deckhand on their shrimp boats, but they'd let him go due to lack of dependability. So it was a surprise to see this larger-than-life legend sitting across from him, grinning like a long-lost friend.

"I hear you almost got your boat ready," Gator said.

"Yeah, I'm making progress."

"You got a deckhand lined up yet?"

"Well, the boat's not going to be ready until March. I was just starting to think about it."

"Think no further. I'll do it. I'll be your deckhand. We'll be great together. Most of these shrimpers are old-timers now. They don't know how to have fun, but we'll have a blast together, won't we? It'll be like back in high school. Hey, I hope there are no hard feelings about that little initiation we had for the football team." Gator chuckled and lifted his Budweiser. "What do you say?"

"I'd have to ask my father about it. He's part owner of the boat," Nick lied. He still remembered the taste of the pogy oil he was forced to drink as part of the hazing ritual for the new players on the football team when he was a sophomore.

"Well, don't take too long to make up your mind. I've got other offers to consider. And one other thing," he said, rising from his chair, "if I decide to work for you, there are two things I don't do. First, if we are out shrimping and 'Free Bird' by Lynyrd Skynyrd comes on the radio, I don't work while it's on—I have to stop and pay my respects. Second, I don't go out shrimping if the Florida Gators are playing on television."

"I'll take all that into consideration," Nick said. He shook Gator's hand as the big man stood up.

Jason arrived just as Gator was walking away.

"What did Gator McDougal want?" Jason asked as he sat down at the table.

"He wants to work for me," Nick said with a laugh. "Can you imagine that?"

"Wow, the mighty Gator McDougal working for you. My, how times have changed."

"Yeah, well, I don't know if that is going to happen. The word is that he is not very dependable. Can you imagine me having to fire him? He'd probably tie me up and make me walk the plank on my very own boat."

Jason was a small guy, about five-foot-eight, and weighing about one hundred and forty pounds, soaking wet. But he possessed a big smile and infectious personality. Although he didn't play sports in high school, Nick and the rest of his buddies liked to hang out with him after the games because he was so funny.

The Ocean under the Moon

Jason adopted the voice of a pirate and pretended to be Gator. "Ahoy, ye mateys. I'm commandeering this here shrimp boat in the name of drink and debauchery. Our goal will be to rape and pillage in every town along the coast. Now, come on, women, surrender the booty!"

Nick laughed at the imitation, but he was going to have to get serious about finding a deckhand.

They relaxed, drinking long-neck Buds out of the bottle, and catching up on what was going on in their lives and jobs. They sat next to the jukebox and listened to songs like "Piano Man" by Billy Joel, which Nick thought could have been written about the Palace, because it matched the vibe of the place. Every now and then, when an appropriate song came on the jukebox, Anna, one of the barmaids, would break out in song.

After awhile, three burly men came in through the swinging doors, and sauntered their way to a table in the back of the bar next to the restrooms. Nick recognized one of the men as the guy that he and his father had outbid for the *Resurrection*. The man was still wearing the same Georgia hat. After the men sat down, he couldn't help but notice them glowering over in his direction, and he told Jason about the guy who'd tried to buy the boat and lost.

He'd seen these men from a distance earlier in the week at the city marina. They were on a shrimp boat called *Dixie Heritage*, flying a Georgia state flag and a Rebel flag, and the writing on the transom said the boat was out of Darien, Georgia.

There was no love lost between the Florida shrimpers and the Georgia shrimpers, since each ventured into the other's territory from time to time to poach each other's shrimp. Most of the time, the boats docked in their home territory, but this boat may have been down here getting supplies from Standard Marine, he surmised.

He tried to ignore the men tonight, as Jason chattered away. He and Jason continued to talk about girls, their jobs, and Nick's reclamation project of the *Resurrection*.

After an hour or so, Nick knew he was going to have to make a trip to the restroom, which would take him right past the glum-looking men at the table in back. He told Jason where he was going.

"Keep an eye out for trouble," he said. "Just in case—I don't know if they're up to anything, but they don't look real friendly." He knew his friend wouldn't be much help in a fight, but maybe he could call for help, if the need arose.

He started to make his way toward the bathroom. He noticed Gator was still in the bar, chatting up a girl sitting on a stool at the end of the bar toward the entrance. As he reached the bar, he turned and headed down the aisle, between the patrons sitting on barstools to his left and the tables on the right side of the aisle.

He avoided looking at the men at the table and thought he'd made it home free, when the man who had been outbid pushed his chair back, blocking his way.

Nick stopped abruptly and the man stood up, his face coming close to his own.

"That should have been my boat," the shrimper said. His breath smelled of beer and Nick guessed he'd been drinking for most of the day with his deckhands.

"I'm sorry you lost. But the auction was fair and square," he said.

He noticed the man in front of him was an inch shorter than him, but much thicker. Despite his pot belly, the man's arms looked strong, from years of pulling in shrimp nets, and his friends, who stood up out of their chairs behind him, looked just as formidable.

He thought, if it was just this one guy in his face, he would have a more than even chance, since the man was clearly intoxicated to some degree, and Nick wasn't. But he was outnumbered and Jason wouldn't be any real help.

"Your daddy ain't here to bail you out this time, boy, is he?" the man said.

He knew he was in trouble. He would probably get one good punch in before he would be swarmed by the other two men and take a severe beating.

"What seems to be the problem here? Can't you see the boy has got to pee?" Gator stepped in between Nick and the guy in the Georgia hat.

"This ain't none of your business." The man looked up at Gator, unnerved that the odds had changed.

"Well, I'm making it my business, because this here fellow might be my new bossman and I'm considering this a job interview." Gator smiled, relishing the idea of some action and looking with glee at the other two men behind the first man.

"Now, step aside," he commanded.

Gator continued to look down at the man, as the shrimper

stared back, weighing his options. After what seemed like an eternity to Nick, the man finally pulled his chair back toward the table and sat down, with his friends following his example.

Gator ushered Nick to the bathroom and waited outside the door, while he went inside to relieve himself. They then walked back by the men's table without incident, and returned to where Jason was sitting. He'd risen from his chair when the trouble started, but quickly returned to his seat once Gator had stood the men down.

"Man, that was awesome!" he said to Gator as he approached.

"It was nothing," Gator said, grinning. "But you boys need to get out of here and run on home. After a few more beers, those Georgia boys are going to get even surlier, as they realize their manhood was questioned."

Nick and Jason looked at each other, then back at the men sulking over their beers, and realized he was right.

"Let's go to the Paddle Loft," Jason suggested, referring to a new bar that had opened at the Amelia Island Plantation, a resort being built on the south end of the island.

"Good idea," Nick concurred.

Gator walked them to the Palace doors. He slapped Nick on his back as he was heading out the door and said with a wink, "I guess you owe me one, kid. Remember that when you get your boat ready. It's good to have a deckhand that you can depend on."

While he walked out the doors into the dark night, Nick thought about the irony of Gator's last words. Yes, he could be depended on to stand shoulder to shoulder in a fight, and brave enough to withstand even the most savage storm at sea, but could he be depended on to show up to work every day, with his history of drinking and carousing? That would be the question he would wrestle with over the next several weeks, while he was finishing the work on the *Resurrection*.

It was a good thing they left when they did that night, he found out later. When Gator left the Palace at closing time, the three men from Georgia jumped him. As a devout Florida fan and former player, there was nothing he liked better than beating up obnoxious Georgia Bulldog fans. The inebriated Bulldogs were no match for this Gator, who would, to his regret, never get to play in another Florida-Georgia game. He took out his frustration on his opponents, sending all three of them to the hospital for several days, and the legend of Gator McDougal just kept growing.

The Ocean under the Moon

Chapter 18

November 17, 1978

"Gator, pull in the trail net. Let's see what we have," Nick commanded.

"Yes, sir, Captain," he responded. They'd been shrimping on the *Resurrection* together for almost two years now, and they were like a well-oiled machine.

Nick was hesitant to hire Gator, at first, and his father had warned him that he would be nothing but trouble. But being young and optimistic and feeling indebted, due to Gator's intervention in the Palace, he decided to give him a try.

He'd worried that not only would Gator be undependable, but that he would also try to dominate the boat and act as *de facto* captain, telling him what to do. For the most part, however, Gator had been dependable so far. Sure, there was the occasional lapse, and for those times, he'd recruited Willie Cooper, a retired Afro-American shrimper, who still liked to go out on occasion and was always available at the last minute.

Once on the boat, Gator did the work of two men. Most large shrimp boats have a crew of three men, a captain and two crew members. The *Resurrection* was mid-sized and with Gator on board, the two of them could manage the boat with ease. With his

The Ocean under the Moon

boundless energy and strong physique, he never seemed to slow down, even when he was hung-over from a night of carousing before they headed out to sea.

His hard-working habits were good enough for Nick to overlook the occasional lapse in dependability and also his quirkiness onboard the boat. He brought a large boom box on board the boat, which was always playing music loudly while he worked. He said it made the day go by faster. For Nick's part, it was a lot more fun than shrimping with his dad, which had always been conducted in silence, except for the weather channel crackling over the VHF radio.

Gator loved to listen to the Greaseman, a radio disc jockey, on the fifty-thousand-watt Jacksonville AM radio channel 69.1, the "Big Ape," in the mornings. Sounding on the radio like the biggest, rudest fifty-year-old redneck out there, he was a precursor to the shock radio jockeys that would come after him. He had hilarious bits on the radio like "Sergeant Fury," in which he relived his supposed time in Vietnam, "South of the Border," where he told stories of his time in Mexico, and the "Hobo-doo-ga-ga Handbook," in which he gave pointers on how to pick up women and have sex.

Nick and Gator would be rolling on the deck of the shrimp boat in laughter at his outrageous embellishments. The disc jockey kept his private life separate from his radio personality and nobody but a few people who worked at the radio station knew what he looked like. It would be years later, after he moved to Washington, D.C., to dominate that market, that Nick would learn he was really a slender, blond-haired man named Doug Tract, who had been in his twenties when they were listening to him, and wasn't anything like the character he portrayed on the radio.

After the Greaseman went off the airways at ten o'clock in the morning, Gator would switch his boom box to the FM station, Rock 105. The "Big Ape" played pop songs all day long, the same twenty or so songs over and over. Rock 105, on the other hand, played hard rock and the longer songs like Skynyrd's "Free Bird."

True to his word, every time that song came on the radio, Gator became a man possessed. As soon as he heard the first organ notes at the beginning of the song, he would stop what he was doing and go grab the broom from the pilothouse.

When the slow start to the song began, with the wailing guitar chords, he would run to the back of the boat and jump up onto the stern and start singing into the wooden end of the broom, as if it was a microphone.

Then, when the fast part of the song kicked in, he would turn the broom around and start playing air guitar with it. He would race around the boat, hopping from spot to spot, while keeping time with the music. For the big, three-guitar crescendo at the end of the song, he would end up on the roof of the crew's quarters, right behind the pilot house, as if on a stage playing to a sold-out crowd of seagulls and porpoises. After the song was over, Gator would bow to his imaginary, adoring fans and then jump down on the afterdeck and get right back to work.

Some shrimpers might think this interruption of work would be an aggravation to the captain of the boat, but Gator's gyrations and the seriousness with which he performed this ritual never ceased to amuse Nick.

He once asked Gator why the song affected him so much.

The Ocean under the Moon

Gator explained that when the song cranked into the fast section, the accelerating guitar licks were like musical heaven to him. The building crescendo of sound released endorphins inside his body that made him want to run through the brick wall of life. It was similar to the adrenaline rush he used to get when he played football and made a great play—like he was king of the world. Now that his knee no longer allowed him to play football, the song allowed him to relive his past glory, by getting his juices flowing again.

There was also another reason why the song seemed to speak to him personally, he told Nick. The summer after the football season in which he injured his knee, he was back in Fernandina still on crutches, having just flunked out of school. He'd just arrived from Gainesville and after visiting with his parents a little bit, he decided to head down to the Palace to drown his sorrows. He was sitting at the bar about ten o'clock at night, talking to a charter fishing captain named Taylor Edwards. Gator asked him why the bar was so dead, since they were the only two people in the bar beside the barmaid.

Taylor told him it was because the Lynyrd Skynyrd band was performing a fundraiser concert to raise money for a band member's uncle, who was running for sheriff of Nassau County. The chance to hear a famous band like Lynyrd Skynyrd, whose members were from the nearby westside of Jacksonville, had drawn everybody to the auditorium at the Atlantic Avenue Recreation Center.

Gator liked the Southern rock band that emerged as a successor to the Allman Brothers. Lynyrd Skynyrd spoke to the rebel that was in all the young men of the South at the time. He, in particular, liked the song "Give Me Three Steps," about a cuckolded man who is about to shoot a fellow who unwittingly fooled around the wrong woman. He said the song reminded him of some of the situations he'd been involved in.

So Gator and Taylor decided to go down to the rec center and see if they could get in somehow. The concert had started at eight-thirty and now it was close to ten-thirty, so they hoped to be able to sneak in for the end of the show.

When they got to the auditorium, they saw an overflowing crowd spilled out the front door, onto the front portico and steps. The two of them realized they would never get in that way, so they went around back to the small side door that entered the auditorium, just to the left of the stage. Due to the packed crowd and oppressive heat inside the auditorium, the side door was open and people had spilled outside to cool off and smoke cigarettes or pot.

They'd arrived right in the lull between the pseudo-end of the concert and the encore. Because there were more people spilling out of the door than trying to get in, nobody questioned their entrance into the auditorium. Since Gator was still using his crutches, the concert-goers moved out of his way and they were able to maneuver up to the front of the stage, right in the center.

It wasn't long before the band members started coming back out and the audience went crazy. They were surrounded by fired-up fans that'd waited for this moment. Ronnie Van Zant, the lead singer, came out and walked right toward them, stopping at the microphone right in front of them.

The Ocean under the Moon

"All right, Nassau County. Don't forget to get out and vote. Now, we're going to wrap this up," he said, to the cheers of the crowd.

With that, the band started into "Sweet Home Alabama," and they substituted the name Fernandina for Alabama, when it came up in the lyrics. The crowd sang along with the band, emphasizing the word Fernandina.

There was a brief lull after the song for everyone to catch their breath. Then, the first, soulful notes of "Free Bird" began and the crowd erupted in appreciation. The hair stood up on the back of Gator's neck and he got the same feeling he used to get when he ran out of the tunnel into the full stadium of adoring football fans back in Gainesville. Ronnie Van Zant, bearded and wearing a black cowboy hat with a feather in front, sang with soul into the microphone, sweat running down his face.

When the fast part of the song began, Ronnie stepped back and the three guitar players stepped forward. The guitar licks started coming faster and faster. With the center guitarist, arm's distance away, right in front of Gator, and the other two guitarists off to the side, he had felt like he was at the epicenter of the concert, the sound piercing his brain, coming in from all directions, as if he was wearing stereo headphones.

Toward the end of the song, the crowd reached a frenzied pitch, as if experiencing a religious experience and a pagan ritual, all at once. Gator had goose bumps by the end of the song, and that night was why he could never listen to the song without jumping around and reliving that awakening.

Besides, he told Nick, since Ronnie Van Zant died in that

185

tragic plane accident in the fall of 1977, along with guitarist Steve
Gaines and vocalist Cassie Gaines, he'd promised himself to keep
their memories alive by always performing his ritual when the
song came over the radio.

He also stuck to his promise of not working if the Florida
Gators were on television. This was not a major issue when they
first started working together, as at the time the Gators were not
that good, usually winding up in the middle of the pack of all the
Southeastern Conference teams. Plus, before the proliferation of
cable television, there was only one SEC game of the week shown
on Saturday afternoon. Since Nick was a Florida fan himself, he
didn't mind adjusting their shrimping excursions around the
occasional Saturday afternoon SEC game of the week, when the
University of Florida was picked to be one of the teams broadcast
on network television.

But besides those two quirks, Gator had turned out to be a
pretty dependable deckhand. Once aboard the boat, there was an
unspoken rule that there would be no drinking. Nick wouldn't
allow it and Gator wouldn't try it. Both men maintained too much
respect for the job at hand and the dangers of the sea. But in port,
he would revert to his hard-drinking ways. Therefore, in order to
minimize temptations, and also because they were two single men
with no family responsibilities, they would stay out on the boat for
four, five, even six days at a time, shrimping night and day, if the
shrimping was good.

Once returning to port, and after the last shovelful of
shrimp was shoveled out of the icebox, dumped into a plastic
laundry basket and hauled out of the hold into the fish processing

house, Gator would be off to his small, rented apartment on North Second Street which was just across from the fish processing house. After a quick shower and change of clothes, he would return to the *Resurrection*, still docked at the fish house, to collect his share of the week's work. Nick would be sitting at the navigation table in the pilot house, figuring up the expenses and dividing up the cash.

Normally, on a shrimp boat, after the catch is sold to the fish processing house, the expenses for fuel, groceries, and ice are deducted. Then the proceeds are divided, with one-third going to the crew, usually split between two deckhands, and two-thirds for the owner-operator. If the owner of the boat has several boats and has to hire a captain, then the ratio is fifty percent of the profits to the crew, including the captain, and fifty percent to the owner of the boat. The boat owner pays for dockage, boat payments, if there are any, insurance, permits, and maintenance expenses.

In Nick's case, since he didn't have any mortgage payments on the boat and docked at the family docks for free, he was able to pay Gator forty percent of the net profits after the basic expenses. This made Gator very loyal to his situation on the *Resurrection*.

On a good week at the peak of the shrimping season, when the shrimp were plentiful and easy to catch, Gator would leave the boat and walk the two blocks to the Palace with up to three thousand dollars in his pocket. He would stroll into the bar about four in the afternoon, plop a big roll of bills on the bar, and start buying drinks for the few people in the bar at that time. If Nick visited the bar later that night, his deckhand would still be sitting on the same bar stool, a girl on each side, with a small crowd gathered around him, regaling them with stories of his past exploits.

Nick tried to counsel him on not frittering his money away, but the brash young former football player liked to live for the day—living with urgency like he was going to die the next day. He did everything full-bore, whether it was work, carousing, or drinking. That's what made him a good football player; his motor ran at redline all the time.

Nick, on the other hand, was quite frugal. After he paid back the four hundred and fifty dollars his father had loaned him to help buy the boat and paid for the repairs to make it seaworthy, he started saving what he could to buy materials for a cottage he planned to build on the vacant lot next to his parent's house.

***

Nick and Monica had continued to see each other whenever they could over the last three years. She was now a senior at the University of Georgia, majoring in elementary education. Caroline thought her daughter would have put the young shrimper in her rear-view mirror once she went to Athens and was swallowed up by all the college activities and fraternity boys, but somehow the young couple's love endured, despite their separation.

They'd developed a yearly routine of seeing each other for the two weeks each summer during the Johnsons' beach vacation in Fernandina. Then he would go up to Hazlehurst for a visit, the weekend before she would head back to school in the fall. They wouldn't see each other again until the Florida-Georgia football weekend at the end of October.

The Ocean under the Moon

Fernandina always came alive on Florida-Georgia weekend or Georgia-Florida weekend, as it was called, depending on which team you supported. The "World's Largest Outdoor Cocktail Party," as it was also called, was played in Jacksonville, only thirty miles away. Since Fernandina was on the border between Georgia and Florida, it became a divided town for the games.

Many of Fernandina's long-time residents were originally from Georgia and maintained an allegiance to the Georgia Bulldog football team. Also, since Fernandina and Amelia Island are north of Jacksonville, most of the old wooden beach houses that had been on the beach for decades, along with the new condominiums that were starting to spring up, were rented by Georgia fans who were down for the weekend.

Every year, the fans would start arriving in town on the Wednesday before the game, roll out their Georgia flags on the front porches or balconies of where they were staying, and begin a four-day party. The locals who were Florida fans did not appreciate this invasion. Gator, in particular, did not enjoy his town being taken over by these, at least in his mind, detestable Bulldog fans.

Every year, Nick knew Gator wouldn't work Florida-Georgia weekend, because some of his old football buddies would always get him a ticket for the game and have a big tailgating reunion at the stadium. He would behave himself, in the days leading up to the game and before the game started. However, if Florida was losing in the fourth quarter, or after the game if they had lost, pity the first Georgia fan who stuck his finger in his face to rub in the victory. Nick had already gone down to Jacksonville to bail him out of jail after the game at least once since they'd been working together.

Nick was also a fan, but not nearly as devoted as Gator. He was more of a casual fan of the Gators, since he didn't actually go to school there. But it still wasn't easy for him to sit in the Georgia section when Monica came down to the game with her family.

The Johnson family would come down for the game in their big motor home, towing a trailer upon which sat a Georgia Bulldog golf cart. They would drive down on Wednesday and wait in line to get into "RV City," a huge, cordoned-off parking lot reserved just for motor homes right outside the stadium. Once allowed inside the lot, they would stake out a space, unload all their gear, and begin a four-day tailgating experience, riding around in their golf cart, visiting friends, grilling out, and having a big time.

Nick always felt out of place, hanging out with her family and friends that weekend. Buck and his cohorts tried to convert him over to their side and to wear Georgia colors, but he in good conscience could not do so, and always wore neutral colors, one of the few in the stadium on game day to do so.

At the time, the Florida-Georgia game and the Texas-Oklahoma game were the only two college regular season games to be played at a neutral site where the crowd was split fifty-fifty. On game day, right before kickoff, the inside of the stadium was a sight to see with both full bands from each school playing and the stadium evenly demarcated by the blue and orange of Florida on one side and the red and black Georgia colors on the other side,

The Ocean under the Moon

distinctly separated at the aisles that divided them.

The energy in the stadium at kickoff was equal to the adrenalin rush of the start of the Daytona 500, or the beginning of a much anticipated heavyweight boxing match between two champion boxers.

Nick always felt conspicuous in his neutral clothes and Gator chided him about not being brave enough to wear his blue and orange amongst the Georgia throng. Nick felt he was in "no man's land" — not bold enough to show his true colors and not willing to join a new side.

Gator often kidded him that if Nick and Monica got married, as Nick often talked about, their marriage, according to their college allegiance, would be a mixed marriage. Like two dogs from different breeds, their kids would not be "purebred." But Nick reminded him that offspring between two separate breeds often bring forward the best qualities of both breeds and strengthen the gene pool.

After the Florida-Georgia weekend, Nick and Monica would get together for Christmas. They would meet, either in Fernandina or Hazlehurst, and exchange presents. She would stay through New Year's Eve to celebrate the arrival of a new year with him, and then head back to school for winter quarter.

At the end of winter quarter, she usually went somewhere on spring break with her girlfriends, most of the time either Daytona Beach or Panama City. He didn't really mind, figuring it was part of college life. He planned on marrying her one day, and he did not want her to have any regrets. Besides, for the last two springs, he and Gator had left Fernandina on the *Resurrection* for a spring break of their own.

Since the white, roe shrimp don't show up off the beaches of Amelia Island until mid-April to the beginning of May, they had taken the *Resurrection* down to Key West to get an early start on the season by catching pink shrimp, also called Gulf shrimp, in the fertile waters around the Dry Tortugas, off of Key West.

Taking Gator to Key West was not one of his best ideas. Gator rampaged his way through the bars on Duval Street like the second coming of Ernest Hemingway, only in a non-literary way. It was all Nick could do to get him to go to sea, and once there, he would keep the boat out several days, in order to keep Gator out of the bars. But eventually, they would have to return to port to sell their catch and get more fuel, ice, and food. Gator would then, again, go on a two- or three-day rampage.

Nick tried his best to keep up with his friend, and to keep his deckhand out of trouble. But he had neither the stamina nor the constitution to keep up with Gator, who was in a league of his own. He would head back to the boat, around one or two in the morning. Gator, on the other hand, would show up at the boat at four or five in the morning, with one or two, sometimes three girls in tow. They would wake him up and try to get him to continue the party.

Most of the time, he didn't care for the bar-flies that his friend would bring home and would try to go back to sleep. Occasionally, Gator would run across some sorority girls from Kentucky, Ohio, or elsewhere, down on spring break, and Nick did give in to his desires a couple of times. Gator was proud of him, but he felt nothing but remorse, and confirmed his love for Monica to himself each time.

The Ocean under the Moon

Finally, as May approached, he would crank up the *Resurrection* early in the morning and be off the East coast of Florida, around Miami, before Gator would wake up out of his drunken stupor, unable to protest their exit. He was worried both of the years they went down there that Gator would never leave and he would lose his deckhand.

This year they were not going to Key West for spring break and catching the pink shrimp. Nick realized the fuel they burned getting down there and back, plus the money they spent in the bars, ate up a large percentage of the profits for the trip, making it hardly worth their while. Secondly, and more importantly, this year Monica was coming to Fernandina with a couple of friends for her spring break and he was going to propose to her.

"Damn," Nick said out loud, seeing that the trail net was empty. "Put it back down," he ordered.

"Aye, aye, Captain," Gator said with a wink, as he was already in the process of lowering the net back down into the water, having anticipated Nick's order.

The Ocean under the Moon

Chapter 19

March 15, 1979

"Hand me that wrench," Nick said. He pointed at a wrench on the deck next to Gator's foot. He was down in the engine room getting prepared to change the engine oil. Gator was sitting on an overturned five-gallon bucket, next to an opened tool box on the afterdeck, staring down at him, the large engine room hatches having been opened up.

"Are you sure you really want to propose?" he said. "Haven't you ever heard the saying, why buy the cow when you can get the milk for free?"

"Well, in case you haven't noticed, I haven't been drinking a lot of milk lately. Pass me that collection pan, would you?"

"If you're not drinking enough milk, it's your own damn fault. I've brought you plenty of milk cows home."

"Yeah, that's a pretty good description of the women you bring home. Milk cows, that's exactly what they are."

Gator responded by throwing an oily rag down at him, hitting him in the back of the head.

"Well, who wants to have one percent milk all the time, when you can have skim milk, or even whole fat, once in awhile."

"I like my one percent milk."

The Ocean under the Moon

"You better, because that's all you'll be getting for the rest of your life."

There was a lull in the conversation, as Nick got the drain plug free, and oil started draining into the pan.

"Don't you know that by Florida divorce law, married women own half of all their husband's money, and by natural law, women already own all the vaginas in the world. So what chance does a man have in a marriage?" Gator asked.

"Well, with an attitude like that, you're never going to get married," Nick said.

"That would be fine by me." Gator took a sip of beer from his can.

Nick didn't allow drinking on the boat, while under way, but when they were sitting at the dock, doing minor repairs or just shooting the breeze after a day of shrimping, he would allow it and even join in by having a beer or two.

He pulled himself out of the engine compartment to wait for the oil to drain into the pan. He sat on the afterdeck, next to the opened hatch, with his legs dangling down into the engine compartment. He took a long sip of his cool beer.

"So, do you know what to do on Saturday night?"

"Yeah, I know what to do," Gator said half-heartedly. "You know, if I can't talk you out of it, at least let me be your best man."

"You got it." He was planning on asking him anyway.

The two men clicked beer cans to seal the deal and each took a sip of beer.

"You know, this means I get to throw you a bachelor

party," Gator said with a sly grin, focusing on the only positive, for him, of his buddy getting married.

"That's what I'm afraid of," Nick said.

He clicked beers again with Gator, who now had a fiendish grin on his face, the wheels turning about the party.

Chapter 20

March 22, 1979

Nick looked into the mirror staring at his reflection, staring back at him, and wondered if he was brave enough to make the commitment he was going to make tonight. He'd been dreaming of marrying Monica ever since the day they met, but he had to admit he was experiencing "cold feet" that he hadn't expected. He didn't doubt that she was the woman for him, but marriage meant he would be casting off his youth and assuming all the responsibilities and restraints of a married man.

Still, she would be graduating in May and would need to start looking for teaching jobs in the fall. He didn't want her to take a job teaching in Georgia somewhere, and meet some young, hunky football coach. What if he lost her?

Nick had arranged for Monica and two of her friends to come down to Fernandina for spring break and stay for free in a beach cottage located near Main Beach. The cottage was owned by the parents of Dan Lowe, a good friend of his. The Lowe family had been in Fernandina for generations and owned the local grocery store. Nick and Dan had known each other since they were ten years old and spent many days playing football and baseball or fishing together. In high school, they spent a lot of time cruising

197

around town talking about girls and where their lives were heading. Then Dan headed down to the University of Florida to get a business degree, while he stayed in town to shrimp with his father. Dan had graduated the previous June and was now selling copiers in Jacksonville, so the young men had drifted apart somewhat, but Dan was happy to help him out by talking his parents into the use of one of their cottages.

The Lowe family owned two cottages on a piece of property one block south of Main Beach. The girls would be staying in the "Lowe Tide," closest to the water, a one-story, wooden cottage on pilings. It used to be a two-story home, but Hurricane Dora, in 1964, took out the bottom floor. However, the Lowes had been able to salvage the top floor and reset it on top of the pilings. The other cottage, which had two stories and stood a little further from the ocean, was called "High Tide."

Nick took one last look in the mirror. Tonight was the big night. Monica and her friends, Mary and Rita, had driven down last Friday night, a week ago. It had been a good week. They, like all college students on spring break, just wanted to lie out in the sun and drink beer. The weather was just getting warm enough to do that, but there was still a bit of coolness in the air. That allowed the girls to stay out on the beach all day, without getting too hot or sunburned as they would have in the summer.

During the day, Nick and Gator had to go out shrimping, but at night, Nick would hang out with Monica and her friends, bringing along some of his other friends. He'd even brought the girls down to the Palace one night and introduced Mary and Rita to Gator, who they thought was wild and funny. Despite their allegiances to different football teams, they got past their initial dislike for each other's schools and Gator was soon leading the girls in drinking games, shooting pool, and dancing.

After the Palace closed for the evening, the party continued over at the Lowe Tide. Then, after some more tequila was consumed that night, the last he saw of Gator, he was walking, arm in arm with Mary and Rita, down to the beach.

But tonight was going to be Nick and Monica's night. He'd made reservations at eight o'clock at the swank Amelia Inn, the new, oceanfront restaurant at the Amelia Island Plantation, an upscale resort recently established on the south end of the island. Once slated to be strip-mined by the Union Carbide Company for some mineral in the sand, the land was saved from that fate when it was purchased by Charles Frasier and the Sea Pines Company, developers of Harbour Town on Hilton Head Island, South Carolina. Frasier had recently built twenty-seven holes of golf, a beach club, and the Amelia Inn, a large structure sitting on a sand dune overlooking one of the golf holes and the ocean.

He picked Monica up at seven-thirty. She plopped down into the bucket seat of the Firebird and gave him a quick kiss on the cheek.

"Finally, a night alone," she said with a sigh.

"What are Rita and Mary doing tonight?" he asked.

"They said they were going to meet Gator down at the Palace for one last blowout."

He began the scenic drive down A1A, toward the south end of the island. The intersection of Atlantic Avenue and South Fletcher Avenue, near where Monica was staying, marks the

northernmost tip of the famous State Road A1A, which runs, for
the most part, beside the beach from northeast Florida to Key West.
Although the scenic and historic coastal highway starts thirty miles
west of Fernandina, in Callahan, it is the sections that run along
Florida's beaches that have made it well-known.

"So, what do you have in mind tonight?" she asked.

Having kept his plans a secret, he answered in a half-
truth.

"Well, first candlelight dinner for two, while watching the
moon come up over the ocean at the Amelia Inn. Then, I thought
we would go to the Paddle Loft for awhile, and after that, maybe
we could meet up with Gator and the girls for a nightcap at the
Palace."

"I like it, all of it except going to meet them at the Palace. I
want you all to myself tonight." She gave him a little wink.

"I like the way you think," he responded, his right hand
giving her left thigh a little squeeze.

They drove down South Fletcher Avenue, past all of the
beach houses and the beach access called Peter's Point, and turned
left on the Amelia Island Parkway. The parkway was a new road
that Amelia Island Plantation built, at its own expense, as a
shortcut and scenic drive to the property. Soon they were back on
A1A and then reached the entrance to the Plantation. After the
security guard confirmed that Nick had a reservation at the inn,
they were allowed to enter the property.

They followed the winding road through the lush foliage,
and noticed the stop signs, instead of being red, were green to
blend in more with the surroundings. When Nick pulled up under

the covered portico of the inn and they exited the car, he handed his keys and a tip to the valet. They walked into the grand entrance, went past the reservation desk, past the lounge, to the *maitre d'* standing at the desk at the far end of the lobby. Nick announced his name and they were escorted to a table for two next to the window.

Night had fallen. He could see the scheduled full moon beginning to peek out from behind the ocean, and he knew the view would improve as the night progressed. Pleased, he gave the *maitre d'* a tip for presenting them with a proper table.

"Oh, it's beautiful," Monica exclaimed, gazing from the white linen tablecloth, lighted candle, and centerpiece of palm fronds and hibiscus flowers, to the sweeping view out of the window.

"Only the best for you, my dear," he said, in his best James Bond imitation.

The wine steward showed up with his list and Nick ordered a bottle of wine. Their waitress came to explain the specials and the menu and then left them alone for a few minutes to make their choices.

He decided on the buttered, peppercorn-encrusted rib-eye and she chose the pecan-and-butter-glazed grouper. After placing their orders, they turned their attention to each other.

"It's been a wonderful week. I wish I didn't have to go back to school," she lamented.

"Well, you've only got one more quarter until you graduate."

"Yeah, but I've got to do my student-teaching next quarter, so I'm a little nervous about that."

The Ocean under the Moon

"You'll do fine. How hard can thirty screaming third-graders be, anyway?"

She didn't answer and picked up her wine glass. She'd thought she might get a ring at Christmas time, but instead he gave her a diamond necklace. She knew he loved her, but he was always talking about the future as if it was a long way off. First, he had to get a boat so he could earn a living, now he was working on building the cottage. She appreciated his efforts to be stable and productive before they got married, but she just wanted to be with him. She loved him with all of her heart.

These last four years when she was away at college, only seeing him once in a while, had been tough on her. She didn't care if they would have to stay with his parents and grandmother in the big, white house, while he finished the cottage next door. She just wanted to wake up next to him in the mornings. She wanted more than just a week here and a weekend there, with him.

"You look preoccupied," he said.

This broke her away from her thoughts.

"I'm just thinking how glad I'll be, to finally be out of school," she said.

"Well, if you get a job teaching, you'll still be in a school. Just this time, you'll be getting paid, and you'll be doing the teaching, instead of the studying."

"Yes, it'll be nice, making some money of my own for a change," she said.

"I bet Buck will be glad to get you off of his payroll." He grinned at her.

"That's what I've got you for," she said. "I'm going to

202

slide right from his payroll to yours," she added, with a mischievous smile.

"Are you now?" He arched one of his eyebrows. "What if my payroll can't support any new employees?"

"Well, I think this employee can be quite an asset to your company." She was staring into his eyes now. She kicked off her right shoe and started rubbing the instep of her foot against his calf.

"In fact, this employee can cause a growth stimulus to the company, which will send production through the roof, rendering the aforementioned employee priceless."

"I could see how such a valuable and knowledgeable employee could definitely be a benefit to my company," he said. He felt a stirring down below.

The waitress brought their salads and she lowered her foot.

Monica decided that maybe she needed to crank up the heat with him. Despite all of the time they had spent together, they'd never fully consummated their relationship. She was an old-fashioned girl and wanted to wait until their wedding night. After her disappointment at not getting engaged at Christmas, she had begun to wonder if he was one of those guys who just couldn't commit. Some guys needed to be forced into making a decision. She did not want to have to give an ultimatum, but maybe she could give a more open invitation.

After they finished their entrées and the table was cleared, the waitress asked if they were having dessert. They listened to the dessert menu and settled on splitting an Amelia Mud Pie.

While they waited for it to arrive, she stared at him,

thinking how great it would be if he proposed here. The setting was perfect, the timing was right. She kept her gaze on him as if, at any moment, he would slide out of his chair, get down on one knee, and present her with a ring.

"What?" he asked. "Do I have parsley between my teeth?"

"You're so handsome. I just like looking at you," she said, recovering her composure.

The waitress returned and placed the dessert between them, with a spoon for each of them. The chocolate ice cream pie, with whipped cream and chocolate sprinkles on top and a chocolate cookie crumb crust, was delicious, becoming more so as it melted, and they took their time eating it. Her imagination getting the best of her, Monica savored every mouthful. She wondered if maybe he had hidden a ring for her in the mud pie, and she wouldn't want to accidentally swallow her engagement ring.

When he offered her the last bit of pie crust, she couldn't help but feel a little bit disappointed. But as he raised his hand to catch the server's attention, signaling that he was ready for the check, he told her he had a little surprise for her.

"What is it?"

"You'll have to wait and see."

When they were outside and the valet had retrieved their car, Monica turned to Nick.

"Where are we going?"

"You'll see."

Nick tipped the valet and slid behind the wheel. He drove the Firebird away from the inn entrance, through the small valet parking lot, and into an adjoining lot that the signs designated as

parking for the Beach Club. He pulled up a slight rise and into a
parking space in the otherwise deserted area.

"Here we are," he said, proudly.

"You're taking me parking? That's your big surprise?" She
looked around at the dark parking lot. "I thought you said the
Beach Club was closed for the winter."

"It is." He got out and came around to open her door.
"We're not going to the Beach Club, we're going to a secret
location, known as the Sunken Forest."

"The Sunken Forest?" she said, wrinkling her nose. "It
sounds foreboding, like the forest in the Wizard of Oz with the
flying monkeys."

"No, it's a magical place known only to a privileged few.
Now close your eyes."

"Why do I have to close my eyes?"

"Because it is a secret place."

"It's called the Sunken Forest, not the Secret Forest."

"Just humor me, please?"

She did as he asked and shut her eyes. His arm around her
waist, he guided her around to the back of the car, then asked her
to stop, while he retrieved something from the trunk of the car.

She opened her eyes a bit, but didn't see anything, as she
was facing away from him. She did hear, however, a slight
clinking, like two glasses being touched together.

"No peeking," he commanded. "I knew you wouldn't be
able to refrain from peeking, so I came prepared."

She felt a soft blindfold going across her face and being
tied from behind.

The Ocean under the Moon

"You don't trust me?"

"I don't want you to spoil the surprise."

She heard the trunk slam shut, and then she felt his right hand in the small of her back, gently pushing her forward, while he grasped her left elbow with his left hand to steady her.

"Okay, we are going to go about thirty paces, straight ahead," he said.

After thirty paces, she felt the terrain change, as he guided her down an asphalt path. The asphalt soon turned into a boardwalk and she could hear her high heels clanking against the wood. Now Nick was leading her by the hand.

First, they went down some steps and then they turned to the right, then back up some steps, and turned to the left. He told her when to step up and when to step down. After winding around for awhile, they started ascending some very steep steps. Thirty or forty of them—she lost count; she didn't know there was any place on the island with this much altitude. She felt like she was on a stairway to heaven.

Finally, they stopped and she could hear him rustling around, his feet scraping on the sand on the boards.

"What are you doing?" she asked in exasperation, about to explode with anticipation.

"Hang on, almost ready." She heard a match strike, then another few moments later, she felt his hands begin to untie her blindfold.

"Are you ready?" he whispered into her ear.

"Oh, yes."

He lowered the blindfold and the sight before her eyes left

her speechless. They were standing on a wooden platform, an observatory, on top of a very tall sand dune, just to the north of the Beach Club. The platform had a wooden rail around it and he'd placed six small, round candles on the rail to heighten the romantic effect. The full moon had now sprung free of the horizon and sat out over the ocean like a big, yellow ball. Its light reflected off the calm ocean right toward her, or so she thought.

Looking to the north, she could see the lights of American Beach, and, following the curve of beach farther north, she could see the lights of South Fletcher Avenue and Main Beach. Then looking southward, she saw the Beach Club down below her, then further south the Amelia Inn, and then beyond that, the newly constructed Beachwalker condominiums. Way in the distance, beyond the southern tip of the island, she could make out the glow of the lights in Mayport, a fishing village two islands away.

"It's wonderful... so gorgeous," she said.

"And so are you," he replied.

He wrapped her shoulders in a blanket he'd brought with him. She turned to him and their lips met, as she wrapped the blanket around them both.

"How about some champagne?" he asked.

"Are we celebrating something?"

"Every day with you is a celebration."

She lifted her face for another impassioned kiss.

He led her over to a basket he had brought, and he retrieved a bottle from the basket and placed it on the railing. He next bent over and pulled out two champagne glasses, which he put on the rail. He grabbed the bottle and opened it, with a loud pop, champagne spewing out the neck. He poured the two glasses half full and gave one to Monica.

"To us," he toasted.

"To us," she repeated.

Her heart pounded with excitement, as she knew he was going to get down on one knee and propose at any moment. This was the perfect time and the perfect setting. She looked out at the brilliant full moon, the shimmering sea, and white curve of the coastline illuminated by the moon. The loveliness was surreal and she wanted to remember it forever.

He guided her over to a wooden bench where they sat down and he held her hand, the blanket draped across their shoulders.

"You know I love you," he said seriously.

"Yes, I do."

He fell silent, gazing out to sea. She occasionally glanced sideways, to try and gauge what he was thinking. He was staring at the waves, sipping his champagne, as if lost in thought. She felt a shiver of nervousness. Maybe he was going to break up with her.

Just then he turned to her and asked, "What do you want out of life?"

"I know I want you." She gave his hand a squeeze.

"What else?"

"I don't know. Just a teaching job for now. Then maybe a little house with a white picket fence, followed by a couple of healthy kids."

"Do you think you could be happy with a shrimper?"

"There is no better occupation than to earn your living

from the land or sea. Look at my father ... he has provided quite
well for our family off of the land. I'm sure the sea will be just as
kind to you, as it has been for your father and grandfather. I don't
care if I have to sleep on the boat all of my life, I just want to be
with you."

She leaned over and put her head on his shoulder.

"A friend of mine who's a lifeguard at the Beach Club,
told me this was the best view on the island," he said, after awhile.

"The view's spectacular," she agreed. "I bet he brings all
of the tourist girls he meets at the Beach Club up here. How many
girls have you brought up here, while I was away at college?" she
asked, with mock indignation.

"None. I was saving this view for one very special girl."

He leaned over and kissed her. Maybe it was the romantic
setting, maybe it was the champagne, but soon her body was
responding with even more passion than ever before. She was
second-guessing her vow to wait until she was married for full
intimacy, when he spoke suddenly.

"This is wonderful," he said. "But I have one more thing
to show you." He stood up, offering her his hand.

She stared at him, regaining her composure, but not
wanting to leave this romantic spot.

"But, Nick—" she began.

"No buts," he said, smiling. "I've got one more very
important thing to show you."

"But it's too beautiful here—why don't you just show me
here?"

"No, what I want to show you is not here."

"If we must, but I warn you I'm leaving under protest," she said.

"It'll be worth it, I promise."

"It better be, because I can't imagine what could be better than this." She stood up, a little giddy from the champagne.

He blew out the candles, dumped the hot wax off the tops and put the candles, along with the champagne bottle and glasses, back into the basket. Arms around each other's waists and the blanket still draped over their shoulders, they made their way down the dark boardwalk back to the car. He put the basket back into the trunk, but instead of opening the car door, he guided her toward the Beach Club.

"Wait—I thought you said this place is closed," she said. "Why are we going that way?"

"You'll see." He sounded a little breathless.

They went down the short boardwalk toward the dark building. The pool lights were on, however, giving the surroundings an eerie glow. They walked past the shuttered lifeguard station and the closed-down game room, and soon were on the beach boardwalk.

"Why are we going to the beach?"

"Because I want to show you something."

"Can't we just can't see it from here?"

"No, we have to get closer."

"Wait a second then, let me take my shoes off," she said, reaching down to remove her high heels. They continued walking, with her in her bare feet, holding her shoes.

Once on the beach, she started dancing around like a little

girl, the cool sand feeling good on her bare feet and the champagne having made her giddy. The brilliant moonlight illuminated the scene so they could just make out their surroundings.

"Dancing in the moonlight…" she began singing the lyrics to the King Harvest song from a couple of summers before. He watched her whirling around in the moonlight, and was never more sure of any decision he had made in his life, than to make this woman his wife.

Finishing the song, she leaned against him. "Now, what was it you wanted to show me?"

"It's just down the beach a little bit."

It was low tide and the beach was wide. They walked down to the shoreline, then headed south, holding hands.

"I never get tired of seeing the ocean in the moonlight. It's so different from south Georgia … it's like another world," she said.

"You should see it out on the water, like we do, when we're out shrimping all night."

"Maybe I'll go out night shrimping with you some time."

"Yes, I think I could make a deckhand out of you," he said with a smirk.

"What, you don't think I can take orders from you?" she asked. "But I'm just here to serve you." She gave him a hug, a quick kiss and a playful grin.

After they had walked about two hundred yards, he turned away from the water and said, "Let's go this way."

He led her up the wide, flat beach toward the dunes. She could just make out the shadows of three automobiles near the dunes.

"Where are we going now?"

"Come on, you'll see," he reassured her.

They walked across the hard-packed, slightly damp sand toward the soft white sand that was beyond the high-water mark, but in a moment, he stopped short, pulling her to him.

"Monica, you know I love you and I always want to be with you. There is something I want to ask you." He clicked a lighter on with his left hand, behind his back without her seeing it. Almost immediately, the headlights of the vehicles facing them turned on.

Startled, she turned toward the headlights, then looked down at the flat, hard-packed sand in front of her, just before the softer, looser sand began. Somebody had used a hard object to write a message in the sand in huge letters. Illuminated by the three pairs of headlights, she could clearly make out the words:

Monica,

Will You Marry Me?

She turned to him, her hands raised to her mouth in surprise. He had stepped back when she turned toward the headlights and now he knelt on one knee. He removed a jewelry box from his pocket and held it out. She opened the little box, revealing a diamond ring inside.

"Oh, Nick! Yes, of course I'll marry you," she said. She pulled him to a standing position, so she could kiss him.

She hugged him and he slipped the ring on her finger as a

crowd of people piled out of the vehicles, clapping and whistling.

She looked over at the people coming toward her in the beams of the headlights. There were her parents, who had driven down from Hazlehurst, aware of Nick's plans. His parents and grandmother were there too, beaming widely. Behind his parents was Gator, who had written the message in the sand, followed by Mary, Rita, Dan Lowe, and an assortment of Nick's friends.

The crowd gathered around them, giving him handshakes and her hugs. After much back-slapping and congratulations were dispensed, they all made their way back to their vehicles.

Abe, Isabelle, Buck and Caroline piled into Abe's International Scout. Nick and Monica, along with Rita and Mary, jumped into the back of Gator's truck. Dan and the rest of Nick's friends got into Dan's Chevrolet Blazer.

The caravan headed south on the beach toward the end of the island, where there were no houses or condominiums, just sand dunes and maritime forest. Once they got to a deserted area, they pulled up and started unloading chairs, coolers and wood for the bonfire.

When the fire was blazing and the chairs circled around it, Nick's friend David Green, who played at local bars and restaurants to earn extra money, pulled out his guitar and started strumming away.

It was a perfect setting, good friends, close family, and a cool, but windless night, and a full moon over the sea. Nick and Monica sat side by side in the sand on a blanket, next to the fire, and enjoyed the celebration. Both sets of parents seemed truly happy about the engagement and joined in the revelry. Buck, in particular, seemed to be enjoying himself, singing along with the music.

Toward the end of the night, after much drinking and singing, Nick and Monica strolled down the beach a little way to have a respite from the party. When they got far enough away from the group, he pulled her to him, giving her a long kiss, while embracing her tightly. After a few heated moments, he pulled back and gazed into her eyes.

"You know, I would do anything for you," he began. "I swear, under this beautiful moon, that I will be the best provider I can. I'm going to build you that house with the white picket fence, and we are going to have beautiful babies together and live happily ever after."

"I believe you," she said. "I know we will."

She hugged him tight again and, with shining eyes, she gazed out at the moon over his shoulder as if she was staring into the future. "I know we will."

The Ocean under the Moon

Chapter 21

June 14, 1979

Nick, standing at the altar, thought he was going to burst with pride when he saw Monica enter the back of the church through the large, wooden double doors. In her white silk gown, with the late afternoon sun beaming in behind her, she looked to Nick like an angel descending on earth. She wore the lovely antique wedding gown that Caroline had worn, and Caroline's mother wore before her.

Their wedding was held at St. Peter's Episcopal Church on Centre Street. The stucco and plaster structure with its medieval, almost castle-like appearance, had been built almost a century before by some of the wealthiest families in Fernandina, during the town's Victorian age. The high ceilings were patterned after the inverted hull of a ship to reflect Fernandina's seafaring spirit in a unique design of open timbers lining the ceilings.

Father Ralph Kelley, or Pop Kelley as he liked to be called, who married the couple, was a burly, heavy-set man who looked more like an aging professional wrestler than a priest. A former policeman and merchant marine, he'd come to the priesthood later in life. He became the parish priest when Nick was a young boy, and had watched him grow up. Pop Kelley had even coached him in football, as a volunteer coach to the junior high school football team. He presented himself as a tough disciplinarian, but was actually a teddy bear of a guy. However, he wasn't above an occasional kick in the butt on the practice field.

Buck, with his daughter holding his arm, grinned from ear to ear. He and Nick had grown close from their hunting excursions and fishing forays, so he wholeheartedly supported her marriage to the dependable and likeable young man.

Caroline, despite her initial misgivings, had grown to accept him. The handsome young man was hard-working and reliable, even if his status in society wasn't up to her original desires for her precious daughter. So her feelings were bittersweet that day, her smile not quite as large as Buck's.

Nick's parents were ecstatic about having Monica in the family. Isabelle was particularly happy to have another female in their family, a daughter-in-law to go shopping with and take to lunch. Abe was also smitten with her and felt that Nick had done very well for himself.

The wedding went off splendidly, the Harrison pipe organ playing beautiful hymns. The late afternoon sun streamed in the colorful stained glass windows that had been imported from New York City many years before.

Nick, to his later chagrin, was talked into wearing an all-white tuxedo by the salesman at the local tuxedo rental store. At the reception later, Gator told him he looked like Boss Hog from the "Dukes of Hazzard" television show. The groomsmen, however, looked very dapper in their dark tuxedos. All of them had just about recovered from Nick's bachelor that Gator had thrown for him.

Even Gator, the best man, looked respectable in the tuxedo, his long hair pulled back into a tight ponytail. Gator had threatened, two nights before at the bachelor party, to speak up in protest at the part where the preacher asked if there is any reason why these two people should not be wed in holy matrimony. But, at the critical time, Nick glanced over at Gator, who just winked back and remained silent.

After the ceremony, most of the crowd headed off to the reception while the wedding party stayed behind to take the formal pictures. Thirty minutes later, after numerous poses, the bride and groom and their attendants piled into their vehicles for the trip to the reception several miles away on the island's south end.

Walker's Landing, the reception site, was a spacious lodge built on a small bluff overlooking Walker's Creek, on the southwest edge of the island, inside the Amelia Island Plantation. The wooden structure contained a huge room with a fireplace and wooden floors perfect for dancing, along with a kitchen. Wide picture windows faced west, revealing a two-mile view over the marsh and the Amelia River to the mainland. Sunsets were beautiful here and they planned a late-afternoon wedding, so the guests could get to the reception and watch the sun go down. Outside the lodge, overlooking the marsh was a large deck, complete with picnic tables and fire pits for roasting oysters.

To reach Walker's Landing, the visitors drove into the Plantation's main entrance, then circled back across the small overpass that went over A1A. After winding through a tree-lined residential section, they turned down a short, crushed oyster-shell road to the shell parking lot.

It was hot and humid earlier in the day, but now, around seven at night a steady, southwest wind was keeping the temperature down and the bugs away. It was also a rare summer evening where the clouds had not built up to the west, so the guests would be treated to a spectacular sunset.

The two hundred-plus guests had all arrived by the time the wedding party got there and were spilling out of the lodge onto the deck and even into the parking lot. Some still mingled inside where a three-piece band was playing, but most were out on the deck, munching on the fresh shrimp cocktail provided by the Stamos family from a recent catch.

Milt Shirley, mayor of Fernandina Beach at the time, and his wife, Sutzie, had loaned the bride and groom the use of a limousine they owned, so they could arrive at the reception in style. Nick, Monica and their parents climbed out of the limousine and were engulfed by well-wishers. Then the entire wedding party slowly made its way through the throng of people, stopping for hugs, handshakes, and congratulations, and finally making it into the side doors of the lodge.

At the sight of the bride, the band stopped playing a song and launched into its rendition of "Here Comes the Bride." The crowd inside the lodge turned and applauded the newlyweds, and again, they were swarmed by people wanting to offer their congratulations. Nick was kept busy introducing his new wife and her parents to all of the local people from Fernandina that they hadn't met yet.

Since the crowd exceeded the number of tables that could

be set up and still have room to dance, there was not a formal sit-down dinner. But people were eating in shifts, or wherever they could find, including the picnic tables out on the deck. Abe had the affair catered by a friend of his, Chef Michael, and the entrées included shrimp creole, baked grouper, and steaks for the non-seafood people.

After the meal was over, Caroline nudged Buck and he reluctantly walked over to the band, which stopped playing so he could get behind the microphone.

"In case you don't know me, I'm Buck Johnson from Hazlehurst, Georgia, father of the lovely bride," he said as some mild feedback squealed. "I want to thank everybody for coming on this glorious night to help us celebrate this merging of these two families.

"You know, I have to tell you a story about the first time we met Nick, because this wedding almost never came about. Nick drove up from Fernandina, one fall, several years ago now, to meet us and take Monica to her homecoming dance. Well, to get to know any of Monica's suitors and to test the mettle of the young man, I always like to take them hunting with me, so I can judge their character. Nick, being an expert fisherman, but a novice hunter, bravely agreed to accompany me on an early morning hunt the morning after the homecoming dance." Buck grinned and some of Nick's friends chuckled.

"Now, I knew he wouldn't get much sleep that night, since the dance lasted past midnight, and I woke him up at five in the morning to go hunting. He passed the first test as he gamely got out of bed and accompanied me and my son, Bud, to the hunting

219

club.

"We got Nick a gun, told him what to do, and stuck him up in a tree stand. Before long, he could hear something large making its way through the underbrush. He raised his gun, put his finger on the trigger, and looked through the scope ready to shoot whatever stepped out. Now, I have to tell you, many people get trigger-happy in that situation, particularly when it's their first deer. The adrenaline is flowing, the senses are heightened, and the anticipation is too much for some people to bear, and they shoot too quick. Nick just knew it was going to be a trophy buck, and me and Monica would be so proud of his kill."

Buck paused for a second, looking toward Nick, who was turning red.

"Well, what he didn't know was the farmer next to the hunting club had a dog who liked to unlock the gate on a corral, letting a horse out, and the horse would head to the food plot for a free meal. So the animal heading through the woods was not a trophy deer, but a big, black horse. Can you imagine what I would have thought about him, if we went deer hunting, and he shot a *horse*?" he asked.

The crowd guffawed.

"But, fortunately, he did not pull the trigger, showing patience and good judgment and later on he did shoot a nice buck, so here we are," he concluded his story.

"Now, I'd like to make a toast." He raised the champagne glass he had been holding.

"To Nick and Monica, may their marriage be as blessed as Caroline and mine's, and to the merging of the land and the sea, the

220

farming family and the shrimping family... may God be kind to both of us."

He took a big gulp of champagne, then announced, "Now it's time for the first dance."

Nick and Monica rose from their table as the band started playing the Commodores' song, "Three Times a Lady." They were aware that everyone's eyes were upon them, which made them feel awkward, but they tried to concentrate on each other and how happy they were. About halfway through the song, their parents came out on the dance floor and Abe broke in to dance with Monica, Nick began to dance with Caroline, and Buck and Isabelle danced together.

After that song, the band picked up the pace, and Gator and the rest of the groomsmen and bridesmaids joined in on the dancing. Soon the entire dance floor was packed.

When the band took a break, Monica and Nick cut the cake, while photos were taken of them stuffing cake into each other's mouth. Gator, of course, could not resist and a mini food fight broke out.

The band played for another hour of dancing, until it was time to throw the bouquet and shoot the garter. After a melee and a wrestling match on the dance floor, one of Monica's sorority sisters caught the bouquet. Nick retrieved the lacy garter amid much hooting and hollering as Monica exposed her leg, and his friend Dan caught the garter, but immediately tried to give it to someone else, so as not to be "next in line."

During the band's final set, Nick and Monica went to change their clothes to leave on their honeymoon. Since she was not working yet, and all of his spare cash was going into the cottage he was building, they had decided just to do a week's driving trip down the east coast of Florida.

Their wedding night, however, was going to be spent only about a mile away. The Pool Villas were a newly built complex of one-story condos inside the Plantation, overlooking the marsh on the point of land just north of Walker's Landing.

While they were changing their clothes, they could hear the band coming to a fevered pitch. They knew Gator was entertaining the crowd by doing his famous dance. When the appropriate song, like "Shout" by the Isley Brothers or "Disco Inferno" by the Trammps, was played, he would flop down on the floor in the middle of the crowd and do the "Gator."

The dance got its name because when he flopped down on his belly and moved his arms and legs up and down, it looked like an epileptic alligator. Then, he would flop onto his back, still gyrating his arms and legs, like a dying cockroach. Invariably, other men in the crowd would join in the impromptu dance, in kind of an uncoordinated free-for-all.

They finished changing out of their wedding finery and into their street clothes. Nick gave his tuxedo to his father to turn back in to the rental store, and Caroline carefully wrapped the wedding dress for safekeeping.

The band was finishing up when they came back into the lodge. Nick spotted Gator, all inebriated and sweating after doing his dance.

"Be careful with my boat," he said. Gator had hired a deckhand and was going to captain his boat for a week while Nick was gone on his honeymoon.

"Don't worry about a thing, Captain. The *Resurrection's* in good hands with me. I know how to treat a boat right. We're going to set the boat's record for shrimp caught, while you're gone."

Looking at his disheveled friend, Nick was having second thoughts about his decision to let him use his boat while he was out of town. But he didn't have time to argue with Gator, plus he needed to keep the boat busy, to cover his expenses, while he was away. He shook Gator's sweaty hand and made him promise, again, to look after his boat, and to be prudent.

"Like I said, don't worry about a thing. Besides," Gator said with a wink, "you're going be too busy for the next few days to worry about your boat."

Monica caught up with Nick and they stepped out on the deck, where the attendees had made a long gauntlet all the way out into the parking lot.

With a whoop from him and a squeal from her, the couple took off running hand in hand, with rice showering down on them from every possible angle. They jumped through the open door into the back of the limo, which was decorated with a big "Just Married' sign in the back window and cans tied with string to the back bumper. Milt was at the wheel and Sutzie was in the front passenger seat, and they took off, with Abe and Isabelle following in Nick's car.

They followed the dark, winding road that had led to Walker's Landing, past the golf clubhouse and the driving range, and turned down Sea Marsh Road, another long, winding road. Finally, they reached the secluded Pool Villas. The young couple thanked the Shirleys for the use of the limousine, and got out to say goodbye to Nick's parents. After one last hug, his parents hopped into the limousine, so Milt could take them home. They'd parked the Firebird in front of the villa, with Nick's and Monica's suitcases already packed in the trunk.

After the limousine pulled away, he pulled her to him, his arm around her waist.

"Alone at last," he said with a sly grin.

"Just because we're married now, don't think I'm going to be easy. You still have to carry me across the threshold."

He scooped up her slender body into his arms and carried her to the door of the villa. Once at the door, he held onto her, while he fumbled for the key to the villa in his pants pocket.

"Be prepared to be amazed," he announced.

"Are you talking about the villa or your prowess?"

"The villa, silly," he answered.

"Too bad." Monica reached behind him and gave his buttocks a squeeze.

He almost fumbled the key to the ground, but managed to locate the keyhole and get the door open. He carried her through a small alcove, past the small kitchen, and into the living room.

Her eyes widened. "Nick!" She kissed his cheek and stared around the room. "This is amazing."

Just beyond the living room, through sliding glass doors, a small, rectangular pool shimmered in turquoise brilliance. He had been by the villa earlier in the day to turn on the chandelier light in the living room, on low, and he had turned on the heater and underwater lights to the pool.

The Ocean under the Moon

He put her down and she headed for the sliding doors, opened them and went outside onto the pool deck. She noticed the pool lights casting eerie reflections off the solid stucco wall beside it. The pool was screened in, to keep mosquitos and leaves out, and afforded total privacy as two long walls, one on the far side of the living room and one to the far side of the pool, extended all the way to the marsh. Only the blue herons and other wading birds could see in.

The most astonishing thing, she noticed, was that the end of the pool away from the marsh extended under a glass wall and into the large bedroom.

"Oh, my gosh! The pool goes into the bedroom!"

"Yes, it does," he said.

"I'm not in Hazlehurst anymore," she joked. She noticed steam coming off of the water, even though it was a sultry June evening.

Nick told her how he had managed to rent the expensive villa for the night. His friend Scott was a golf cart attendant, whose father, Dutch Hood, was head professional at the Amelia Island Plantation Links golf course, and Scott had rented the villa, under his name, getting a significant employee discount.

"You mean every night as Mrs. Nick Stamos is not going to be like this one?" She made a gesture at her surroundings.

"I'm afraid tonight will only live on, in your memory."

"Then, in that case, we better start making some memories."

She looked at him seductively and let her sundress fall to the ground.

The Ocean under the Moon

She stepped toward him and pulled him close to her. She pressed her body against his, and he caressed her as they kissed. After awhile, she pushed him away and jumped into the pool.

"Come and get me," she teased.

He hurriedly removed his clothes and dove in after her.

An hour later, they lay exhausted and naked on a deck chair beside the pool, fully satisfied and reveling in their newfound intimacy.

After a prolonged silence, cuddling in the deck chair, listening to the crickets chirping loudly, and gazing up at the stars, she broke the silence.

"Promise me you will never leave me."

"Why would I leave after that?"

She elbowed him in the ribs for his comment.

"You know what I mean. When I'm old and I'm fat and you don't want me anymore."

"You see that star up there? The one that's brighter than all the others in the Little Dipper?" He pointed skyward.

"Well, yes, I see it."

"That's the North Star, part of Ursa Minor constellation. It's used in navigation by sailors in the northern hemisphere, because it always points to true north. It's under that star, that this night, I pledge to you that I will never abandon you."

She turned to him and gazed into his eyes for several seconds.

"I believe you, Nick Stamos." She returned to her original position, and they stayed close together, contented in the quiet darkness.

The Ocean under the Moon

Chapter 22

March 17, 1980

They had enjoyed a wonderful honeymoon. After the night at the pool villa, they'd driven halfway down the Florida coast and spent the night in Cocoa Beach. Just south of Cape Canaveral, Cocoa Beach was a bedroom community for NASA workers and had been the location of the 1960s "I Dream of Jeannie" television show.

The honeymooners enjoyed a romantic dinner at a restaurant at the end of the wooden pier, with surfers "shooting the pilings," by slaloming between the pilings of the pier, underneath the restaurant, while they dined. The next day, the young couple drove down to the Fontainebleau Hotel in Miami Beach for two days — going to the beach, hanging out at the pool, and taking in the Latin cabaret show in the hotel at night.

After that, they drove on to the Florida Keys, stopping in Islamorada, the sport-fishing capital of the United States. He rented a boat and they went out for a day. She worked on her tan, while he tried his luck fly-fishing for the renowned, but elusive, bonefish. He didn't have much luck with them, but did hook several tarpon, or "silver kings." Not good to eat, the tarpon are famed for their fighting ability as a game fish — known for rocketing out of the water and shaking their head violently in order to dislodge the hook. He got several good jumps out of the tarpon he had hooked, before he brought them to the boat and released them.

After Islamorada, they traveled all the way down the chain of islands to Key West and checked in at the Casa Marina Hotel. They spent three relaxing days in the "Conch Republic," going to the beach, shopping on Duval Street, and visiting bars like Sloppy Joe's and Captain Tony's.

After driving back up to Fernandina Beach, the honeymooners settled into the big house with Abe, Isabelle, and Catherine. Nick still had to do a lot of work on his cottage, and he was eager to complete it. But it was summer time and he was too busy shrimping; plus, the heat and the afternoon thunderstorms made it difficult to work on the building in the summer. He would have to wait until winter, when the shrimping season was over and the weather was cooler and drier, to complete the cottage.

It wasn't the perfect situation for the young couple, to have to live with his parents and grandmother, but he was used to it and she blended into the family quite well. Catherine and Isabelle enjoyed Monica's company, and she filled the role of the daughter that neither of the older women ever had.

Monica was offered a job teaching third grade at Emma Love Hardee Elementary School. She kept busy buying school supplies, meeting with the principal and other teachers, and getting ready for the upcoming school year.

Nick, for his part, got back into his usual routine of getting up early and going shrimping with Gator. But he cut back on the all-night shrimping and being out for days on end, so he could be back home with Monica in the evenings, particularly when the afternoon thunderstorms chased them in early.

Gator gave him a hard time about coming back to the docks early, good-naturedly chiding him about being "p-w'd."

"Man, we used to stay out shrimping all the time, before you got married," he said one afternoon. "Guess it's okay for you, but it's taking money out of my pocket and I can use more for the Palace, you know." He rubbed it in that, while Nick was on his honeymoon, he and his hired deckhand had done quite well, staying out shrimping almost the entire week and coming back with a hull full of shrimp.

He did not let Gator's trash-talking get to him. Even though he could have used the extra money to finish the cottage, he wanted to get his marriage off to a good start by spending time with Monica in the evenings and not leaving her alone for long periods of time with his family.

Nick and Gator would get up at five-thirty every morning, be on the boat by six o'clock, and have the *Resurrection* out the channel and shrimping by seven o'clock in the morning. They would shrimp most of the day, until about three or four o'clock in the afternoon, depending on the afternoon thunderstorms. They would try to be back to his dock by four or five in the afternoon.

Nick would get cleaned up and take Monica to the movies, or out to eat, or to the skating rink at Main Beach. Sometimes, if the weather was good and there was a cooling sea breeze, they would work on their new home.

He had already done most of the structural work, including the foundation, plumbing, electrical, framing, and the roof. Now, the interior work needed to be done, including the sheet rock, trim, flooring, painting, and cabinets. He'd put off this part, both to save up the money to pay for the material and to get Monica's input on the interior decorating and finishing. She was anxious to finish the cottage and she'd already made several trips to Fernandina Lumber Supply and Amelia Paints and Hardware to get ideas about flooring, trim, and paint colors.

While shrimping only in the mornings and early afternoon was good for him and Monica spending time together, it had a flip side, as it allowed too much time for Gator to get in trouble. Since they usually made it back to Nick's dock by about five o'clock, Gator had time to take a quick shower at his apartment downtown and then make it to the Palace Saloon for happy hour every day.

He would sit at the end of the bar, drinking long-neck beers, joking with the regulars, and teasing the barmaids. Around seven-thirty he would have his regular dinner of boiled shrimp and a barbecue sandwich at the bar. Then, after consuming several more beers, he would stagger back to his small apartment by eleven o'clock and pass out. This allowed him to sleep off the alcohol in time to wake up and go shrimping again, early the next morning.

Nick and Monica tried to get him to change his bad habits, knowing it was not good for his long-term health to drink so much. But he seemed to have the constitution for it, because he never seemed to gain weight or develop a beer belly, and he always managed to drag himself down to the dock on time in the mornings

As newlywed couples are often wont to do, they tried to fix him up with a "nice" girl, so they could double-date. He would have none of it, and preferred to pursue the local barflies and the occasional, unsuspecting tourist girl, for casual relationships, with no strings attached.

Nick and Gator fished hard during the fall shrimping season. The weather, for the most part, was good. No hurricanes came close to northeast Florida that fall and even the nor'easters were few and far between. Fernandina was pretty well located as far as bad storms were concerned, which was a good thing, since their dock and boats could be destroyed by one rogue hurricane.

Nick knew it was Fernandina's geographical location, which helped protect it from hurricanes, that, plus its natural deep harbor, were what made it a popular port back in the nineteenth century. He knew two factors combine to help protect this part of Florida from direct hits from hurricanes. First, Fernandina sits just about at the apex of a long concave arc formed from Cape Hatteras, North Carolina, to Miami. Then, there is the Gulf Stream, a warm, powerful, and fast-moving Atlantic Ocean current that starts in the Gulf of Mexico, shoots through the Straits of Florida, and follows the coastline of the southeastern United States before crossing to northern Europe. The Gulf Stream, which is only a mile or so off the beach from Miami to Stuart, Florida, is forty to eighty miles off the beach in Fernandina.

The long, shallow continental shelf off the coast of north Florida, which makes a great place for shrimping, also helps protect the area from hurricanes. Since hurricanes follow warmer, deeper waters, the hurricanes that form off of North Africa near the Azores, then barrel west across the Atlantic picking up speed and energy, either tend to go south into the Caribbean and Gulf of Mexico or barrel over the Bahamas toward south Florida.

The Ocean under the Moon

Then, depending on the high pressure areas over the continental United States, a hurricane usually does one of two things. It either continues across south Florida or it follows the Gulf Stream up toward South Carolina or North Carolina. The highest winds and main energy are concentrated just to the right of the eye of the hurricane due to its counterclockwise flow, so as a hurricane passes up the coast of north Florida, following the Gulf Stream offshore, Fernandina tends to get just a glancing blow of high winds and tides, but not the full fury of the hurricane.

But hurricanes are unpredictable due to varying atmospheric conditions and don't always follow the usual plan. Nick remembered, in 1964, northeast Florida did receive a direct hit from the east in the form of Hurricane Dora. Three people in the Jacksonville area died from the storm, and in Fernandina Beach several beach houses and a section of the beach road were lost to the storm.

Fortunately, his father prepared well for that storm, taking his shrimp boats up the St. Mary's River and tying them at all four corners to trees along each bank of its river. Nick and the rest of the family were sent to his maternal grandparents' farm outside of Waycross to ride out the storm. Abe stayed in the house at Old Town to watch over it, and the house as well as the boats came through the storm without any problems.

Hurricane Dora made a strong impression on Nick, who was only eight years old at the time. When he returned to Fernandina after the storm and observed the destruction along the beach, he was amazed. The view of naked pilings in the sand, where houses once stood, and roads washed away showed the

232

young boy the true power of the ocean. It reinforced what his father and grandfather also taught him: Always respect that power, because if you don't, the ocean can overwhelm you in an instant.

During that fall, Nick tried to make as much money as he could, since the shrimp were plentiful, so he could finish the cottage. Living with his parents wasn't bad, but he and Monica craved the privacy that their own cottage would provide them.

Monica spent her time getting used to her classroom, students, other teachers, and the administration. She found that she enjoyed teaching, and the interaction with students, particularly third-graders, who were at the perfect age for her to make a difference in their lives.

After the fall shrimping run, he turned his attention to the cottage. His plan was to have the cottage finished by the end of March, in time for the spring shrimping season. Gator offered to help him through the winter for just a small stipend of drinking and eating money. Monica did what she could to help on weekends and after school.

First, Gator and Nick tackled putting the sheetrock on the interior walls. After they got a room completed, dried and sanded, Monica would swoop in and paint it, after school or on the weekends, with one of the colors she picked out at the hardware store. Next, they installed the electrical sockets, light fixtures, and ceiling fans, and then turned to installing the wood floors. Nick bought some heart pine wood that had been reclaimed from a church near Savannah. After they laid it down, they went through the laborious process of sanding the wood and varnishing it to restore its original beauty.

The Ocean under the Moon

It was during the sanding of the floors that Gator threatened to go on strike, but Nick kept him happy by bribing him with an occasional beer and kept him moving to the loud music coming from the ever-present boom box that Gator always kept around when he was working.

The next job was installing the kitchen cabinets and bathroom vanities that Monica had picked out, and then all of the appliances, like the stove, refrigerator, washer, and dryer.

Finally, on St. Patrick's Day, Nick was able to carry Monica across the threshold of their new home. They celebrated that night with a small housewarming party, consisting of an oyster roast and green beer, with Nick's parents, his grandmother, Gator, and a few of their close friends.

Now that the cottage was finished, Nick's winters, in the future, would be spent working on the *Resurrection* or on the nets, getting them ready for another shrimping season, or taking a well-deserved vacation. But despite all the extra work they put in the last several months to earn extra money and then finish the cottage, the look on Monica's face when he had carried her across the threshold of her new house, made all the sacrifice and hard work worthwhile.

The Ocean under the Moon

Chapter 23

April 7, 1980

"You're crazy, Butch. There's no way pink shrimp taste as good as the white shrimp found here. Why don't you go back to Texas, if you think that way?" Gator said to his fellow shrimper.

Butch Rollins worked as a deckhand on the *Sea Warrior* and was originally from Texas, until a slow shrimping season forced him to look for work elsewhere four years ago.

"I know y'all are biased around here toward the white shrimp, but I grew up eating the shrimp caught off the coast of Texas and I say they are the best," he repeated.

"Greg, why do you let a traitor like Butch work on your boat?" Nick asked of Greg Turner, captain of the *Sea Warrior*, who was sitting across the table from him.

"That's because, if the son-of-a-bitch is too dumb not to know north Florida white shrimp are better than Texas pink shrimp, he's too dumb to ask for a raise," Greg responded, eliciting guffaws from everyone at the table except Butch.

The shrimpers were seated at the big, round table just inside the entrance to the Marina Restaurant. Also seated at the table was Patricia Toundas, in her usual spot going through the bills of the restaurant, while directing traffic.

The Ocean under the Moon

Nick had always admired Patricia, the benevolent dictator of the restaurant, who decides who sits where and when, and keeps the restaurant running smoothly. The feisty woman of Greek descent had worked at the family-run restaurant since the age of thirteen. That's when she had to lie about her age to get a driver's license when her parents, the owners of the restaurant, both had heart attacks. She had been instrumental in running the restaurant ever since, and it routinely won awards in the local paper.

The Marina Restaurant, just across the railroad tracks from the city docks, was a beloved local hang-out. The decor was all nautical, including a large shrimp boat mural on the wall, a six-foot copper lighthouse by the door, a mounted sailfish, and a wooden pelican wearing Mardi Gras beads by the cash register. Nick knew the two-story brick building had been built in the mid-1800s as a feed store and also to house the first Customs House in Florida. Later the building had housed the *Florida Mirror*, the oldest newspaper in Florida, which eventually became the present local weekly paper, the *Fernandina Beach News-Leader*.

In the early 1900s, a restaurant had been established in part of the building. It passed through several owners until Patricia's parents, Alice and Michael, acquired the restaurant. Nick, and his father, Abe, before him, had been eating at the restaurant for years, especially for lunch when the weather was too bad to go out shrimping. Gator, due to his single life, ate there often, to enjoy its home-style cooking since he had nobody else to cook for him.

"So much for the opening of the shrimping season," Greg lamented as he glanced out the front glass door of the restaurant at the rain coming down sideways, pushed by the strong wind. Last night and this morning, a strong front was making its way through the region, delaying the shrimpers' plans for the beginning of the season.

Yesterday, on Easter Sunday, they'd had the annual blessing of the fleet in gorgeous weather, but last night the weather turned ugly. Now with the weather so bad, the shrimpers could do nothing but enjoy their lunch and discuss the merits of shrimp species.

"I've got tourists that travel here from all over the globe and most of them say that the shrimp here is the best they ever had," Patricia said by way of debate to Butch.

"Well, Miss Patricia, I know the shrimp here are mighty good, but it may be just where I was raised. I still like Texas shrimp better," he said politely.

"Everybody knows that white shrimp, with that sweet taste and firm, almost crunchy meat, are preferred by chefs and shrimp connoisseurs from all over the world," Gator said, as if stating a fact.

"What are you, a damn shrimpologist? Or is that just the company line?" Butch retorted.

"Both," Gator answered.

Nick's and Gator's livelihood was tied to the white shrimp, the main type harvested along the northeast Florida coast. From watching his grandfather and then his father, Nick knew the life of a shrimper follows the seasons and life cycle of the shrimp they are trying to catch. Also, in an effort to know his competition, he knew that there were five species of shrimp commercially harvested in the waters around Florida, categorized by their shell and color type.

The white shrimp were the main catch in his area. Although called white, their shells are actually blue-grey in color, until cooked, when they turn pink. Nick and his buddies were well familiar with its life cycle. White shrimp spawn in the spring, usually about four miles off the beach in about forty to sixty feet of water. The female, on average, will release about five hundred thousand to one million eggs into the ocean.

Within twenty-four hours the fertilized eggs will hatch into shrimp larvae. Following the ocean currents and tides, the shrimp larvae will migrate in through the waterways, into the marshes throughout northeast Florida and southeast Georgia.

The larvae shrimp hide in the estuaries and marsh grass, feeding on algae, small animals and organic debris, until they mature about four months later. Then, in the fall, the mature white shrimp migrate back out the oceans and head south for the cooler months.

The next spring, the surviving shrimp return to the area off the beaches of Amelia Island, to become part of the new spawning stock. Therefore, Nick and the others knew the shrimp to be a naturally renewable and sustainable source of protein, which reproduces in a hurry, as the average life cycle of a shrimp is only just over one year.

"I'll give you this, the white shrimp taste better than the brown shrimp," Butch offered. On this point, everybody at the table could agree.

Nick knew from experience that Florida brown shrimp, named after their reddish-brown shells before cooking, could be harvested year-round in both the Atlantic Ocean and Gulf of Mexico, but the highest yields are during the summer months, June through August. The meat of a brown shrimp has a firmer texture than the white shrimp and a stronger flavor due to its iodine content. He knew that brown shrimp, however, do not typically bring as good a price at the docks, because their taste is not as sweet as the white shrimp.

"I still think pink shrimp are the best and y'all are not going to change my mind," Butch repeated, defiantly. By the reaction around the table, he might have as well told a Southerner that unsweetened tea tastes better than sweet tea.

Nick was familiar with the pink shrimp from his and Gator's time spent catching shrimp around Key West. He knew pink shrimp are the most common type of Florida's wild-caught shrimp, and they're caught in the southern waters of Florida and along the Gulf Coast all the way to Mexico. Feeding in the clean coral sand off both coasts of south Florida gives them their distinctive color and when cooked, their shells turn an even deeper shade of pink. In his opinion the meat has a fairly firm texture, with white and pink tones, and a mild flavor that is blander than the white shrimp.

"The boys down in St. Augustine will say the royal reds have the best taste," Greg countered.

"They're only special because they are so damn hard to catch," Gator said.

The shrimpers knew that the Florida royal reds were a unique shrimp species, only harvested in the deep waters off the coast of St Augustine. Royal red shrimp are harvested in the late summer and into the fall, fifty miles off the coast, in deep water. At about twenty-five hundred feet deep, they are the most difficult to harvest.

"I don't think they taste as good as our white shrimp, but with their deep red color and high salt content, we use them in the restaurant for making colorful sauces," Patricia explained.

"What about rock shrimp?" Butch asked.

"Is that even considered a shrimp?" Gator asked, dismissively.

Nick knew Butch was talking about the last shrimp species caught off Florida's Atlantic coast, the rock shrimp, so called for its rock-hard shell. Also called the "baby lobster" due to the likeness of its shell to a lobster's, it boasts the firm texture of a lobster with the sweet taste of a shrimp.

Because the royal reds and rock shrimp require special equipment and nets, Nick and Gator, like the majority of the local shrimpers, had always concentrated on the white shrimp and brown shrimp, except for their earlier March trips to Key West to catch the pinks. They had settled in to a schedule of catching the roe white shrimp coming back to spawn off the coast of Amelia Island around the beginning of April until the end of May, then catching mostly the brown shrimp, or brownies as they are called, during the summer months of June, July and August. When the larval white shrimp that had been hatched in the spring and matured in the marshes during the summer began their exodus back out to sea, then the major shrimp run of the year would begin, from September through the end of December.

"Well, I think there's one thing we can all agree on. This

weather sucks," Nick said, as they all turned to see the rain still coming down sideways beyond the glass front door.

"Amen to that, brother," Gator concurred.

"Want some more tea, Nick?" Susan, the long-time waitress, stood next to the table holding a pitcher of sweet tea.

"Might as well, Suzy. It doesn't look like we're going anywhere anytime soon," Nick said with a sigh.

The Ocean under the Moon

Chapter 24

November 17, 1982

"Nick, my water's broken!" Monica said to him, as she tried to rouse him out of his deep sleep.

"What?" he said groggily.

"My water's broken," she repeated. "We need to get to the hospital."

He jumped out of bed and started putting on his jeans.

"Are you okay?"

"I'm fine, just hurry," she said. A look of pain came across her face.

"How far apart are the contractions?"

"About six minutes apart, I think."

"We'd better get going. Good thing the hospital is not far," he added.

They'd been delighted to find out that she was pregnant almost seven months ago. She'd waited a year after moving in the cottage to try and get pregnant. They had wanted to enjoy being a young married couple and doing things with their friends, before having children and settling down.

She figured she'd get pregnant right away, her life having been so wonderful since they'd been married. Her job was going

The Ocean under the Moon

well and she loved teaching the third-graders.

The cottage was beautiful, with a nice view from their bluff, overlooking the Amelia River, to the west. They would sit on their screened-in back porch, with the ceiling fan going overhead and have a beer or glass of white wine, and watch the sun go down over the expansive marsh to the west.

He'd built a brick fire pit out back of the cottage where, when the weather was cooler, they would have guests over for an oyster roast. She had fun decorating the cottage with a beach motif, buying paintings and knickknacks from the specialty stores in downtown Fernandina. She also bought a lot of things during the annual Shrimp Festival, where artists and craftsmen set up booths down each side of Centre Street.

Growing up in south Georgia, she'd always dreamed of living near the beach. Even though their cottage wasn't on the beach, instead overlooking the river, the beach was only a mile and a half away on the other side of the island and she could go anytime she pleased, after school or on the weekends. While they enjoyed their evening cocktail watching the sunset most evenings, she reveled in the fact that her view now consisted of the red ball of the sun sinking behind the miles of marsh, instead of the view of a cow pasture and pine trees that she'd had growing up in Hazlehurst.

Now, all they needed to make their lives perfect was a baby. She thought she would get pregnant as soon as she went off birth control pills, but that didn't happen. It was almost another year later before she was able to surprise him with the good news. Nick had been ecstatic, even later on, when he found out it was

243

going to be a girl.

Monica went into nesting-mode and painted the nursery pink. Caroline was also excited by the pending arrival of her first grandchild. She threw her daughter a baby shower in Hazlehurst, and one of Monica's teacher friends threw one in Fernandina. Soon the baby's room was packed with stuffed animals, a crib, a bassinet, a mobile, diapers and other baby paraphernalia.

Now, he grabbed the bag full of extra clothes and toiletries that they had kept next to the bed for the last month in anticipation of their trip to the hospital. He then brought his car around out front, helped her down the steps and into the car and loaded the bag into the car.

The good thing about living on an island is that nothing is very far away. Even though the county had moved the hospital from its location where he was born, which was just a mile down North 14th Street from his home in Old Town, to a new location on Lime Street that was just a mile farther down the road. At this late hour, there were very few cars on the road and in just over five minutes, he pulled the car up the circular drive to the hospital's front entrance. He helped Monica out of the car and through the entrance to the front desk. A wheelchair was brought around and she was rushed off to the maternity ward, while he went back out to park the car.

When he returned and located her room, he noticed there seemed to be a beehive of activity going on in the room. He saw three nurses, one doing an ultrasound, one working on the baby's heart rate monitor, and the third one, the head nurse, met him as he tried to enter the room.

The Ocean under the Moon

"Mr. Stamos, we are going to have to ask you to wait in the waiting room for us, please," the stout nurse said. She stepped in front of him, blocking his entrance.

He looked over the nurse's shoulder and saw a terrified look on Monica's face.

"What's going on? Dr. Anderson said I could be present at the birth," he began.

"I've already called Dr. Anderson. He'll be here shortly. There are some complications, however, which Dr. Anderson will explain later. In the meantime, we have to work to save your baby, so please wait in the waiting room."

"Can I at least speak to my wife?"

"Just for a minute." The nurse stepped aside.

He went over to Monica's side and clasped her hand. She looked up at him, her eyes full of shock and disbelief.

"Everything will be okay," he began, wanting to reassure her and wanting to believe what he was saying would be true. "Just remember, whatever happens, I love you with all my heart." He leaned over to the bed and kissed her on the cheek.

She just nodded her head and mumbled a weak, "I love you, too."

She was in shock and seemed disconnected from the activity buzzing around her.

He could not bear to see the "deer in the headlights" look on her face any longer so he did as the nurse requested and left the room. He only made it halfway to the waiting room before he spotted a men's restroom and went inside the empty restroom and began sobbing. He knew in his heart that something was drastically wrong.

Seven months of happiness, anticipation, preparation, and now this, he thought, his arms supporting his slumping body, as he stared at his red eyes in the mirror. He wondered what could have gone wrong. The doctors and nurses all through the pregnancy had said everything was going fine.

He washed his face and composed himself and went out to the waiting room. His parents were there to greet him. He'd called them from his house before leaving for the hospital because he knew they would want to be present for the birth of their first grandchild.

Abe and Isabelle took one look at the expression on his face and knew something was terribly wrong. He walked over, and without a word, began hugging his mother as his father put a reassuring hand on his shoulder. He informed them that he didn't know exactly what was going on, but it didn't look good.

After forty-five minutes of nervous waiting, Dr. Anderson came out through the double doors from the interior of the hospital. Nick had immediately liked Kevin Anderson when he first met him six months ago. The young doctor had done his undergraduate studies at Georgia Tech, then medical school and his gynecology and obstetrics residency at Emory University and Grady Memorial Hospital in Atlanta. Dr. Anderson was a big Georgia Tech football fan and Nick and the doctor liked talking football during Monica's well-visits.

Tonight, however, he wore a defeated look on his face. He walked over toward Nick and his parents, who all stood up as he approached.

The Ocean under the Moon

"I'm afraid I have some bad news for you," he said. "The baby was stillborn."

"What happened? Everything was supposed to be going according to plan," Nick said.

"Have you ever heard of *vasa previa*?" the doctor asked in a gentle voice.

All three of them shook their heads.

"It's a rare condition in which the fetal blood vessels traverse the fetal membranes, or bag of waters, as they are more commonly known, across the lower part of the uterus between the fetus and the cervical opening," he said. "It happens in less than one in three thousand births, but unfortunately it has a high mortality rate for the infant, over fifty percent.

"When Monica's water broke, it tore these fragile blood vessels, causing the fetus to exsanguinate, or bleed out. By the time you got to the hospital, the nurses could not find a heartbeat, and that's why they kicked you out of the room. I arrived soon thereafter, induced the delivery, and used a vacuum extraction to speed up the delivery. We tried to resuscitate the fetus, for over fifteen minutes, but were unsuccessful. I am very sorry for your loss, Nick." He put a hand on Nick's shoulder.

Nick dropped his head and his parents hugged him. He had one more question for Dr. Anderson.

"When can I see Monica?"

"Well, we sedated her pretty heavily right after the birth, so she can recover both physically and mentally," he said, looking at his watch and noting it was almost four o'clock in the morning. "She won't wake up for at least twelve hours, the way we have her sedated. So I suggest you all go home and try to get some rest, then return later on this afternoon."

After Dr Anderson left them, Nick looked at his watch. He knew it was going to be impossible for him to sleep after what had happened. There was nothing else for him to do, however, but to try and rest and come back to the hospital around noon, so he would be sure to be there when Monica woke up. This was a tough blow for him, but he knew it would be devastating for her, with all her well-laid plans and expectations now in shambles; it would be a heartbreaking loss.

He shook his head in disbelief and, with an arm around each one of his parents, walked out of the waiting room toward their cars.

The Ocean under the Moon

Chapter 25

November 21, 1982

Angela Olympia Stamos was buried on a drizzly and gloomy Tuesday afternoon. The weather was a perfect match for Nick's and Monica's mood. The funeral service for baby Angela was held at the small, white chapel at Oxley-Heard Mortuary on Atlantic Avenue next to the primary school that she would have attended.

He didn't want to have the services at St. Peter's Episcopal Church where a larger crowd might have showed. No, he wanted a smaller, private affair. The service had been a quick and solemn one. What can you say about a life that was over, before it began outside the womb?

They say the quality of your life is determined by how well you live the dash between your birth date and your death date. The dash represented the years in between. Nick thought for his little daughter, there really wasn't a dash, her birth date and death date being one and the same.

They couldn't make sense of their tragic loss, other than to think God needed a new angel that was pure of this world, and that he took her before she could be corrupted. In that case, she would have lived up to her name that they had chosen for her earlier, Angela, meaning angel-like, and Olympia, meaning heavenly.

The Ocean under the Moon

That was the only comforting thought that he could think of, as they laid her to rest in her tiny coffin in the Stamos plot under the cedar trees at Bosque Bello Cemetery. Grandfather Eber's headstone was on the far left as one faced the family plot.

Next to him was Grandmother Catherine, who had died just three months ago. Nick's beloved Grandma Catherine, who had been fighting cancer for several months, had been ecstatic about Monica's pregnancy and desperately wanted to cling to life long enough to see the baby. She didn't make it. Now he was relieved that she wasn't around to witness the tragedy.

He stood looking at the cemetery plot with his parents, his wife, and close friends who gathered around while the preacher said a few last words as the rain drizzled down. This made him realize his own mortality. Seeing his grandparents buried on one end of the plot and his baby on the other end, then the space in the middle intended for his parents along with Nick, Monica, and maybe some more children, made him think about the continuum of life. How time marches relentlessly forward, and how fragile and short life really is.

He grabbed his wife's hand and squeezed, trying to reassure her, but wondering, himself, if they could ever get over this tragedy.

Chapter 26

September 19, 1990

"Wa.........aaah."

The first wail of the baby was music to Nick's ears. Almost eight years had passed since baby Angela had been stillborn. It had been a rough eight years emotionally for his wife. The joys of marriage and setting up house in their perfect, little cottage had been replaced by the irony of her working with other people's children, all day, while she had none of her own.

Nick looked at the contented smile on her face as she held their newborn child and he had never been more proud of her.

Two miscarriages along the way had only heightened her frustration and disappointment. Both times her initial elation, and the rest of the family's hope, had been cruelly dashed by nature's vagaries. She had no idea why God was punishing her so and began to question her faith, although she still attended services every Sunday at St. Peter's.

But God works in esoteric ways and just when they were ready to give up and adopt, she found out she was pregnant again. This time she was taking no chances. With Nick's blessing, she took a year-long leave of absence from her teaching job, even though her salary had helped give them a steady income, while his income

251

fluctuated with the availability and market price of shrimp.

The last eight years hadn't been easy for him either. The heydays of the shrimping industry had given way to changes in the shrimping industry in the latter part of the 1980s. The government was trying to impose use of turtle extruder devices, or TEDs, which reduced the shrimper's productivity, and the local shrimpers were facing increased competition from imported shrimp. Unlike his father, who had ushered in Nick to the world during the "Golden Age" of shrimping, the younger Stamos was not certain catching shrimp would be viable as an occupation for his son in the coming decades.

His newborn son's future occupation was the last thing on his mind, however, as he looked around at Dr. Anderson's relieved smile and Monica's glowing and proud face. The nurse handed his son to him, swaddled in a blue baby blanket, crying and squirming. He looked down at his healthy baby boy and was never prouder or more grateful for anything in his life.

"What are you going to call him?" the nurse asked.

"Matt, short for Matthaios," Nick responded.

Matthaios Galen Stamos, they'd named him. Matthaios meant "gift of God" in Greek and this baby was certainly that, a gift from God for them. Galen meant "calm seas" in Greek. They hoped that the boy's middle name would always bless him with a smooth and untroubled life.

However, Nick realized, from all his years at sea, that life, like the ocean, tends to vacillate between smooth sailing and rough seas. The ocean, as well as life, can be deceptive at times, like the calm seas and blue skies that precede a hurricane. Since the low pressure of the eye of a hurricane sucks in all of the clouds, rain, and winds to form a tight, counter-clockwise pinwheel of energy, the weather just before and just after a hurricane is full of blue skies. Before the advent of modern meteorology, sailors and townspeople along the shoreline would be fooled by the deceptively good weather, only to face the full fury of a hurricane twenty-four hours later.

He knew that sometimes the meaning of a name was only wishful thinking. But he also knew, as he looked down at his young son, that he would do anything for this little boy, to smooth his way through a turbulent world.

The Ocean under the Moon

Chapter 27

May 30, 1992

Monica had only been back to work for three months when she
found out she was expecting again. After all her struggles, she
hadn't expected to get pregnant so fast, but neither had she been
taking any precautions. She'd heard of many couples who
experienced trouble having their first child, then after either
adopting or finally having their first child, the pregnancies seem to
come fast and furious, one after the other, but she didn't expect it to
happen to her.

This time, she kept working until about two weeks before
the delivery. Andonios Zotikos Stamos was born at Baptist-Nassau
Hospital in a quick and easy delivery, as if he was anxious to see
the outside world. They intended to call him Andy, for Andonios,
which meant "invaluable" in Greek. It soon became apparent,
however, that maybe the boy's middle name, Zotikos, or "full of
life" in Greek, was a more appropriate moniker.

It was Abe who first started calling the boy Zoti, and
noticed that Nick and Monica's second child was going to be very
different from the first. Matt had been the perfect baby, seldom
crying, only when hungry or wet. He was also a good sleeper,
sleeping through the night, except for right after being born and

then a little later, when he was teething. They could take him with them to a restaurant in his little carrier and it seemed like the louder the restaurant, the better he would sleep through the meal.

Abe and Isabelle were getting into their late sixties when Zoti was born, but they were still spry enough to babysit. Abe had retired from shrimping a few months ago and now he considered watching Matt and Zoti his full-time job. It was a convenient arrangement for Nick and Monica to have them right next door. Monica was able to go back to work quicker this time and did not have to worry about putting the boys in a nursery or preschool, like the other young mothers.

She was pleased with the situation, which allowed Abe and Isabelle to bond with the boys, and for the children to get to know their grandparents, so they would love and remember them, when their grandparents were gone. And keeping the boys out of daycare kept them healthier. It seemed all of her friends who were teachers were always having to leave school to pick up their sick child from daycare, as it seemed at least a third of the kids in daycare were sick at any given time and just passing the germs around to each other.

Just Matt was easy for Abe and Isabelle to watch; adding Zoti to the mix more than doubled the work for them — it went up exponentially. Zoti was a demanding baby, always crying or squirming, and rarely slept, it seemed. Add that to the fact that Matt was nearing the "terrible two's" and in the inquisitive stage, where the toddler walks around trying to get into everything, and the grandparents had their hands full.

When they got overwhelmed or just worn out, Buck and

Caroline were more than happy to come down and stay at Nick and Monica's for a week or so to help out. Also, during Monica's summer vacation or Christmas break from school, she would take the boys up to Hazlehurst to visit the farm and spend time with her parents.

It was a good thing that Nick and Monica had plenty of help, since Zoti would not sleep completely through the night for the first five years of his life. With work and children, the young couple always seemed tired and on the move.

Nick talked to people whose kids were grown and they would always say to him to enjoy his kids while they were young, because they grow up so fast. But, for him, he couldn't wait until his boys got older and more independent. It would be years later before he could appreciate what the people had been trying to tell him.

The Ocean under the Moon

Chapter 28

October 22, 1994

Gator sat down on the top of the crew's cabin, his feet dangling off the back, breathing very hard. He'd just finished another rendition of "Free Bird," as it had played on his trusty boom box. He had made his trademark lap around the boat, playing air guitar, then finished with his *tour de force* finale, singing to the ocean and sea birds, off his "stage" on the back of the roof of the crew's cabin.

"You're getting old," Nick remarked. He never got tired of watching Gator perform his Free Bird ritual. Fortunately, the length of the song prevented it from being played often on the radio, so it never got too redundant. Gator, of course, could have bought a cassette and played it whenever he wanted, but that would have spoiled the spontaneity, so he never did. Also, the pure joy and kid-like enthusiasm that he displayed during the ritual kept Nick from getting mad at him for breaking from his work.

"I've still got it," Gator said, then immediately started coughing.

Nick laughed at his friend's bravado, but he'd been trying for years to get his friend to cut down on his drinking and late-night carousing. Lately, there had been signs of him slowing down a little.

The Ocean under the Moon

About a year ago, Gator had bought an old, run-down, Key West style cottage on White Street a couple of blocks from where Nick lived. It was away from the waterfront, where land was much cheaper. He had been trying to renovate the cottage as time and money allowed. Nick tried to help Gator whenever he could, in order to pay his friend back for when he helped Nick build his house years earlier. The doting father tried bringing his sons, now four and two years old, respectively, but they wanted to try and do everything themselves and kept getting in the way, so Monica would bring them over for a little while, then take them back home, so Nick and Gator could actually get some work done.

About six months before, Gator had also started dating a girl, steady, for the first time in his life. Nick was glad Gator was finally sticking with one woman for more than one week at a time. Gator told Nick all about his new girlfriend during the long days they spent out shrimping on the *Resurrection*.

* * *

Brandy O'Reilly was a striking auburn-haired girl with green eyes. She was twenty-five years old and the daughter of a tavern keeper from Chicago. She was from a large Irish Catholic family dominated by the men in her family. Her mother had run off with one of the patrons of her father's tavern, leaving her father to raise her and her three older brothers.

Brandy grew up a tomboy and knew how to be around, and handle, men. Despite her outward appearance, which was all female and girlish, she was tough as nails, from dealing with her older brothers growing up, and then later, from working in her father's bar and dealing with the mostly male customers. She was a

The Ocean under the Moon

Chicago Bears fan, who grew up loving sports of all types.

About a year before, while working in the tavern, she had met a slick young investment banker from Miami, who was in Chicago on business. The young businessman was very handsome in a dark, Latino way. She'd grown tired of the over-protectiveness of her father and brothers and the monotony of her job. After dating a few times on his frequent trips to Chicago on business, she jumped at his invitation to come back and live with him in Miami.

Her father vehemently objected to her plans to move. For her father, she was doing to him what her mother had done years before, abandoning him for another man. Her brothers were none too thrilled either and threatened to go to Miami to beat up the guy.

Despite their protestations, Brandy felt it was something she had to do at that point in her life, to get out and see the world and get out from under her family's protective umbrella. So she piled everything she owned into her car and took off for Miami.

At first she was enthralled by the city's exotic lifestyle. Her boyfriend, Juan, lived on the twentieth floor of a high-rise luxury condominium complex near downtown Miami, overlooking Biscayne Bay. As she told Gator later, the first time she walked out on the balcony and looked out over the shimmering, aquamarine waters of the bay, she was glad to have left dreary Chicago, and wondered who would not want to live in south Florida. Juan took her out in his Ferrari to all of the best restaurants and night clubs in Miami, and at first, she was mesmerized by the tropical night air and Latin beat of the clubs.

After about three months, however, she was not quite so thrilled with her situation. Her boyfriend was getting more and more possessive. He wouldn't even let her get a job. He wanted her to be at home, waiting for him, when he got off of work, which was sometimes eight or nine at night. She got bored, sitting around all day long, and waiting for him to get home. She wanted to leave, but she didn't know where to go. The lonely and confused young woman hated to go back to Chicago and face the "I told you so" that she would get from her father and brothers.

But she had to do something. Juan, who was so romantic and attentive at first, was getting more paranoid and possessive. She found out, about six weeks after she moved down to Miami, that he was using cocaine. She'd walked in on him one day in the bathroom by accident, and there he was with a line of the white powder spread out before him and with some of the powder around his nostril.

She had blown up with rage and he apologized and promised her he would quit. She never saw him do it again, but she was beginning to have her doubts with the continuation of his paranoia and possessiveness.

The final decision to leave was made for her when DEA officers burst through the door of the condo when Juan was at work. They initially put her in handcuffs while they searched his condo for drugs. The DEA officers informed her that another group of officers was simultaneously arresting Juan at the bank where he worked, for money laundering.

She denied any knowledge of drugs or money laundering and when the search of his condo came up clean of any drugs, the officers took the handcuffs off her, but said she would have to go down to the station and make a statement.

The Ocean under the Moon

At the station, she found out that Juan was in big trouble and was probably going to jail for quite some time. It turned out that he was one of several Miami bankers working with a rather large drug cartel to launder a portion of their ill-gotten money. She'd always wondered how her boyfriend, who was only twenty-nine, had gotten so successful, so fast. She'd just assumed he was a very astute businessman, but now she knew the truth.

It was lucky for her, that after her blow-up at him over the cocaine, he'd moved his stash to his office. If the officers had found drugs in the condo, she would have been arrested, also.

Since they hadn't found anything, they let her go, but only after getting her contact numbers, in case she needed to testify later. She went straight back to his condo and packed her things into her car, and left town. The sooner she could see south Florida in her rear-view mirror, the better, she thought at the time. She headed up the east coast of Florida on I-95, initially headed for Chicago. The Latin beat of Miami had been fun at first, but the difference in culture and the language barrier had worn on her, making her feel like a stranger in her own country.

After driving for six hours up the peninsula, she was at the last exit in Florida before crossing over into Georgia. Tired from her eventful day and all the driving, she decided to pull off the interstate to get some gas and find a hotel for the night. She pulled into the lone gas station at the interstate exchange, exhausted, since it was almost nine o'clock at night now.

"Where's the nearest decent hotel?" she asked the gas station attendant.

"Well, the best hotels around here are going to be in

261

The Ocean under the Moon

Fernandina Beach, about ten miles east of here on the coast. Or, you can drive north into Georgia," he responded.

She considered getting back into her car and driving up to the first exit in Georgia, but for some reason, she didn't quite want to leave Florida yet.

She decided to drive to the coast and hang out for a day or two and contemplate her future. She had plenty of money. Juan was always generous with his cash. He'd given her a healthy allowance, then paid for almost everything himself, so she'd been able to squirrel away a small nest egg of savings.

She drove into Fernandina, found a bed-and-breakfast inn in the historic downtown district, and settled in for the night. The next day, she woke up refreshed and feeling liberated from the strong, male forces that usually surrounded her. She decided to spend some time in Fernandina to think about her future.

She had breakfast at the inn, then wandered around downtown, browsing through the shops in the historic district. That afternoon, she went to Main Beach. Unlike Miami Beach, the beach here was not crowded. She found a secluded spot, laid out her beach towel and reclined on it, then let out a little sigh as the sun rejuvenated her body.

Soon, she started appreciating the laid-back, relaxing atmosphere of this little town, after the hustle and bustle of Miami. The big city of Miami, with its glitz and glamour, was a nice place to visit, but you wouldn't want to live there. At least that's what this Midwestern girl concluded, as she lay on the warm sand, listening only to the seagulls crying and the relaxing roar of the ocean as the small waves crashed upon the beach.

The Ocean under the Moon

Later that evening, she had a delicious seafood dinner at the Marina Restaurant, and wandered down to the Palace Saloon. This place looks interesting, she thought, as she approached the old building with its swinging saloon doors. It reminded her of her father's tavern and some of the other bars from back in Chicago, so she decided to go in.

She walked through the front doors and felt at home. The musty, old saloon had much the same feel as her father's tavern, where she had grown up working. She sat on a bar stool at the end of the bar closest to the entrance. Since it was only eight o'clock in the evening, the time between the happy hour crowd and late night crowd, the bar was just about empty. Two couples sat at tables along the wall, next to the jukebox, sipping on some kind of specialty drink out of souvenir cups.

At the far end of the bar, with a girl sitting on each side of him, was a handsome man with a long, blond ponytail, laughing and joking with the barmaid. The barmaid didn't see Brandy at first, because she was enthralled with a story or joke that the tall man was telling. Soon the barmaid and the two girls beside the man erupted in laughter, and the barmaid turned and noticed her sitting at the other end of the bar all by herself.

The barmaid, a rather plain-looking woman in her thirties, came over to Brandy and asked her what she wanted to drink. Brandy pointed over at the tourists drinking out of the souvenir cups and asked the barmaid what they were drinking.

"Oh, that's a Pirate's Punch," the barmaid responded. "It's gin, two types of rum, Rose's lime juice, orange juice, and I could tell you the rest, but I'd have to shoot you, because it's a secret recipe." She laughed at her own joke.

"I'll try one of those," Brandy responded, not normally following the tourist route, but figuring, what the hell, it could be her last night in Florida.

The barmaid brought her a Pirate's Punch, complete with small plastic pirate sword with a skewered wedge of orange, pineapple, and a cherry, sitting on top of the drink. It surprised her that the drink was so good, and she could hardly taste the significant amount of rum and gin, masked by the tropical flavor of the drink.

By the end of her first Pirate's Punch, she had fallen in love with the Palace Saloon and its magical drink. The saloon's nearly century-old ambience made her feel at home, as though she was in the Chicago tavern, without her father and brothers around to tell her what to do.

When the barmaid brought her a second Pirate's Punch, Brandy asked her if they were looking for any help in the bar. The barmaid said, as a matter of fact, a bartender had just quit and they were looking for some help. She left and returned with an application and a pen.

"You got any experience?" the barmaid asked.

"Just all my life," she responded.

She filled out the application while nursing her second drink. Out of the corner of her eye, she noticed the large, muscular man with the pony-tail get up off his barstool and walk to her end of the bar.

"You're not from around here, are you?"

She had heard every pick-up line working in her father's

bar and was not impressed with that lame opening line.

"That's the best you can do? You sound like an old spaghetti western," she said.

She kept filling out the application, not even looking up at him. She had studied this guy from afar earlier and liked the looks of him, but she thought he might be a little old for her, gauging by the creases around his eyes. Besides, she was swearing off men for awhile, after her last fiasco.

He seemed to realize that this girl was no push-over and tried a different tack.

"Hi, my name's Gator."

"Well, of course it is," she responded, still being sarcastic. "What else would you be called, in this little hick town. Next, you're going to tell me you got your name because you wrestle alligators for a living."

"No, I got my name because I used to play football for the Florida Gators and actually, I did wrestle a gator when I was a kid." He grinned widely.

"Were you any good? At football, I mean."

"Well, I was, before I wrecked my knee."

"What do you do now?" she asked.

"Now, I ply the seas for shrimp."

"Then shouldn't your nickname be Shrimp now, instead of Gator?" she asked with a chuckle.

"Very funny," he said. "Do you mind if I sit down?"

"Won't your little harem over there miss you?" She pointed at the two girls he had been sitting with.

"Oh, them? They're just friends of mine. Drinking

buddies, more or less." He pulled out the stool next to her. "May I?"

"It's a free world," she replied.

She never wanted to drink alone. She also wanted to pump information from this local guy to see if she wanted to stay in this "hick town," as she had called Fernandina.

"Be careful with those Pirate's Punches. Three or four of those and you will be dancing topless on top of the tables," he said, as he slid onto the barstool.

"We'll see about that," she said. She took another sip of the potent drink.

She never did dance topless on the tables that night, but they did stay till closing time, pounding down drinks and telling each other their life stories. By the end of the night, it was clear both had found their soul mates—not just drinking buddies—and she had decided she would stick around for awhile in this little "hick town." Little did she know that Amelia Island had a hold of her and would never let her go.

The Ocean under the Moon

Chapter 29

April 14, 1995

Gator and Brandy were married on a warm, Saturday evening the following spring. To appease her father, and also her brothers, who'd traveled to Amelia Island from Chicago for the big event, the wedding ceremony was held in St. Michael's Catholic Church. Named for the patron saint for those at risk, like the sick, soldiers in battle, and sailors at sea, the parish had been established in 1872, at the corner of Fourth Street and Broome Street in downtown Fernandina.

After the long wedding service, complete with communion, the wedding party adjourned to Tiger's Point Marina back in Old Town. Tiger's Point was a new marina built on the long neglected south bank of Egan's Creek, just east of Nick's land.

The marina had a long dock, parallel to the creek, for sailboats, and sport-fishing boats to tie up to, short term and long term. The owners had also built a party house to hold functions such as wedding receptions and reunions. The wooden structure was built on pilings, over the marsh, and had a beautiful view. The building was open on three sides, with porches overlooking the creek to the north and the Amelia River to the west.

Two nights before, Nick paid Gator back by throwing him

a bachelor party. He'd rented a limousine and Nick, Gator, Brandy's father and brothers, and a few friends piled into the car and made the rounds of all the strip joints in Jacksonville. Gator and Brandy's brothers, being the professional drinkers that they were, enjoyed a tremendous time and the whole crew stayed out almost to dawn. The revelers had just recovered in time for the rehearsal dinner the next night, and were still feeling the effects even the night of the wedding.

The wedding reception site was perfect. A clear, blue sky gave way to a brilliant sunset, and then the cool, evening breezes kicked in. Sean McCarthy, a well known local musician, who'd played in Nashville, played his guitar for the couple. Sean played music similar to Jimmy Buffett and had written several original compositions about island life. But one of the hits that evening was his rendition of "Brandy" by Looking Glass. The lyrics, "Brandy, you're a fine girl, what a good wife you will be, yeah, your eyes could steal a sailor from the sea," delighted the crowd.

The joyous evening went long into the night. Brandy, beautiful in her long, white flowing gown, seemed to be twirling and dancing with someone, every time Nick looked up. He was very happy for his good friend, Gator, who'd finally met his match in a woman. She seemed down to earth, with a good head on her shoulders, and was very pretty to boot.

Gator was clearly a happy man. Maybe now, he would settle down a little bit. Gator had never let it affect his work, but all those late nights and drinking had to be taking some toll on his body. As strong and formidable as he was, now that he was nearing forty years old, he needed to settle down a little bit. As his friend and employer, Nick was happy to see his friend calm down some.

Just after he watched Gator and Brandy slow-dancing to the end of a ballad, Sean launched into his version of "Shout" and soon Gator and the O'Reilly brothers were "gatoring," flopping down on the dance floor. He shook his head in both dismay and delight. Some things never change.

The Ocean under the Moon

Chapter 30

May 1, 2005

Nick looked up at the action on the ball field after the crack of the bat. He'd been concentrating on eating his messy cheeseburger and French fries with ketchup all over them. He was sitting on a lawn chair beside the bleacher with his knees pressed together and the food balanced on his lap. Monica was in the bleachers talking with two girlfriends, most likely about their kids. Matt was out on the ball field, pitching. Zoti was behind the bleachers in a small grassy area kicking a soccer ball around with his friends.

"Come on, Matt. One more strike," Nick yelled toward the field with his mouth half-full of food.

It seemed like yesterday that Nick had been at Gator's wedding. The years changed, however. The people who'd said "enjoy your kids while they are young, because they grow up so fast" had been right. Before Nick knew it, a decade passed. The decade had been a whirlwind of school functions, soccer games, baseball games, church functions, birthdays, and trips to Disney World.

All of a sudden, it seemed to him, Matt was fourteen years old and Zoti was twelve. Matt had grown into a strapping young man. Big for his age, he both pitched and caught for his senior league baseball team. Possessing superior velocity for his age, he struck out nearly two out of every three batters he faced, and when he wasn't pitching, as a catcher he threw out nearly ninety percent of the runners who tried to steal on him. Nick was very proud of Matt's baseball accomplishments, even though he couldn't always make it to all of his games due to his shrimping schedule.

He loved going up to Buccaneer Field to watch the games, however. It seemed like the whole town turned out at the ball fields near Central Park in the spring, to watch their children play Little League, Senior League, and girls' softball games. With four ball fields laid out in each compass direction, their home plates positioned near a central concession stand, this large circle of ball fields became the epicenter of social life for couples with children.

Getting a cheeseburger and fries from the concession stand and then sitting in your lawn chair watching your son play baseball on a beautiful spring evening, there was nothing better than that, Nick thought. Plus the slow pace of a baseball game, with its many breaks between innings, allowed a lot of time for moving around, socializing, and catching up with what was going on in town and with other people's lives.

Zoti, on the other hand, had no use for the slow pace of baseball. His two loves were surfing and soccer, in that order. He'd always loved the ocean. Even when he was only two or three years old, whenever they would take the boys to the beach, Zoti would head straight for the water and try to go as deep as he could. When a wave pounded the boy, knocking him from his feet, he would just get up, squeal with laughter and head back out again.

Nick had to be constantly by his side, at this stage, to keep

271

the young boy from drowning himself. When they would leave the beach that day, no matter how long they had stayed, the boy would always throw a fit not to leave.

For self-preservation, Nick taught Zoti to swim at a very young age, in the pool at the Atlantic Avenue Recreation Center. As he grew older, he quickly graduated from riding a boogie board, to a small tri-fin surfboard, to winning his age group at surfing contests. They traveled to places like Cocoa Beach and Sebastian Inlet to compete in contests.

To practice surfing, Zoti would wake up at dawn and ride his bike to the beach, carrying his board, with his dog, Pepe, running by his side. Pepe was a medium-sized mongrel dog that Zoti acquired for free, when a neighbor's dog had puppies. He'd brought the puppy home and talked them into keeping it, promising that he would do all the work to take care of the dog. From that day forward, the two became nearly inseparable.

Pepe grew up to look like the dog in the "Benji" movies and was just as smart as Benji. When Zoti rode his bike around town, Pepe would run, unleashed, at his side, following his commands. The only time he was forced to put Pepe on a leash was when he went into a store, because he would try to follow Zoti inside. If not leashed to a post outside, the dog would dart in when someone else opened the door.

Zoti had told his father what happened the first time Pepe accompanied him surfing, when the dog almost drowned. Despite Zoti's forceful commands to stay at the water's edge, after thirty seconds of hesitation, Pepe had started trying to swim out to where he was sitting on his board, gazing out to catch an oncoming wave.

The Ocean under the Moon

When Zoti turned around, he could see the desperate animal dog-paddling, just as a wave broke over his little head. His head disappeared for what seemed like an eternity, but finally his head popped back up like a cork, his mouth gasping for air.

Surely, the dog will turn back to the beach now, Zoti had thought. Pepe, however, spotted his master and began his struggle anew. Zoti paddled over to the panting dog before the next wave could strike and carried him to the beach. He had to leash him to his bike to keep the dog from following him back out to the surf. It would take several more trips to the beach to teach him to be content enough just to stay at the water's edge, dodging the small waves and chasing the seagulls along with the skimmer birds.

* * *

While things had been going great on the home front for Nick in the last decade, the years continued to be bad for the domestic shrimp industry. He had become the unofficial leader and voice for the Fernandina Beach shrimpers. He'd attained that position, mainly, for his willingness to spend his own money to travel to Tallahassee on state issues or to Washington for federal issues.

He had it better than most shrimpers. He learned from his research on behalf of the shrimping industry that the average shrimper was a fifty-two-year-old male with over twenty years of fishing experience, earning about forty thousand dollars a year after expenses. About half of shrimpers didn't have health insurance and also, about half had no income from a spouse.

He was lucky in that his wife worked as a school teacher, earning about forty thousand dollars a year, and they were able to get health insurance through her employment. He also enjoyed an advantage over most other shrimpers in that he had free dockage behind his house. Therefore, he felt an obligation to help his friends, some of whom were having very rough times.

Around 1995, after much litigation, the turtle extruder devices became mandatory for all U.S. shrimp trawlers larger than twenty-five feet. Nick, as leader of the local shrimpers, had fought a long fight against the use of TEDs. It wasn't that he and his fellow shrimpers were against saving sea turtles or other by-catch. Like most fisherman and hunters, they realized that over-fishing or over-hunting any species works to the detriment of the entire ecosystem and is bad in the long term.

He and Gator had always worked hard to reduce the by-catch death by returning the by-catch to the ocean as soon as possible, and checking their nets more often, since turtles can only hold their breath for five or six minutes.

What the independent and hard-working shrimpers objected to was being told by the government what to do; that, and the fact that TEDs reduced their bottom line. When a turtle or other large fish pushed open the hard trap door on the back of the net, invariably some of the shrimp escaped also.

The shrimpers claimed they lost thirty percent of their catch with a TED; the government claimed it was ten percent. The truth was probably in between at around twenty percent. This meant the shrimpers, with the same amount of fuel costs and time and labor spent, lost twenty percent of their catch and hence, profit.

Also, while use of TEDs had become mandatory in the U.S. waters, the use of TEDs was very limited in the rest of the world, putting U.S. shrimpers at a competitive disadvantage.

Despite their fight to keep devices from being mandatory, once they were required by law, Nick learned the U.S. shrimping industry eventually reached a ninety-nine percent completion rate and a ninety-seven percent reduction in sea turtle deaths, according to government figures.

The other, bigger issue that had become a concern over the last decade was that by 1995, eighty percent of the U.S. consumption of shrimp was in the form of low-cost, imported shrimp. The vast majority of these shrimp were farm- or pond-raised shrimp from tropical countries around the world. Unlike the wild-caught shrimp that grow up and are harvested in areas that are pristine and free from pollution, the farm-raised shrimp are raised in stagnant pools.

Along the southeastern Atlantic coast and the Louisiana and Texas coasts, the salt marshes, along with providing the young shrimp a place to hide and find nutrients, act as a natural filtration system to keep pollutants from land, like fertilizers, from affecting the saltwater estuaries. In south Florida and in tropical countries like Vietnam, India, Thailand, Ecuador, Malaysia, and south China, it is the mangrove forests along the coast that provide the natural shrimp habitat along with many other species of fish.

Unfortunately, in certain parts of Southeast Asia and South America, large areas of mangrove forests were being converted into massive shrimp farms. Nick was shocked when he learned how it worked. First, an area of mangrove forest, salt flat, or some other ecologically valuable saltwater estuary must be converted into a saltwater pond.

The Ocean under the Moon

Then as many as one hundred fifty thousand shrimp larvae are dumped in a one-acre pond, which can yield as much as fifteen thousand pounds of shrimp in three to six months. Because of this density, the waste that they swim in, and all the nutrients added to make them grow faster, the stagnant pool has to be treated with algaecides, fungicides, and pesticides.

Also, there have been many instances of contamination from farm-raised shrimp. White spot virus, salmonella, and Taura virus syndrome are just a few of the diseases that have had known outbreaks due to contaminated shrimp from the stagnant pools of poorly-run aquaculture farms. In order to prevent these kinds of outbreaks, excessive, strong antibiotics are used — sometimes even chloramphenicol, which is banned for use on edible animals in the United States, because it can cause aplastic anemia.

At one of the meetings that he had attended in Washington, Nick heard of rice paddy fields that had been converted into shrimp farms, in some Southeast Asian countries. Because of the toxic sludge and salinity that builds up at the bottom of the paddy fields after several years, the areas had to be abandoned, as they would not support shrimp or any agriculture any more.

He'd also learned that, besides the shrimp farms destroying the mangrove forests, two to four pounds of sea life have to be caught and ground up as feed, for one pound of shrimp. In a vicious cycle, the loss of fish estuaries and over-fishing for seafood for shrimp-feed, turn even more indigenous fishermen to shrimp farming for a living.

Nick didn't know anyone who, given a choice, wouldn't

choose a wild-caught shrimp, spawned and harvested from a natural marine environment, free from pollution, and handled and packaged following U.S. standards, over a foreign, pond-raised shrimp with questionable oversight and cheap labor.

He knew in a taste test, side by side, American consumers would prefer fresh wild-caught south Atlantic and Gulf shrimp for their sweet and succulent taste and firm texture, over the bland taste and mushy texture of foreign pond-raised shrimp that have to be imported from great distances.

While Nick and Gator unloaded the boat in the evenings, he sometimes looked at the catch and shook his head as he pondered the situation. The problem, he thought, is that the American consumer is not being told where their shrimp comes from by restaurants and grocery stores. Most restaurants and supermarket owners just care about the price. They assume that for most consumers, a shrimp is a shrimp. Covered with batter, cocktail sauce, ketchup, or some other condiment or sauce to mask the taste of the shrimp, what difference does it make? Just sell them the cheapest products they can get their hands on.

In Nick's opinion, this is like saying a steak is a steak. He assumed most American consumers would know that if they go to dinner at the Ritz-Carlton or a fine steakhouse, the cut of meat and taste will be above the norm and will not be similar to the taste of a steak at a budget steakhouse, and the consumer is willing to pay for that difference.

But the consumer is not given the choice on shrimp, because consumers have no idea where it comes from. Ironically, he knew of restaurants in Fernandina that sold foreign, pond-raised shrimp, instead of fresh, wild-caught Florida shrimp, because they could buy it cheaper from their wholesalers than they could buy it straight off the boat from Nick and his friends without any middlemen.

What made him really mad was his experience at Fernandina's annual Shrimp Festival, which was supposed to be a celebration of the town as the "birthplace of modern shrimping" — and yet most of the vendors and charities manning the food booths were selling cheap, inferior foreign shrimp. Only a few of the booths, like the Nassau Sports Fishing Club and St. Michael's Church, served real Fernandina shrimp.

He knew, from prices at the dock, that despite his costs going up, the international dumping of farm-raised shrimp on the market was forcing the price of shrimp downward. Over the previous five years, he had watched the dockside price of shrimp go down almost two dollars per pound, while his fuel costs, price to repair nets, ice, and labor had all gone up.

No doubt about it, if the local shrimp industry, indeed the entire American wild-caught shrimping industry, was going to survive, they would have to differentiate their product from the imported pond-raised version.

Fortunately, for him, he had made some valuable contacts with the chefs at Amelia Island Plantation and the Ritz-Carlton Amelia Island, plus some of the owners of the fine restaurants downtown, like Brett's Waterfront Café and the Marina Restaurant, to sell shrimp from his boats and some of his friends' boats, directly to the restaurants.

He also had his little black book of local residents who

liked to be called when he came back with a particular good catch. They would soon show up at his dock, coolers in hand, and leave with ten to fifty pounds of shrimp. In addition, he had a list of regional restaurants and private individuals that he would ship shrimp to, packed in dry ice, at their request.

At his meetings involving shrimpers associations from other states, he learned that, due to international dumping of shrimp in U.S. markets, forcing the price per pound to go down, the domestic shrimp industry was losing shrimpers at an alarming rate. In the 1970s, there were almost fifteen hundred trawler licenses sold in Georgia, but last year he'd heard that it was down to only about five hundred. Texas had almost five thousand vessels licensed for shrimping at the beginning of the 1990s. At the end of the decade, there were less than three thousand licensed.

The ironic thing to him was that in 2001, shrimp passed tuna as America's favorite seafood, by consumption. So the shrimper's product was in great demand, and more people were eating shrimp than ever before in the United States, it just wasn't United States shrimp. Even with the great demand, it was getting hard for domestic shrimpers to sell the shrimp at a price that would cover their costs and allow for a decent living. While the price of shrimp was going down, fuel costs, boat insurance, dockage, and other costs were going up. These factors were threatening people like him, some of whom had been shrimping for generations, and now their very livelihood was at stake.

* * *

"Strike three!" said the umpire behind home plate.

"Way to go, Mattie," Nick said, as he crammed another

279

The Ocean under the Moon

French fry into his mouth. Nothing like baseball to take your mind off your troubles, he thought.

The Ocean under the Moon

Chapter 31

May 7, 2005

"Come on, Zoti. Hurry up. We're going to miss the best tide for the waves," Terry Sneed called from his bike, as he looked back over his shoulder at him.

Terry and Zoti had grown up together, in the same grade at school, and been best friends since Mrs. Tester's first grade class. The boys were always together; usually surfing in the morning when the swells were smooth from lack of wind, and playing soccer in the afternoon, after the sea breeze turned the waves choppy.

"We're coming," he responded. He was referring to himself and Pepe, who was trotting happily at his side.

He hadn't felt well this morning when he woke up. Usually, he couldn't wait to get up and head to the beach to surf the waves. The boys' parents wouldn't let either of them go surfing alone, just in case one of them hit their head on the board or something, so the boys made a pact to meet at sunrise on days that the waves were supposed to be good, to go together. This particular morning the waves were supposed to be four feet, glassy, with a light, west wind.

Since Terry lived on the way to the beach from Zoti's

house, it was Zoti's job to get up first, then go by his friend's house and wake him up. This morning, however, he'd fallen back to sleep; therefore, he was running about fifteen minutes behind schedule. When he'd woken up for good this morning, he felt fatigued. He also noticed the neck area under his right jaw bone was swollen and was a little tender to the touch, when he pressed on it.

Maybe he was starting to catch a cold, or even the flu. But he wasn't going to let a little cold stop him from experiencing one of the best surfing days that had come along in awhile.

He prided himself on his stamina. Surfing had built up his upper body, giving him broad shoulders for his age and the characteristic V-shaped back of a proficient surfer. Soccer had built up his legs, along with his lungs and heart. He'd become quite a specimen of health at his age. He also looked the part of a surfer dude. Unlike Matt, who had the dark, curly hair of his father, Zoti had straight, sun-bleached blond hair like his mother, and a dark tan from days spent out on the water.

This morning, however, he was finding it hard to keep up with his friend, who was pedaling down the sidewalk on Atlantic Avenue in his hurry to get to the waves. Soon the two boys and the dog had made it to Main Beach. Terry got there first and jumped off his bike, letting it fall to the ground in the grass in the park, right before the sand dunes that led to the beach. He tucked the surfboard under his arm and headed for the waves. Zoti was close behind, with Pepe barking and running circles around his legs.

The sight of perfect waves hastened the boys' run across the beach. The boys dashed into the water, running splay-legged

282

through the shallow water, jumping over the smaller waves until
they got too deep to run. Then they hurtled themselves forward,
pulling their surfboards under their chests, landing with a thud,
with their momentum propelling them toward deeper water.

Pepe, as he had finally learned to do, stopped when the
water got up to his chest and stood barking furiously at the boys, as
he jumped over the small waves that approached him.

The boys had surfed about an hour and the red sun had
pulled itself clear of the horizon and now was a yellow ball, fully
up in the sky, making the boys squint as they stared into its
blinding reflection, searching for the best waves. Zoti usually
caught nearly twice as many waves as Terry.

He was what the older surfers called a wave-hog. He
would ride any wave that came near him. He believed that quantity
would eventually lead to quality. But he always worked harder
than most surfers. With an uncanny eye to spot the best swell
coming in from the deep ocean, he would paddle, parallel to the
beach, to get himself in the proper position to catch the wave, just
as it peaked, before it broke, and also to be at the spot just to the left
or right of the curl of the wave.

On this day, however, he was being more selective. He
just didn't have his usual energy, so he was content to sit on his
board, like the other surfers, and let the waves come to him. He
was floating, squinting into the early morning sun, when he felt a
warm liquid run down from his nose into his mouth. It tasted salty
and he just thought it was seawater until he wiped above his upper
lip with his hand and was surprised to see blood on his hand.

About that time, Terry, who'd been sitting on his own

board just a few feet away from him, looked over.

"Dude, you're bleeding," he said, in astonishment. "Did you hit yourself?"

"No, it must be a nose bleed," Zoti said, puzzled, never having one before.

"Well, you better go in before you attract sharks," Terry said, half-kidding and half-serious.

"I've never heard of a shark attack here," Zoti said.

"Well, I don't want to be the first. Why don't you go on to shore? When you get the bleeding stopped you can come back out."

He reluctantly agreed and paddled back in towards the shore, catching a breaking wave and riding on his belly, on his surfboard, all the way to the beach. Pepe greeted him in the shallow water, running alongside him, as he rode all the way in until his skeg touched bottom.

He jumped off his board and ran over to where he had dropped his towel on the beach earlier. It took him quite awhile, and ruined his towel, before he could get the bleeding to stop.

Zoti never did return to the ocean that morning — he just didn't feel up to it. He must have been pushing himself too hard, between the soccer and the surfing. If he just rested for a day, he felt maybe he would be back to his old self. Tomorrow was Sunday, so he would be able to rest all afternoon after going to church in the morning. If he didn't feel better by Monday, he would ask his mother to take him to the doctor.

But for right now, he just lay back on the blood-stained towel and soaked up the warmth of the early morning sun. Soon he

The Ocean under the Moon

fell asleep on the warm sand.

Chapter 32

May 8, 2005

Zoti, did not feel better the next day; in fact, he felt worse. He woke up feeling hot and Monica measured his fever at one hundred and one. She sent Matt and Nick to church, while she stayed home to care for him. She made him chicken soup for breakfast and forced him to eat some of it. She told him that this was what he got for "overdoing it" and that he shouldn't always get up so early to go surfing.

He felt confident that if he just stayed in bed for a day, he would bounce right back. Not that he would mind staying sick, for awhile, so he could miss school for a day or two.

So he lay there all day, watching bad TV re-runs and all the sports that come on TV on Sunday afternoons. His fever, however, didn't change. It didn't get worse, nor did it get better. His mother informed him that if his fever continued, they were going to see the doctor Monday morning. This didn't displease him, because it was always good not to have to go to school on a Monday.

He didn't really care for school. He loved being outside enjoying nature. In school, he felt like a caged animal. All he wanted to be was a professional surfer. He wanted to travel the world, riding the waves in all the best places. He knew the odds were stacked against him. The waves on the east coast of Florida are not the best to breed a professional surfer. The waves were often small and mushy, limiting his practice time. The waves in this area only approach the types of waves he would see at professional tournaments when a hurricane or tropical depression runs up the coast, staying far enough off shore to generate swells, but not so close as to incur the winds that would chop up the water.

If professional surfing didn't work out for him, he could always try soccer, and if that didn't work out, at the very least, he knew he could go to work for his father, running one of his shrimp boats.

Monday morning, he was no better, and his mother took him to the doctor. Not too long ago, in order to try and save some money on medical insurance premiums, the Nassau County School Board had switched from a traditional insurance to a health maintenance organization, or HMO, insurance.

She and most of the other teachers had not been happy with the switch, but it was the school board's decision and if they wanted to keep their group insurance through the school board, the teachers had to go along with the decision. Since Nick, as a self-employed shrimper, did not have access to group insurance and an individual policy was very expensive, they didn't have any choice but to join the HMO.

Since Dr. Evan Hardy, the boy's pediatrician since birth, did not accept the HMO, due to his already busy workload and the HMO's low reimbursement rates, she had to find another primary physician that accepted the HMO and was on their panel.

The Ocean under the Moon

Monica was loyal to Dr. Hardy, who had always provided great care for her sons and hated the fact that the insurance company could come between the doctor-patient relationship. Zoti, although he'd always liked Dr. Hardy, was embarrassed, now that he was older, to have to sit with the little kids in his waiting room, so he was kind of pleased to be switching doctors.

Monica had decided on Dr. Hunter Davis, a young, new doctor, who'd come to town just six months before and was eager to accept new patients. He was from Macon, Georgia, and had gone to Mercer University in Macon for his undergraduate degree, medical school, and residency in family medicine. He was from her mother's hometown, and Monica was well-acquainted with the town from her visits to her grandparents' home when she was young. She felt he would be easy to talk to and they would have a lot of common ground.

She was right. Both she and Zoti liked him and had a nice visit with the young doctor. Zoti was impressed with Dr. Davis's youth and love of sports. She enjoyed talking to him about people and places in Macon they both were familiar with.

He reassured her that Zoti probably just had a virus or touch of the flu. But just to be safe, he took a throat culture and drew some blood for further analysis to rule out mononucleosis or something more complicated, the earnest young doctor explained. Then he wrote a prescription for some antibiotics for her son to take, prophylactically, until the test results could be analyzed.

Dr. Davis said he would try to get the lab to rush the results of his blood work, but the HMO was contracted with just one lab in Jacksonville to do all of its work in the Jacksonville, area, so he didn't know how big the lab's backlog was or how effective his request would be.

In the meantime, he wanted Zoti to stay out of school, in case he had mononucleosis, and wrote him a note, excusing him for the rest of the week. This pleased Zoti to no end, but Monica assured him that she would be visiting his teachers at the middle school and bringing home his work for him to do.

* * *

Zoti spent the next three days resting, watching TV, and doing the school work that his mother brought home for him. On Friday, Dr. Davis called Monica, after she'd gotten home from school and was sitting with Nick.

"The good news," Dr. Davis began," is that Zoti's monospot and Epstein-Barr antibody test came back negative, which means he doesn't have mononucleosis. However, if he doesn't get better in the next ten to twelve days, we'll have to repeat the test. Sometimes, if the blood is drawn early in the infection, the antibodies may have not shown up in the blood yet, leading to a false negative.

"The bad news, however," the doctor continued, "is that his white blood cell count is up and his red blood cell count, hemoglobin, and platelet count are all down. This means there is something going on in his blood system. I want y'all to go to Nemours Children Hospital, at ten o'clock Monday, for further testing. The HMO is not going to like me referring it out so soon, but I want to get a differential diagnosis as soon as possible from the specialists, so we know how to deal with this."

"Is it serious?" she asked, alarmed by the doctor's concern

289

and the term "specialists."

"I don't want to speculate until we have a definite diagnosis," he answered. "In the meantime, just keep him resting and taking his antibiotics."

"That's easier said than done, on both counts," she said. "He's already going stir crazy."

"Well, the antibiotics he's taking will make him photosensitive, so be sure he doesn't get out in the sun at all and definitely, no surfing. He needs to rest as much as possible so his body can recover."

The doctor knew, if the boy had what he suspected he had, that the antibiotics were just a placebo effect and to help prevent any secondary infections. It was going to take something a lot stronger and more toxic to the human body, than antibiotics, to get rid of his disorder.

The fever, fatigue, swollen lymph nodes, the nose bleed, the high white blood cell count, and the low red blood cell count, added up to one possible diagnosis in his mind. It was not a diagnosis any doctor wanted to tell the parents of a child, particularly, the child of a nice woman like Mrs. Stamos. Now, he was supposed to tell this woman her son had a disease that might kill him. Medical school doesn't really teach you how to do that.

No, it was better to let the specialist confirm the diagnosis with a bone marrow aspiration and biopsy. Then, once the diagnosis had been confirmed, the specialist could break the bad news.

Besides he wasn't one hundred percent sure of the diagnosis. While most signs and symptoms pointed toward leukemia, there were a couple of factors that didn't fit. First, at twelve years old, Zoti was older than most children who developed leukemia, the average age of onset being between three and seven years old. That is why he'd suspected mono at first, which was much more consistent with his age group. His older age of onset worked for him, as far as not likely to be leukemia, but if that diagnosis was confirmed, his prognosis would be worse now than if he was younger.

The second factor that puzzled him was Zoti did not have any signs of pallor of the skin, or petechiae, which were tiny red spots under the skin. His dark tan from surfing, however, may have masked these two signs, he assumed. These two factors left enough doubt in his mind, to justify not telling Mrs. Stamos of his tentative diagnosis.

"You'll be seeing Dr. Christopher Lindstrom down at Nemours. He is a very good doctor and I will be in constant touch with him about Zoti's condition. In the meantime, enjoy your weekend and make sure he gets his rest," he concluded.

"Thank you, doctor. I will." She was still not certain whether she should worry or not. She didn't know how she was going to keep him inside all weekend; he was already "bouncing off the walls" and living up to his name, Zotikos—full of life.

She put the phone down and stared off into space. She had no way of knowing that her son had a disease that would test the very premise of his name.

The Ocean under the Moon

Chapter 33

May 16, 2005

"Listen to this," Monica began. "The Nemours Foundation runs one of the largest pediatric healthcare systems in the country. The system presently consists of the Alfred I. duPont Hospital for Children in Wilmington, Delaware, numerous clinics in Delaware and parts of Pennsylvania and New Jersey. In Florida, Nemours runs children's clinics in Jacksonville, Pensacola, and Orlando. Now, Nemours employs over four hundred physicians and four thousand employees."

She was reading from a brochure that came in the new patient packet she'd received from Nemours a few days ago. They were driving down I-95 on their way to the clinic in Jacksonville.

The family had left their house thirty minutes earlier. Nick was driving, Monica was in the passenger's seat, and Zoti was sleeping in the back seat. Nick had let Gator take out the *Resurrection* with Willie Cooper as his deckhand, because Monica insisted that he accompany her today.

He didn't know why he had to go with them today. Zoti probably just contracted some "bug" and, with rest and the antibiotics, would be fine in a few days. In fact, his son had started feeling better over the weekend and it took both of them to keep an eye on him, to make sure he didn't sneak out of the house to go fishing or whatever.

It's not that he didn't trust Gator with his boat—by now his deckhand could run it just as well as he, himself, could. But Nick had never been sick a day in his life and he detested the idea of sitting in a clinic all day, waiting for Zoti to be seen. He was used to being outside, working in the fresh air and sunshine. The very thought of sitting in a crowded waiting room, then some holding room, waiting for a test to be performed, made his skin crawl.

He remembered when Matt had his tonsils out and when Monica had her delivery problems, the days of hanging around the hospital. He'd been like a tiger in a cage, pacing back and forth. The thought of doctors and hospitals brought on a phobia for him, as if he entered a hospital, he would catch some malady and never be allowed to leave alive.

Monica was still glancing through the brochure. "It says that the Nemours Foundation got its start from a trust from one of the duPont heirs that moved to Jacksonville, Alfred I. duPont," she said, interrupting Nick's thoughts. "When he died, in 1935, his estate was valued at over fifty-six million dollars. Since he was orphaned, while young, and also had been blind in one eye and suffered from serious hearing loss, he always had great empathy for disabled children, so his will left the bulk of his estate to the trust to provide the treatment and care of ill and disabled children."

They pulled up at the front of the large, impressive Nemours Children's Clinic at 807 Children's Way. The twelve-story building was just off I-95, near the south bank of the St. John's

293

River. It was connected by a pedestrian suspension bridge to the Wolfson Children's Hospital on the other side of the freeway.

As they walked toward the clinic, Nick wondered why they needed such a prestigious place to discover the source of Zoti's malaise. Dr. Davis had said they were just going to do more extensive testing. The young doctor told them that the doctors at Nemours were going to draw blood again, to repeat some of the blood work already done, but also that Zoti was going to have a bone marrow aspiration and biopsy.

Dr. Davis had explained that this procedure was a little more invasive than just drawing blood and involved using a long needle to withdraw bone marrow from Zoti's hip bone. He said this was being done just to rule out anything more serious than just a virus. The young doctor didn't elaborate on what they were ruling out and Nick and Monica didn't ask, because they didn't want to worry Zoti or themselves unnecessarily.

They walked into the large, expansive waiting room on the first floor. Monica went up to the reception desk while Nick and Zoti plopped down on a couple of soft chairs in the waiting area. She presented the receptionist with Dr. Davis' HMO referral letter and was asked to have a seat, until they were called.

Nick watched the people coming and going while Zoti and Monica picked up a couple of magazines to read. He noticed all kinds of children with their parents. He looked over beside the elevators where a large sign listed the specialties: Urology, Orthopedics, Endocrinology, Oncology, Otorhinolaryngology, Pulmonology, Genetics, General Surgery, Ophthalmology, and more. He hadn't realized that children could have so many problems.

He tried to guess which children were coming for whatever condition. He surmised the obese children were probably headed to the diabetic clinic on the endocrinology floor. The orthopedics were easy to spot with their casts, crutches, and limps. But the saddest and most obvious were the oncology kids, with their bald heads covered by hats, and their sunken eyes, giving them a thin, holocaust victim-like appearance. He couldn't help but stare at these kids. How sad it was that their lives were being threatened, before they could really get started.

After about a twenty-minute wait, Zoti's name was called and all of them stood up and approached the reception desk. They were told to go up to the eighth floor to the hematology department. They rode the elevator up and entered another smaller reception area. After approaching another reception desk, they were asked to have a seat and were told Nurse Bradwish would be right with them.

Soon, Nurse Evelyn Bradwish, a petite, efficient looking woman in her forties, approached them, introduced herself and asked them to follow her. In a small treatment room, she asked Zoti to sit on the treatment table, and guided Nick and Monica to a couple of empty chairs in the corner.

"First, we are going to be drawing some blood," she said, matter-of-factly. "Let me see your arm."

The nurse took his wrist and turned his palm up. With her other hand, she thumped the vein in the crook of his right elbow with her forefinger to make the vein stand out. After swabbing the area with alcohol, she inserted a syringe and withdrew a vial of his

The Ocean under the Moon

blood into the cylinder. Monica had to turn her eyes away, but Zoti watched the whole thing without batting an eye.

She put the vial in a plastic bag for processing later. Then she picked up a clipboard with some forms on it and handed it to Nick.

"This is the informed consent to do the bone marrow aspiration and biopsy. Look it over carefully and sign at the bottom."

Nick, with Monica looking over his shoulder, read the two-page form, which described how Zoti would lie down on his right side on a table. A local anesthetic would then be applied to his left lower back, and a long, thin needle would be inserted into the rear left hip bone and aspire a small amount of bone marrow, which looks like blood. After the blood marrow aspiration, the doctor would then take a large needle further down into the bone and wiggle the needle from side to side to loosen a larger sample for biopsy.

The form went on to say that this is a very common and safe procedure, but like any procedure, there was always a chance of infection and other possible complications, which it listed. They read through the entire form. Then, Nick looked up at the nurse.

"It sounds kind of invasive. Is this procedure really necessary?"

The nurse frowned at the question. "Didn't your primary doctor explain why we are doing these tests?"

"He just said we were doing them to rule out other things that were more serious than a viral infection. He didn't go into all the possibilities, he said, because he didn't want to speculate,"

The Ocean under the Moon

Monica said.

The nurse cringed at Monica's explanation. The experienced nurse realized these people were clueless and wished their primary doctor had been more forthcoming with them. She hated being the bearer of bad news; even though she worked in a clinic that dealt with the toughest childhood illnesses, she never got used to it. She didn't want to scare these people, but she needed to scare them enough to get them to sign the release form.

"According to your son's previous blood work, your son is anemic. One possible cause of anemia in children is leukemia. In order to rule that out, we need to do these procedures," she said, in a tone as though it was just a routine procedure, belying her true suspicions.

Upon hearing the word leukemia, Nick and Monica glanced over at each other. All he could think about, when he heard that word, was the sullen, walking-death look on some of the kids' faces in the lobby.

"Leukemia?" he said.

"Yes," she said. "Your son has a lot of the signs and symptoms of leukemia, but he is a little older than its usual age of onset, so we need to do these tests to rule it out."

He liked the sound of "rule it out." Surely, his beautiful, youngest son, who was so full of energy and life, did not have leukemia. That was impossible. Hopefully, this test would prove that. He signed the form and gave it back to the nurse. The nurse took back the form with a look of satisfaction on her face. Her mission was accomplished.

"Now, you two can go back to the reception area, while I

take Zoti to another room where the procedure will be performed."

They did as they were asked and watched as Zoti disappeared down the hall with the nurse. Nick thought about asking if he could accompany them, but the image of watching a long needle go into his son's hip did not appeal to him.

Zoti returned to the waiting area after a short time, limping slightly, with Nurse Bradwish not far behind. He sat down gingerly on a chair beside his parents, while she approached.

"The biopsy went well. We got what we needed," she said. "His hip will be sore for a day or two, then it will be back to normal. We are going to analyze the blood work and the biopsy. We have a conference scheduled here with Dr. Lindstrom Thursday to go over the test results. So go home and get some rest and we will see you Thursday, at three o'clock."

"Can we go get something to eat now? I'm starving," Zoti said, like a true child, only worried about his stomach.

"Sure," his father said, glad Zoti still had his appetite. Nurse Bradwish looked at them and gave him a wistful smile.

"See you on Thursday," Monica said to her as they turned to leave.

* * *

The next few days went by slowly. At first, Zoti said he liked missing school, but now, he was bored and missed his friends. Monica had to go back to work, so Nick stayed home with him, letting Gator run his boat for a few more days. She left Nick all the schoolwork Zoti's teachers had given her, and it was like pulling teeth to get him to do his work. After Zoti did his schoolwork in the mornings, Nick let him watch television. But the weather outside was beautiful and both of them were going stir-crazy.

Nick wished his mother and father were still alive. They wouldn't have minded watching Zoti. But Abe had died of colon cancer three years before, and Isabelle had died a year later of a heart attack—although Nick thought it was a broken heart and lack of will to live, after her husband had died. Now they were buried in the family plot at Bosque Bello, side by side, with Eber and Catherine.

They had practically raised Matt and Zoti when the boys were younger. The boys were quite close to their grandparents and were hit hard by each of their deaths. It was the boys' first experience with death and reality.

Now, he did not know what the future held for his son. They had spent the last few days skirting the issue, not really wanting to come with grips with the fact that their youngest son might have cancer.

"That wouldn't be fair, would it?" he had asked of his wife.

Fair or not, it was what they were facing. They were hoping it was just a false alarm. That's why they didn't call Buck or Caroline to come down and help watch Zoti, while they worked. Monica didn't want to alarm them. Therefore, all they knew was that he was "a little under the weather."

Thursday rolled around and they headed back down to Nemours for their conference with Dr. Lindstrom. All three of them were quiet on the ride over to Jacksonville, lost in their thoughts.

Again, they rode the elevator up to the eighth floor, and

strode up to the reception desk. At the reception desk a pretty, young girl with short brown hair received them with a warm smile.

"We are the Stamoses. We're here to see Dr. Lindstrom," Nick said.

"Yes, Dr. Lindstrom is expecting you. However, he's still with a patient. I'll show you to his office and he will be with you in a few minutes," the girl said.

She led them down a hallway to a small office containing a cherry desk with three chairs in front of it. The walls were lined with plaques and bookcases. Zoti and Monica sat down, while Nick inspected the plaques and diplomas on the wall.

He ascertained that Dr. Lindstrom went to Duke University for both undergraduate and medical school. Another diploma showed the doctor had gone to Johns Hopkins University for a residency in internal medicine, with a subspecialty in hematology.

Finally, Nick sat down and noticed a family portrait on the bookcase behind the desk. He assumed this was a portrait of the good doctor and his family. The doctor appeared to be a portly man about forty-five years old with a balding head and wearing spectacles. His brunette wife looked much younger and prettier than the man deserved, if he hadn't been a successful doctor. The son and daughter in the picture appeared to be about ten and twelve years old, respectively, and were a little on the pudgy side.

Just then the door to the office burst open, startling him, and Dr. Lindstrom rushed in, looking exactly like his picture.

"Sorry for the wait, but my schedule has me just a little behind today," he began. "I'm Dr. Lindstrom, head of the hematology department here at Nemours." He shook hands with each of them.

After sitting down behind the desk and grasping the folder in front of him, he let out a sigh and began talking.

"Hematology is the study of blood disorders. Most of the time, our blood system works wonderfully well and we take it for granted. Sometimes, however, things can go awry. Unfortunately, Dr. Davis was right to send Zoti over here for further testing. The blood work and biopsy confirm that your son has Acute Lymphoblastic Leukemia, also called Acute Lymphocytic Leukemia, or ALL for short."

"Oh, my God," gasped Monica.

Nick's and Monica's hearts sank with the word, leukemia. Zoti blithely took the news, assuming, as kids tend to, that he was invincible. He would overcome this disease, whatever it was, and would soon be back surfing. That was his main concern.

"I've got a big surfing tournament in a month. Will I be well by then?" he asked.

"Well, I'm afraid it's not quite that simple," the doctor began. "Zoti, I know you may not feel it yet, but you are a very sick young man," he continued.

"Have any of you ever heard of ALL before?" All three of them shook their heads from side to side.

"Leukemia is a type of cancer that begins in blood cells. Your bone marrow, specifically your red bone marrow, produces blood cells in the form of red blood cells, platelets, and white blood cells. The red blood cells' purpose is to carry oxygen from the lungs to the rest of the body. The platelets are important in blood clotting.

The white blood cells protect the body against infection. In people with leukemia, the bone marrow produces abnormal white blood cells which, in time, crowd out the red cells, platelets, and the normal white cells."

Nick frowned, trying to follow all the details. Monica reached for his hand, as she stared at the doctor.

"In Acute Lymphoblastic Leukemia, which is the most common type of cancer in children, the immature blast cells, which ordinarily develop into healthy blood cells, are arrested in their development. These abnormal cells then crowd out the normal cells. Normal bone marrow contains less than five percent blast cells because the blast cells are constantly turning into red blood cells, platelets, and white blood cells. Unfortunately, Zoti's biopsy showed that abnormal blast cells constitute forty-nine percent of his bone marrow." The doctor paused and then continued.

"The amount of abnormal blast cells in his bone marrow explains the results of his blood work. Zoti's platelet count is low, hence the nose bleed. His red blood cell count and hemoglobin are down, therefore his fatigue and general feeling of malaise. His white blood cell count is up, but they are the wrong kind of cells. The body is fighting infection, both real and imagined, hence the fever. The biopsy confirms that he has ALL and also explains all of his symptoms.

"Any questions so far?" he asked.

"What causes it?" Nick asked.

"We don't know," he answered. "We do know it only affects about one in twenty-five thousand children every year in the United States. It affects boys more than girls and Caucasian children more than Afro-American children."

"Can it be treated?" Monica asked.

"Yes, with modern treatment options the cure rate for ALL is about sixty-five to ninety-five percent. The treatment is not simple, however. It involves several months of intensive chemotherapy treatments. Zoti is going to feel worse before he feels better, due to the invasive nature of his treatments."

Monica took a deep breath and put an arm around Zoti's shoulders.

"The first phase of treatment lasts about one month and is called inductive chemotherapy," Dr. Lindstrom said. "The goal of this is to achieve a remission. He probably has close to one hundred billion leukemia cells in his body right now. Our goal is to kill at least ninety-nine-point-nine percent of the cells within one month with the chemotherapy. This will be enough to achieve a remission, which will allow his body to start producing normal blood cells again. We are able to achieve this type of remission in about ninety-five percent of children after about a month of therapy.

"The problem is, even after killing ninety-nine-point-nine percent of the cancer cells, that still leaves about one hundred million leukemia cells in the body. The goal of the next phase of treatment, which is called the consolidation or intensification phase, is to kill these remaining cancer cells. Chemotherapy and several drugs are used in combination to prevent the remaining bad cells from developing a resistance to the medication. This phase will last about four to eight months," he said.

"If the consolidation phase works, as confirmed by another biopsy, then the maintenance phase will begin. That phase is to kill any leftover leukemia cells that weren't killed in the first two phases. The presence of just a few cells can result in a relapse, if they are not completely eradicated, so the maintenance phase continues for about two to three years."

"So, I guess the surfing tournament is out," Zoti said ruefully.

"I'm afraid so, Zoti," the doctor said. "You'll probably be feeling really ill in about one month, from all of the chemo drugs. Plus, you are going to be at great risk for infection, after we kill all of your white blood cells, so we are going to have to keep a close watch over you. You may even have to stay in the hospital during this time."

"Aah, man," he said. "I hate hospitals."

"You might as well get used to it, Zoti. You and I are going to be seeing a lot of each other in the next couple of years. I know this is not what you want to be doing at this age. You should be out surfing and having fun. But this is what you have to do, if you want to stay alive."

One in twenty-five thousand, Nick thought. Why did his son have to be that one in twenty-five thousand?

Monica, in shock, looked at her son. His sun-bleached hair and lingering tan belied the fact that he had a serious disease. He'd always been her rambunctious child, so energetic and lively. It was hard to imagine that deep down inside his bones, his bone marrow was rapidly producing these defective cells that could kill him. She turned away and started sobbing.

"Now, now, Mrs. Stamos," the doctor said in a consoling manner. "Remember, we have an overall chance of about eighty-five percent of beating this disease."

She heard this, and trying to compose herself, nodded her head in agreement. She did this for Zoti's sake only, because as a mother all she heard was her son had a fifteen percent chance of dying.

The Ocean under the Moon

Chapter 34

June 15, 2005

"How are you feeling, Zoti?" Dr. Lindstrom asked.

Zoti was sitting in front of his desk, flanked by his parents. He looked quite different than the boy the doctor had seen just one month before. Gone were the blond, surfer-boy locks. He was wearing a Jacksonville Jaguars hat to cover up his bald head. Also gone were his tan and healthy appearance. The boy sitting across from him was pale, thin, and stared back at him with sunken, almost pleading eyes.

The doctor had witnessed his transition from a healthy, sun-kissed surfer to a boy who was bald and looked near death, during his treatment over the last month. The sympathetic doctor hated that about his job. In order to save his patients, sometimes he had to push them almost to the brink of death. The goal of the initial treatment, after all, is to achieve remission by destroying millions of cells—the leukemia cells—so normal cells can grow again.

Over the last several weeks, he'd given Zoti weekly doses of two strong chemotherapy drugs. Viacristine is a mitotic inhibitor derived from the Madagascar periwinkle plant, while Daunorubicin is from the anthracycline family and intercalates with the DNA molecule of the rapidly growing cancer cells, inhibiting DNA replication. He knew that chemo is like poison to the body, and the normal bone marrow cells are killed along with the bad ones, leaving the patient weak, pale, and nauseous.

Zoti had been a regular visitor to Nemours over the past month and even spent a couple of weeks in Wolfson Children's Hospital, across the interstate, to manage the side effects and complications from his treatment. Besides dealing with the usual side effects from chemotherapy treatment, hair loss, mouth sores, loss of appetite, nausea, and vomiting, he'd endured blood and platelet transfusions to treat anemia and to prevent bleeding. The chemo drugs had nearly killed off all of his red blood cells, white blood cells and platelets, and it would take awhile until his bone marrow could recover and produce some normal ones.

Another reason for his hospital stay during this time was to keep close watch out for infection, since he possessed very few white blood cells to fight infection. The doctor put him on antibiotics during this time as a preventive measure, because infections were the leading cause of death for ALL patients during this early phase of treatment.

During his stay in the hospital, Zoti also underwent intrathecal therapy. Because the central nervous system can serve as a region for the leukemia cells to hide from the other chemotherapy, he had to have a spinal tap and a triple cocktail of methotrexate, hydrocortisone, and cytosine arabinoside was injected straight into his spinal fluid. This procedure can have severe side effects, so Dr. Lindstrom watched him very carefully during this time.

The Ocean under the Moon

Zoti weathered the storm of the intensive chemotherapy, and its terrible side effects, and he was sitting in Dr. Lindstrom's office with his parents now to see if all of their efforts had achieved the desired effects.

"Good news, Zoti," Dr. Lindstrom began. "Your latest blood work shows that your blast cell count is four percent. Your blast cells are the immature cells that ordinarily develop into healthy blood cells. Remember, before starting treatments your blast cell count was at forty-nine percent. Normal bone marrow contains five percent or less of blast cells. This means you are officially in remission."

Nick looked over at Monica, who gasped in relief.

Zoti leaned forward and fist-bumped the doctor in celebration.

"Does this mean I can start surfing again?"

"Well, I'm afraid you're not out of the woods yet. This remission just means we got your bone marrow back to functioning normally, because we've eradicated ninety-nine-point-nine percent of the cancer cells. However, it's like trying to rid your lawn of weeds. You can pull the weeds by hand or spray with herbicides, but if you don't get every little seed and spore, the weeds can pop back up.

"This just means we move on to the consolidation therapy phase, where we use some of the same drugs, but the treatment regimen is a little different," the doctor said. "You will still have to travel over here for regular treatments, but you won't have to stay in the hospital, unless we run into some complications. This phase will last about four to eight months depending on how well you do.

The Ocean under the Moon

If all goes well, then we will move on to the maintenance phase where you will take your chemotherapy by pills, instead of intravenously, and at that time you can probably resume your normal lifestyle."

"Ah, man, I've got to wait another four months before I get to surf again?" he asked, in disgust.

"I know you want to get back to surfing as soon as possible, but I want you to wait until we finish the consolidation phase before you return to surfing. You are going to be anemic and weak at times from the chemotherapy. If you overdo it now, it may send you into relapse and extend the consolidation phase, and we have to start all over. So expend your energy now with getting caught up with your school work.

"I know this has been tough on you not being able to go to school, see your friends, and do the things you like to do. But you are fighting for your life and we need to give up some things now so you will have a long, healthy life in the future. Do you understand, Zoti?"

"Yes, Dr. Lindstrom. I understand."

Nick and Monica also nodded their understanding at what the doctor had said, as he stood up.

"We're making progress, but we still have a long way to go. Now, Zoti, it's time for another chemo treatment to see if we can get rid of that last one-tenth of a percent of leukemia cells."

Chapter 35

January 18, 2006

Nick sat at a small desk in the corner of the spare bedroom that served as his office. Spread on the desk before him were bills of all types. Between his shrimping business and Zoti's medical treatments, he seemed to be receiving three or four bills a day. The majority of the bills were for Zoti's treatment and were to be paid by his medical insurance for the most part.

Thank God they were able to get insurance through Monica's job. He, like most shrimpers, couldn't afford insurance through individual policies and Zoti's medical care would have forced them to sell their home and boats, to provide for his care. As it was, even with their HMO coverage, it was a battle to get all of the bills paid.

At first the HMO denied the bills, saying that Zoti had a pre-existing problem that should have been discovered while he was on his previous plan, before the school board switched to the HMO. Nick had to get Dr. Davis and Dr. Lindstrom to write letters saying this wasn't the case. Even after that, Nick was forced to write to the insurance commissioner's office and get them involved, before the HMO acquiesced and started paying the bills.

And even then, there were still co-pays and extra

treatments that the HMO didn't pay for entirely. The HMO's protocol for treating ALL and Nemours' protocol were quite different. Nick told the doctor that he wanted Zoti to have the finest of care, regardless of the cost, and he'd taken out a home equity line on his house to pay for the extras.

Still, it was confusing. He was receiving bills every day. He'd always been one to pay his bills in a timely fashion. It bothered him to keep receiving copies of bills that said they had been forwarded to his insurance for payment, but they seemed to take forever to get paid. Then when they did get paid, there always seemed to be some overage that he was forced to pay.

So even with the HMO's coverage, he'd run up a nearly one hundred thousand dollar debt on his home equity line. Fortunately, the house and his boats had been paid off, so this was a debt he could handle, even though the shrimping industry was not doing so good.

Catching the shrimp wasn't the problem. Nick and Gator on the *Resurrection* and Billy and Marty on the *Island Girl* had been coming back lately with their hulls full of shrimp. He'd sold the *Amelia Queen* after his father died; it made him too sentimental to look at the boat, because it reminded him of his father.

The problem was not the quantity of the shrimp, it was the price they were getting from the seafood processing plants. It was just enough to cover their basic expenses, with nothing left over for unusual expenses, like net tears, not to mention making a profit. Thank goodness for his little black book of loyal customers and his connections with local restaurants — with them, he was still able to eke out a meager living.

The Ocean under the Moon

Now as he stared at the mound of paperwork before him, he was just glad his son was getting better. It'd been a total of eight months since Zoti was first diagnosed with leukemia. At their last meeting with Dr. Lindstrom a week ago, he had seemed pleased with Zoti's progress.

In fact, this week, Zoti was starting the maintenance therapy, where he would take the chemotherapy by pill, so they wouldn't have to drive down to Nemours every week like they'd had to do for the last eight months. Dr. Lindstrom said if Zoti lasted three years on the maintenance therapy without a relapse, then he would in fact be "cured."

So even though he faced an hour or two of writing out bills, Nick did so with the relief that, for now, it seemed his precious, youngest son might have a normal life and get back to his usual exuberant self.

The Ocean under the Moon

Chapter 36

April 7, 2007

Zoti leaned back in his beach chair, closed his eyes, soaking up the warmth of the early-morning sun on his face and body. It'd been over one year since he'd started on the maintenance therapy for his leukemia. He had endured taking daily oral doses of mercaptopurine, plus oral methotrexate once a week, and a once-monthly five-day course of intravenous vincristine and oral corticosteroids.

When he wasn't feeling too sick from the side effects or receiving his intravenous therapy, he went to school. If it wasn't a school day, he would go surfing when he felt well enough. He never went surfing alone. His parents always insisted Terry or one of his other friends went along with him, to look after him. Of course, his dog always tagged along also. Pepe had missed going to the beach and following his energetic owner around town.

While Zoti was undergoing the initial treatments and staying in the hospital, Pepe, like many dogs do, sensed there was something wrong with his owner, particularly after Zoti lost his hair. Whenever he was home, Pepe would follow him around the house, right on his heels, no matter which room he went into. Even if it was just to get a glass of water or go to the bathroom, his dog would be right there behind him. When he sat down, the dog would sit next to him on the couch, put its head on his lap, and look up at him with big, sorrowful eyes.

Zoti's goal of being a professional surfer had suffered a serious set-back. But he was determined to make up for lost time and as soon as he felt well enough, he was back on the waves. It was tough at first; he'd lost most of his stamina. Just paddling out through the waves would leave him exhausted. He would have to rest and catch his breath for awhile before he could even think about catching a wave. Even after resting, he could only catch about a third of the waves he normally would, because he had to rest in between rides.

After awhile he had enough stamina back that he started competing again in local surfing tournaments. He was a natural on the waves and surfing came easy to him. He seemed to be in tune with the ocean and always in the right spot to catch the best waves, which is the secret to doing well in the contests.

This Easter weekend, they'd driven down to Cocoa Beach, so Zoti could compete in the 42nd Ron Jon Easter Surfing Festival. This event was the "Daytona 500" of the East Coast Surfing Association's series of contests, held during the spring and summer and culminating in the East Coast Championships in Virginia Beach, Virginia, in late August. Held for over four decades, always on Easter weekend, this surfing festival was always a resurrection or renewal of a new surfing season.

A large contest with events for men, women, boys, and girls, from ages six to sixty, the festival was a professionally run tournament, held at the same time in two locations on the beach.

The Ocean under the Moon

One was the Cocoa Beach Pier and the other was just south of the pier at Shepard Park. At both locations there were tents for the competitors, committee members, surfboard manufacturers, and clothing manufacturers. A booth for the announcers and a stage for the trophy presentations were also set up. All of this led to a festive atmosphere, almost like a medieval jousting tournament held by the ocean.

The weather always seemed to be good for the event, which was well appreciated by the people from up north, who had traveled down to the festival after a long winter. On this sunny Saturday morning, his parents had spread out their beach blanket and set up their beach chairs and umbrella in the soft, white sand. On the beach was a throng of people with their colorful beach chairs, umbrellas, and coolers.

The ocean was calm, but the swells were four to five feet, thanks to an offshore storm. These were good waves for Florida and perfect for the day's competition. Zoti was competing in the boys' short-board, fourteen-to-sixteen-year-old, amateur category. This was going to be his first big competition since he had been sick.

He had been doing well in competitions, before his illness. Competing in the ten-to-twelve-year-old division when he was twelve, he'd placed in the top three in several events in Florida and been in the top ten at the championship in Virginia Beach, at the end of that summer.

But now, for a whole year he hadn't been able to train at all. Even when he got the go-ahead from Dr. Lindstrom to start surfing again, it took quite awhile to get his stamina back. In the

315

last six months, however, he'd felt his strength returning. What he never lost, however, was the ability to make the surfboard do what he wanted it to beneath his feet. It was if the board was glued to his feet and whatever maneuver he tried, he could pull it off with ease.

He was hoping this weekend would announce to the other competitors that he was back in the game, that he could be competitive with the other elite amateur boys again. Yesterday, during the practice session, he'd gotten reacquainted with several of his former competitors from the younger age group. Most of them had heard about his illness and were glad to see him back out on his board again.

Today, however, he was competing against forty other boys. The boys would surf in four twenty-minute heats, in groups of ten. The top two surfers of each heat would advance to the final heat, consisting of the top eight. The final heat would last thirty minutes and decide the first-, second- and third-place winners.

* * *

Nick and Monica stared into the strong, early-morning sun. The surfing contests were always held early in the morning to take advantage of the clean waves, before the wind picked up and made them choppy. Their son's heat was getting ready to start. They squinted into the glare, trying to keep their eyes on him, as he bobbed among his nine competitors maneuvering for position within the marked-off area, waiting for the horn to blast, signaling the beginning of the heat.

Finally, the air horn blasted and all eyes of the beach-goers trained in on the competitors. Nick just hoped with all his heart that Zoti finished in the top two of his heat and made it to the finals. That would be victory enough. After all his son had been through, he didn't expect him to be that competitive with the other boys. But he knew if Zoti didn't make it at least to the final heat, his son would be very disappointed. He didn't want him to have any more disappointments in life, after the last couple of years.

Nick kept his eyes trained on his son and saw that he was doing very well. Zoti was working hard to get himself in the best possible position and had caught several nice waves. He beat several of the other boys to the inside position, next to the curl of the wave, which renders the best points. The twenty minutes went by fast and soon the air born blew again, signaling the end of that heat.

Zoti soon came running up to them, board under his arm, dripping wet, but with a big grin on his face.

"You looked good out there," Nick said as he approached.

"Man, it was awesome. I'm so stoked to be out there doing my thing again. The waves were perfect!"

"How do you think you did?" his mother asked.

"I don't really care," he said. "I just had the best time of my life. But, you know, I think I did pretty well. I caught some nice waves and seemed to be in the right position at the right time."

"You looked great out there," she said, tears welling in her eyes.

"Ah, man. Don't get mushy on me now. If I make it through to the final, I still got a lot of surfing to do," he said.

"Well, sit down and rest," Nick said. "It's going to be a while before the results come out. There's still one more heat to do in the preliminary round."

The Ocean under the Moon

* * *

Zoti sat on the blanket, drank a bottle of water, and then lay back to rest in the warm sun. He hadn't felt this good in a long while. His strength had started to come back in the last six months and now he felt back to his usual self. It'd been a long, hard road, but if he could do well in his tournament, it would signify that he was back in form.

After another twenty-minute heat and about another twenty minutes to tabulate the results, the surfing officials posted the results on the scoreboard.

"Yes!" he said, as he pumped his fist, when he saw his name listed among the finalists.

"Congratulations," Nick said.

"Good job, honey." Monica smiled and patted Zoti's shoulder.

Now, he needed to get ready for the finals. If he could just place in the top three and get on the podium, he would be ecstatic. He studied the names of the other competitors in the top eight, and recognized most of the names from the boys he used to surf against before he got sick. He knew from his past experiences, and also from the talk on the beach, that his toughest competitors were going to be Andy Lopez from Sebastian Inlet and Brian Williams from New Smyrna. Last year, Andy had dominated the circuit and if Andy didn't win, then Brian did.

He knew that even if he did his best, the most he could hope for was third place. But even that would be a good accomplishment for him, because of his time off and the quality of the rest of the field. While he was standing there looking at the list

318

of names, Andy came up beside him to check out the board.

He glanced over at Andy, who'd been just a skinny little kid when they last competed against each other in the ten-to-twelve-year-old division. Now he noticed that Andy was much more muscular and mature.

Andy turned from the board and saw him.

"Zoti? Is that you?"

"Yeah, it's me, man."

Andy came over and clasped his hand in an upraised handshake.

"It's good to see you, man. I saw your name on the board. It's hard to forget that name. It's good to have you back out here. I heard about your illness. Are you doing better now?"

"Yeah, dude. I'm good, now."

"Well, glad to have you back out here, man. Good luck to you out there today," he said. He gave Zoti a pat on the shoulder, as he turned to head back toward the water.

Zoti headed back to their spot on the beach, to wax his board one more time. He was pleased that Andy had remembered him. After all, it'd been over two years since he'd competed and Andy was the dominant surfer now. It was good to see that all of Andy's success hadn't gone to his head.

After he had waxed his board, and after receiving his parents' well-wishes, he headed out on the water. Since Andy was the dominant surfer in the group, Zoti took up a position close enough to him to keep an eye on him, but not so close as to get in his way. However, most of the other surfers possessed the same idea, so Zoti decided to paddle out of the pack to get some clear water away from the group.

He saw a good swell coming just as the horn went off to signal the beginning of the heat. He paddled to his left to get in position to catch the wave in the proper spot. He got to his chosen position just in time, sat up and swiveled his board toward the beach. With a few quick, sharp strokes he was being propelled toward the shore by the cresting wave.

He stood up on his board the second before the wave broke. He raced down the face of the wave, staying in front of the curl. When he reached the bottom of the wave, he made an abrupt turn back up the face of the wave and then when he reached the crest, he did another one-hundred-eighty-degree turn and raced back to the bottom of the wave. He made a few more sharp maneuvers before the wave petered out.

A good start, he thought. He gathered the board beneath him to start paddling back out.

But as he glanced to his right, he saw Andy cutting up a nice wave with sharp, crisp maneuvers. He knew he was going to have to surf his best, if he was going to keep up with Andy. This just made him more determined, as he paddled to get out past the breaking waves and get back into position to catch a wave before it broke.

He worked hard during the thirty-minute heat. As soon as he finished riding one wave, he would turn around and paddle back out to catch another. He also tried to work each wave to get in as many maneuvers as possible. Whenever he glanced over at his competitors, it always seemed Andy was up, slicing across a wave. This just spurred him to try harder and he was surprised how well his stamina held up during the competition.

Finally, the horn blew, signifying the end of the heat and it was only then that he realized how hard he had been working and that he was spent. He realized that he'd given it his all and now it was up to the judges to see how he would place. He felt confident that he'd done pretty well. He had caught some nice waves and carved them up pretty good. It was the best he felt on his surfboard since he was competing back when he was twelve, before his illness. He was just happy to be back competing. If he made it back to the podium, as one of the top three places, he would be surprised.

He came running out of the water, surfboard under his arm, back to where his parents were sitting. They stood up out of their beach chairs as he approached.

"Good going, son." Nick slapped Zoti on the back when he bent over to lay his surfboard on the blanket.

"You looked so good out there," his mother added. She gave him a hug after he laid down his surfboard.

"Thanks," he said, embarrassed by the attention.

"How do you think you did?" Nick said.

"Pretty good, I think. But I saw other guys doing well also. The judges don't know me anymore since I haven't been competing, so who knows where they will place me."

"Well, we're proud of you," Monica said.

"Thanks, Mom," he said. He appreciated her effort, but didn't put much stock in it, knowing she was biased.

"Well, lie down and rest for awhile," she said. "The awards ceremony is not until four-fifteen. We'll find out how you did then."

He realized how tired he was now that the competition was over and decided to listen to his mother and did as he was told. The blanket was warm from the sun and the sand under the blanket was soft. He was satisfied with his effort in the competition, so he fell quickly asleep.

At four o'clock, his father nudged him awake with his foot.

"Zoti, wake up. It's time to go to the awards ceremony."

Zoti started to protest, then he remembered the situation and rose to his feet while rubbing his eyes.

They walked through the soft sand toward to the big tent where the competitors and a throng of onlookers had gathered. There'd been over three hundred competitors in all the divisions. All kinds of people had competed in the different divisions. There was Men's Longboard, Women's Longboard, Paddle Board, Skim Board, Men's Shortboard, Women's Shortboard, Girls' Shortboard, Boys' Shortboard, and Men's Longboard Legends. Between the competitors, their families and friends, and curious onlookers, the crowd for the awards ceremony was over one thousand people.

Zoti and his parents watched patiently as the awards for some of the other divisions were presented. The first categories announced were the paddleboard divisions, then the skimboarders. The middle-aged announcer in the Hawaiian shirt was saving the surfing divisions for last, since they were the most popular events.

The paddleboarders were mostly older competitors, who'd given up competitive surfing. They were mostly tall and broad-shouldered from the paddling. The skimboarders were mostly skinny young boys and some girls who were light enough to skim across the beach on the thin layer of water trapped underneath their boards, thrown onto the beach as the waves recede. They were kept thin by all of the running, jumping, twisting, and turning that skimboarding required.

Finally, the announcer said it was time to announce the winners of the boys' and girls' surfing divisions. The crowd had built even larger during the awards ceremony because people were coming to hear the live band that was going to play following the awards ceremony. The announcer, who was wearing sunglasses and trying to look as hip as he could despite his age, quieted the crowd. The younger age groups were announced first, and they started working toward the older groups.

"Now we come to the Boys' Fourteen-to-Sixteen Shortboard Division. Pay attention to these names because they are going to be the professionals of tomorrow. You'll be hearing a lot more from these guys in the future," the announcer said.

"In third place, from New Smyrna Beach, Florida, is Brian Williams."

Brian came forward through the crowd as the crowd clapped politely. He received congratulations from some of the other competitors as he made his way to the podium. He seemed happy, but not overly enthused about his third-place finish. He made it to the podium and jumped up on the box reserved for the third-place finisher. A pretty blond girl in a bikini, wearing a "Miss Ron Jon Festival" sash and a tiara, came and handed him his trophy and gave him a peck on the cheek.

"Now this next competitor has been off the surfing circuit

for a couple of years, because he has been battling illness, but it's great to see him recovered and returning to the circuit with a splash. Let's hear a big round of applause for Zoti Stamos!" the announcer said, his voice rising on Zoti's name.

The crowd erupted in applause. Zoti raised his fist in triumph and turned and hugged his mother, who had started crying when his name was announced. He turned and shook his father's hand, and could tell his dad was having trouble holding back the tears himself. It was a triumphant moment for his family, who had been through so much in the last two and a half years.

He started through the crowd toward the podium. The crowd continued to clap and he high-fived and fist-bumped his way toward the front of the crowd. He burst free of the crowd and leaped up on the podium for the second-place finisher and waved at the spectators, who were still clapping their approval.

Nick and Monica put their arms around each other's waists and strained to see above the crowd, tears streaming down both of their faces, as their hearts swelled with pride.

"Miss Ron Jon" came and gave him the obligatory kiss on the cheek, but also a congratulatory hug. Then she handed him his trophy, which he held aloft for everyone to see, evoking another big round of applause.

"That's what this contest is all about, right there, folks," the announcer said. He seemed touched by the outpouring of appreciation for Zoti's accomplishment.

"But we do have another winner in this division. In first place, from Sebastian Inlet, Florida, last year's champion in this division, who repeats again this year, is Andy Lopez."

The Ocean under the Moon

The applause was polite, but not as big as Zoti's reception.

Andy made his way through the crowd and leaped onto the podium. After the Ron Jon girl gave him a brief kiss and handed him his trophy, he held it up to a nice round of applause. Then he pulled Zoti up beside him and raised his arm to indicate that he was a champion also.

The crowd erupted in their approval for Andy's good sportsmanship and Zoti's recovery and competitiveness. The photographers in front of the podium went crazy snapping shots of the two boys on the podium, realizing a great photo opportunity.

* * *

Nick turned to Monica and hugged her. He squeezed her tight, overwhelmed by emotion, and then gave her a tender kiss, as tears streamed down both their faces. After the agony and worry of the last few years, he realized that this was the first truly happy moment that they'd had since his son was diagnosed with his disease.

He hoped that, with Zoti's recovery, they were finally seeing the light at the end of the tunnel and exiting a dark era for a better one. Between Zoti's illness and the shrimping industry woes, it had to get better. But he didn't want to think of what the future might hold. He only wanted to enjoy this moment.

After talking with Andy and Brian for awhile, Zoti returned to where they were standing. Monica gave him a big hug. Then Nick shook his hand and took the trophy from him. He held the trophy up in front of him, admiring his son's name on the brass plate.

The three of them stood through the rest of the

presentations, as the announcer progressed through the men's and women's professional divisions. Zoti wanted to stay for the live band that followed the awards ceremony. He wanted to celebrate with his reunited friends.

Nick wished Matt could have been here so the whole family would have been together. Matt, however, had a baseball tournament to play in, so he'd stayed behind, staying with a friend's family.

But this was Zoti's moment to shine. Nick thought back to all the chemotherapy and other treatments he'd endured, always with an upbeat attitude and a competitor's spirit. It did not surprise him that Zoti was beating this disease. He knew his son was a competitor and a winner. But he had to admit, there were times right after Zoti's diagnosis, and also during the intense chemotherapy treatments, where they feared the worse. Those times were in the past now, though, and he was ready to forget them.

As the band started playing after the conclusion of the ceremonies, Zoti ran over to be with his friends. Nick and Monica walked back to their spot on the beach and sat down in their chairs. From here, they could hear the music and watch the festivities, without being overwhelmed by the noise and crowds.

The sun was still beaming, but not quite so strong in the late afternoon, with a gentle, sea breeze blowing. Nick held hands with Monica as they gazed out over the sea, enjoying the view and listening to the wailing guitar from the band. He thought how life can mimic the ocean, being beautiful and serene one moment, then angry and hostile the next. They had weathered the storm of Zoti's

The Ocean under the Moon

illness, now he hoped they had clear sailing ahead.

He shut his eyes and leaned his head back, enjoying the cool, ocean breeze and the special happiness of this afternoon. Soon, however, a series of squalls, and a final hurricane in his life, would have him questioning God and his own existence.

The Ocean under the Moon

Chapter 37

August 1, 2007

Nick was feeling good this morning. The warm, summer sun
illuminated his face as he steered the *Resurrection* out through the
channel for another day of shrimping. He looked through the
pilothouse window, watching Gator secure the lines on the bow of
the boat.

He was proud of his friend. After years of carousing,
partying, and burning the legendary candle joyfully at both ends,
he'd settled down to be a true family man. Nick wasn't sure if it
was Brandy, Gator's age, or the combination of the two that caused
him to settle down.

The man, who'd chased girls in bars, treating them like
disposable objects to be used and discarded, now treated his wife
like a queen and his daughters like little princesses. Gator, who did
everything to the maximum, whether it was playing football,
drinking, or chasing women, now turned his considerable energy
to being a father and a husband.

Nick liked the "new" Gator, who'd been settled down for
about a decade now. Unlike the old Gator, who he was never quite
sure would be showing up for the day, he knew that this Gator
would show up for the day's shrimping trip, fresh, and not hung-

over.

Gator doted on his two girls, Megan, now ten years old, and Mandy, seven. Megan was a tomboy, who liked going surf-fishing with Gator and playing softball. He was an assistant coach on her girls' softball team. She'd inherited his athletic ability and was the star of both her softball team and her basketball team.

Mandy, on the other hand, loved ballet, dancing, and dressing up. As the baby of the family, she was Daddy's little princess and Gator proudly sat through her dance recitals.

They made a striking family now. Gator, despite being past fifty years old, was still tan and muscular from working on the shrimp boat. Not as imposing as he once was, his long blond hair now streaked with grey, he still looked good for his age.

Brandy, despite nearing forty and having two kids, had retained her good looks and trim figure. Megan was growing tall and athletic from all the sports she played. Mandy was all curly blond hair and sass. She carried herself like a young Shirley Temple, bossy and wise beyond her years.

Nick had seen the family all together recently as Gator had talked him into attending one of Mandy's recitals for Mrs. Bean's School of Dance, held at the local middle school auditorium. Nick hadn't really wanted to go, as these things can be kind of tedious affairs, even if you have kids performing, but Gator talked about it on the boat for a week and he'd finally relented.

Once there, however, he'd enjoyed the performances and was amused by how excited Gator was when it was time for Mandy to appear. Since they had only boys, it gave Nick and Monica an insight on what it would have been like to have a girl, and it made Monica a little sad that they never had one.

Nick's mind returned to the task at hand, as he steered the *Resurrection* clear of the white can buoy that marked the end of the jetties and turned the boat south toward his favorite shrimping area. He liked shrimping in the summer time. The ocean was usually calm in May, June, July, and early August. Unlike March and early April when the winds were blustery, the fall when there were hurricanes and nor'easters to deal with, and the winter when there were cold fronts and strong northwestern winds, the summer months were usually benign. True, there were the occasional thunderstorms, but they were almost always formed only in the afternoons. The mornings in the summer were almost always clear and calm, and this morning was no exception.

The other thing he liked about the summer was they didn't have to travel far to get to where they would be shrimping. Their normal routine in the summer was to stay about four to six miles off the coast of Amelia Island to catch the brownies and white roe shrimp that were coming back from the ocean depths to the coastal estuaries to spawn.

Although the number of shrimp was not great, as in the fall shrimp run, the shrimping in the summer was steady, and usually enough shrimp could be caught to make it worth their time.

After the *Resurrection* had cleared the jetties, he headed south about half a mile before he and Gator readied the boat to lower the nets. After years of shrimping together, they rarely had to say a word to each other about what they were doing. Each man had his own tasks, and the years of working together they'd refined their actions into a silent, synchronized performance of efficient maneuvers.

By noon, they'd already experienced a successful day. They had just pulled in their third load of shrimp. The nets were over half full each time, which was good for the summertime. Gator was sitting on an overturned five-gallon bucket near the stern of the boat, separating the shrimp from the by-catch, when "Free Bird" came on the boom box sitting on the ledge behind the pilothouse. He stood to attention when he heard the first organ notes radiating from the boom box.

He walked over, turned the volume up, and grabbed the broom, which was leaning against the back of the pilot house. Nick chuckled and shook his head — Gator would never get tired of this. He could envision his deckhand still giving the performance at eighty-five.

Gator returned to the back of the boat and kicked some of the by-catch out of the scuppers. He then started to stroke his broom to the slow beginning part of the song. He, of course, knew all the words and bellowed out the song in his strong, baritone voice, which could be heard above the sounds of the wind and the drone of the engine.

Nick continued to drive the boat, but would occasionally sneak a peek at Gator's act, as it never ceased to humor him. As the fast part of the song began, Nick could hear and feel him jumping and running around the back of the boat. Eventually Gator skipped his way up to the bow, like a performer at a concert working every angle of the stage.

At the bow, he gyrated for his imaginary audience in front of the boat. Nick watched his silhouette from behind, through the pilothouse window as he was steering the boat. He felt like he was watching a rock star from backstage, serenading the audience.

As the song reached its crescendo, Gator turned and ran down the side of the pilothouse, to get in position on the roof for the big finale. He ran past Nick, gave him a wink, and Nick could see the pure joy on his face as he sped past.

Nick heard the thumps of him jumping on the icebox, then onto the top of the crew's quarters behind the pilot house. He could hear Gator jumping to the rhythm of the song as the three-guitar round-robin built towards the song's impressive conclusion.

Thump, thump, thump. The jumps were keeping time with the music. Nick could just imagine the glee of his friend's face as he played to the imaginary audience, now all around him from his perch on top of the roof.

Then Nick heard a very loud thud as if someone or something had fallen. After that, he heard only silence, except for the music from the boom box, now coming to the final crescendo of the guitar battle.

That's strange. He always finishes the song to its conclusion.

He realized something was wrong. Looking ahead to make sure his path was clear, he put the boat on autopilot, and rushed out of the open doorway of the pilot house. He ran around to the back of the crew's quarters, jumped up on the icebox, and saw his friend sprawled onto his back, his arms spread out like a snow angel.

"Gator!" he yelled.

"Gator!!" he shouted even louder.

The Ocean under the Moon

There was no response from the big man lying prone. He scampered up onto the roof and ran to his side thinking, if this was one of his pranks, he was going to kill Gator himself.

He reached Gator's side and shook him to make sure he wasn't joking around. Seeing no response, he felt for a pulse. Monica had forced both Nick and Gator to take CPR courses from the Red Cross, just in case of such an emergency. He knew what he was supposed to do, but it's different when your best friend in the world is the victim.

He panicked for a moment. He glanced around and saw no other boats in the area, as his own boat steamed south away from the harbor entrance, on autopilot. The ocean was calm, the day was beautiful, and it seemed incongruous with the situation at hand.

His training kicked in. He knelt down beside Gator and tilted his head back and lifted his chin so he had an open airway. Then he bent over and pressed his mouth tightly over Gator's open mouth and gave two quick breaths.

He then moved further down his torso and felt for the bottom of his sternum. Then, putting the heel of his right palm two finger-widths above the bottom of the sternum and placing his left palm on the back of his right hand, Nick gave him thirty compressions to try and get his blood pumping.

He looked at his friend's face as he did his compressions. His face looked serene, as if he was sleeping, but every time Nick did a compression his head would move as if he was nodding in agreement.

"Come on, breathe, dammit!" he shouted.

The Ocean under the Moon

He went back to his head and gave him two more breaths of air. Then he went back to his big chest and did thirty compressions. He repeated this cycle for a few minutes.

He knew that once you start CPR you are not supposed to stop until help arrives. However, he knew there wasn't any help on the way, and the boat was still heading away from the entrance to the harbor. Seeing he wasn't making any progress, as Gator still lay motionless beside him, he decided to stop for a moment. He jumped off the side of the roof and ran to the pilothouse.

He disengaged the autopilot and turned the wheel hard to the port side. Once he had completed a one-hundred-and-eighty-degree turn and was heading north, he re-engaged the autopilot, and pressed the pre-set waypoint for the entrance to Cumberland Sound.

He then grabbed the microphone to the VHF radio and turned the tuner to the Coast Guard channel. He called out a Mayday distress signal over the radio. When the Coast Guard Station at Mayport responded, he gave them details of his predicament and the latitude and longitude of his position. He also told them he was headed toward the entrance of Cumberland Sound.

The dispatcher told him to continue on his course and that the dispatcher would call the fire station in downtown Fernandina and have a couple of EMTs meet the Coast Guard auxiliary boat that was kept, at ready, at the city marina. The Coast Guard Auxiliary boat would rendezvous with the *Resurrection*, somewhere near the entrance to the St. Mary's River channel at the eastern edge of the sound, and transfer Gator to the much faster auxiliary boat.

The Ocean under the Moon

Once on the auxiliary boat, the EMTs could work on Gator, while they made their way back to the dock, and then transfer him to a waiting ambulance. They would then rush him to the local hospital, which was only a couple of miles from the city marina.

He acknowledged the plan and rushed back up to where his friend was lying, knowing that the human brain can only go about four minutes without oxygen before starting to suffer brain damage. He noticed Gator's pale skin color and slightly bluish lips, as he knelt over him to give him two quick breaths. He started back on his cycle of two breaths and thirty compressions.

Soon he was dripping sweat, as he furiously worked on his friend.

"Come on! You can't leave me!" he yelled out loud, as if the unconscious man could hear him. He found himself mad at his friend, as if Gator somehow had a choice in this matter.

"You just had to put on a show, didn't you," he chastised Gator, whose head kept nodding in agreement with each compression he performed.

He worked on him for about twenty minutes, as the boat continued its steady progress toward the entrance to the channel. Every now and then, he looked up from his duties to make sure the autopilot was keeping them on course. He was getting fatigued from his constant exertion, but he had to keep it up, despite no signs of progress. At one point, he felt again for a pulse in his friend's neck, but couldn't find one.

Every so often, after giving him his breaths, he would pause and turn his head sideways and place his left ear just above nose and mouth to listen for signs of Gator breathing on his own.

The Ocean under the Moon

At the same time, he watched Gator's sternum for signs of movement. Every time, he would be disappointed by the lack of response and have to start his actions all over again.

The alarm on the autopilot warned him that they were nearing the waypoint in the middle of the channel, just east of the jetties. He glanced down the channel to see if the Coast Guard Auxiliary boat was coming. He could see the bow of a boat a mile to the west.

He assumed that this was the auxiliary boat heading his way. He left Gator and scrambled off the roof and back to the pilot house to reset the autopilot to head towards a waypoint at the western end of the channel. He surmised that their boats should meet about halfway into the channel just offshore from Fort Clinch.

He wanted to get away from the eastern end of the channel, where the ocean and river met. Even on calm days, this area of the channel, where the ocean and river collided, could be quite volatile, particularly when the tide and wind were going in opposite directions. Therefore, he wanted to head further into the channel, where the water was calmer, which would make transferring Gator from boat to boat easier.

Once the course of the boat was reset, he scrambled back up to the roof to resume CPR. After about five minutes, he noticed the boats were close enough that he would need to go back down to the pilothouse and disengage the autopilot.

He made his way to the pilothouse. He turned off the autopilot and grabbed the wheel of the boat. He pulled back on the throttle and allowed the *Resurrection* to slow down, so the shrimp boat was just making headway. He threw a couple of car tires, attached to ropes, over the side to use as fenders between the two boats. The Coast Guard Auxiliary boat was a twenty-five-foot cabin cruiser, privately owned, and manned by volunteer retirees who'd been trained and certified by the Coast Guard, to help out and be on call for emergencies. The captain of the cabin cruiser indicated to Nick, by hand signals, that he would circle around behind the *Resurrection* and come up along the side of his boat, traveling in the same direction.

The first mate on the auxiliary boat threw a couple of fenders over the side of the cabin cruiser and the captain pulled the boat up alongside the *Resurrection*. Two EMT guys climbed up onto the shrimp boat and the first mate passed them a back board and other equipment, then the auxiliary boat pulled away from the *Resurrection*, so the two boats wouldn't bang together.

Nick reset the autopilot and helped the men on board and pointed to where Gator was up on the roof. The men scrambled up on the roof and knelt beside him.

"How long has he not been breathing on his own?" one of the men asked him.

"About thirty minutes," Nick responded.

The man nodded. He didn't appear enthused by that news. Then both men set about checking for Gator's vitals.

"No pulse," the tall EMT kneeling beside Gator said, to his shorter partner. Then he lifted one, then the other, of Gator's eyelids.

"Pupils fixed and dilated," he announced.

The tall guy, whose name tag indicated his name was Joe, took scissors out of the first aid kit and cut Gator's t-shirt up the middle to expose his bare chest.

"Hand me the AED," he said to his partner, referring to the automated external defibrillator device they brought with them.

Nick watched as Joe opened up the AED and started placing the pads, each containing an electrode and connected by a wire to the device, on Gator's chest—one pad just above his right nipple and the other just under his left nipple.

"Patient is asystolic," he announced to his partner, while looking at the graph on the device that revealed Gator's heart had flat-lined and was in a state of no cardiac activity. The AED device only worked if the patient was in ventricular fibrillation, or ventricular tachycardia.

"Give me the epinephrine," he said.

The shorter guy reached into his medical bag and produced a syringe with a long needle. He removed the plastic covering that kept the syringe sterile and removed the hard plastic cap that protected the needle. He handed the syringe to his partner, who plunged it into Gator's chest and pushed down on the plunger.

Nick had to look away when the needle started going into Gator's chest, as this was not something he wanted to see happening to his friend.

Immediately after the injection, the EMTs started doing two-man CPR. Joe kept his eye on the AED device to watch for heart activity, while he did compressions. The other EMT used a breathing device, consisting of a face mask and hand-compressed bellows, to give Gator breaths after every fifteen compressions.

After two minutes of CPR, the two men paused to check

for signs of life. Not seeing any, Joe told Nick to wave the other boat over. The EMTs rolled Gator over onto the rescue stretcher that they'd placed beside him on the roof and strapped him to the stretcher. They left the AED patches on him and placed the AED device on the stretcher between his legs.

The two men then lifted the stretcher with the big man on it, careful not to let the AED fall off with the boat rocking back and forth. The men spread their legs wide to steady themselves under Gator's weight and the rocking of the boat. They slowly made their way to the edge of the roof and then put the stretcher back down on the roof.

Then Joe jumped off the roof onto the top icebox and grabbed the end of the stretcher and pulled it towards him. He passed the end off the stretcher to Nick, who was standing on the deck, and then went and retrieved the other end of the stretcher from the short guy, who was bent over at the edge of the roof of the crew's cabin.

Nick carried his end of the stretcher over towards the side of the *Resurrection*, where the auxiliary boat had pulled alongside again. Joe jumped off the icebox with his end of the stretcher and followed him over to the rail of the boat.

The other EMT retrieved his medical bag and scrambled down into the auxiliary boat. He met them at the side of the *Resurrection*, to take Nick's end of the stretcher. It wasn't easy to pass Gator, on the stretcher, between the two boats going up and down in an unsynchronized rhythm.

Joe passed his end of the stretcher to the first mate on the auxiliary boat as the captain tried to keep the two boats from banging together, but close enough. The men put the stretcher down on the deck of the auxiliary boat and Joe jumped down onto the deck of the boat beside Gator.

Nick took one last look down at his friend. Gator's ponytail had come loose in the commotion and his blond hair was spread out on the stretcher beside his head. He looked like an aged Viking who'd succumbed in battle. His massive chest was bare except for the electrodes and still not moving. How ironic, that this guy with the massive heart and appetite for life might be undone by the failure of his big heart.

He watched as the boat sped away, with the EMTs resuming the CPR for the trip back to the dock and to the waiting ambulance.

He went back to the pilothouse and turned off the autopilot. He grabbed the wheel of the boat and noticed his hands were shaking. He hadn't realized how much energy he'd exerted, because the adrenaline had kicked in, but now that it was over, he felt exhausted.

He reached for his cell phone, which was on the bridge in front of the steering wheel. He searched for Gator's home phone number on his contact list on the phone, while he drove the boat. He found the number and pressed the call button, hoping Brandy would be at home in the middle of the day.

"McDougals' residence," Mandy answered, sweetly.

Nick's heart fell. He had forgotten the kids were out of school for the summer. He remembered how he felt when his grandfather had the heart attack, when he was about Mandy's age. He prayed that they could do something for Gator when he got to the hospital.

"Mandy, this is Uncle Nick. Is your mother home?" he said, trying to stay calm.

"Yes, she's washing clothes. I'll go get her for you," she said, helpfully.

Nick was "Uncle Nick" to Gator's girls and Gator was "Uncle Gator" to Nick's boys. It had always been that way, ever since the children were young.

"Hello," Brandy answered the phone, cheerfully.

"Brandy, this is Nick. Gator's had an apparent heart attack," he began.

"What?" she said in disbelief. "Is he okay?"

"I don't know," he answered, somewhat truthfully, although he expected the worse.

"He should be at Baptist-Nassau Hospital in about fifteen minutes. We've just transferred him off the *Resurrection* to a faster boat and he should be at the city docks in about five to ten minutes and the hospital, shortly thereafter. I'll call Monica and see if she can come down and watch the girls for you."

"Oh, my God," she said.

They both hung up at the same time, since they both had things to do. She had to get ready to go to the hospital and he needed to call Monica.

So he dialed the number for Monica's cell phone, hoping she would be home. She had mentioned she was going to the grocery store that morning before he left, asking him if he needed anything. When he called, she'd just returned from the store and was putting the groceries away.

The Ocean under the Moon

She knew something was wrong the second she heard him on the phone. He never called this early. He usually waited until they were coming back to the dock, about four or five in the afternoon. And she could tell from the cracking in his voice that something bad had happened.

"It's Gator," he began. "He just keeled over on the boat. It looks like a heart attack and it doesn't look good."

"Oh, no!" she gasped. "Does Brandy know?"

"I just called her. Can you go down to her house to watch Megan and Mandy, while she goes to the hospital?"

"Certainly. I'll head right down there. Are you okay?"

"I'm fine physically. Emotionally? Not so good. It's hard to see your best friend keel over before your eyes. It also brought back bad memories of my grandfather's heart attack."

"I'm so sorry," she said.

"Well, I'll be at our dock soon. Then I'm going straight to the hospital. I'll let you know about his condition as soon as I find out anything."

"I love you," she said.

"I love you, too."

He soon pulled the *Resurrection* past the pogy plant and into the mouth of Egan's Creek. He circled past the dock and came back into the current to make docking easier, since he was by himself. He eased the bow of the boat up to the dock, then hustled up to the bow and jumped off the *Resurrection* with the bow line in hand. He secured the bow line to the cleat on the dock. The incoming current pulled the boat close to the dock and he ran down the dock to secure the stern line to the dock. He hastily secured

342

some spring lines from each cleat to the middle of the boat and then took off running down the dock. He raced through the back yard, around the side of his house, to his driveway. He jumped into his car, noticing that Monica's car was gone already, and headed to the hospital.

He raced down Fourteenth Street, exceeding the speed limit. The first mile of the trip to the hospital went quickly since there weren't any red lights or much traffic on North Fourteenth Street. But the last mile, once he crossed Atlantic Avenue onto South Fourteenth, was a frustrating series of several red lights. It seemed to take forever for him to cover that last mile, but in reality it was only a few minutes.

He exited his car in the parking lot and rushed through the double doors that led to the emergency room waiting area.

Brandy was sitting alone, bent over, with her head in her hands, crying. When he burst in, she looked up at him with sad eyes. She just shook her head, side to side, to indicate that it was not good news.

"He's gone, Nick," she said. She stood up and he embraced her in a hug to comfort her and himself.

"Gator's gone," she repeated through sobs, as if she couldn't believe what she was saying.

"What did they say happened to him?" he finally asked, as she cried on his shoulder.

"The doctor said he had a massive heart attack. He said that he didn't have a chance. That they probably couldn't have saved him, even if he had been a minute from the hospital," she said between sobs.

The Ocean under the Moon

He was stunned and devastated to know his friend was gone for good. Gator's death was going to leave a huge void in his life. There was a small consolation, though, in the fact that he couldn't have done anything else to save his friend.

He felt tears streaming down his face and he kept hugging her, both to comfort her and to keep her from seeing his own anguish. He hadn't cried since his grandfather died, those many years ago, not even when his father died. But now the tears streamed forth.

They stayed embraced for a long time, each one's head on the other's shoulder, comforting each other as they would a child awakened from a bad dream.

Eventually, he pulled back and looked into her red, tear-filled eyes.

"Brandy, go home and give your girls a hug. Gator will always live within them. I'll stay here and make all of the arrangements. Do you want him sent to Oxley-Heard?" he asked.

"Yes, I suppose so," she said, as if in a daze. She started to turn to walk away and then she turned back to say something to him.

"Thank you, Nick. You've always been a very kind to us. You know, Gator told me several times that if it wasn't for you and the *Resurrection*, he would've drunk himself to death many years ago."

He nodded his head in appreciation, worried that he was going to break out crying again.

"Gator told me the same thing about you and the girls," he said. "I guess we were both lucky to have him as long as we did."

She nodded solemnly and walked toward the double doors of the exit, her shoulders shaking from the sobbing. He watched her walk away, with sadness in his eyes, as he realized that she and the girls would be all alone now.

Chapter 38

August 4, 2007

Gator's funeral was three days later. Since he did not attend any particular church regularly, the funeral service was held at the small, white chapel adjoining the Oxley-Heard Funeral Home. Nick made all of the arrangements. Brandy was still too distraught over her loss to function properly, and the girls were beside themselves with grief.

He paid for the casket, the funeral arrangements, and a small family plot at Bosque Bello Cemetery. It was the least he could do, since shrimpers do not have a company 401(k) plan or life insurance benefits. Fortunately, a couple of years ago he'd forced Gator to attend his annual meeting with his insurance agent and he had coerced his friend to sign up for a modest one hundred twenty-five thousand dollar life insurance policy. Nick always carried a million dollar life insurance policy on himself and he'd renewed a ten-year level term insurance policy at that time.

One hundred twenty-five thousand dollars was not much for the rest of her life, but it would allow Brandy to pay off the balance owed on their modest house and have some left over for the girls' college fund. If she got a job to pay for their everyday living expenses, they would be able to scrape by. She wouldn't get the money from the life insurance policy for a few weeks, and he felt responsible as her husband's employer, so he went ahead and paid for all funeral expenses.

Oxley-Heard was located on Atlantic Avenue, next to the elementary school that Gator had attended as a child. The funeral home occupied the historic John Denham Palmer House that had been built in 1891. The white, two-story house with large porches on both floors was an icon in the community. The chapel adjoining the main house was built more recently, in the mid-1980s. The chapel seated over one hundred people, but on this day it was overflowing with all the seats filled and people lined up along the walk and out onto the porch, out front.

Nick arranged for Father George Young, from St. Peter's Episcopal Church, who'd taken over after Pop Kelley's retirement, to preside over the ceremonies. The service started out solemnly with the usual perfunctory prayers. The chapel was quiet, except for sobs coming from Brandy and the girls. Nick, Monica, Zoti, and Matt were seated beside them, and Nick could not look over at them, without breaking up in sorrow himself.

After the prayers and a couple of hymns, the first of several eulogists stepped up to the pulpit. One friend of Gator's from childhood related the famous story about how Gator acquired his nickname by wrestling the alligator. There were a couple of stories about all the mischief he got into as a child. There were also stories about his substantial prowess on the football team in high school, how he almost single-handedly won several games as a hard-hitting middle linebacker, and a hard-charging, not to be denied, fullback.

The Ocean under the Moon

Another friend told the story of Gator's impassioned halftime speeches to his teammates during his senior year that propelled that team to the regional play-offs and one of the Pirates' best seasons ever. Nick was familiar with all of these stories as he had been on that team as a young sophomore.

Eric Jackson, one of Gator's teammates from his college days from the University of Florida, spoke about their college days. Eric had been a fellow linebacker and one of Gator's closest friends on the team. He spoke of their first day of practice in pads as freshmen at the University of Florida.

"Every year, as an initiation and reality check for the incoming freshmen, the coaches would run a drill called 'Bull in the Ring' where the seniors on the team would form a circle around a lone freshman and the freshman would have to try and break through the ring of seniors surrounding him," he said.

"The normal process was that the smaller and less physical freshman would be repeatedly tossed back into the middle of the circle, by the larger seniors, until the freshman was exhausted in defeat and the coaches would whistle in the next victim. The previous victim would usually leave the circle to derisive jibes and cat-calls from the older players."

Nick looked over at Brandy and the girls, who had stopped sobbing and were drying their tears as they listened intently to the speaker's story.

"When it was Gator's turn, he strode, cockily, to the middle of the circle and, like a great bull from Pamplona, circled warily looking for a means of escape. But instead of looking for the weakest link, he had chosen the largest foe, an offensive tackle named John Milton, who had been first team all-SEC, the year before, as a junior.

"He charged the bigger man, who was several inches taller than him. Gator, who was built like a tank and all muscle, got his helmet under the big man's shoulder pads and hit him with the crown of his helmet right in the tackle's sternum. This knocked the wind out of the senior and sent him reeling backward. I would never forget the look on the coaches' faces as they looked at each other in astonishment, as if to say 'look what we got here.'"

Nick chuckled at the story. He thought he'd heard all of the stories about Gator over the years, but he had never heard this one before.

The former linebacker, a rather large man himself, continued.

"It was truly tragic that Gator got hurt. There was no doubt he was destined for big things on the football team for the University of Florida. I had a pretty good career in college and even played a couple of years in the NFL, but Gator was a much better linebacker than I was. If it hadn't been for the injury, there was no telling what he could have accomplished."

Some of the men in the pews nodded their heads in agreement, knowing that Gator was the best football player they ever saw.

"But he was more than just a great football player; he was also a fun-loving guy. I'll never forget, our freshman year, when some sorority girls broke into our dorm during Thanksgiving break and stole underwear from several of the players in the dorm. The girls then hung a sign up outside the student union with the underwear on a string and each player's name below their respective briefs. The writing on the sign above the underwear asked the question: 'Do the men in Robert's Hall measure up?'

"The picture of the sign with Gator, and some of us teammates looking up at it, made it into the school newspaper. To get back at the girls for their prank, the Gator and I went to the local bait shop and bought a large bucket full of crickets," Eric said, grinning.

"One Saturday night, when all the girls were out on dates, we snuck into the girls' sorority house and ran down the halls, throwing a handful of crickets into each girl's room. When the girls returned that night and turned their lights out to go to sleep, the crickets would start chirping and the girls couldn't sleep because of the noise. The girls had to move out of the sorority house for a week, while the exterminators fumigated the place, giving us our revenge."

The crowd laughed at the prank, momentarily lightening the mood.

"Those were good times," he said wistfully. "I'm just sorry they had to end."

The big man started sobbing and had to be helped back to his seat.

After his college teammate spoke, a couple of Gator's drinking buddies, one after the other, got up and related some stories. Nick was a little worried about what they might say. But both of them cleaned things up in their stories, which were mainly about Gator coming to their rescue in several bar fights that would have ended badly for them, if he had not intervened.

The Ocean under the Moon

There was a lot of laughing, and some crying, at all of the stories about Gator, who'd clearly led an interesting life. Finally, it was Nick's turn to speak as the final eulogist of the day. He walked up to the podium and began to speak, but he became overcome with emotion as he looked over to Brandy and her daughters.

Father Young came over and consoled him with an arm across his shoulder, while he composed himself. After a brief delay, he got hold of himself and started talking. He talked about how he first met Gator, when Nick was a freshman on the high school football team and he was the star senior. He spoke of how intimidated he was of him and how he never dreamed that they would eventually work together.

He told of how Gator had also saved him from a bar fight with the disgruntled shrimper from Georgia, and how Gator then coerced him to accept him as his deckhand—and how unsure he was at the time, but how grateful he became over the years that he made that decision.

He spoke of Gator's penchant for dancing around the boat to "Free Bird." He even did a short imitation of Gator's antics during the song, which drew big laughs from the attendees. "It is appropriate that his last breath was doing something for the pure joy of it, as that was how he lived his life," Nick said.

He told the audience that Gator was not a rich man, but he had a wealth of friends.

"If wealth was measured in friends, Gator would truly be a rich man today." He gestured to the large crowd in attendance.

He quoted Abraham Lincoln, who said, "In the end it's not the years in your life that count. It's the life in your years."

The Ocean under the Moon

He paused to collect himself. Then looking at Brandy, he uttered his final words.

"Gator had a lot of life in his years," he concluded, while Brandy nodded her head in agreement.

A hush fell over the audience, after Nick's final salute to his fallen friend. Everyone tried to collect themselves after the rollercoaster of emotions, from crying to laughing, then back to crying. Several sobs could be heard from the audience as he made his way back to his seat.

Father Young got up and said one final prayer, then announced to the audience that there would be a short graveside service at Bosque Bello Cemetery. The mourners slowly made their way out of the chapel to their cars. Brandy's car had been pulled up to the front of the circular drive beside the funeral home, with Nick's car second in line. After he and the other eulogists, who were also the pallbearers, had carried the casket out to the waiting hearse in back of the funeral home, they piled into the cars in the circular driveway on the side of the building and the procession began.

With a Nassau County Sheriff deputy in the lead, the long procession made its way to Bosque Bello. Nick had bought Gator a small family plot under the shade of an old cedar tree, surrounded by ancient oaks. A canopy was set up next to the gravesite and metal, folding chairs had been placed beneath the canopy.

Nick and the other pallbearers removed the casket from the hearse and placed it on a stand above the gravesite. Brandy and her daughters were seated in front of the casket, Nick, Monica, and their sons beside them in the front row.

The Ocean under the Moon

Father Young said a few more words. Then Megan and Mandy got out of their seats and each placed a rose on Gator's casket. The girls were crying and Nick felt it was the saddest thing he had ever seen, knowing that these girls were going to be without a father they adored.

When the ceremony was over, and after the final condolences, hugs, and handshakes, Nick told Monica he wanted to stay awhile and say his final goodbye to his friend privately, and that he would walk home, since the cemetery was just down the street from Old Town.

Soon, everyone had left, except a couple of workers from the cemetery, whose job it was to fill in the dirt over the casket. Now that everyone had left, he opened a cooler, which had a six-pack of long-neck Budweiser beers in it. He gave each of the workers a cold beer and asked them to give him a few minutes alone at the gravesite, before they started their work. The two workers happily accepted the bottles and excused themselves to a safe distance, under an old sago palm, to drink their beers.

He placed one of the folding chairs next to the open grave and sat down on it, with the small cooler next him. He pulled out one of the cold bottles of beer. He opened the cap on the bottle and poured the contents onto Gator's casket.

Then he reached into the cooler, took out a beer, and opened it for himself.

"Here's to you, my friend," he said, solemnly, as he raised the bottle in a toast.

He took a long draw from the bottle, the cold beer going down very smooth, and greatly appreciated, after a long, emotional afternoon. Nick couldn't believe his friend was really gone, and so suddenly. He shook his head, in disbelief.

"How am I'm going to carry on without you, buddy?"

He took another swig from his beer.

"I can find another deckhand. But it won't be the same without you. It damn sure won't be as much fun without you. You just had to dance to that song, didn't you?"

He knew he would never be able to listen to that song again. It would be too painful a memory for him. He glanced over at the headstone that he'd purchased for the grave. He and Brandy had agreed on the epitaph for the headstone. The headstone read:

Travis "Gator" McDougal

March 29, 1954 – August 1, 2007

"If I leave here tomorrow, will you still remember me?"

The epitaph was the first lyric from the "Free Bird" song that he'd loved so much, which, now, took on a new meaning.

"Damn right, Gator. We are going to remember you," he said.

"I'll bring you a beer once a week," he promised his friend.

With that, he stood up and tossed the last two beers from the cooler, unopened, into the grave on either side of the casket. With his nearly finished of bottle of beer in his hand, he began the lonely walk back to his house, tears streaming down his face.

The Ocean under the Moon

Chapter 39

October 13, 2007

"Pull on that line, Neal. Harder!" Nick gave instructions to the young deckhand, as they tried to maneuver the net over the deck of the *Resurrection*, in order to dump out their catch.

"Steady it there," he said. He had to yell above the engine noise, as he released the catch onto the afterdeck.

"Watch out for the blue crabs, stingrays, and the jellyfish," he warned his young deckhand, before he waded into the mass of sea life, to separate the by-catch from the shrimp.

He'd settled on the young, inexperienced Neal Bollard after trying a couple of older shrimpers. The first one he had hired, Stanley Wilson, kept getting severe kidney stones, which would send him to the hospital for several days at a time. He even incurred a couple of attacks while out shrimping, which caused Nick to cut his day short to rush back, so the elderly shrimper could go to the emergency room.

After Stanley, he tried another old shrimper named Jeremiah Green, who turned out to be just as undependable, this time because of alcoholism. He would show up late, still half-drunk, and when Nick caught him taking a swig from a flask while on the boat, he fired Jeremiah on the spot.

The Ocean under the Moon

After the fiascoes with the older shrimpers, he decided to hire Neal, a greenhorn, who was just out of high school. He figured Neal would be a blank slate, without any ingrained bad habits— somebody that he could mold into what he wanted.

What he really wanted was one of his sons, either Matt or Zoti, to take an interest in the business and follow in the family tradition. Both boys were still in school, however, and when they were off from school, Matt usually had baseball practice or a game, and Zoti just wanted to go surfing.

When circumstances allowed it, and he needed the help, he would drag one of the boys, or both, out with him on the *Resurrection*. Like most teenagers, the boys acted bored and wanted to be with their friends, doing something else, instead of out on a boat trying to catch shrimp. They complained all day, kept checking their text messages on their cell phones, or slept in the shade of the crew's quarters while the nets were out.

Despite their lack of motivation, he was glad to spend time with the boys, especially Zoti. His youngest son was doing well now. He was officially in remission and had received good blood work for over two years now. Two months ago the doctors stopped his maintenance therapy and he was officially "cured." Dr. Lindstrom warned, however, that there was still a small chance of the leukemia returning, but for the last couple of months, his blood work continued to look good.

It wasn't any too soon, as far as Nick's finances were concerned.

But for now, despite his financial worries, he was just going to revel in the fact that his son was cancer-free and concentrate on training Neal.

"Hey, Neal. Don't use your foot to push those stingrays over the side of the boat. Use the shovel. Their barbs will go right through your boots."

Neal nodded his head and then moved to get the shovel, but not before he kicked one more stingray over the side with his foot.

Nick just shook his head in amazement. All teenagers are alike, stubborn. He put his boat on autopilot and started over to help Neal.

"Gator, I sure do miss you, buddy."

The Ocean under the Moon

Chapter 40

November 3, 2007

"Sit down, honey. I have some bad news for you," Monica began. It was around five o'clock in the afternoon. Nick had returned from shrimping and just walked into the kitchen, after showering and changing into clean clothes.

She was stirring pasta into a pot of boiling water on the stove, as she was making spaghetti for dinner. Matt was at baseball practice and Zoti was at soccer practice, so neither boy would be home for another hour or so. After he sat down, she turned to face him and he could see that she had been crying.

"Principal Woods called me into her office today and told me they won't be renewing my contract to teach next year."

"What? How could they do that?" he blurted out. He was struggling as it was, trying to keep two boats running with the shrimping industry doing so badly. Now their source of steady income from her teaching job was threatened.

"The principal said it was a perfect storm of three things. First of all, because the economy is doing so poorly throughout the country, people aren't traveling on vacation like they normally do. Since Florida needs that sales tax money from tourism, the state has a huge deficit in their budget for next year and they're having to slash what they send the counties to support education," she explained, between sniffles.

"And then, you know how bad the housing market in Florida has gotten. With all the foreclosures and home values going down, the county school system is getting less tax money, since the taxes come out of homeowner's property taxes.

"The third thing is that new high school in Yulee that opened last year—it's siphoned off around half of the students that were going to our local high school, so our school needs fewer teachers. Some of them have gone over to the Yulee High School, but others with seniority have gone down to the middle school, and in turn, some of the middle school teachers with seniority have been bumped down to elementary school."

"This is unbelievable," Nick said, and put a hand on her shoulder to comfort her. Distraught, she turned away from him, shaking her head.

"In my grade, believe it or not, I'm the less senior teacher. Judy Tester has over thirty-three years with the school system and Betty Harper has almost thirty years. Therefore, I'm the odd person out in my grade, since I have only twenty-eight years of service," she said.

"They can't do that, can they? What does the teachers' union have to say about that?" he demanded.

"I already talked to the union representative about my situation and they said that as long as there is no discrimination and it's based on seniority, there is no recourse."

"What about our insurance? We can't do without it, in Zoti's situation."

The Ocean under the Moon

"According to the union rep, under the COBRA laws, the school board has to allow us to continue our insurance coverage for up to eighteen months, but we have to pay all of the premiums ourselves."

"But with Zoti's condition, I'm having trouble just paying for our portion of the premium now and all the overages. How are we going to pay for the whole thing if you're not working?"

"Well, hopefully, I can find another teaching job. Maybe up in Georgia, in Camden County — they pay better anyhow," she said, optimistically. "Plus, Principal Woods said there was a good chance I could do some substitute teaching, although that doesn't qualify me to receive benefits, like insurance."

He got up from the table and walked over to the refrigerator. He wouldn't drink this early in the evening on a normal day, but this was an exception. He reached into the refrigerator and pulled out a cold beer in a bottle.

"Would you like a beer, honey?" he asked.

"No, but I would like a glass of wine." She poured the steaming pasta and water into a colander in the sink.

He took a half-full bottle of white wine from the refrigerator and poured some into a wine glass.

He walked over toward the sink where she was working. She turned around to accept the glass from him, but he just kept coming closer, then slipped the glass of wine onto the counter behind her, and embraced her in a tight hug.

"Monica, what are we going to do?"

"Don't worry. I'll find another job," she said reassuringly, although she wasn't that sure herself.

The Ocean under the Moon

"Let's go out back and watch the sun go down," she suggested, as if that would make things better. "Just let me put the spaghetti in the pot to simmer."

After dumping the pasta into the pot, stirring the contents with a wooden spoon, then adjusting the temperature down some, she grabbed his hand and led him to the deck chairs on their back porch. They sat down and continued to hold hands, reassuring each other things would be all right.

One of the couple's favorite things to do was to sit on their back porch and watch the sun go down. When the weather was good and there weren't too many clouds off to the west, their view from their back porch, sitting on the high bluff overlooking the Amelia River and the eight miles of marshes to the west, would reward them with spectacular magenta sunsets.

Tonight, however, they sat still, staring at the sun until it faded below the horizon, not appreciating its beauty while they contemplated their unknown future.

The Ocean under the Moon

Chapter 41

March 27, 2008

Zoti's cancer came back with a vengeance. One day, two months ago, he'd woken up with a fever. Nick had hoped it was just a touch of flu, but Dr. Lindstrom quickly confirmed that the leukemia was back.

He'd explained that somewhere deep inside Zoti's bone marrow there had remained a few dormant cancer cells that somehow managed to survive all those years of previous chemotherapy. These few cells managed to stay dormant and hidden away in the billions of normal red blood cells for the last couple of years. Now those cells had started to replicate again and were rapidly reproducing themselves in his body.

Zoti's therapy would have to be even more aggressive this time, Lindstrom told them, since the survival rate for the reoccurrence of leukemia was not good. They had been devastated by this news. Zoti didn't seem to grasp the reality of the situation and was more bummed that the chemotherapy would interfere with his surfing competitions, than he was worried about any long-term implications.

But they started the twice-weekly trips to Jacksonville again, for the intravenous chemotherapy treatments. Soon Zoti's

362

hair fell out again and he started losing weight due to the nausea associated with the chemotherapy. Nick and Monica, who'd thought they were out of the woods concerning his health, could not believe they were going to have to go through this again.

Not only were they watching their son wither away, they were also watching their financial situation grow more dire. Due to the competition from all the other laid-off teachers, she'd not been able to find another full-time teaching position. She'd only been able to get the occasional substitute-teaching job and had also been working part-time at Wadsworth, a downtown haberdashery that sold upscale men's clothing to the tourists.

As for his business, it wasn't doing much better. Although he was still catching shrimp on the *Resurrection*, shrimping had become a Sisyphean task due to the low prices at the dock caused by the dumping of low-cost, pond-raised shrimp from abroad.

He'd recently sold his other boat, the *Island Girl*, to Billy Sutton, who had been working as its captain all these years. Since Billy didn't have the money to buy the boat outright, Nick agreed to owner-finance its purchase. After a small down payment, Billy would make a monthly payment for the mortgage of the boat and dockage at his dock. This, at least, would give him some steady income, as long as Billy could afford to make the payments.

Nick would need all of the help he could get because, after Monica lost her job and his son was doing better, he'd let the family's health insurance lapse. It was not a decision he had taken lightly at the time. The premium for the family's coverage had risen to over two thousand dollars a month. That was like having to pay a mortgage on a three hundred thousand dollar house. He'd taken a gamble by not paying the premium and letting the insurance lapse, hoping that Monica would get another job and then they would reinstate their insurance.

She'd warned him not to let the insurance lapse; it was too big a risk. He, however, thought the worst was behind them as far as their son's health was concerned. At that time, Zoti looked recovered, with his long blond hair grown back and his body tanned from surfing. Dr. Lindstrom reassured them that Zoti was doing well. His strength returned and he was dominating the local surfing competitions and doing well in the ESA events that they traveled to up and down the east coast.

Nick was used to taking chances with nature and the elements out on his shrimp boat. His work bred an independent spirit and a can-do attitude. He was used to taking gambles, like when he salvaged and bought the *Resurrection*. He always felt that with hard work and a positive attitude any obstacle could be overcome. He'd been confident that Zoti had beaten the cancer, so he decided to take the calculated risk of letting the insurance lapse temporarily, when he'd been faced with having to dip into his home equity line again, just to pay the premium.

He'd gambled and lost.

Fortunately, back in 2005, at the height of the real estate market, he had secured from his local bank a home equity line of nearly six hundred thousand dollars against his property. He'd already spent over a hundred thousand dollars of the line on Zoti's first round of treatments. Now he would have to dip into the equity line again, this time for much more, as he would be paying one hundred percent of the cost. He told Dr. Lindstrom, however, that he wanted his son to have the best of care, no matter what the cost.

At the height of the real estate market, he'd been approached by a developer who offered him one million dollars for his property. The developer wanted to build condominiums with boat slips on the property. He refused at the time because he wanted to keep the property in his family and have a place to dock his boats. Now, looking back, maybe he should have taken the deal. It was too late now, however, since the real estate market had soured and all of those kinds of deals were on hold.

Now, his son was in a fight for his life and he was going to do whatever was necessary to help him. Even if he had to sell his property and the *Resurrection*, he was willing to do that, if it would save his son's life.

The local community rallied around the fight to battle the return of Zoti's leukemia. The local downtown businesses put glass jars, with his picture on it, next to their cash registers to collect donations. Also, the shrimping community held a fund raiser at Ten Acres, with a concert by Sean McCarthy and his friends. The event raised over fifteen thousand dollars and was appreciated, but unfortunately, that amount would only be a fraction of what would be required to try and save his life.

The Ocean under the Moon

Chapter 42

April 4, 2008

"All of you are probably wondering why I called you to my office today," Dr. Lindstrom said, as he looked into the faces of Zoti, Nick, Monica, and Matt staring back at him from across the desk.

"I think it is time we considered allogeneic stem cell transplantation," he said. "We've been able to knock the cancer back with the intensive consolidative chemotherapy Zoti has been taking, but every time we try to reduce the dosage, the cancer pops back up. If we want to completely eradicate all of the cancer cells in his body, we are going to have to do very intensive chemotherapy, followed by full-body radiation to kill all of the cancer cells.

"Unfortunately, this also kills the normal cells found in the bone marrow. Stem cell transplantation allows us to treat the leukemia aggressively, with the chemotherapy and radiation, to destroy the diseased bone marrow, then, infuse the patient with healthy stem cells from a suitable donor. In a successful transplant, the new stem cells migrate to the cavities of the large bones, engraft themselves, and start producing normal blood cells." Dr. Lindstrom held up a diagram to illustrate.

"Stem cells for a transplant come from either bone marrow or from the peripheral blood. Bone marrow transplants used to be

366

more common, but now they have been largely replaced by peripheral blood stem cell transplants. The stem cells can come from either the patient or from a matched donor. Stem cell transplants using stem cells from the patient are called autologous stem cell transplants, while a transplant from a donor is called an allogeneic stem cell transplant. In a transplant using a donor, the donor's stem cells must match the patient's own as perfectly as possible.

"Matt, this is why you are here today. Previous blood work indicates that you would be an excellent donor. There are advantages and disadvantages to using donor material. The advantage is that using stem cells from another person seems to help fight any remaining leukemia cells through an immune reaction, which is called a graft-versus-leukemia reaction. The disadvantage with an allogeneic transplant is that if the genetic match is not good enough, the donor's stem cells can perceive the patient's body as foreign material to be attacked and destroyed. This is known as graft-versus-host disease or GVHD, which can prove fatal. Alternatively, the patient's immune system may destroy the new bone marrow, called graft rejection, leaving the patient susceptible to infections. This can also be life-threatening."

Nick took a deep breath and realized he was squeezing Monica's hand hard. She did not seem to notice.

"So, you see, this transplantation is not without its risks and it also is not cheap," Dr. Lindstrom said. "Because the risk of infection is so great, once we kill off all of his blood cells, including the white blood cells that fight infection, he will have to stay in a special, sterile ward we have here at the hospital, under close observation until his white blood cell count reaches over one thousand again.

"Stem cell transplants usually cost well over one hundred thousand dollars, and require a long hospital stay. Some insurance companies consider them experimental and don't pay for them, but these procedures are quickly becoming the standard of care. Since you are self-pay, you don't have to worry about the insurance issue—you know already you will have to handle the full financial brunt of this procedure and his follow-up care. Therefore, I want you to go home as a family and discuss whether you want to proceed from here. Any questions?"

"I'm in the middle of my senior season playing high school baseball," Matt said. "How is this going to affect me?"

"Good question, Matt. With bone marrow transplants, we used to put the patient to sleep under general anesthesia and use a long needle to extract the bone marrow from the hip bone. Now, using the peripheral blood process, we can just withdraw some of your blood, and through a process called apheresis, separate out what we need," the doctor said.

"You may feel anemic or weak for a few days afterward. And beforehand, you'll have to have daily, subcutaneous injections of granulocyte-colony stimulating factor to mobilize your stem cells to move from your bone marrow out into the peripheral circulation. But I think the impact to your season will be minimal, except for a few days of weakness, which we can work around your schedule."

Matt nodded and seemed satisfied with the answer, with the typical teenager's outlook—what mattered most was his own little world and whether he would get a baseball scholarship by the end of the season.

"Any other questions?" Dr. Lindstrom asked.

Zoti, already weak and defeated by the ongoing chemotherapy, sat silently, resigned to his fate.

Monica was silent also. Nick knew that she was feeling stunned by yet another turn of events that could have grave consequences for their son.

"You said that the procedure would cost well over a hundred thousand dollars?" Nick asked. "Is that what we can expect?"

"That's if everything goes well. If we run into complications, like GVHD or rejection, it could run two or three times that amount."

"If it was your son, Dr. Lindstrom, what would you do?" Monica asked.

"Well, if it was my son, knowing that our current treatments have all eventually failed, resulting in relapse, I think the best option of eradicating the leukemia completely lies with the stem cell transplant, regardless of cost."

They thanked Dr. Lindstrom for his time and Nick and the boys each shook hands with the doctor. He promised Dr. Lindstrom that he would call him the next day with their decision. But for now, he just wanted to go home and be with his family. They had a lot to talk about.

Chapter 43

April 4, 2008
8:00 p.m.

"But why do we have to do it during baseball season?" Matt asked, in that whiny way teenagers so often have.

"Because Zoti's health can't wait. You don't want him to die, do you?" Nick asked.

Nick, Monica, and Matt were sitting around the dinner table. Zoti, who was too nauseous from past chemo treatments to eat, had retired to his room to play video games.

"But I'm trying to get a baseball scholarship. Don't you guys want that? With all of the money you spent on Zoti's treatments, I know you don't have the money to send me to college."

"We'll find a way, dear," Monica said.

"No, you won't. Dad probably doesn't even want me to go to college, so he can use me as a free deckhand for the rest of my life."

"That's not true," Nick said, louder than he'd intended. If things were different, he would have loved Matt to be the fourth generation of his family to work the ocean for shrimp, but since there was so little profit in shrimping now, he wholeheartedly supported Matt's college ambitions.

"Your mother and I want you to go to college," he said, in a more composed voice. "It's just that Zoti's needs are more pressing right now. We are talking about his life."

"Yeah, but what about my life?" Matt said. "The next two games are against Bishop Kenny and Bolles. They are the two best high school teams in the Jacksonville area and there are going to be a lot of college scouts there. Don't you want me to be at my best?"

"Of course, honey," said Monica as she grasped his hand. "We are not putting Zoti's needs above yours. We love you both equally."

"We'll ask Dr. Lindstrom if we can put off the collection of the stem cells from you, until after your two big games," Nick said. "He said he would work around your schedule, and if I remember correctly, he said they would need to give Zoti several days of very intensive chemotherapy, then full body radiation. So it may be awhile before they need the stem cells anyway."

"Now, who wants some of my Amelia Mud Pie?" Monica asked, cheerfully. She had gotten the recipe from a chef at Amelia Island Plantation several years earlier, and in her world, Amelia Mud Pie made everything better. It would be just what they needed to lighten their moods, and take their minds off of the serious business ahead.

The Ocean under the Moon

Chapter 44

April 15, 2008

Zoti had never looked worse, Nick thought to himself as he entered the hospital room at Wolfson Children's Hospital. He could barely acknowledge their arrival as Nick, Monica, and Matt entered his room. His head was bald and his eyes were sunken with dark circles underneath them.

"Hey there, champ. How are you feeling?" Nick approached the side of the bed and reached out to put his hand on his son's shoulder.

"Not so good," he whispered back, his response taking all of his effort.

"Hey, honey," Monica said. She bent over to kiss him from the other side of the bed from her husband, with a look of concern on her face.

"Have you been eating anything?" she asked.

He just shook his head. Nick looked at the tubes coming out of his body. There were two in the right arm and two in the left arm and a large catheter coming out of his chest, just above his heart. Dr. Lindstrom had explained that this flexible tube, inserted into a large vein, allowed the medical staff to administer the chemotherapy drugs, other drugs, and then the stem cells, into his blood system, directly. It also allowed the staff to withdraw the hundreds of blood samples required during the course of treatment, painlessly, without the use of needles. Looking at the tubes in his arms, Nick surmised that they were feeding him intravenously since he was too weak to eat.

"How'd you do?" Zoti whispered to Matt, who'd been hanging back, shocked at the sight of his brother.

"I went three-for-four against Bishop Kenny and then pitched a two-hitter against Bolles," Matt said.

Zoti gave him a weak smile and slowly raised his hand into a thumbs-up position.

Matt returned his brother's smile, but he felt guilty that he'd put his own concerns ahead of his brother's. Dr. Lindstrom, however, said it was fine that he'd played in the two games before he donated his stem cells, because for the last week and a half, Dr. Lindstrom had been getting Zoti ready to accept the new stem cells. Zoti was undergoing the conditioning, or preparative regimen, as it is called. He'd underwent several days of intensive chemotherapy, using dosages much stronger than previously used, and also radiation, to destroy his old bone marrow, and the cancer cells within, to make room for the new bone marrow.

Now, Zoti's bone cavities were a "blank slate" upon which Matt's stem cells would hopefully engraft themselves and start producing normal, cancer-free blood cells. That was what Matt was here for today, to go through apheresis, and donate his stem cells.

Matt had been undergoing daily injections to stimulate his stem cells to move into his peripheral blood system. Dr. Lindstrom wanted to wait a couple of days after the termination of the chemotherapy and radiation treatments, for Zoti's body to recover somewhat, before infusing the new stem cells into his blood system.

Because the treatments also crippled Zoti's immune system, the family was required to wash their hands with antiseptic soap and wear protective gowns, gloves, and masks before entering the room to visit him. Because his brother was in such a weakened condition, Matt was hesitant, at first, to get too close.

Now, he approached the side of Zoti's bed and Monica stepped back to allow him room to sidle up to the bed.

"I'm going to give you my best stuff," he said. "With these stem cells, you'll be back surfing in no time."

Then he raised a gloved, clenched fist for a fist-bump. Zoti raised his hand and gently knocked knuckles with his brother; it took all of his effort. Matt turned away from his brother, so Zoti wouldn't see him crying, and left the room.

The Ocean under the Moon

Chapter 45

May 13, 2008

It was now almost four weeks since Zoti was infused with his brother's stem cells. Nick sat in the corner of the hospital room reading a book, wearing a hospital gown, gloves, and a mask. Every now and then, he would look up from his book, checking on his son's monitors and breathing, then go back to his reading. Not that he knew anything about the monitors, but he could always watch the rise and fall of Zoti's chest to reassure himself that his son was still alive.

Monica was downstairs in the cafeteria to getting something to eat. Over the last several weeks, they'd taken turns spending as much time with their son as possible during visiting hours. Buck and Caroline had come down to help them and visit with Zoti, but they were in their late seventies now and didn't have the stamina to sit for long stretches of time, so they soon returned to their farm.

Dr. Lindstrom had told them that the two to four weeks following the transplant were the most critical. While he and his staff waited for the stem cells to migrate to the cavities of the large bones, to engraft and start producing normal blood cells, Zoti was at risk of infection and internal bleeding. Multiple antibiotics and blood transfusions would be administered to him to help prevent and fight infection. Also, transfusions of platelets were being administered to prevent excessive bleeding. Furthermore, during this time, the doctor said Zoti would be watched for rejection and graft-versus-host disease.

So far, things had been going pretty well. Zoti's blood work had showed signs of improvement, indicating that the engraftment was occurring and he was starting to produce his own normal blood cells. He was still very weak and sick, however.

Dr. Lindstrom explained to them what Zoti was going through in terms of someone who had the flu. When healthy people get the flu, they suffer from nausea, vomiting, fever, diarrhea, and extreme weakness. Now, he said, imagine having the flu, not for several days, but for weeks on end. That is what a transplant patient has to go through, he explained.

Not only was Zoti feeling sick most of the time, he was also feeling isolated. Extraordinary precautions had been taken over the last few weeks, to minimize his exposure to viruses and bacteria. He was in a private room with special air-filtering equipment to purify the air. Flowers, plants, fresh fruit, and raw vegetables were prohibited in the room, because they might contain fungi and bacteria that could pose a risk of infection for him.

His friends were not allowed to visit, only immediate family, to reduce the risk of infection. He felt helpless and lonely and kept telling them that he just wanted to go home. Dr. Lindstrom told him he would have to wait until his new bone marrow was producing a sufficient number of healthy red blood cells, platelets, and most importantly, white blood cells.

The Ocean under the Moon

During his better moments, they'd tried to encourage him to walk to the bathroom and put on his mask and walk down the hall, but this seemed to require more energy than he possessed. Nick had to be content to watch his formerly vivacious son just be able to breathe and sleep.

It didn't take Matt long to recover from donating part of his blood. He'd felt weak for a day or two and had to sit out a couple of practices, but by the next game, he went two-for-three in his at-bats.

One week ago, he was offered a partial scholarship to play baseball at Jacksonville University. Matt, who'd attended Coach Terry Alexander's baseball camp the previous two summers, had fallen in love with JU's beautiful baseball field, nestled by the St. John's River, surrounded by mounds and old oak trees. Nick and Monica appreciated the coach's strict, tough-love approach and his advice about studying hard and staying away from drugs and alcohol.

Nick knew Matt was really excited about JU's offer. It was where he wanted to go. A couple of community colleges, Gulf Coast Community College and Chipola Community College, both in the Florida Panhandle, had offered better scholarships. But his heart was set on JU, plus they would only have to drive forty-five minutes versus five hours to watch their son play.

The only problem was how they were going to pay for it. Jacksonville University, a private school of about thirty-four hundred students, was very expensive. Normal tuition was about eighteen thousand dollars per year. Even with the partial scholarship, they were looking at about ten thousand dollars a year for tuition and books, not to mention dormitory and food.

But if he could spend so much on Zoti's health, surely he could find some room in his rapidly diminishing home equity account for Matt's education, Nick thought. But he didn't want to worry about his finances now.

He leaned his head back and rested it against the wall. If Zoti could just come out of this healthy, and get back to his normal high-spirited self, Nick would not ask God for anything else. Money problems were not foremost upon his mind; he just wanted his son to get well.

The Ocean under the Moon

Chapter 46

May 27, 2008

It was a glorious day for the Stamos household. Monica and Caroline were scurrying about getting everything ready for Zoti's arrival. The last couple of weeks had been nothing short of miraculous for him. The engrafted stem cells morphed into fully functioning bone marrow that was producing normal, healthy blood cells. Now, his blood cell counts also returned to normal.

An improvement in his physical condition mirrored the improvement in his blood cell counts. His cheeks returned to their rosy hue, instead of the ashen color they'd been. The dark circles were gone from under his eyes and his hair and nails started growing again.

His energy level also improved dramatically over the last two weeks. He went from barely able to raise his head or arms, to doing push-ups in his room in order to regain his muscle tone for surfing. By the end of the two weeks, he was "bouncing off the walls" and pestering Dr Lindstrom to allow him to go home.

The doctor had assured him that once his white and red blood cells, and platelet counts, returned close to their normal levels, he would consider letting him leave the hospital. Every day he asked the doctor and the attending nurses what his numbers were after his daily blood tests. He looked at it like a surfing competition and he was determined to come out on top.

Finally, yesterday, Dr. Lindstrom had come into his room with a big grin on his face. The pleased doctor then told Nick, Monica, and Zoti that he could go home the following day.

Monica called her parents and they'd driven down from Hazlehurst the night before, to help her prepare for a small welcome-home party.

Caroline and Monica had been in the kitchen all morning, cooking and baking, and Nick, Buck, and Matt went to pick Zoti up from the hospital in Jacksonville and bring him back to Fernandina. Since it was Saturday, Monica had invited a few of his closest friends, including Terry, his surfing buddy, to welcome him home. Because Zoti was still at risk for infection, she invited only three of his friends, and gave each one a hospital mask to wear, when they arrived.

Pepe could sense something was about to happen. The dog followed Monica around the kitchen, as she scurried about, and he gobbled up the scraps of food that accidentally fell to the floor. He also barked loudly as each of Zoti's friends arrived.

Her cell phone rang. It was Nick on his cell phone telling her they were about fifteen minutes from arriving. She had Terry and his other friends go out on the front porch and hang a welcome home banner over the front door.

She was beside herself with joy. She was getting her son back—hopefully, a healthy son at last. Dr. Lindstrom had been amazed at Zoti's rapid recovery over the last couple of weeks, but he warned them that their son was not out of the woods yet.

The Ocean under the Moon

Though he was well enough to leave the hospital, his recovery was far from being over. Weekly visits to the clinic would be necessary to monitor his progress, to check for infections, and to administer any medications or blood products needed.

To be safe during this period, he would have to refrain from going to crowded public places like school, movie theaters or grocery stores. He would have to wear a mask if he went out in public.

Dr. Lindstrom also warned him that it would be six months to one year to recover fully from the transplant and during this time he would still be at risk for rejection, relapse, and graft-versus-host disease.

But Monica didn't want to dwell on the negative or think about what the future might hold. She just wanted to concentrate on this happy moment and kept glancing out of the kitchen window, hoping to catch a glimpse of Nick's car approaching.

Finally, his car pulled up in front on the house and stopped in a cloud of dust. Nick and Buck got out and Nick ran around the car to the rear passenger door. After waiting for the dust to settle, he opened the rear door and they assisted Zoti out of the car. He was wearing jeans and a surfing t-shirt, and he had on a protective mask.

The crowd on the porch started clapping and cheering. With his father on one side and grandfather on the other, he slowly made his way toward the front porch. When they'd made it only halfway up the sidewalk to the front porch, Pepe recognized Zoti behind his mask. The dog bolted off the front porch, and headed straight for him.

The Ocean under the Moon

Nick tackled Pepe before the charging dog jumped on Zoti and knocked him down or scratched him with his claws. Zoti knelt down and his father allowed the dog to advance, so he could lick his owner behind his ears and on his neck, since his mask prevented the dog from licking him on the face.

He stood up and walked toward the porch, with his dog running circles around him, after his father let go of Pepe's collar. Zoti ascended the stairs to the porch, and his mother was the first one to give him a hug. She gave way to his grandmother, Caroline, who also hugged him.

Then he walked over to his friends, who had been lingering back on the porch to give his family first rights on the greeting.

"What a crew!" Zoti said to the three boys. "You guys look hilarious, all lined up with those masks over your faces." Everyone laughed.

How good it was to hear Zoti laugh, Monica thought. She couldn't remember the last time she'd heard him laugh. It'd been quite awhile. Nick walked up and put an arm around her shoulder, and she smiled up at him. Their son was home with them. Maybe they could finally put this nightmare behind them.

"Let's go inside, everybody," she said. "We've fixed a fabulous lunch. Let's go eat, before it gets cold."

The entire merry crowd made its way inside the Stamos home. But like the beautiful light radiating off the surface of the ocean under the moon, Zoti's newfound healthy appearance belied the dangers underneath the surface.

The Ocean under the Moon

Chapter 47

June 4, 2008

Zoti's downward spiral started with a rash on his palms and soles
of his feet. He'd been home a week and things appeared to be going
well. But as he was brushing his teeth that morning, he noticed red
splotches on the palm of his right hand. He looked at his left hand
and noticed it also exhibited some lacy, red marks.

He assumed it was a reaction to one of the many
medications he was taking. He would tell Dr. Lindstrom about the
rash at their next appointment, which was in three days. He did not
feel bad; in fact, he was feeling better every day.

He was so glad to be out of the hospital, where he'd felt so
bored and isolated. At home, at least, he could see his friends,
although they each still had to wear their protective masks. But
Terry and some of the other guys could come over and play video
games, and he resumed some semblance of his former life.

He didn't make it the three days until his appointment
with Dr. Lindstrom. The day before he was supposed to see the
doctor, he woke up with a rash on his face, and his skin and the
whites of his eyes had taken on a yellow hue. On top of that, he had
a belly ache.

Alarmed, his mother called Dr. Lindstrom's office as soon

as it opened and was told to bring him in, right away. Nick was out shrimping on the *Resurrection* with Neal. She decided not to call him until after they met with the doctor because she didn't want to alarm him if it wasn't necessary.

After getting dressed, she and Zoti made the forty-five-minute drive over to the doctor's office at Nemours, where they were rushed into one of the examination rooms. After a short wait, Dr. Lindstrom strode into the room.

"Good morning, Zoti, Monica. How are y'all today?" He walked up to Zoti and started examining him.

The doctor noted the erythematous rash on the boy's face and the yellow color of his skin and sclera of both eyes. He grasped Zoti's hands and turned his palms up to examine the rash on the boy's hands. He had Zoti remove his shoes and socks and examined his feet, noting a rash on the soles of both feet.

Then Dr. Lindstrom asked him to lie flat on the examining table.

"Does this hurt?" he asked as he applied pressure to the boy's lower abdomen.

"Ouch!"

"I'll take that as a yes," the doctor quipped. "Have you experienced any diarrhea?"

"Yes, the last three days have been really bad," Zoti said.

The doctor gave him a disposable thermometer and told him to place it under his tongue.

"What's wrong with him?" Monica asked.

"Remember us talking about graft-versus-host disease or GVHD, for short?"

The Ocean under the Moon

"Yes, vaguely."

"Well, it's a complication in which the newly transplanted material attacks the transplant recipient's body. If it happens within one hundred days of the transplant, it's called acute GVHD. It can affect the skin, liver, and intestinal tract, hence his rashes, jaundice, abdominal pain, and diarrhea," the doctor said.

"This is a common complication of transplant patients, although he is starting a little later than most cases for acute GVHD. We've had him on low doses of immunosuppressive drugs every day, in order to suppress this response. Mild GVHD can actually be beneficial, however, to the recipient, because it can attack the remaining leukemia cells in the blood system. But it looks like he's developing the more virulent form of acute GVHD and this can be dangerous."

He pulled the thermometer out of Zoti's mouth and looked at it.

"One hundred and one degrees," he announced. "You have a mild fever, Zoti. I'm afraid we are going to have to keep a close watch on you. This means you're going to have to go back into the hospital."

"Oh, man! Do I have to?" he asked, with a disgusted look.

"Yes, you have the classic triad of GVHD: dermatitis, enteritis, and hepatitis. We are going to have to put you on stronger immunosuppressant drugs. When we do that, you are going to be at risk for infections. We're going to have to watch you closely, both to get the GVHD under control and to watch out for the secondary infections. I am not going to lie to you—this is a very serious situation and it may get worse before it gets better."

The Ocean under the Moon

Monica raised her head at the doctor's last statement.

"He will get better, won't he?"

"Yes, if he responds to the medications appropriately, and doesn't get any secondary infections, then he should be all right."

"But what if he doesn't?"

"Let's try to be positive, shall we. Zoti is going to get the best care possible. We've handled these types of complications before. Matt was such a good match for him. I'm kind of surprised that his body is having this strong of a reaction. But, like I said, some GVHD reaction can be beneficial to kill off any residual leukemia cells, so maybe this is a good thing. We are just going to have to be sure it doesn't get out of control. But in the meantime, let's go over to Admitting and we will get him checked back into the hospital."

Monica and Zoti followed the doctor out of the examining room, but neither one of them wanted to do so.

He, particularly, wanted to make a break for the exit to the stairs instead of following the doctor into the elevator. He wanted to escape down the stairs and out of the hospital and run into the sunshine and fresh air. The hospital felt like a prison to him, and he felt like he was being returned to his jail cell.

He had been battling this leukemia for nearly three years. Whenever he thought he was getting past it, he was sucked back in. He looked at the doorway to the stairwell, hesitating momentarily, then followed Dr. Lindstrom and his mother into the elevator.

Chapter 48

June 18, 2008

Zoti had been in the hospital for two weeks now and his condition had only gotten worse. The prednisone, a strong steroid and an anti-inflammatory drug to fight the GVHD, made him swell. His face was moon-shaped and he didn't look like himself. Nick and Monica could barely recognize their own son.

Worse yet, the strong anti-inflammatory drugs, which were helping to stave off the GVHD, were making him susceptible to secondary infections. He developed an infection from the cytomegalovirus, or CMV. Dr. Lindstrom had explained to them that CMV is a common virus that is dormant in most people, but in an immunosuppressed patient like Zoti, or in AIDS patients, the dormant virus would activate and begin to proliferate throughout the body, in a process called reactivation. This viral infection was causing him to have lung and liver problems, and he had been put on the drug acyclovir to try and control the advance of the virus.

He was in a catch-22. When Dr. Lindstrom reduced his immunosuppressant drugs to help fight his infections, then the GVHD disease would flare up, attacking his liver and intestines. If the doctor increased the dosage of immunosuppressant to help the GVHD, then the CMV would advance and cause fever from an infection of the virus in the liver, and diarrhea, blood in the stool, and abdominal pain from inflammation of the colon.

He developed spots and blurred vision in his left eye, as the virus invaded the retina. Because of this infection, he was taken over to the ophthalmology department, and an introvitreal acyclovir implant was surgically placed inside his eye, next to the retina, to deliver a steady flow of the drug to fight the virus.

He was very despondent. Over the last two weeks it had seemed it was one thing after another. He became convinced he was not going to leave the hospital alive this time. He knew he should have listened to his inner voice and made the break for freedom, when he had the chance, before they admitted him to the hospital.

Now, here he was, almost blind in one eye. He maintained a constant fever of around one hundred and two, with severe abdominal pain, and he was also losing his hearing on his left side. Because of viral pneumonia and previous damage to his lungs from the radiation treatment, the nurses periodically had to drain fluid from his lungs. His breathing was not bad enough to be put on a ventilator yet, but Dr. Lindstrom told them it was just a matter of time, before it would be necessary.

One day while Nick and Monica were sitting with him, Zoti told them that he didn't want to live if he could not live a quality life. He insisted he did not want any heroic measures taken to prolong his life, if there was not any chance of recovery. He also informed his doctor of his wishes, and a few days later, his parents were asked to sign DNR, or Do Not Resuscitate, consent forms.

It was when the nurse brought them the DNR forms that

The Ocean under the Moon

Nick and Monica fully grasped the gravity and consequences of the situation. Up until that time, through their son's entire three-year ordeal, they had always kept an upbeat attitude, believing that with good patient care and the Lord's help, he would eventually overcome this disease. Now, they were faced with the reality that the disease might win and that they might have to decide when to call it quits and let the disease have its final victory.

They could not bring themselves to sign the forms yet. Nick asked the nurse if they could take the forms home and think about it, before signing them. She agreed that it would be all right if they kept the forms overnight, but cautioned them not to delay too long, because even though their son was stable for now, things could change in a hurry. They thanked the nurse for her compassion and took the forms home, to try to develop the courage to sign them.

The Ocean under the Moon

Chapter 49

June 20, 2008

On Sunday morning, the family sat together in Zoti's hospital
room—Nick and Matt wearing suits and Monica, a pretty yellow
summer dress. They had decided to bring the church service to Zoti
today. They'd brought their Bibles and hymnals and Monica was
leading them in prayer and song.

Nick and Matt were a little self-conscious at first, singing
in low, soft voices. However, when a nurse appeared at the
doorway and reported that the other patients had requested that
they sing a little louder, so the patients could hear, they started
belting out the songs. Zoti was going in and out of consciousness.
He would wake up and smile at them, then drift back off to sleep.

Zoti had experienced a bad day yesterday. After much
soul-searching and debate, they had brought back the signed DNR
forms yesterday. When they got to the hospital, they'd found out
that his fever had spiked up. Dr. Lindstrom wasn't sure what was
causing this, so Zoti had spent the day undergoing a battery of
tests, which, coupled with the fever, left him tired and exhausted.
Because of the fever, he'd slept fitfully that night, tossing and
turning. Nick had stayed overnight with him, while she'd gone
home to get some rest and to bring Nick's Sunday clothes when she

and Matt returned the next day.

Now, she'd opened the curtains to the window to let the morning sun come in and illuminate Zoti's bed, but had to draw the curtain closed slightly, however, to keep his head in the shadow as he was still photophobic from the CMV retinitis.

They sang and prayed for over an hour and a half. His parents held hands and prayed kneeling at his bedside. Matt fought back tears, feeling guilty that it was his red blood cells, that he had donated, which were attacking his brother's body with the graft-versus-host disease.

Was he not a good enough match for his brother? Was there something defective in him? Had he done something wrong?"

He'd drunk a couple of beers the weekend before he donated the stem cells. He wondered if that had any effect on Zoti's condition. He prayed hard that the GVHD would go away and that the doctors would then be able to get the infection under control.

Later that afternoon, Dr. Lindstrom came to the open doorway of their room. Seeing that Zoti was asleep, the doctor motioned for Nick and Monica to join him in the hallway.

"We got back the results of Zoti's blood work and other tests, and it does not look good," he said.

"His white blood cell count is extremely elevated and the tests show that his bowel is perforated, which is leaking bacteria into his body, which his body, in its present state, is defenseless against. We are going to pump him full of antibiotics, but if he turns completely septic, it will only be a matter of time until he has multi-organ system failure and we will lose him. I just thought you ought to know, to give yourselves time to prepare," he finished, with tears in his eyes.

"Thank you, doctor, for being so honest," Monica said, her voice breaking.

"I'm so sorry. We're doing everything we can. I've never seen a patient go awry as quick as he has. It seems that for every tack we take, the disease has an answering maneuver."

"Well, whatever happens, I know we've had the best of care," she said. She reached out and patted his wrist gently.

The doctor's eyes welled up with tears again. He knew that he'd done everything possible and according to protocol, but when people lose a loved one, particularly a child, they often look for something or someone to blame. The fact that she was reassuring him, instead of blaming him, showed what kind of person she was.

He composed himself, and asked them to accompany him to his office.

"I hate to ask you to do this at a time like this, but I have some consent forms for you two to sign, before we can proceed further."

After his parents walked down the hall with the doctor, Matt sat pondering the words he'd just heard, that his brother was probably going to die. Even though the discussion had taken place in the hall, with the hard tiled floor echoing the sound, he could clearly hear the entire conversation.

As he sat in a hard chair, beside the foot of the bed, he was surprised to see his brother's hand move, motioning him to come closer. Matt stood up and walked forward, then leaned over to him.

"Promise me," Zoti began in a low whisper. "Promise me that you will not let me die in this hospital."

"What can I do?" Matt stared at him, dumbfounded.

"Tomorrow, I want you to take me to the beach," he said, between coughs. "Bring Terry, Pepe, and Terry's long board. I want to go surfing one last time."

Matt wasn't sure if Zoti was hallucinating or not. He looked at the tubes and catheters coming out of his brother's body, and all of the monitoring equipment, and he thought that what his brother was requesting was impossible.

"But you'll die if we disconnect this stuff," he said.

"I'm dying anyway." Zoti's eyes were pleading. "Please grant me this last wish. I'm tired, so tired. I just want to catch one more wave and then go to Heaven."

"But it will kill you." his brother said.

"Please, please, let me die, my way. It's the only thing I have left," he whispered, grabbing his brother's shirt in his clenched fist with his last bit of energy before falling back in exhaustion.

"Okay, brother, I promise." Matt laid his hand on his shoulder, as his younger brother drifted off to sleep.

The Ocean under the Moon

Chapter 50

June 21, 2008

Matt and Terry pulled up outside Wolfson Hospital at five-thirty in the morning. They had Terry's long board strapped to the racks on top of Matt's car and Pepe was spinning around in circles in the back seat. The dog sensed something exciting was about to happen, and when he saw the surfboard being put onto the car earlier; he knew he was going to the beach.

The night before, Matt had gone out to his car and called Terry on his cell phone. He'd told him what Zoti had said, and Terry was happy to help Zoti fulfill his final wish.

Nick and Monica had decided to come home from the hospital on Sunday night and get some rest for what was probably going to be some long days ahead. After spending Saturday night at the hospital and all day Sunday, Nick was exhausted and the hospital staff assured them that his son was stable and they would call them if there were any major changes during the night.

They planned to get up early and be back at the hospital by eight o'clock in the morning. Matt told his parents that he was getting up early to go surfing, before school, which was half of the truth.

Now, outside the hospital, dressed in hospital scrubs that

Matt had previously used as pajamas, the boys were trying to get up the nerve to exit the car and enter the hospital.

"We could go to prison for this, you know," Matt said.

"But it's Zoti's dying wish, dude. You have to fulfill his wish."

"I know — but it's kidnapping, maybe even manslaughter."

"It's neither, if that's his wish, dude," Terry said. "They are holding his body hostage, but we need to get his soul free."

Matt nodded. He knew that Terry shared with Zoti the bond all surfers have with the Mother Ocean, and the feeling of being one with nature and the universe, while riding the waves.

"But maybe Zoti will recover," he said.

"You said last night the doctor said there wasn't much hope of that. Besides, this is what Zoti wants. He made the decision. You shouldn't feel guilty about what happens."

"You're right. It's his decision."

The two boys walked toward the front entrance and waited until some hospital workers arrived at the entrance. They entered right behind the others, as if they worked there also. The middle-aged security guard gave the group a casual glance, but no more than that.

Once inside the lobby, Matt spotted an unattended wheelchair that was used to usher patients out when they are dismissed from the hospital. He moved it over to near the stairway entrance, which was around a corner and down a short hallway, out of sight from the lobby receptionist. He parked the wheelchair near the stairway door, so it would be ready for their return.

The Ocean under the Moon

Then the boys went through the door into the stairwell and started climbing the stairs up to the third floor. Yesterday, after Matt's conversation with Zoti, he had scouted out the situation. Fortunately, Zoti's room was positioned at the end of the wing, straight across from the stairway entrance. Matt had told his parents yesterday that he was going to the cafeteria to get some food, but on the way there, he went down the stairs to make sure the path was clear and that no alarms went off on the stairway doors.

He'd noticed the day before that since the room was at the end of the hall, it could not be seen directly from the nurses' station. He thought if he could get his brother out of the room quickly, he could get across the hall and carry him down the stairs before the nurses could stop him. At the bottom of the stairway, he would put him in the wheelchair and wheel him out into the lobby. Then, they just needed to get past the security guard and they would be out of the hospital.

They arrived at the door of the stairway that exited into the hallway across from Zoti's room. Matt motioned for Terry to stay back, then cracked the door open to peek down the hallway. He didn't see any nurses in the hallway, nor did he see anybody in Zoti's room through the open door to his room.

"Come on," he whispered, motioning with his hand.

They slipped across the hall and into Zoti's room.

"Zoti, Zoti, we're here!" Matt kept his voice hushed as he went over to the bed.

Zoti opened his eyes and gave a weak wave with his hand in greeting.

The Ocean under the Moon

"Hang in there, Zoti, we're going to the beach," Matt said. His brother seemed to be even weaker than yesterday.

He pulled out a pair of sharp scissors from his back pocket.

"Now, when I cut these plastic tubes, I want you to grab his legs and I'll grab under his arms and we'll carry him out," he told Terry. "We'll have to move fast, because when I cut these tubes, it may make the monitors go off and alert the nurses' station."

Terry positioned himself beside the bed so he could grab Zoti's legs.

"Ready?"

Terry nodded his head in affirmation.

"Ready, Zoti?" Matt looked down at his younger brother, who opened his eyes and gave a weak thumbs-up signal.

Matt clipped the tube closest to him that was going into his brother's left arm. Then he reached over and cut through the clear rubber tube going into his right arm. Finally, he cut the catheter that was coming out of Zoti's chest. He wasn't sure of the consequences of his actions, and he just hoped his brother wouldn't die before they reached the beach.

"Now!" he said.

He was surprised how light Zoti had become. He remembered overhearing his mother telling his father that he was down to around one hundred and ten pounds.

Terry grabbed Zoti's legs and encircled them with his arms. Matt ran his hands under his brother's armpits and clasped his hands together across his chest. Their hold on him was awkward, but manageable, since he was so light. They quickly traversed the hallway and began the descent down the stairs.

At the nurses' station, the monitor alarms for his room began to go off. A heavy-set nurse, who had been trying to complete her paperwork for the end of her night shift, reluctantly got to her feet, but not before finishing what she was writing. As she came around from behind the counter, she thought she caught a glimpse of the door to the stairway closing at the end of the hall.

That's odd, the nurse thought. Maybe she was imagining things. It'd been a long and busy shift on her floor. The last thing she needed was another emergency right before her shift ended. She slowly made her way down the hallway.

When the nurse stepped inside the open doorway to Zoti's room, she was startled to see that the patient was not in his bed. Maybe he somehow got out of bed and made it to the bathroom, she thought at first. She glanced toward the bathroom, but its door stood open and the nurse could see that no one was in there. She then took a couple of more steps toward the bed and picked up one of the tubes that had been going into his arm and saw that it was cut.

"My God!" she said aloud, startling herself into action.

The nurse hurried out of the room and across the hall and opened the stairway door. She peered down the stairwell. She heard the shuffling of feet going down the stairs and some muffled voices. Then, looking down through the open space between the descending flights of stairs, she could make out the shoulders of two people carrying a third person down the stairs. Alarmed, the nurse ran down the hall, as fast as her chubby legs could take her, to the nurses' station.

By then, they had made it to the bottom floor and loaded Zoti into the wheelchair. He'd moaned and groaned all of the way down the stairs with all of the jostling. He was floating in and out of consciousness. The boys straightened him up in the wheelchair and calmed their own breathing for a second, then pushed him down the short hallway and into the lobby, heading for the front entrance.

The nurse, back on the third floor, was reaching for the phone to call down to the lobby.

Matt, pushing Zoti in the wheelchair, and Terry walking alongside had already reached the front entrance by the time the phone started ringing at the receptionist's desk in the lobby. Matt and Terry nodded at the security guard standing next to the entrance. The guard nodded back at them with a somewhat puzzled look on his face, but he did not stop them.

The boys made it all the way past the set of glass double doors when they looked back and saw the receptionist standing up behind her desk with the phone in one hand and pointing at them. They saw the security guard turn and start to come toward them, and they looked at each other and then started running. Matt pushed Zoti as fast as he could to his car, which was not parked far away.

He stopped the wheelchair by the rear passenger door, then pulled his keys from his pocket and opened the car doors with his remote key. He tossed his keys to Terry and told him to start the engine. He opened the car door, then scooped up his brother in his arms and placed him in the back seat. Pepe jumped up in his master's lap and started licking his face.

Just as Terry started the ignition, Matt slammed the rear door closed and glanced back to see the security guard about halfway from the hospital entrance to their car, closing as fast as he could, which at his age was not very fast. Matt opened the front passenger door and slid into the front seat.

"Go! Go!"

Terry shifted the car into drive and squealed out of the parking lot. Matt turned around and looked out the window and saw the security guard run up to where their car had been parked. The guard stared in their direction, trying to read the license plate on his car.

Terry drove up the entrance ramp and onto Interstate 95. They traveled less than a mile on the interstate before exiting on Beach Boulevard and heading east toward the beach.

Matt pulled out his cell phone and called his parents, who he knew were on their way to the hospital by now. Nick, indeed, was driving his car on the way to the hospital and was almost to the hospital, when Monica's cell phone rang.

"Hello, honey," she said after seeing Matt's name as the incoming call on her cell phone.

"Mom, this is Matt. I have Zoti with me. We have to do something. It was Zoti's wish," he blurted out and then hit the button to disconnect the call. Then he turned his cell phone off altogether.

"There, maybe that will get the cops off our back," he said, hoping his parents would explain to the staff when they got to the hospital.

The Ocean under the Moon

After about four miles, instead of going straight on Beach Boulevard, which would have taken them to Jacksonville Beach, he instructed Terry to turn north on Southside Boulevard. Soon they were crossing the Dames Point Bridge, a large suspension bridge spanning the St. John's River.

"Are you okay?" He turned around to look at Zoti.

Pepe, sensing his master was not his usual self, settled down and was lying close beside him with his head in his lap. Zoti was leaned back in his seat with his head propped against the window looking out at the scenery, as though it was the last time he would see it. He was breathing laboriously.

"I'm good," he said matter-of-factly, even though it was clear he was not.

Matt gave Terry a glance and motioned him to speed up.

They made it over the bridge and then turned right on Heckscher Drive, the scenic, winding road that hugs the north bank of the St. John's. They were headed to Huguenot Park, Zoti's favorite place to surf. The boys arrived at the entrance to the city-owned park and paid the one dollar admission fee.

A spit of sand that separates St. John's inlet from Fort George Island inlet, Huguenot is a mecca for surfers and beachgoers with its wide, flat beach where the sand meets the ocean on the east side. On the west side, which faces the calm waters of Fort George inlet, kite surfers and jet-ski riders commonly criss-cross the surface of the water.

One of the allures of Huguenot Park is that you can drive your vehicle right out onto the hard-packed sand of the beach, so it looks like a parking lot on the weekends. The long, flat beach also makes for smooth-breaking, long-riding swells, unlike other, more populated areas along the coast, where they had to pump sand onto the beach to battle erosion to protect houses, leaving the beach steep, with a shore-break that is not good for surfing.

The boys drove down the road winding between the small sand dunes of the narrow isthmus that separates the shallow bay on the left from the deep, fast flowing St. John's River on the right. Across the river, Zoti could see the Mayport Naval Station, with its large surface ships in the harbor and helicopters and planes buzzing over the base.

The sun was up just past the horizon, a huge orange ball, beginning its day's work. It was going to be a beautiful morning, Zoti thought, a perfect day for surfing. The wind was calm and the river and bay were glassy smooth. If only there was a bit of a swell in the ocean, conditions would be perfect.

Zoti's condition was far from perfect, however. He was tired, so very tired. An exhaustion similar to climbers on Mount Everest, trying to take their last few oxygen-deprived steps toward the summit, where every step they take, they fear will be their last one, before they fall face-first into the snow and die.

His breathing was becoming loud and wheezy. He was coughing hard between each breath. Matt and Terry gave each other concerned looks. Terry drove the car off the end of the pavement, onto the hard-packed sand on the bay side, and then they passed between the tall sand dunes to the Atlantic side, where the ocean awaited them.

The beach was nearly deserted, since it was a Monday morning, and they saw only a couple of retirees surf-fishing, down

402

the beach. The sky was clear, the warming sun was making its way up from the horizon, and the ocean was smooth as glass. There was a long, clean two- to three-foot swell that normally would be too small for good surfing, but for their purposes today, it would be perfect.

Terry pulled the car down toward the water, noting that the tide was going out. He parked parallel to the edge of the water with Zoti's side of the car facing toward the ocean. He started to unstrap the surfboard from its rack on top of the car, while Matt opened Zoti's door. Pepe jumped out of the car and immediately ran off down the beach after a seagull. They took off their scrubs and threw them into the car, revealing the bathing suits they had worn underneath.

"Here we are, Zoti. How are you feeling?"

"It's beautiful, man," he said softly, tears welling up in his eyes at the sight of the ocean.

"Perfect day for surfing!" Matt agreed, exaggerating for his brother's sake.

The irony of Zoti's appreciation of the natural world, which he would not long be inhabiting, was not lost on Matt. Unlike many people in the world who are just interested in getting ahead, making money, and buying more material things, here was someone who could fully appreciate a beautiful sunrise and a perfectly-formed wave. Yet he was scheduled to die and these other people would go on living.

It's not fair, Matt thought, as he bent over and slid one arm behind his brother's back. He slipped his other arm under the crook below Zoti's knees and picked his emaciated brother up in a

fireman's carry.

When he neared the edge of the water he laid his brother down on the beach to wait for Terry to finish getting the surfboard waxed and ready to go. Matt went back to the car and retrieved a life-preserver from the trunk. He figured, in Zoti's weakened condition, just falling off the board could result in him slipping under the water and drowning.

Even in his enfeebled state, Zoti started chuckling and shaking his head from side to side, when his brother approached with the life preserver.

"No way, man," he said, as Matt approached.

"You might drown if you wipe out."

"I can think of worse ways to go," Zoti responded, between coughs. "No life preserver. Unless you got a life preserver for leukemia."

Matt tossed the life preserver up on the beach toward his car.

"Are you sure you want to do this?" he asked his brother, giving him one last chance to back out.

Zoti simply nodded in affirmation, as he gazed out onto the ocean.

Matt picked him up again and Terry lifted the heavy board, put it under his arm, and they walked toward the rising sun, out into the water. When they got to crotch-deep, Terry put the board down on the water. Matt placed Zoti in a prone position on top of the wide and stable long board.

Zoti weakly gripped the rails of the surfboard with his hands and could just raise his head up to see the small waves approaching. Terry had to stand next to the board and reach across him to stabilize the board and keep him on it as the incoming waves slid underneath.

"Since you're a better surfer than me, Terry, why don't you take him out a little further and get him started on the good part of the wave? I'll stay here in the shallow water and catch him as he comes in," Matt offered.

Terry nodded and started guiding Zoti out to deeper water.

"Just like old times, me and you, going surfing, isn't it?" Zoti whispered.

"Yes, it is." Terry pulled on the front of the board, facing forward, so Zoti could not see the tears in his eyes.

He made it out to chest-deep water and spun the board around so Zoti was facing toward the beach.

"Ready for the ride of your life?" he asked.

"Well said," Zoti said with a smile.

"Here comes one now!" Terry said as a smooth swell started cresting into a perfect two-foot wave. "Hang on, Zoti."

He gave the board one last big push to propel it forward with enough force to catch the wave.

Zoti knew he was too weak to stand or even kneel on the board. His goal was to just once again feel the power of the ocean pushing his body and the board along, in harmony, knowing that he had harnessed the energy of the ocean for his own enjoyment. If he could just stay, lying on the board, making the subtle balance movements to keep the board going straight toward the beach, without falling off, then he would once again be in control of his life and in harmony with Mother Nature and closer to God.

All of his senses were heightened. He could feel the warm sun on his back. The salty taste of the seawater was in his mouth. The light crescendo of the small waves hitting the shore and the cries of the seagulls rang in his ears.

He felt the power of the small wave swell up behind him and then his friend's final push. Soon the board was skimming along in front of the wave. He started laughing. His joy at feeling the power of the ocean was immense. His mind was free from the illness; it no longer existed.

As the wave picked up the back of the board, it tried to turn the board sideways. He knew this would happen and was ready for it. He leaned with all of his might on one rail to try and straighten the board. When this didn't completely straighten the board perpendicular to the beach, he slipped his foot off the board on that side and used it like a rudder to straighten the board.

Terry and Matt both raised their arms and yelled in triumph, as they saw him riding the wave. Matt hustled over to the spot where he was heading, to intercept him before he hit the beach. He splashed through the knee-deep water and intercepted Zoti just as the skegs on the long board were about to scrape on the bottom.

"That was awesome!" Matt said.

"Again!"

It was all he could say. He was exhausted from his efforts.

Matt turned the board around and started pushing his brother and the board back out to deeper water. Terry came in part of the way and took control of the board from Matt, when he reached waist-deep water.

"Great ride, Zoti!" he said.

"Thanks," he mustered, his breathing becoming more laborious.

Terry pulled him back out to deeper water, taking care that Zoti did not fall off the board with each passing wave. Finally they reached the appropriate depth where the waves weren't quite breaking yet, just a smooth swell passing that hadn't quite crested. Terry turned the board around and pointed its nose toward the beach.

"Are you ready to go again?"

"I was born ready," he whispered, with false bravado.

Terry saw a good wave coming and moved Zoti slightly to the right, so he would be in the best part of the wave that was beginning to crest. He gave the board a final push and the wave picked up the board and carried it forward.

Once again Zoti rode the wave perfectly, riding on his belly on the board, steering by dragging either foot in the water as needed to keep the board straight. Matt again reached the board as it entered knee-deep water to keep the board from crashing into the beach. Pepe was running around in the shallow water, jumping up and barking, as he approached on the board.

This time Zoti had been more subdued on his ride in. Matt noticed a tired look in his eyes and a grim determination on his face that looked like it was taking all of his strength just to hold onto the board.

"Are you okay, bud? Do you want to rest on the beach for awhile?" Matt asked as he stopped the forward momentum of the surfboard.

"No! Again!" he demanded, a worn, but determined look on his face, as if time was running out.

Matt knew better than to argue with his strong-willed little brother, so he started pushing the board back out. Zoti put his head down on the board and tried to conserve his energy. He was nearing exhaustion. The lining of his lungs had been damaged by the full-body radiation that killed the last of his bone marrow. Over the last several weeks his lungs had become stiffer and stiffer, losing the elasticity that allowed them to expand and contract. Now he was gasping for air and suffering from the paranoia that comes from not getting enough oxygen.

Zoti looked at his hand in front of his face out of his good eye as his brother pushed him toward his friend. He noticed his skin was a weird yellow color like a person who had used a cheap, fake tan cream. He knew, however, it was jaundice, from the GVHD attacking his liver. His skin felt like there were tiny little bugs crawling underneath his skin, all over his body, also the effects of GVHD. Worse of all was the cramping in his gut, as the disease attacked his intestines, which was making it hard for him to lie on his stomach on the surfboard.

One more ride. Then he would go rest on the beach.

"Gonna go again?" Terry asked.

"One last time," he whispered, barely able to raise his head.

"Okay, buddy. I'm going to find you a perfect wave."

He once again pulled Zoti out through the white crests of each oncoming wave. Zoti kept partially sliding off the board with each passing wave and Terry had to keep re-centering him on the board. Finally, they made it out past the breaking waves. Terry thought that it was a good thing the waves were small today, otherwise Zoti would never have been able to stay on the board.

Out about neck deep in the water now, Terry had to hold onto the board with each incoming swell as the water got too deep for him to touch bottom, only for his feet to hit bottom again after each swell passed. He rotated the board between swells so Zoti was pointed toward the beach. His face was very close to Zoti's now as he held onto the rail of the surfboard looking out into the ocean for the perfect wave.

"I love you, man," Zoti said. "We've had some good times together, haven't we? Thanks for coming today."

Terry looked over at his friend; his peaceful blue eyes were staring at him, but seeming to look right through him.

"There'll be plenty more great days ahead," he lied, averting his eyes from Zoti's. "Here comes a good one now."

"Is it perfect?"

"It's perfect," Terry confirmed. With tears in his eyes, he gave the back end of the surfboard a gentle, but firm, push to catch the wave.

His board caught the wave, but Zoti no longer possessed the energy to keep his head up to see where he was going. His eyes looked in the direction his face was pointing as he rested his head on the surfboard.

He could see the green, clear water rushing past the side of the board. He could see the small wall of white water stretched out behind him pushing him toward shore. He could see the blue sky and hear seagulls screeching overhead. Off in the distance, a skimmer bird was flying toward him, its lower beak skimming through the shallow water trying to intercept a minnow or two.

He didn't want to leave this life. It was too beautiful, but he had no choice in the matter.

Matt could see his brother was in trouble. The board quit tracking straight and veered suddenly to its right, dumping him into the water. He ran as fast as he could through the thigh-deep water. The empty surfboard zoomed past him advancing, upside down and sideways, in front of the wave.

When he got to the spot where Zoti went off the board, he spotted him rolling, face down, just beneath the surface in the turbulent water. Matt reached into the water and plucked him from the sea. He started dragging his limp body toward shore.

"Zoti ... are you all right?" he asked.

When they got to shallow water, Pepe was there to greet them, hopping around and barking.

He pulled Zoti out of the water and laid him on the soft sand, just past the water's edge. Pepe rushed up and started licking Zoti in the face. There was no response from him. Matt pushed the dog aside and slapped his brother gently on the face.

"Zoti... Zoti... Wake up!"

He slid his hand down the side of his brother's neck and felt for a pulse, like he had been taught, while learning first aid in the Boy Scouts a few years ago. He did not feel a pulse. He lifted one of Zoti's closed eyelids. Even with the bright early-morning sun, he could see the pupil did not constrict to light exposure and was fixed and dilated. He lifted the other eyelid and saw the same

The Ocean under the Moon

result. He knew his brother was gone.

"Arrrr...gh," he groaned to the sky.

He grabbed his brother under the armpits and raised his upper torso. He sat down behind him and splayed his legs to either side of Zoti's body and leaned his brother's upper body back against his chest. He wrapped his arms around Zoti in a bear hug.

Terry slowly walked up and saw the two brothers facing the ocean, tears streaming down Matt's face, rocking back and forth in their embrace. Pepe was running circles around them, barking excitedly, and sometimes darting in and tugging on Zoti's shorts with his mouth, as if to implore him to get up and play. But there would be no more playing for Zoti, his life was over.

Matt sat there hugging his brother, not wanting to let him go, staring at the rising sun and wondering how life could be so cruel.

Chapter 51

June 25, 2008

Nick sat in the front pew, quietly sobbing, while holding Monica's hand. She sat between him and Matt, gripping both of their hands. With his free hand, Matt wiped away tears of his own. Hundreds of people had showed up at St. Peter's for the funeral—far beyond the capacity of the church—which seated only about two hundred fifty people. Once the sanctuary was filled, people spilled out into the courtyard, where the ushers put up folding chairs and speakers that were normally used for the overflowing Easter service.

Terry spoke in eulogy at the service, as well as Andy Lopez and Brian Williams, Zoti's buddies from the surfing circuit.

Nick, however, was too distraught to make a speech, without breaking down. He, Monica and Matt appreciated the kind words and stories, but their sadness over losing their energetic, younger son and brother was overwhelming. Every few seconds one of them, or all three, would break out sobbing over some word or memory that was being invoked.

After an exhausting, nearly two-hour service, the long caravan moved slowly to Bosque Bello Cemetery.

There, beside the grave in the shade of the old cedar trees and oak trees, the mourners heard Father George recite a poem,

The Ocean under the Moon

"Death Is Nothing at All," by Harry Scott Holland, who was canon of St. Paul's Cathedral in London around the turn of the previous century.

Death is nothing at all.
I have only slipped away into the next room.
I am I and you are you.
Whatever we were to each other,
that we still are.

Call me by my old familiar name.
Speak to me in the easy way you always used.
Put no difference in your tone.
Wear no forced solemnity or sorrow.

Laugh as we always laughed,
at the little jokes we enjoyed together.
Pray, smile, think of me, pray for me.
Let my name be ever the household name that it always was,
Let it be spoken without effect, without the trace of a shadow on it.

Life means all that it ever meant.
It is the same as it ever was.
There is unbroken continuity.
Why should I be out of mind,
because I am out of sight?

The Ocean under the Moon

I am waiting for you, for an interval,
Somewhere very near,
just round the corner.

All is well.

Father George concluded the graveside service, and the family accepted the final condolences from the mourners. After awhile, the crowd dwindled, leaving just the immediate family and a few of Zoti's closest friends lingering behind, as the workers lowered his casket.

Nick stood beside the open gravesite as the casket was slowly lowered to the bottom of the grave. Terry came up beside him and tossed in an unused bar of surf wax after the casket had reached the bottom of the grave. Another of Zoti's friends came up on the other side of him and threw in Zoti's old surfing leash.

"You can't go surfing in heaven without these things," Terry said, out loud, to Zoti's casket.

Pepe, having been let out of the car by Matt, now that the crowd was gone, came running up to the edge of the gravesite. He began barking and pawing at the dirt at the edge of the grave. Matt had to put him on his leash and drag him away from the grave site.

Monica grabbed Nick's arm and told him they needed to get home, because they had people coming over to the house. He said he wanted to stay a little longer with his son and for her to take the car, along with Matt and Pepe, home. He would walk the short distance home in a few minutes. She nodded her understanding and with a pat on his arm, headed for their car.

He said a short prayer on the open grave, then threw a key into the grave on top of Zoti's casket. It was a spare key to the *Resurrection*. It was his dream that he would give that key and the ownership of the family's shrimping business over to his son one day. Since Zoti loved the ocean so, it was his assumption that Zoti would be the one to carry on the family's seafaring legacy. Now that dream was dead.

He stepped back from the edge of the grave and nodded to the two workers who were impatiently waiting to get on with their business. He retreated to the shade of one of the old cedar trees and watched them go about filling in the grave.

He gazed out at the family cemetery plot. There was Grandfather Eber's headstone on the left end of the plot and next to him was Grandmother Catherine's headstone. To the right of her headstone was Nick's father Abe's headstone, along with his mother Isabelle's. Then there was an open space for three more graves — intended for Nick, Monica, and Matt. At the far right end of the plot was Zoti's grave, which the workers were tossing dirt into with their shovels. Next to his grave was little baby Angela's small headstone.

He looked at the grassy spot, just to the right of his mother's headstone. He came face to face with his mortality. He was next in line. That was the way it was supposed to go, in orderly fashion, wasn't it? Death wasn't supposed to go for the youngest, he thought, as he moved his gaze across the grassy open spot to where the workers were tossing dirt on his son's casket.

He shook his head at the cruel twist of fate his family had

endured. He'd lost his youngest son and the shrimping industry was falling apart around him. He couldn't help but remember the last few lines of the poem Father George had recited.

"I am waiting for you, for an interval,
Somewhere very near,
Just around the corner,
All is well."

"I'm coming, Zoti. I'm coming," he whispered, and then began the lonely walk home.

The Ocean under the Moon

Chapter 52

July 13, 2008
8:05 a.m.

Nick woke up with a start. He had not intended to, but he'd fallen back to sleep for a few short minutes. He looked over at Monica, who was still sleeping beside him. For a second, doubt crept into his mind about what he needed to do.

He laid his head back down on the pillow and thought about what he just dreamt about. His grandfather's death, his courtship with Monica, his finding and restoration of the *Resurrection*, teaming up with Gator, the birth of his children, Gator's death, and Zoti's death—all had flooded before his mind like a kaleidoscope of memories.

Maybe they are right about your life flashing before your eyes before death. He intended to die this evening and his life had passed before his mind, in his dreams; a life bittersweet. It had started off sweet, but lately it'd been quite the opposite.

When does a man know he has been defeated? Is it when he loses his best friend? When he loses his son? Or is it when he loses his livelihood?

In the last couple of months, gas prices soared to over four dollars a gallon. He could catch all of the shrimp he wanted, but with the rise in fuel costs, coupled with the depressed price of shrimp from the influx of cheap, farm-raised, foreign shrimp, his career was not a profitable venture any more. So now, he not only had lost his youngest son, he was becoming unable to provide for his wife and his other son.

He buried the back of his head, deeper into the pillow, and pondered his situation. Matt had recently graduated high school and was preparing to go to Jacksonville University on his partial scholarship, but where was the rest of the money for tuition, books, and living expenses going to come from?

Worse yet, how was he going to pay the mortgage on his house? The credit line payment, secured by the equity in his house, had steadily risen from the huge medical bills from Zoti's long, unsuccessful battle with leukemia. His son had waged a brave, but expensive, fight against cancer, one that he'd lost. Modern medicine does not come cheap, and there is no refund at the end if that battle doesn't conclude with a victory.

Their son's long struggle cost them total medical bills of over five hundred thousand dollars. Monica was unaware the bills had accumulated so high. He'd been paying all of the household bills throughout their marriage and he kept her shielded from the true extent of their indebtedness. He'd been paying the medical bills by using the existing credit line on their house and land.

He had developed a good relationship with his local bank from years of doing business with them. The rotund bank manager, Richard Mallet, gladly set up a home equity line using their home and choice piece of property as collateral, back when Zoti first got sick and real estate was booming on the island.

The Ocean under the Moon

But in the last year, the recession had taken its toll on the real estate prices on Amelia Island, just like the rest of the country. Richard called him about two weeks before his son's death to inform him that the bank was not going to be able to lend him any more money against his property, and that his home equity loan was maxed out against the adjusted price of his property.

The ironic thing, he thought, as he lay there staring at the ceiling, was that two years ago, he'd received that offer from the real estate developer for over one million dollars for his property. This was back when real estate was still strong. At that time, Zoti was going into remission and he didn't have any idea that his son's final medical bills would be so high, so he turned the developer down. Now, with twenty-twenty hindsight vision, it looked like he should have taken the deal.

He shook himself from his random thoughts and rose to get out of the bed. He wanted his last day on earth to get off to a good start, so he decided he would go down to the Marina Restaurant for a hearty breakfast, while his wife slept in late. He showered, shaved, and got dressed in some decent clothes. He decided he would change into his shrimping clothes when he came back after breakfast.

He left his house and drove to downtown Fernandina. As he drove down Centre Street past all the shops now occupying the bottom floors of all the historic buildings, he wondered how the shops were doing in this poor economy. It seemed to him that there were fewer tourists in town the last two summers. He'd noticed on a drive through town, a couple of evenings ago, that the only place that seemed busy was the fudge and ice cream shop. He surmised that even in a recession, or maybe because of the recession, people still wanted to satisfy their sweet tooth, because it made them feel better for awhile.

Seeing that all the parking spaces in front of the Marina Restaurant were full, he pulled around the side of the building and parked in an unmarked space next to the railroad tracks that only the locals know about. He walked around to the front of the restaurant, and noticed the three park benches there, which were normally full of people this time of year waiting their turn to get into the restaurant, were nearly empty.

He pushed the door open and saw Patricia at her usual spot, working on her bills at the big round table, just inside the door.

The usual assortment of working men also occupied the round table. A lawyer, a store owner, and a mill worker were all enjoying their breakfast and talking politics, and solving the world's problems.

Patricia looked up when he walked in and her face brightened.

"Well, looks what the cat's drug in," she said, with a smile.

He'd not been in the restaurant since his son had died and she was glad to see him getting out again.

"Well, y'all know you can't solve the world's problems without my input," he said, as he approached the table.

All the men at the table stopped talking and stood up and greeted him with smiles and handshakes. He made his way over to Patricia and gave her a big hug, and she gestured for him to sit next to her on her right side. The men soon went back into their debate about politics.

"How have you been doing?" she said. She had a concerned look on her face and leaned in to Nick.

"It's tough, Patricia, real tough. You don't expect to bury your youngest child. But we just keep muddling along. That's all you can do."

She patted his hand in understanding, then changed the subject.

"How's the shrimping been?"

"Well, we've been catching them okay, but the price at the dock isn't what we need to make a profit. Now with gas up so high, it's hardly worth cranking up the boat," he said.

"Tell me about it," she agreed. "People aren't traveling like they used to. With the price of gas what it is and the recession going on, my business is down twenty percent. However, I'll buy two hundred pounds of shrimp from you on your next run. You set the price to whatever you need. I'd buy more, but as you can see, my business is down, too."

"That's very kind of you," he said. He felt bad that it would be the one order he would not be able to fill, if he completed his plan.

"Oh, it's not charity," she said. "I need the shrimp. Plus, at least if I get them from you, I know they're fresh and not from some shrimp farm in China or wherever."

"Thank you, Patricia. You're a good friend," he said, patting her arm.

They turned their attention back to the men's conversation

going on around the table about how oil speculators were artificially driving up oil prices for their own greedy gains, at the expense of the American consumer.

He sat back and listened to heated banter among the men and one woman, at the table, and realized how much he was going to miss this.

The Ocean under the Moon

Chapter 53

July 13, 2008
9:30 a.m.

Nick was back at his house after having left the restaurant. He'd brought his wife a take-out order of scrambled eggs, bacon, grits, toast and a small slice of watermelon. He assembled the meal on ceramic plates, and placed a single cut red rose, from the rose bushes in front of the house, in a small vase on top of the tray. Once the presentation was just right, he carried the tray into the bedroom.

"Wake up, sleepyhead," he said in a soothing voice, as he entered the room.

Monica, who was lying on her back in the strong, early-morning sun, opened her eyes.

"What's the occasion?" she asked.

"No occasion. Can't I just do something nice for my beautiful wife?"

She sat up in bed, raised an eyebrow, and gave him a questioning look. He came over to her and placed the tray across her lap and sat down on the edge of the bed beside her.

"Neal got called to do jury duty today," he said. "Can you imagine that? Neal, sitting in the jury box, with someone's fate in his hands. That's a scary thought." He shook his head in disbelief.

"Well, anyway, I thought I would sleep in and go out shrimping later. But I couldn't sleep very late, because I'm too used to getting up early. So I decided to go down to the Marina and get us some breakfast."

"Where's your food?" she asked.

"Oh, I ate down at the Marina with Patricia and the boys."

"How is she doing?"

"She's doing fine, but the restaurant is struggling a bit due to the lack of tourism this summer. She did promise to buy two hundred pounds of shrimp from me, however, so I'm going to take the *Resurrection* out in a little bit and see if I can catch enough shrimp for her order and then some."

"You're going out alone?"

He knew she did not like him shrimping alone. She felt it was unsafe. She always asked what would happen if he got his hand caught in the winch or got knocked overboard. There would be no one there to help him. That's why she had always insisted Gator, Neal, or one of the boys went with him.

"I don't want you to go alone."

"But Neal's got jury duty and it's too late to try to find someone else. I'll be fine. I'm just going to get enough shrimp for Patricia's order. I'll be home by nightfall."

"Well, maybe just this one time."

He leaned down toward her and kissed her on the forehead.

"You know I love you, always have, and I would do anything for you, don't you?"

The Ocean under the Moon

She nodded her head in acknowledgement.

"I still see you as that sixteen-year-old girl on the beach, whom I fell in love with the first time I laid my eyes on you."

"First, breakfast in bed, now profession of your love. What are you doing? Trying to get lucky?" she said with a mischievous grin.

"I'm already lucky. I have you."

He leaned in to kiss her and it became a long passionate kiss. They made love. He knew it would be for the final time, so he went slow and savored every moment of their encounter. She, aroused by his words, and secure in their love for each other, responded in kind.

Afterward, she lay beside him, her head on his chest listening to his heartbeat. He lay on his back, looking at the ceiling, stroking her hair. Tears were rolling out of the sides of his eyes, because he knew this sweet embrace would be their last.

The Ocean under the Moon

Chapter 54

July 13, 2008
11:14 a.m.

Nick backed the *Resurrection* away from his dock, then rotated the boat so he was heading north. He motored at slow speed past the mouth of Egan's Creek, past the dilapidated docks at the old pogy plant, then past the campground at Fort Clinch State Park at the northwest corner of the island. He guided the boat into Cumberland Sound and the channel that separated the two islands. This was his daily commute and he loved every minute of it.

Unlike the millions of commuters who were stuck in traffic in the large cities around the country, cussing and stressing, he got to see a beautiful sunrise coming up over the Atlantic every morning and enjoy the wide open spaces of the ocean, instead of jostling with cars and other people.

Once in the channel, he looked to the north and could see the wide, sandy beach of the south end of Cumberland National Seashore. He spotted a group of wild horses, descendants of horses brought to the island in the seventeenth century, grazing on the sea oats. If he looked south, he could see the large, brick walls of Fort Clinch, highlighted by the mid-morning sun.

Yes, he had enjoyed a wonderful life. Being free to do

what he wanted to do, in such a beautiful environment. But now his life was falling apart. He was saddled with debt, and market forces beyond his control would not allow him to work his way out of the debt. It's ironic; here he was, healthy, from working in an enjoyable, outside environment, but about to kill himself. Meanwhile, the commuters in the big city were slowly killing themselves with stress, cholesterol, and high blood pressure.

He had always provided for his family and he would make the ultimate sacrifice to do so again. He knew that if Monica and Matt knew of his plans they would have stopped him. They would rather be bankrupt and still have their husband and father, respectively. But he'd taken an oath, when he married his wife, to provide for her.

He could not imagine having to sell his family's land and having to go live with Buck and Caroline. He would feel like a failure, and not being able to send Matt to college was another failure he was unable to face. To see the disappointment in his son's face, and to watch Matt take a job he didn't want to do and not realize his dreams, would be too much for him to take.

To bolster his own courage, and to enhance the perception that his upcoming actions were truly an accident, he had brought aboard a cooler full of beer. He reached into the cooler and pulled out a cold beer. He was about to break one of his cardinal rules, which was not to drink on the boat while working. He popped open the top and took a healthy draw from the beer, and set the can down in front of the steering wheel on the bridge of the boat.

He looked up at the sun that he was heading toward, then noticed that he had passed the white can buoy marking the end of the south jetty. He turned the boat southeast and headed toward his shrimping grounds. The ocean was calm, the water was clear, and there was just a hint of breeze to cool things off.

It was going to be a great day to kill oneself. He pushed the throttle forward.

The Ocean under the Moon

Chapter 55

July 13, 2008
12:03 p.m.

Nick's plan was to shrimp all afternoon and then stage his
"accident" in the early evening. To make it look like an accident, he
wanted the hold of the boat to be full of shrimp to prove that he
had been shrimping all day and had no intentions of suicide. He
also wanted to be seen shrimping by the other boats, and he would
make sure to banter with the other captains over the radio
throughout the day.

There was a camaraderie between the shrimp boat
captains based out of Fernandina. Sure there was some
competition, about who could catch the most shrimp, but there was
also a lot of information sharing over the radio about where the
shrimp were located. Also, there was a lot of loaning of equipment
between boats, when something broke down, to keep the boats
running. He was going to miss his fellow shrimpers.

He arrived at his shrimping grounds, about four miles off
the beach about halfway down the island. He set the boat on
autopilot, then went back and lowered the nets into position. He
didn't bother with the trail net on this day. Either he was going to
catch shrimp or he wasn't.

The Ocean under the Moon

He set the nets out wide, returned to the pilothouse, flipped the autopilot off, and took control of the wheel. This was his element, guiding the boat through the sea, engine droning steadily, as it pulled its heavy load through the water.

He couldn't believe his way of life was about to end. Not only for him personally, but for his industry as a whole. An industry that had its beginning in the waters around Amelia Island almost one hundred years ago, was soon going to be extinct. And, unlike the buffalo hunters of the plains over a hundred years ago, whose industry died because of over-harvesting and loss of habitat, coastal shrimping was sustainable. No, shrimping on boats like his would disappear from reasons that were truly unjust.

Why weren't the legislators in Washington helping out the shrimp industry more? Were they too busy chasing the waiter at their fancy cocktail parties, to get a free shrimp cocktail, to worry about where the shrimp comes from? He'd often joked that the only time legislators move quickly and effectively was when there was free food to be had or if there was a good publicity-shot opportunity.

But the congressmen help the farmers, even paying them subsidies not to grow crops on their land. The shrimpers, however, weren't asking for a handout—just a level playing field. But they'd never get that. Unless the U.S. government allowed the domestic shrimpers to destroy the marshes of the southeastern United States, the mangroves of south Florida, and the bayous of the Louisiana and Texas to build shrimp farms, and allowed them to disregard all environmental regulations, the playing field would never be level between domestic shrimp and foreign pond-raised shrimp.

The Ocean under the Moon

He'd learned from going to meetings and his previous lobbying efforts that up to thirty percent of some tropical countries' mangrove ecosystems had been converted into shrimp farms, and another one to two percent were being lost per year. He was not a biologist, but from his years of studying nature, he knew this could not be a good thing for those nations' ecology. He knew that the mangrove forests, just like the marshes, protect shorelines from erosion, storms, and hurricanes — as well as providing food resources, habitat, and spawning grounds for many types of fish and wildlife.

One study, he remembered, said the tropical mangrove forests were vital habitats for the young of eighty percent of all commercial seafood species. So destroying the mangrove forests to implement shrimp farms not only robs other species of spawning grounds, but also threatens the livelihood of fishermen, who make their living catching other types of seafood.

He knew the mangroves act as a filtration system to prevent run-off of fertilizer and other pollutants from the land from entering directly into the sea. When these ecosystems are destroyed and shrimp farms installed in their place, eutrophication can be a problem. The introduction of large amounts of nutrients into the water, to encourage shrimp growth, also causes plant growth to explode, and when the plants die, the resulting decomposing bacteria depletes the oxygen and results in large fish kills.

He finished his beer, crumpled the aluminum can in his hand and tossed the can in a plastic five-gallon bucket in the corner of the pilothouse. He reached into the cooler and retrieved another cold beer and popped its top. Cautioning himself not to drink too fast, he took a small sip. He planned on a long day and he didn't want to pass out before he could complete his task.

The Ocean under the Moon

Chapter 56

July 13, 2008
1:28 p.m.

Nick was on his third beer and second dragging of the nets. His
first drag had resulted in only about fifty pounds of shrimp. He
was hoping the second drag would be more successful. He worked
the winches that pull the nets onto the boat, and positioned the nets
over the afterdeck. He released the lever to open up the nets and
dumped the catch out onto the afterdeck. The contents of the nets
spilled out onto the deck and the pile flattened in every direction,
like salt being poured onto a table.

A good haul, maybe over three hundred pounds. The
catch was over ninety percent shrimp with very little by-catch.

"Ahhh, look at that shrimp," he said out loud.

"Isn't that beautiful?" He wished Gator could be here to
admire it with him.

He sat down on a small stool and started separating the
by-catch out of the pile of shrimp. He tossed the trash fish toward
the scuppers on the back sides of the boat. From there he would
push the fish through the scuppers with his shovel or shovel them
over the side, where the live ones would swim away and the dead
ones would be consumed by the sharks and seagulls that followed

the boat.

In the ocean, everything gets recycled. Soon, it would be his turn. He imagined crabs picking at his body and it made him shudder. He started to have doubts, but then he thought about it some more. He'd always made his livelihood from the sea, it was only right that he gave something back.

He picked up one of the shrimp and examined it. The shrimp was still alive and its little legs, called pleopods, were flying back and forth, as if it would soon get traction and crawl across the boat like a centipede and make it back to the sea.

He sat there on his stool admiring the little creature. Shrimp were the perfect food. Built with a head and carapace that can be easily twisted off, the body of a shrimp is one big muscle loaded with protein and naturally low in fat. The tail makes a perfect handle for eating them by hand or they can be chopped up into pieces to be put in many different recipes. He could still remember the famous lines about the versatility of shrimp expressed by Benjamin Buford Blue, otherwise known as Bubba in the movie "Forrest Gump."

"Anyway, like I was saying, shrimp is a fruit of the sea," Bubba had said. "You can barbecue it, boil it, broil it, bake it, sauté' it. Dey's, uh, shrimp-kabobs, shrimp creole, shrimp gumbo. Pan-fried, deep-fried, stir-fried. There's pineapple shrimp, lemon shrimp, coconut shrimp, pepper shrimp, shrimp soup, shrimp stew, shrimp salad, shrimp and potatoes, shrimp burger, shrimp sandwich. That's, that's about it."

He had loved that movie and its portrayal of the shrimping industry's ups and downs, from boom times to

The Ocean under the Moon

hurricanes.

He looked down at the magnificent creature in his hand again. He knew that ancient Greek and Roman peoples were fond of shrimp, which were called *squilla* in ancient Latin. People had always loved shrimp. Originally the shrimp were hard to catch and were considered a rare delicacy, in ancient times. With the advent of motorized boats and trawl nets it became easier to catch shrimp, around the beginning of the twentieth century.

Then the inventions of manufactured ice and refrigeration made it possible to ship the shrimp to larger markets. That was when the golden age of American shrimping began. His grandfather and father had enjoyed mostly good times catching shrimp, due to the high demand and relatively low supply, because all of the shrimp had to be wild-caught. Eber and Abe always enjoyed their days as "cowboys of the sea," going out into the open ocean and "rounding up" the shrimp and bringing them to market.

The best part was that shrimp could not be over-fished, thanks to their short life cycle and prodigious reproductive ability. Shrimp were like a crop, such as wheat, one that can be replaced every year.

"Pink gold," he muttered to no one, referring to the old-timers' moniker for the creatures, as he looked down at jumbo shrimp struggling in his hands. Fool's gold was more like what it should be called now.

What had happened to the "American Dream"? Through hard work, all things were supposed to be possible in America. Each generation was supposed to be more successful than the previous. If his grandfather, Eber, was alive today he would be

435

shaking his head at what was going on in America. People getting laid off from their jobs, unemployment rising, long-time companies going bankrupt, globalization robbing America of jobs — he was sure Eber would be dismayed.

But hadn't Eber survived the Great Depression, then a World War right on the heels of the Depression? Surely America would survive this recession; it'd always bounced back from adversity. But even if America overall recovered from the recession, he wasn't sure about the prospects of the domestic shrimping industry. The globalization of the industry with the dumping of cheap, imported shrimp into the United States was threatening to ruin everything that his grandfather and father had worked to accumulate.

How were he and other American shrimpers supposed to compete with the international producers with their cheap labor and lack of regulations? He had turtle extruders and three-mile off the beach limits to deal with, while many foreign countries had no environmental regulations at all.

He and his friends had fought with the government for years for labeling to differentiate wild-caught shrimp from farm-raised shrimp. He felt that if the public was educated on the differences, the public would be willing to pay a little more for wild-caught shrimp, just as they do for other organic foods, as long as the labeling is clear as to its origins.

In 2005, he and his associates thought they'd won a major victory when the USDA imposed regulations requiring producers to put labels on their products indicating whether the shrimp were wild-caught or farm-raised. But due to a loophole that "processed" shrimp doesn't have to be labeled, in fact, most of the shrimp is still not labeled. Also, restaurants and the majority of shrimp sellers, like seafood markets, are not required to label—so what's the point, he thought.

Shrimp, as a food source, had become a victim of its own success. With its reputation as a delicacy, once the price came down, due to greater supply, shrimp became America's favorite seafood. Now America's chain seafood restaurants could offer nine-dollar-ninety-nine-cent all-you-can-eat shrimp, due to an endless supply of cheap, farm-raised shrimp.

He was getting giddy now, from the beer he was sipping in between thoughts. If the public was only aware of what they were eating, the wild-caught shrimp industry might be able to distinguish their product from their foreign competitors and get a decent price for their product enabling them to continue to make a living.

He laughed suddenly. He had just pictured a fancy restaurant in his mind, and a waiter talking with a couple of diners.

Waiter: "We have two appetizers for your dining enjoyment tonight. The first appetizer is a shrimp cocktail from an unknown foreign country, far away. These shrimp are pond-raised in unknown conditions. We do know they are lightly dusted with antibiotics, algaecides, pesticides, and with just a hint of fungicide. The shrimp are then frozen and flown or shipped over many miles, for your culinary pleasure. These shrimp have a mushy texture and bland flavor and are best eaten with plenty of overlying cocktail sauce. This shrimp cocktail is six dollars and ninety-nine cents.

"The second appetizer is also a shrimp cocktail. These

local shrimp are caught in open waters, stored in ice, and brought fresh to the table. They have a firm, almost crunchy texture and a sweet, succulent taste. These shrimp have no additives since they were raised in a natural environment. This shrimp cocktail is nine dollars and ninety-nine cents.

"Which one would you prefer?"

He laughed again and drained the last bit of beer from his can. He pitched the can into the plastic bucket.

If only the millions of shrimp-lovers knew the whole story. The new packaging guidelines didn't seem to be working effectively and the Food and Drug Administration, which is responsible for food safety, inspects less than one percent of the one billion pounds of imported shrimp per year.

The chain restaurants just want an endless supply of cheap shrimp that they can mark up for a healthy profit. The consumers just want shrimp at the lowest price and unless they are fortunate enough to live in the coastal areas, where they have access to real, wild-caught shrimp and appreciate the difference, most people are unaware of the difference in quality.

He looked down at the pristine shrimp in his hand that was trying to flip its way out of his hand using its strong back muscle. It's just not right. Restaurants and grocery stores label wine for the region in which the grapes are grown and with the winemaker's name and price accordingly. Most people understand the difference in quality and taste in wine, why not for shrimp?

Restaurants don't charge just one price for wine, then try to find the cheapest source possible. Why do they treat shrimp this way? It used to make him mad to see the mild fraud being perpetrated at certain seafood restaurants with their décor and pictures of shrimp boats on the wall—and no hint that what's being served came from stagnant ponds in an unknown place. This would be akin to going to the Bordeaux region in France and being served inexpensive, inferior foreign wine under the guise that it was local wine.

But none of this was his concern anymore. He'd done all he could do to change the situation and his voice had fallen on deaf ears. He tossed the shrimp onto the pile in front of him and started separating the rest of the shrimp from the by-catch.

Chapter 57

July 13, 2008
5:05 p.m.

He had gone from exuberant to melancholy. After doing his
frenetic Gator dance almost two hours earlier, he'd fallen asleep for
awhile. Now, after being startled awake by a seagull's cry, he
realized it was getting later in the day and he knew his time was
running out. It didn't help that he'd consumed so much beer. The
beer at first had given him self-confidence, but now it just made
him depressed and sorrowful.

How could he kill himself? Wasn't that a sin in God's
eyes? If he killed himself for the insurance money, was that
providing for Monica and Matt, or was he just abandoning them?
What was their reaction going to be? Anger? Sympathy?
Bafflement?

He, like most Christians, felt it was morally wrong to
commit suicide. After all, in the Middle Ages, it was not
uncommon for people to desecrate the suicidal corpse, deny the
person a Christian burial, and confiscate the deceased's property. If
a literal interpretation of the commandment "Thou shall not kill" is
taken, then suicide is an unrepentant sin.

Therefore, it was important to him that the upcoming

event was not a suicide, but an accident. It would be an assisted accident, but an accident nonetheless, in his mind.

He did not even know if his plan would work. He was hoping it would. He would be gone in a flash, before he could change his mind. The alternative was for him to "accidentally" fall overboard while the boat was on autopilot. Drowning, however, was a slow death and he wasn't sure he had the courage for that. Besides, there was a chance of rescue in the drowning scenario and he certainly didn't want that to happen.

His hope for a quick demise lay in the old gasoline engine that powered the *Resurrection*. He'd stubbornly refused to change it out for a safer and more economical diesel engine. His father had always warned him about how dangerous it was to have a gas engine on a boat. Soon, he was going to find out if that axiom was true.

But first, he wanted to enjoy his last few hours of being alive. The knowledge that his time was running out heightened his awareness of his surroundings. He put the nets back out for another drag and was guiding the *Resurrection* north, parallel to the beach, just over three miles off shore. He was sitting in the captain's chair, guiding the boat with one hand on the steering wheel, and nursing another beer in his other hand.

He watched a couple of porpoises playing in the bow wake. The porpoises were gliding effortlessly in front of the wake, swerving side to side, as if body-surfing the wave. He thought of Zoti, who'd loved surfing so much, and it brought tears to his eyes. Maybe, just maybe, if humans were reincarnated into animals, as the Hindus believed, Zoti would be reincarnated into a porpoise.

The Ocean under the Moon

That would only be fair, after his son's life had been cut so short.

He saw a pelican dive-bomb into the ocean off the starboard bow, evoking a big splash. Of all the sea birds he'd watched over the years, he liked to watch the pelicans the most. When he, Zoti, and Pepe went to the beach so Zoti could practice his surfing, he would watch the sea birds, in between watching his son catch waves.

He categorized the birds according to their behavior. The seagulls were loud, obnoxious, and always looking for a handout. One didn't dare to throw a bread crumb, left over from a sandwich, to the one lone seagull that always seemed to be hanging around, unless you wanted thirty of his friends to arrive, almost instantly, after the free handout, expecting the same treatment.

The skimmer birds were sleek and elegant, but aloof. They would come by flying fast and silent, their lower beaks skimming through the shallow water of receding waves trying to scoop up a minnow in the two- to three-inch deep water. Pepe would take off after them, chasing them, as far as a mile down the beach, as the skimmers effortlessly kept in front of him, before he would realize it was a fruitless effort.

The sandpipers were always kind of fun to watch, skittering in and out of the waves trying to probe for periwinkles and sand fleas before they could re-bury themselves after a receding wave. Pepe, in particular, loved to chase the sandpipers because they would only fly thirty or so yards up the beach before landing, to resume feeding, sending him off again to chase them back into flight.

But Nick's favorites were the pelicans, who he considered

The Ocean under the Moon

to be the B-17's of the sea birds. Like the venerable World War II bombers, pelicans have a large wingspan, are slow-flying, and like to fly in formation.

On calm days, he would watch the pelicans fly in V-formation just above the incoming waves up and down the beach. Their large shadow from their formation would spook some bait fish into revealing themselves with their skittish behavior. Then, one or two of the pelicans would break from the formation and circle up higher, and dive straight down on the unsuspecting fish with a huge splash as they entered the water, like a diver off the high-dive.

As the day progressed, Nick cherished every nuance of his surroundings even more, for he knew it would be the last time he would be experiencing these things. The sun grew lower in the sky and he desperately wanted to push it back up, to gain more time. But it continued its relentless march down toward the western horizon.

The Ocean under the Moon

Chapter 58

July 13, 2008
8:12 p.m.

He had ceased shrimping; there really wasn't any purpose to it any more. The hold was over half-full, which would serve his needs well enough. He had cooked some of the shrimp on a little portable stove that he kept on the boat. He'd sautéed the shrimp in garlic and butter and also cooked some rice. He savored his last meal, eating very slow, while the boat was on autopilot, running parallel to the beach. Now, he was sitting on an overturned bucket near the stern of the boat, finishing his last supper, waiting for the sun to go down.

The sky was cloudless to the west, which was a little bit unusual this time of the year, so he knew he was in for a spectacular sunset. Whether he was on his boat or sitting on the back porch of his house, enjoying a glass of wine with Monica, he'd always enjoyed the time of sunset. The disappearance of the sun over the horizon signified the passage of time, the end of the day, and a time to relax.

He knew she was probably on their back porch, at this instant, watching the sun getting ready to go down over the Amelia River. He wanted desperately to call her, but in his half-drunk state he was worried that he would get too emotional and give away his intentions. He watched the sun get lower and lower.

After debating with himself for awhile, he gave in. He wanted to hear her voice one last time. He went inside the pilothouse and retrieved his cell phone, then returned to his seat on the overturned bucket. He punched the pre-set button on his cell phone.

The phone rang several times and just when he thought it was going to go to voicemail, she answered the phone.

"Hello! Hello!" she said, out of breath from running to the phone.

"Hey, it's me," he said. He tried to sound calm and composed.

"Are you all right? You haven't broken down, have you? I thought you would be back by now."

"No, I'm fine. Everything's okay, the boat's running fine. It's just that the shrimping has been slow up until about an hour ago. The last drag was really good, however, so I'm going to stay out here a while to catch my quota. I'll probably be home around nine," he lied.

"You know I don't want you out there by yourself, particularly after dark." He could hear the concern in her voice.

"I'm just going to make one more pull, then I'll come in."

"I was waiting for you on the back porch, thinking you would be pulling up to the dock any minute, so we could watch the sun go down together. I was hoping that tonight, we would finally be able to see the green flash together."

He chuckled out loud. Watching for the mythical "green

flash" was a standing joke between the two of them. He knew the famous, but seldom seen, green flash was an optical phenomenon that is supposed to occur just as the last part of the sun disappears below the horizon, if the atmospheric conditions are just right. Admiral Byrd and his men on one of his expeditions to the South Pole were supposedly able to observe the phenomenon for an astonishing thirty-five minutes due to the sun moving along the horizon for an extended period of time due to their extreme location. Nick knew many shrimpers and sailors who also said they had witnessed the phenomenon.

He didn't doubt its existence; he'd just never been able to witness it for himself. He understood the science behind other optical phenomenon, like red sunrises and sunsets being caused by the fact that red light has the longest wavelength in the visible spectrum, and due to refraction of light, it's the first light visible as the sun peeks above the horizon in the morning and the last as the sun settles below the horizon in the evening. He was aware too that blue and violet light are the shortest wavelengths in the visible spectrum and due to Rayleigh scattering, the shorter wavelengths are diffracted more severely by the molecules and particles in the atmosphere, hence the sky appears blue.

He didn't quite understand the science behind the green flash phenomenon. He knew it had something to do with dispersion of light into its color spectrum and the green light lagging behind the red light and extinction of the violet and blue light at the extreme angle of sunset. He usually took a few seconds, when he was out on his boat at sunset, to watch for the green flash. When he was at home, it had become a nightly ritual for them to go out on their back porch, sit in their Adirondack chairs, sip wine, and watch the sun set over the Amelia River—hoping to spot the elusive green flash.

"Well, I tell you what," he began. "There's no way I'll make it home in time, since the sun is going to set in about ten minutes. Take your cell phone and go out the porch, and I'll motor south a little bit, past the south end of the island, where I can see the sun set over Nassau Sound and we'll watch the sunset together. Maybe we will see the green flash tonight."

"Ha! Fat chance! You've been telling me about this thing for twenty-five years and neither one of us has ever seen it. I'm beginning to doubt its existence," she said.

"Well, maybe tonight will be different," he said. He felt a catch in his throat, knowing that, indeed, this night was going to be different, due to his actions. He pushed the throttle forward, so the boat would make it past the end of the island before the sun went down.

"All right, I have my glass of wine and I'm in my chair on the back porch," she said.

"I'm sorry I didn't make it back on time and for worrying you," he said.

"That's all right. The sound of your voice is enough. Although, I do wish you were here so I could hold your hand."

He wished he could be there also; he began to have serious doubts about what he needed to do. If he followed his plan, there would be no more sunsets for him, no more holding of her hand. He was tempted to turn the boat around and race back to her and feel her full embrace.

The Ocean under the Moon

He started to turn the boat around and then he remembered that although he would have her, he would probably lose his house, boats, and livelihood. That would be too bitter a pill for him to swallow and the sunsets would become meaningless. He continued on his course toward Nassau Sound.

"You know I love you, don't you," he said. Tears welled in his eyes.

"Of course I do."

"And that I would do anything for you and Matt."

"Why are you getting so serious? We are supposed to be enjoying our sunset together."

"Was I getting serious? I thought I was being romantic."

"Can you see the sunset yet?"

"I'm just now coming to the end of the island. I should be able to see it in a few seconds—wait—there it is! Yeah, it's magnificent, isn't it?"

The sun was just beginning to flatten itself out against the horizon as the bottom of the sun was starting to disappear behind the water and flat land beyond.

"This sunset is almost as beautiful as you are," he told her.

"Aren't you being sweet tonight," she said. "Maybe we should watch the sun go down together over the phone more often."

He cringed at the thought that there wouldn't be any more sunsets together. Tears started streaming down his face and he struggled to keep his voice from cracking.

"You know I love you today as much as that first time I saw you in that little white bikini, with the morning sun outlining your silhouette," he said.

"Well, I doubt I could get into that bikini now."

"Oh, I bet you could. You still look the same to me."

"I wish you were here so I could kiss you for saying that."

"I wish I was there too," he said. In fact, he was second-guessing his entire plan. It would be so easy for him to abandon his plans and head back in, to her open arms.

So what if he had no money or livelihood, he would still have his wife and her love. But would she still love him, if he had no way to provide for her? And what about Matt? His son had dreams of going to college. If he lost his boats and house, how could he pay for that?

He clutched the phone tight in his fist. He would stick with the plan. It would be for the best, this way.

The sun was about halfway down behind the horizon now. He thought how it seemed to take a long time for the sun to get to the horizon, but once there, it seems to move very fast.

Tonight's glorious sunset reminded him of some he'd witnessed in Key West, when he and Gator used to go down there to shrimp. Watching the sun go down there was a major event, with a large crowd gathering at the western end of the island at Mallory Square to be entertained by the street performers and then watch the sun go down. With an unobstructed view of the Gulf of Mexico to the west, the sunsets were spectacular. The moment not only marked the end of the day, but the beginning of the night and time to start drinking, if they hadn't started already. He and his friend had watched many a sunset in Key West together, usually with a drink in hand, but even in that perfect location with altered minds, they never saw the green flash as the sun went down.

He raised his beer in a salute to his old friend.

"I miss Gator. I wonder what he is doing now," he said into the phone.

"Oh, I think he probably bluffed his way into heaven and is probably chasing beautiful lady angels around now."

"And Zoti?" he said.

"Well, he's probably surfing on an endless, perfect wave in heaven, a wave with classic form that never reaches the shore," she said with optimism.

He liked her hopeful view of the after-life; he could only hope that it was true. He would soon find out if it were so.

The sun continued its silent fall. Three-quarters of the circle was now out of view and the sun was getting redder by the minute.

"It won't be long now," she said. "Maybe tonight will be the night we see that flash."

He'd long ago given up hope of seeing the flash, but he still looked for it out of habit, and to humor his wife, who still hoped she would one day see the phenomenon.

"Well, I wouldn't get my hopes up if I was you," he said.

"Aren't you the spoilsport, tonight," she retorted.

"I'm just saying, we don't always get what we want in life."

"Oh, look, it's going down now!"

The sun had almost disappeared behind the horizon. There was only a sliver of the red sun left.

"Here we go!" she said.

The Ocean under the Moon

The sun was sinking very fast now, the last vestiges disappearing exponentially over just a few seconds.

Finally, the sun was gone.

"Did you see it?" she asked.

"No, did you?"

"I didn't either."

"There's always tomorrow," she said, hopefully.

Her words hit him like a ton of bricks. There would be no tomorrow for him.

"Yes, there's always tomorrow," he lied.

The Ocean under the Moon

Chapter 59

July 13, 2008
9:14 p.m.

Now was the time. He'd enjoyed a wonderful day, catching shrimp, and had watched a lovely sunset, but he could procrastinate no longer. He had to do what he needed to do. In his mind, he felt he had no choice. It was the only solution to his predicament. He needed to complete his plan, before he got too drunk and passed out, or lost his nerve.

He wasn't even sure his plan would work. All of his life, he'd been told how dangerous gasoline engines were in a boat. Both his father and all of his shrimping buddies warned him, that if he didn't always use the blower, or exhaust fan, to rid the engine compartment of gas fumes before starting his boat, he could blow his boat out of the water. They were always after him to re-power the *Resurrection* with a diesel engine.

Due to stubbornness or possibly superstition, he refused to switch over to diesel. The boat had come with a gas engine and he'd always maintained that engine, despite its purported hazards. He was about to find out if the alleged claims were true.

He took another sip of beer for courage and steered the boat closer to shore. Now that it was completely dark, he was guided by the lights of the tall condominium complexes. He aimed for the new Ocean Reef Restaurant that had been built between American Beach and the Amelia Island Plantation. He knew people would be dining there, looking out over the ocean. He wanted witnesses to the explosion and to be close enough to shore for debris to wash ashore, so that the cause of the explosion could be easier ascertained.

The *Resurrection* arrived at the appropriate spot he wanted, about two hundred yards off the beach, close enough to be seen, but safely out past the breakers. He cut the engine off and took his half-empty beer and walked out of the pilothouse to the back of the boat.

The wind had fallen and the night was very still. He sat down on the transom and dangled his legs over the stern. A huge, yellow full moon had come up over the horizon after nightfall and was low in the sky to the east, over the open ocean. He'd picked this night for his mission, because of the full moon. He knew the silhouette of his boat would be visible in the reflected moonlight to the beachgoers and to the diners at the Ocean Reef.

He sat there on top of the transom with his beer by his side and stared at the moon. It never looked so big; it seemed twice as close as normal. He could clearly make out the large dark spots on the moon. He remembered from his high school studies that the dark spots, which look like oceans, are actually featureless lunar plains, filled with vast pools of solidified basaltic lava from ancient times.

The moon was bright, the ocean was calm. The light seemed to radiate from its source across the flat ocean right up to the back of the *Resurrection* where he was sitting. It was a beautiful sight, as he sat there sipping his beer. But it reminded him of a saying that his beloved grandfather used to say:

"Life is like the ocean under a full moon ... beautiful on the surface, but there are many hazards underneath."

He looked down at the black water behind the boat. If his plan to blow himself up didn't work, he could always just slip off the back of the boat into the dark water. That would probably be appropriate, because he would be returning something to the ocean in the form of his body, nourishing the sharks and crabs after all these years of him receiving nourishment from the ocean in the form of shrimp.

But he didn't have the courage for slow death by drowning. He wanted his death to be instantaneous and irreversible.

He looked up and saw a few wispy clouds drift across the face of the moon, giving him an ominous feeling.

"It's time," he said out loud, then drained the last of his beer.

He scrambled back over the transom and made his way to the pilothouse. Along the way he checked to make sure he was still safely out past the breakers and that he had not drifted too close to shore.

He settled into the captain's chair behind the wheel and instinctively started to reach for the blower switch, to exhaust any gas fumes out of the engine compartment before turning the ignition. He stopped himself and instead reached for the key to the ignition. He was about to find out if all of the admonishments about gas engines were true.

He turned the ignition key.

Nothing happened, except the engine started running.

"Damn!"

It had been quite awhile between when he'd cut the engine off and then finished his beer on the back of the boat. He surmised that too much time might have elapsed, allowing the gas fumes from the engine room to dissipate. He decided he would drive around in a small circle, running the engine to build up gas fumes, and then immediately try to restart the engine.

He drove the boat in a small circle for about a minute, then cut the engine off. He waited two or three seconds, then turned the ignition key again. Once again all he heard was the sound of the engine coming back to life.

He chuckled to himself. If he saw his father or his friends in heaven, he was going to give them a piece of his mind about all those warnings about gas engines.

He drove the boat in a circle for a little longer, then tried shutting the engine off and re-starting it again without using the blower. No explosion. He tried the process again, over and over, for a total of ten tries. Still, the gas fumes refused to ignite and explode.

"Arrgh!" he moaned in frustration and drunkenness.

"I can't even kill myself properly," he said and hit the wheel of the boat with the palm of his hand. He really did not want to have to try and drown himself.

He decided to take a different tack. He drove the *Resurrection* in a circle for three or four laps to build up the gas fumes in the engine compartment. Then he put the boat on autopilot, parallel to the shore. He grabbed a ball peen hammer and a flashlight out of the toolbox that he kept on the pilothouse floor.

With a wild feeling of determination, he walked back to the center of the boat. Just aft of the crew's cabin were the trap doors in the deck that led down into the engine compartment.

He lifted one of the trap doors and slid down into the cramped engine compartment, turning on the flashlight. He pulled the trap door back down, so it closed over the top of him. The engine room was very small. There was barely enough room for him to move between the engine and the walls. The ceiling was so low he had to stoop over at the waist to keep from bumping his head.

The engine was still running, loudly, and the compartment was stifling hot. The air in the small compartment was filled with gas fumes and it was hard for him to breathe. He figured if he couldn't get the compartment to explode by creating sparks with the hammer, he might just die of carbon monoxide poisoning.

It was so miserably hot in the small compartment that he couldn't wait to die. He started hitting the hammer against a steel support beam overhead, at an angle, trying to create some sparks. About every third or fourth strike, he would see some small sparks fly from the area of contact, but still no explosion. He struck the hammer against the beam twenty, then thirty times, until he was too exhausted to go on.

He sat down on the floor next to the engine, and cried. All of the frustrations of the last few years came flowing out. He sat there, tears flowing from his eyes and sweat pouring out of his body, but the engine compartment was too hot, loud, and unbearable to stay there for long.

Just as he was getting ready to push the trap door open, he gave the engine a hard rap with the hammer on its manifold, out of frustration.

"*Ka-booooom!*"

He saw a brilliant flash of white light that had a strange emerald-green tint to it. He'd finally seen the green flash, just not in the way he had imagined. It was his last conscious thought.

* * *

Meanwhile, inside the swank, oceanfront restaurant, a well-dressed, elderly couple was sitting at a table for two, next to the window. The couple, who lived in the Amelia Island Plantation, had driven just outside the resort to try the new restaurant. The man, obviously a successful, retired businessman, wore a dark, blue suit and still had a full, lush head of silver hair and a smile of even, white teeth. The woman, in an elegant, green cocktail dress, had perfectly-coiffed hair, and layers of pearls around her neck. They were sharing a shrimp cocktail, when they noticed a flash of light out over the ocean.

"I didn't know the Plantation was having fireworks tonight," the woman began.

"I don't recall seeing anything in the bulletin about fireworks," her companion responded.

"That's odd," she said.

"Oh, well. Why don't you have the last shrimp, my dear,"

he said.

"I don't mind if I do."

Then the woman casually remarked, "I wonder if these shrimp are local?"

* * *

At the same moment, a restaurant worker was dumping that night's trash into a dumpster in a private area, hidden by tall fences, beside the Ocean Reef Restaurant. One of the cardboard boxes that he was tossing into the dumpster caught his eye. He noticed the box because he recognized letters from his native country and this made him homesick. The box said, in both English and Vietnamese: "This box contains pond-raised shrimp, imported from the Socialist Republic of Vietnam."

The Ocean under the Moon

August 19, 2008

Matt had his arms full of clothes as he was carrying them out to his car. He was packing to set off for college for the first time. His mother was trying to help him pack, organizing his things so he could take them out to the car, but she was crying more than helping.

She was proud that he was heading off to college to play baseball and further his education. But she was also filled with sadness, that she would now be all alone in the big white house.

They'd been shocked and overcome with grief at Nick's death. Their disbelief turned to anger when the autopsy report on his charred body, which had washed ashore along with the burning hull of the *Resurrection*, showed him to be drunk at the time of the accident. The toxicology report showed he measured a blood alcohol level of 0.15, over the legal drinking limit of 0.08, when the accident occurred. The official Marine Patrol report went on to say that the captain's drunkenness, along with careless use of the gasoline engine, was the cause of the tragedy.

Once again, a large contingent of the town turned out for a Stamos funeral. A couple of his shrimping buddies and then Matt gave moving eulogies, but there was an undercurrent of disturbing pain about the way Nick died.

His remains were buried in the family plot at Bosque Bello, bringing the total up to four generations of Stamos men buried in the plot. He joined his beloved grandfather, his revered father, and his treasured son in the plot. It marked the end of the Stamos family's shrimping dynasty. It had lasted just less than one hundred years.

Monica's anger turned to dismay after she found out about their true indebtedness. After going through the bills on the computer in his small office in the house, she'd been shocked at how he allowed the mortgage debt to accumulate on their property. If she'd known, she would have tried even harder to find a job after the school board let her go. At the time of the funeral, she was in turmoil, mad about what Nick had kept from her, and disappointed that she was going to have to tell their son that he might have to put his college plans on hold.

But things became clear to her a few days later, when she and Matt visited Nick's lawyer's office for the reading of the will.

His lawyer, Grant Daniels, explained that most of Nick's personal effects like clothes, tools, guns, and fishing poles went to his son, while the house, property, and furnishings went to his wife. Then Grant quickly detailed his client's debts and assets.

It was looking to her like they were going to have to sell everything he was leaving to them, just to settle their debts, when the lawyer dropped the bombshell of his client's one-million-dollar life insurance policy.

That's when the true explanation became clear to her. She remembered how sentimental Nick had been on the phone with her, as they watched the sun go down together, right before the accident. At that time, she'd thought it was just the romance of the sunset, but in hindsight, she realized he was subtly trying to say goodbye.

She didn't say anything about her suspicions in the lawyer's office, but in the car ride home, she explained to her son about what she thought had happened. She told him she didn't have any proof, but what looked like a drunken accident might really have been a well-thought-out plan to provide for their future.

She was still mad at her husband for leaving her — she would much rather have him and be bankrupt, than to be without him. But she didn't want her son to go through the rest of his life thinking ill of his father, when his actions might have been an unselfish act to provide for their future.

The man from the insurance company showed up at their door three weeks later with the check. She signed for the check, feeling guilty about accepting it. But to raise her suspicions now would mean his death was in vain, if that was his true intention.

Now, Matt had just about finished packing things into his truck. There was only one last thing he needed, to complete his load.

He sat down on the end of the bed beside his mother, who was clutching a picture of him in his All-Star baseball uniform when he was about ten years old. She was crying and looking at the picture, wondering where all the years had gone.

"It's all right, Mom. I'm going to be less than an hour away. I'll be able to visit you on the weekends and you can come down and watch our baseball games," he said. He put his arm across her shoulders.

"I know. I know. But you are all that I have left."

Mother and son hugged for a moment, and then he said, "I will just be a phone call away."

He stood up and looked at the object leaning against the wall in the corner of his room. The six-foot-long wooden object was the nameplate off the stern of the *Resurrection* that had been salvaged from the remains of the boat when it washed ashore. One of his father's shrimping buddies, who was working on the salvage crew, took it off the boat and presented it to him.

He tucked the heavy nameplate under his arm and walked toward the front door of the house. His mother got up off the bed and followed him to the front porch. She stopped at the front porch and sadly watched him walk toward his truck with the wooden board under his arm.

He stopped halfway down the walkway to his truck and turned and waved to his mother. She waved back.

He walked the last few steps to his truck and laid the nameplate face up on top of the luggage in the bed of the truck. He looked at the board, which he planned to put on the wall of his dorm room. It read "RESURRECTION" in big, gold, ornate letters.

He remembered his father once telling him the story behind the name. His father said he had named the boat that because he was "resurrecting" it from its beaching after hitting the jetty, to join his shrimping fleet, and give it a new life.

Now, Matt was going to hang the sign on his wall to remind him of a different "resurrection." That would be his personal resurrection and the resurrection of the Stamos dynasty.

The Ocean under the Moon

He wasn't sure, however, what the future was going to hold, he wasn't even sure what his major in college was going to be yet.

But there was one thing he was sure of, and that was that his future was not going to involve anything to do with catching shrimp. He got into the truck, gave his mother one last wave, which she returned from her spot on the porch, and he drove away.

The End

LaVergne, TN USA
21 March 2011
221010LV00001BA/119/P

9 781453 865002